Dear Reader,

One of the best perks of being a writer is becoming—
for the time it takes to write the book—someone else.
To write well, you have to climb inside someone else's
skin and personality. In *Daring to Dream*, I got to
become gorgeous and glamorous and gutsy Margo
Sullivan. Not a bad deal.

In *Holding the Dream*, the second book of my Dream
Trilogy, I became Kate Powell. Orphaned at the age
of eight, Kate was raised by the Templetons, and has
vowed never to disappoint them. She's sharp, smart,
a gamine woman with a head for figures. As someone
who failed high-school algebra, this was quite a kick
for me.

I enjoyed focusing on Kate in this story, exploring her
heart and mind, continuing to develop the close and
loving relationship between her and Margo and Laura.
I liked watching her take a more active role in the
running of Pretenses, the unique little shop she and
her sisters of the heart have established. And, naturally, I enjoyed the steps and stages of her romance
with the handsome hotelier, Byron DeWitt. There's a
man, I think, who could make even our practical Kate
forget that two and two are four.

I hope you'll enjoy, as I did, watching Kate's life and
her needs shift and change as she struggles with the
loss of one dream and the beginnning of another.

Nora Roberts

By Nora Roberts

Homeport	Northern Lights	Black Hills
The Reef	Blue Smoke	The Search
River's End	Montana Sky	Chasing Fire
Carolina Moon	Angels Fall	The Witness
The Villa	High Noon	Whiskey Beach
Midnight Bayou	Divine Evil	The Collector
Three Fates	Tribune	The Liar
Birthright	Sanctuary	The Obsession

The Born In Trilogy:
Born in Fire
Born in Ice
Born in Shame

The Bride Quartet:
Vision in White
Bed of Roses
Savour the Moment
Happy Ever After

The Key Trilogy:
Key of Light
Key of Knowledge
Key of Valour

The Irish Trilogy:
Jewels of the Sun
Tears of the Moon
Heart of the Sea

Three Sisters Island Trilogy:
Dance Upon the Air
Heaven and Earth
Face the Fire

The Sign of Seven Trilogy:
Blood Brothers
The Hollow
The Pagan Stone

Chesapeake Bay Quartet:
Sea Swept
Rising Tides
Inner Harbour
Chesapeake Blue

In the Garden Trilogy:
Blue Dahlia
Black Rose
Red Lily

The Circle Trilogy:
Morrigan's Cross
Dance of the Gods
Valley of Silence

The Dream Trilogy:
Daring to Dream
Holding the Dream
Finding the Dream

The Inn Boonsboro Trilogy:
The Next Always
The Last Boyfriend
The Perfect Hope

The Cousins O'Dwyer Trilogy:
Dark Witch
Shadow Spell
Blood Magick

Many of Nora Roberts' other titles are now available in eBook and
she is the author of the In Death series using the pseudonym J.D. Robb.
For more information please visit
www.noraroberts.com or www.nora-roberts.co.uk

NORA ROBERTS

Holding the Dream

piatkus

PIATKUS

First published in the US in 1997 by The Berkley Publishing Group,
A division of Penguin Group (USA) Inc., New York.
First published in Great Britain in 2008 by Piatkus Books
Reissued in 2008 by Piatkus Books
This edition published in 2016 by Piatkus

10 9 8 7 6 5

A CIP catalogue record for this book
is available from the British Library.

ISBN 978-0-349-41170-5

Data manipulation by Phoenix Photosetting, Chatham, Kent
www.phoenixphotosetting.co.uk
Printed in Great Britain by Clays Ltd, Elcograf S.p.A.

Papers used by Piatkus are from well-managed forests
and other responsible sources.

MIX
Paper from
responsible sources
FSC® C104740

Piatkus
An imprint of
Little, Brown Book Group
Carmelite House
50 Victoria Embankment
London EC4Y 0DZ

An Hachette UK Company
www.hachette.co.uk

www.piatkus.co.uk

To family

Holding the Dream

Chapter One

Her childhood had been a lie.

Her father had been a thief.

Her mind struggled to absorb those two facts, to absorb and analyze and accept. Kate Powell had trained herself to be a practical woman, one who worked hard toward goals, earned them step by careful step. Wavering was not permitted. Shortcuts were not taken. Rewards were earned with sweat, planning, and effort.

That, she had always believed, was who she was; a product of her heredity, her upbringing, and her own stringent standards for herself.

When a child was orphaned at an early age, when she lived with the loss, when she had, essentially, watched her parents die, there seemed little else that could be so wrenching.

But there was, Kate realized as she sat, still in shock, behind her tidy desk in her tidy office at Bittle and Associates.

Out of that early tragedy had come enormous blessings. Her parents had been taken away, and she'd been given others.

The distant kinship hadn't mattered to Thomas and Susan Templeton. They had taken her in, raised her, given her a home and love. Given her everything, without question.

And they must have known, she realized. They must have always known.

They had known when they took her from the hospital after the accident. When they comforted her and gave her the gift of belonging, they had known.

They took her across the continent to California. To the sweeping cliffs and beauty of Big Sur. To Templeton House. There, in that grand home, as gracious and welcoming as any of the glamorous Templeton hotels, they made her part of their family.

They gave her Laura and Josh, their children, as siblings. They gave her Margo Sullivan, the housekeeper's daughter, who had been accepted as part of the family even before Kate.

They gave her clothes and food, education, advantages. They gave her rules and discipline and the encouragement to pursue dreams.

And most of all, they gave her love and family and pride.

Yet they had known from the beginning what she, twenty years later, had just discovered.

Her father had been a thief, a man under indictment for embezzlement. Caught skimming from his own clients' accounts, he had died facing shame, ruin, prison.

She might never have found out but for the capricious twist of fate that had brought an old friend of Lincoln Powell's into her office that morning.

He was so delighted to see her, remembered her as a child. It warmed her to be remembered, to realize that he had come to her with his business because of the old tie with her parents. She'd taken the time, though she had little to spare during those last weeks before the April 15 tax deadline, to chat with him.

And he just sat there, in the chair on the other side of the desk, reminiscing. He'd bounced her on his knee when she was little, he said, had worked in the same ad firm as her father.

2

Which was why, he told her, since he'd relocated to California and now had his own firm, he wanted her as his accountant. She thanked him and mixed her questions about his business and his financial requirements with queries about her parents.

Then, when he spoke so casually of the accusations, the charges, and the sorrow he felt that her father had died before he could make restitution, she had said nothing, could say nothing.

"He never intended to steal, just borrow. Oh, it was wrong, God knows. I always felt partially responsible because I was the one who told him about the real estate deal, encouraged him to invest. I didn't know he'd already lost most of his capital in a couple of deals that went sour. He would have put the money back. Linc would have found a way, always did. He was always a little resentful that his cousin rode so high while he barely scraped by."

And the man—God, she couldn't remember his name, couldn't remember anything but the words—smiled at her.

The whole time he was speaking, making excuses, adding his own explanations to the facts, she simply sat, nodding. This stranger who'd known her father was destroying her very foundations.

"He had a sore spot where Tommy Templeton was concerned. Funny, when you think it turned out that he was the one to raise you after it all. But Linc never meant any harm, Katie. He was just reckless. Never had a chance to prove himself, and that's the real crime, if you ask me."

The real crime, Kate thought, as her stomach churned and knotted. He had stolen, because he was desperate for money and took the easy way out. Because he was a thief, she thought now. A cheat. And he had cheated the justice system by hitting an icy patch of road and crashing his car, killing himself and his wife and leaving his daughter an orphan.

So fate had given her as a father the very man her own father had been so envious of. Through his death, she had, in essence, become a Templeton.

Had it been deliberate? she wondered. Had he been so desperate, so reckless, so angry that he'd chosen death? She could barely remember him, a thin, pale, nervous man with a quick temper.

A man with big plans, she thought now. A man who had spun those plans out into delightful fantasies for his child. Visions of big houses, fine cars, fun-filled trips to Disney World.

And all the while they lived in a tiny house just like all the other tiny houses on the block, with an old sedan that rattled, and no trips to anywhere.

So he stole, and he was caught. And he died.

What had her mother done? Kate wondered. What had she felt? Was that why Kate remembered her most as a woman with worry in her eyes and a tight smile?

Had he stolen before? The idea made her cold inside. Had he stolen before and somehow gotten away with it? A little here, a little there, until he'd become careless?

She remembered arguments, often over money. And worse, the silences that followed them. The silence that night. That heavy, hurting silence in the car between her parents before the awful spin, the screams and the pain.

Shuddering, she closed her eyes, clenched her fists tight, and fought back the drumming headache.

Oh, God, she had loved them. Loved the memory of them. Couldn't bear to have it smeared and spoiled. And couldn't face, she realized with horrid shame, being the daughter of a cheat.

She wouldn't believe it. Not yet. She took slow breaths and turned to her computer. With mechanical efficiency she accessed the library in New Hampshire where she'd been born and had lived for the first eight years of her life.

It was tedious work, but she ordered copies of newspapers for the year before the accident, requested faxes of any article mentioning Lincoln Powell. While she waited, she contacted the lawyer back east who had handled the disposition of her parents' estate.

She was a creature comfortable with technology. Within an

hour she had everything she needed. She could read the details in black and white, details that confirmed the facts the lawyer had given her.

The accusations, the criminal charges, the scandal. A scandal, she realized, that had earned print space because of Lincoln Powell's family connection to the Templetons. And the missing funds, replaced in full after her parents were buried. Replaced, Kate was certain, by the people who had raised her as one of their own.

The Templetons, she thought, who had been drawn into the ugliness, had quietly taken the responsibility, and the child. And, always, had protected the child.

There in her quiet office, alone, she laid her head on the desk and wept. And wept. And when the weeping was done, she shook out pills for the headache, more for the burning in her stomach. When she gathered her briefcase to leave, she told herself she would bury it. Just bury it. As she had buried her parents.

It could not be changed, could not be fixed. She was the same, she assured herself, the same woman she had been that morning. Yet she found she couldn't open her office door and face the possibility of running into a colleague in the corridor. Instead, she sat again, closed her eyes, sought comfort in old memories. A picture, she thought, of family and tradition. Of who she was, what she had been given, and what she had been raised to be.

At sixteen, she was taking an extra load of courses that would allow her to graduate a full year ahead of her class. Since that wasn't quite enough of a challenge, she was determined to graduate with honors as well. She had already mentally outlined her valedictorian speech.

Her extracurricular activities included another term as class treasurer, a stint as president of the math club, and a place in the starting lineup of the baseball team. She had hopes of being named MVP again next season, but for now her attention was focused on calculus.

5

Numbers were her strong point. Sticking with logic, Kate had already decided to use her strengths in her career. Once she had her MBA—more than likely she would follow Josh to Harvard for that—she would pursue a career in accounting.

It didn't matter that Margo said her aspirations were boring. To Kate they were realistic. She was going to prove to herself, and to everyone who mattered to her, that what she had been given, all she had been offered, had been put to the best possible use.

Because her eyes were burning, she slipped off her glasses and leaned back in her desk chair. It was important, she knew, to rest the brain periodically in order to keep it at its keenest. She did so now, letting her gaze skim around the room.

The new touches the Templetons had insisted she choose for her sixteenth birthday suited her. The simple pine shelves above her desk held her books and study materials. The desk itself was a honey, a Chippendale kneehole with deep drawers and fanciful shell carving. It made her feel successful just to work at it.

She hadn't wanted fussy wallpaper or fancy curtains. The muted stripes on the walls and the simple vertical blinds fit her style. Because she understood her aunt's need to pamper, she'd chosen a pretty, scroll-sided settee in deep green. On rare occasions she actually stretched out on it to read for pleasure.

Otherwise, the room was functional, as she preferred.

The knock on her door interrupted her just as she was burying her nose in her books again. Her answer was a distracted grunt.

"Kate." Susan Templeton, elegant in a cashmere twin set, entered, her hands on her hips. "What am I going to do with you?"

"Nearly finished," Kate mumbled. She caught the scent of her aunt's perfume as Susan crossed the room. "Midterm. Math. Tomorrow."

"As if you weren't already prepared." Susan sat on the edge of the tidily made bed and surveyed Kate. Those huge and oddly exotic brown eyes were focused behind heavy-framed reading glasses. Hair, sleek and dark, was tugged back into a stubby ponytail. The girl cut it shorter every year, Susan thought with a sigh. Plain gray sweats bagged over a long, thin frame down to the bare feet. As Susan watched, Kate pursed her wide mouth into something between a pout and a frown. The expression dug a thinking line between her eyebrows.

"In case you haven't noticed," Susan began, "it's ten days until Christmas."

"Umm. Midterm week. Nearly done."

"And it's six o'clock."

"Don't hold dinner. Want to finish this."

"Kate." Susan rose and snatched Kate's glasses away. "Josh is home from college. The family's waiting for you to trim the tree."

"Oh." Blinking, Kate struggled to bring her mind back from formulas. Her aunt was watching her owlishly, her dark blond hair curled smoothly around her pretty face. "I'm sorry. I forgot. If I don't ace this exam—"

"The world as we know it will come to an end. I know."

Kate grinned and rolled her shoulders to loosen them. "I guess I could spare a couple of hours. Just this once."

"We're honored." Susan set the glasses on the desk. "Put something on your feet, Kate."

"Okay. Be right down."

"I can't believe I'm going to say this to one of my children, but . . ." Susan started toward the door. "If you open one of those books again, you're grounded."

"Yes, ma'am." Kate crossed to her dresser and chose a pair of socks from an orderly pile. Beneath the carefully folded socks was her secret stash of Weight-On, which had done pitifully little to put more pounds onto her bones. After tugging the socks on, she downed a couple of aspirin to kick back the headache that was just beginning to stir.

"It's about time." Margo met her at the top of the stairs. "Josh and Mr. T are already stringing the lights."

"That could take hours. You know how they love to argue

whether they should go clockwise or counterclockwise.'' Tilting her head, she gave Margo a long study. ''What the hell are you all dolled up for?''

''I'm simply being festive.'' Margo smoothed the skirt of her holly-red dress, pleased that the scoop neckline hinted at cleavage. She'd slipped on heels, determined that Josh should notice her legs and remember she was a woman now. ''Unlike you, I don't choose to trim the tree wearing rags.''

''At least I'll be comfortable.'' Kate sniffed. ''You've been into Aunt Susie's perfume.''

''I have not.'' Lifting her chin, Margo fluffed at her hair. ''She offered me a spritz.''

''Hey,'' Laura called from the bottom of the staircase, ''are you two going to stand up there arguing all night?''

''We're not arguing. We were complimenting each other on our attire.'' Snickering, Kate started down.

''Dad and Josh are nearly finished with their debate over the lights.'' Laura shot a look across the spacious foyer toward the family parlor. ''They're smoking cigars.''

''Josh smoking a cigar?'' Kate snorted at the image.

''He's a Harvard man now.'' Laura affected an exaggerated New England accent. ''You've got shadows under your eyes.''

''You've got stars in yours,'' Kate countered. ''And you're all dressed up too.'' Annoyed, Kate pulled at her sweatshirt. ''What's the deal?''

''Peter's dropping by later.'' Laura turned to the foyer mirror to check the line of her ivory wool dress. Busy dreaming, she didn't notice the winces that Margo and Kate exchanged. ''Just for an hour or so. I can't wait till winter break. One more midterm, and then freedom.'' Flushed with anticipation, she beamed at her friends. ''It's going to be the best winter vacation ever. I have a feeling Peter's going to ask me to marry him.''

''What?'' Kate yelped before Laura could shush her.

''Quiet.'' She hurried back across the blue-and-white-tiled floor toward Kate and Margo. ''I don't want Mom and Dad to hear. Not yet.''

8

"Laura, you can't seriously be thinking of marrying Peter Ridgeway. You barely know him, and you're only seventeen." A million reasons against the idea whirled through Margo's mind.

"I'll be eighteen in a few weeks. It's just a feeling, anyway. Promise me you won't say anything."

"Of course not." Kate reached the bottom of the curving staircase. "You won't do anything crazy, will you?"

"Have I ever?" A wistful smile played around Laura's mouth as she patted Kate's hand. "Let's go in."

"What does she see in him?" Kate mumbled to Margo. "He's old."

"He's twenty-seven," Margo corrected, worried. "He's gorgeous and treats her like a princess. He has . . ." She searched for the word. "Polish."

"Yes, but—"

"Ssh." She spotted her mother coming down the hallway, wheeling a cart laden with hot chocolate. "We don't want to spoil tonight. We'll talk later."

Ann Sullivan's brow furrowed as she studied her daughter. "Margo, I thought that dress was for Christmas Day."

"I'm in a holiday mood," Margo said breezily. "Let me take that, Mum."

Far from satisfied, Ann watched her daughter roll the cart into the parlor before she turned to Kate. "Miss Kate, you've been overworking your eyes again. They're bloodshot. I want you to rest them later with cucumber slices. And where are your slippers?"

"In my closet." Understanding the housekeeper's need to scold, Kate hooked her arm through Ann's. "Come on now, Annie, don't fuss. It's tree-trimming time. Remember the angels you helped us make when we were ten?"

"How could I forget the mess the three of you made? And Mr. Josh teasing the lot of you and biting the heads off Mrs. Williamson's gingerbread men." She lifted a hand to touch Kate's cheek. "You've grown up since. Times like this I miss my little girls."

9

"We'll always be your little girls, Annie." They paused in the parlor doorway to survey the scene.

It made Kate grin, just the look of everything. The tree, already shining with lights, soared a good ten feet. It stood in front of the tall windows that faced the front. Boxes of ornaments brought out of storage sat ready to be opened.

In the lapis hearth decked with candles and fresh greenery a sedate fire flickered. Scents of apple wood and pine and perfume filled the room.

How she loved this house, she thought. Before the decorating was done, every room would have just the right touches of holiday cheer. A bowl of Georgian silver filled with pinecones would be flanked by candles. Banks of poinsettias in gilt-trimmed pots would crowd all the window seats. Delicate porcelain angels would be placed just so on glossy mahogany tables in the foyer. The old Victorian Santa would claim his place of honor on the baby grand.

She could remember her first Christmas at Templeton House. How the grandeur of it had dazzled her eyes and the constant warmth had soothed that ache just under her heart.

Now half of her life had been lived here, and the traditions had become her own.

She wanted to freeze this moment in her mind, make it forever and unchangeable. There, she thought, the way the firelight dances over Aunt Susie's face as she laughs at Uncle Tommy—and the way he takes her hand and holds it. How perfect they look, she thought, the delicate-framed woman and the tall, distinguished man.

Christmas hymns played quietly as she took it all in. Laura knelt by the boxes, lifting out a red glass ball that caught the light and tossed it back. Margo poured steaming chocolate from a silver pot and practiced her flirting skills on Josh.

He stood on a ladder with the lights from the tree glinting in his bronze hair. They played over his face as he grinned down at Margo.

In this room filled with shining silver, sparkling glass, polished old wood and soft fabrics, they were perfect. And they were hers.

"Aren't they beautiful, Annie?"

"That they are. And so are you."

Not like them, Kate thought, as she stepped into the room.

"There's my Katie girl." Thomas beamed at her. "Put the books away for a while, did you?"

"If you can stop answering the phone for an evening, I can stop studying."

"No business on tree-trimming night." He winked at her. "I think the hotels can run without me for one night."

"Never as well as they run with you and Aunt Susie."

Margo lifted a brow as she passed Kate a cup of hot chocolate. "Somebody's bucking for another present. I hope you've got something in mind other than that stupid computer you've been drooling over."

"Computers have become necessary tools in any business. Right, Uncle Tommy?"

"Can't live without them. I'm glad your generation's going to be taking over, though. I hate the blasted things."

"You're going to have to upgrade the system in Sales, across the board," Josh put in as he climbed down the ladder. "No reason to do all that work when a machine can do it for you."

"Spoken like a true hedonist." Margo smirked at him. "Be careful, Josh, you might actually have to learn how to type. Imagine, Joshua Conway Templeton, heir apparent to Templeton Hotels, with a useful skill."

"Listen, duchess—"

"Hold it." Susan cut off her son's testy remark with an upraised hand. "No business tonight, remember. Margo, be a good girl and pass Josh the ornaments. Kate, take that side of the tree with Annie, will you? Laura, you and I will start over here."

"And what about me?" Thomas wanted to know.

"You do what you do best, darling. Supervise."

It wasn't enough to hang them. The ornaments had to be

11

sighed over and stories told about them. There was the wooden elf that Margo had thrown at Josh one year, its head now held on its body with glue. The glass star that Laura had once believed her father had plucked from the sky just for her. Snowflakes that Annie had crocheted for each of the family members. The felt wreath with silver piping that had been Kate's first and last sewing project. The homey and simple hung bough by bough with the priceless antique ornaments Susan had collected from around the world.

When it was done, they held their collective breath as Thomas turned off the lamps. And the room was lit by firelight and the magic of the tree.

"It's beautiful. It's always beautiful," Kate murmured and slipped her hand into Laura's.

Late that night when sleep eluded her, Kate wandered back downstairs. She crept into the parlor, stretched out on the rug beneath the tree, and watched the lights dance.

She liked to listen to the house, the quiet ticking of old clocks, the sighs and murmurs of wood settling, the crackle of spent logs in the hearth. Rain was falling in little needle stabs against the windows. The wind was a whispering song.

It helped to lie there. The nerves over her exam the following day slowly unknotted from her stomach. She knew everyone was tucked into bed, safe, sound. She'd heard Laura come in from her drive with Peter, and sometime later Josh returned from a date.

Her world was in order.

"If you're hanging out for Santa, you've got a long wait." Margo came into the room on bare feet and settled down beside Kate. "You're not still obsessing over some stupid math test, are you?"

"It's a midterm. And if you paid more attention to yours, you wouldn't be skimming by with C's."

"School's just something you have to get through." Margo slipped a pack of cigarettes out of her robe pocket. With every-

12

one in bed, it was safe to sneak a smoke. "So, can you believe Josh is dating that cross-eyed Leah McNee?"

"She's not cross-eyed, Margo. And she's built."

Margo huffed out smoke. Anyone not struck blind could see that compared to Margo Sullivan, Leah was barely female. "He's only dating her because she puts out."

"What do you care?"

"I don't." She sniffed and smoked and sulked. "It's just so . . . ordinary. That's something I'm never going to be."

Smiling a little, Kate turned to her friend. In a blue chenille robe, with her tumbled blond hair, Margo looked stunning and sultry and sleek. "No one would ever accuse you of being ordinary, pal. Obnoxious, conceited, rude, and a royal pain in the ass, yes, but never ordinary."

Margo raised a brow and grinned. "I can always count on you. Anyway, speaking of ordinary, how stuck do you think Laura really is on Peter Ridgeway?"

"I don't know." Kate gnawed on her lip. "She's been dreamy-eyed over him ever since Uncle Tommy transferred him out here. I wish he was still managing Templeton Chicago." Then she shrugged. "He must be good at his job or Uncle Tommy and Aunt Susie wouldn't have promoted him."

"Knowing how to manage a hotel has nothing to do with it. Mr. and Mrs. T have dozens of managers all over the world. This is the only one Laura's gone over on. Kate, if she marries him . . ."

"Yeah." Kate blew out a breath. "It's her decision. Her life. Christ, I can't imagine why anyone would want to get tied down that way."

"Neither can I." Stubbing the cigarette out, Margo lay back. "I'm not going to. I'm going to make a splash in this world."

"Me, too."

Margo slanted Kate a look. "Keeping books? That's more like a slow drip."

"You splash your way, I'll splash mine. This time next year I'll be in college."

Margo shuddered. "What a hideous thought!"

"You'll be there, too," Kate reminded her. "If you don't tank your SAT."

"We'll see about that." College wasn't on Margo's agenda. "I say we find Seraphina's dowry and take that trip around the world we used to talk about. There are places I want to see while I'm still young. Rome and Greece, Paris, Milan, London."

"They're impressive." Kate had seen them. The Templetons had taken her—and would have taken Margo as well if Ann had allowed it. "I see you marrying a rich guy, bleeding him dry, and jet-setting all over."

"Not a bad fantasy." Amused by it, Margo stretched her arms. "But I'd rather be rich myself and just have a platoon of lovers." At the sound in the hall, she shoved the ashtray under the folds of her robe. "Laura." Blowing out a breath, she sat up. "You scared the wits out of me."

"Sorry, couldn't sleep."

"Join the party," Kate invited. "We were planning our future."

"Oh." With a soft, secret smile, Laura knelt on the rug. "That's nice."

"Hold on." Eyes sharp, Margo shifted and took Laura's chin in her hand. After a moment's study, she let out a breath. "Okay, you didn't do it with him."

Flushing, Laura batted Margo's hand away. "Of course I didn't. Peter would never pressure me."

"How do you know she didn't?" Kate demanded.

"You can tell. I don't think you should have sex with him, Laura, but if you're seriously thinking marriage, you'd better try him on first."

"Sex isn't a pair of shoes," Laura muttered.

"But it sure as hell better fit."

"When I make love the first time, it's going to be with my husband on our wedding night. That's the way I want it."

"Uh-oh, she's got that Templeton edge in her voice." Grinning, Kate tugged on a curl falling over Laura's ear. "Unbudgable. Don't listen to Margo, Laura. In her head, sex is equated with salvation.''

Margo lit another cigarette. ''I'd like to know what tops it.''

''Love,'' Laura stated.

''Success,'' Kate said at the same time. ''Well, that sums it up.'' Kate wrapped her arms around her knees. ''Margo's going to be a sex fiend, you're going to search for love, and I'm going to bust my ass for success. What a group.''

''I'm already in love,'' Laura said quietly. ''I want someone who loves me back, and children. I want to wake up each morning knowing I can make a home for them and a happy life for them. I want to fall asleep each night beside someone I can trust and depend on.''

''I'd rather fall asleep at night beside someone who makes me hot.'' Margo chuckled when Kate poked her. ''Just kidding. Sort of. I want to go places and do things. Be somebody. I want to know when I wake up in the morning that something exciting is right around the corner. And whatever it is, I want to make it mine.''

Kate rested her chin on her knees. ''I want to feel accomplished,'' she said quietly. ''I want to make things work the way I think they should work. I want to wake up in the morning knowing exactly what I'm doing next, and how I'm going to do it. I want to be the best at what I do so that I know I haven't wasted anything. Because if I wasted it, it would be like . . . failing.''

Her voice broke, embarrassing her. ''God, I must be overtired.'' Because her eyes were stinging, she rubbed them hard. ''I have to go to bed. My exam's first thing in the morning.''

''You'll breeze through it.'' Laura rose with her. ''Don't worry so much.''

''Professional nerds have to worry.'' But Margo rose as well, and patted Kate's arm. ''Let's get some sleep.''

Kate paused at the doorway to look back at the tree. For a moment she'd been shocked to discover that a part of her wished she could stay here, just like this, forever. Never have to worry about tomorrow or the next day. Never have to concern herself with success or failure. Or change.

Change was coming, she realized. It was barreling down on her in the dewy look in Laura's eyes, the edgy one in Margo's. She turned off the lights. There was no stopping any of it, she realized. So she'd better get ready.

Chapter Two

She got through the days and the nights and the work. There was no choice but to cope. And for the first time in her life, Kate felt there was no one she could talk to. Each time she felt herself tipping, needing to reach for the phone or run to Templeton House, she yanked herself back.

She could not—would not—pour out this misery, these fears to the people who loved her. They would stand by her, there was no doubt about that. But this was a burden she had to carry herself. And one she hoped she could hide in some dark corner of her mind. Eventually she would be able to let it rest, to stop feeling compelled to pick it up, again and again, and examine it.

She considered herself practical, intelligent, and strong. Indeed, she couldn't understand how anyone could be the latter without the two formers.

Until this, her life had been exactly as she wanted it. Her career was cruising along at a safe and, yes, intelligent speed. She had a reputation at Bittle and Associates as a clearheaded, hardworking CPA who could handle complex accounts without complaint. Eventually she expected to be offered a full partnership. When that time came, she would ascend yet another rung on her personal ladder of success.

She had family she loved and who loved her. And friends . . . well, her closest friends were family. And what could be more convenient than that?

She adored them, had loved growing up at Templeton House, overlooking the wild, sweeping cliffs of Big Sur. There was nothing she wouldn't do for Aunt Susie and Uncle Tommy. That included keeping what she had learned weeks before in her office to herself.

She wouldn't question them, though questions burned inside her. She wouldn't share the pain or the problem with Laura or Margo, though she had always shared everything with them.

She would suppress, ignore, and forget. That, she had to believe, would be best for everyone.

Her entire life had been focused on doing her best, being the best, making her family proud. Now, she felt she had more to prove, more to be. Every success she had enjoyed could be traced back to the moment when they had opened their home and their hearts to her. So she promised herself to look forward rather than back. To go on with the routine that had become her life.

Under ordinary circumstances, treasure hunting wouldn't be considered routine. But when it involved Seraphina's dowry, when it included Laura and Margo and Laura's two daughters, it was an event. It was a mission.

The legend of Seraphina, that doomed young girl who had flung herself off the cliffs rather than face a life without her true love, had fascinated the three of them all of their lives. The beautiful Spanish girl had loved Felipe, had met him in secret, walked with him along the cliffs in the wind, in the rain. He had gone off to fight the Americans, to prove himself worthy of her, promising to come back to marry her and build a life with her. But he had not come back. When Seraphina learned he had been killed in battle, she had walked these cliffs

18

again. Had stood on the edge of the world and, overcome with grief, had flung herself over it.

The romance of it, the mystery, the glamour had been irresistible to the three women. And of course, the possibility of finding the dowry that Seraphina had hidden away before she leapt into the sea added challenge.

On most Sundays Kate could be found on the cliffs, wielding a metal detector or a spade. For months, ever since the morning that Margo, at a crossroads in her life, had found a single gold doubloon, the three had met there to search.

Or maybe they gathered not so much in hopes of uncovering a chest of gold as simply to enjoy each other's company.

It was nearly May, and after the jangled nerves she had suffered leading up to April 15 and the income tax deadline, Kate was thrilled to be out in the sun. It was what she needed, she was sure. It helped, as work helped, to keep her mind off the file she had hidden in her apartment. The file on her father that she had carefully organized.

It helped to block out the worries, and the ache in her heart, and the stress of wondering if she'd done the right thing by hiring a detective to look into a twenty-year-old case.

Her muscles protested a bit as she swept the metal detector over a new section of scrub, and she sweated lightly under her T-shirt.

She wouldn't think of it, she promised herself. Not today, not here. She wouldn't think of it at all until the detective's report was complete. She had promised the day to herself, for her family, and nothing would get in the way.

The gorgeous breeze ruffled her short cap of black hair. Her skin was dusky, an inheritance from the Italian branch of her mother's family, though beneath it was what Margo called "accountant's pallor." A few days in the sun, she decided, would fix that.

She'd lost a little weight in the last few weeks of crunch time—and yes, because of the shock of discovering what her father had done—but she intended to put it back on. She always had hopes of putting some meat on her stubbornly thin bones.

She didn't have Margo's height or stunning build, or Laura's lovely fragility. She was, Kate had always thought, average, average and skinny, with an angular face to match her angular body.

Once she had hoped for dimples, or the dash of a few charming freckles, or deep-green eyes instead of ordinary brown. But she'd been too practical to dwell on it for long.

She had a good brain and skill with figures. And that was what she needed to succeed.

She reached down for the jug of lemonade Ann Sullivan had sent along. After a long, indulgent drink, Kate cast a scowl in Margo's direction.

"Are you just going to sit there all afternoon while the rest of us work?"

Margo stretched luxuriously on her rock, her sexpot body draped in what, for Margo Sullivan Templeton, was casual wear of red leggings and a matching shirt. "We're a little tired today," she claimed and patted her flat belly.

Kate snorted. "Ever since you found out you're pregnant you've been finding excuses to sit on your butt."

Margo flashed a smile and tossed her long blond hair behind her shoulders. "Josh doesn't want me to overdo."

"You're playing that one for all it's worth," Kate grumbled.

"Damn right I am." Delighted with life in general, Margo crossed her long, gorgeous legs. "He's so sweet and attentive and thrilled. Jesus, Kate, we've made ourselves a baby."

Maybe the idea of two of her favorite people being blindly in love, starting their own family, did bring Kate a warm glow. But she was bound by tradition to snipe at Margo whenever possible. "At least you could look haggard, throw up every morning, faint now and again."

"I've never felt better in my life." Because it was true, Margo rose and took the metal detector. "Even giving up smoking hasn't been as hard as I thought it would. I never

20

imagined I wanted to be a mother. Now it's all I can think about.''

"You're going to be a fabulous mother," Kate murmured. "Just fabulous."

"Yes, I am." Margo studied Laura, who was giggling and digging at a patch of scrubby earth with her two little girls. "I've got an awfully good role model right there. This past year's been hell for her, but she's never wavered."

"Neglect, adultery, divorce," Kate said quietly, not wanting the fitful breeze to carry her words. "Not a lot of fun and games. The girls have helped keep her centered. And the shop."

"Yeah. And speaking of the shop—" Margo turned the detector off, leaned on it. "If these past couple of weeks are any indication, we may have to hire some help. I'm not going to be able to give Pretenses ten and twelve hours a day after the baby comes."

Always thinking of budget, Kate frowned. The upscale secondhand boutique they had opened on Cannery Row was primarily Margo's and Laura's domain. But as the third partner in the fledgling enterprise, Kate crunched numbers for it when she could squeeze out the time.

"You've got over six months left. That hits holiday shopping time. We could think about hiring seasonal help then."

Sighing, Margo handed the metal detector back to Kate. "The business is doing better than any of us anticipated. Don't you think it's time to loosen up?"

"No." Kate switched the machine back on. "We haven't been open a full year yet. You start taking on outside help, you've got social security, withholding, unemployment."

"Well, yes, but—"

"I can start helping out on Saturdays if necessary, and I've got my vacation time coming up." Work, she thought again. Work and don't think. "I can give Pretenses a couple of weeks full time."

"Kate, a vacation means white-sand beaches, Europe, a sordid affair—not clerking in a shop."

21

Kate merely raised an eyebrow.

"I forgot who I was talking to," Margo muttered. "The original all-work-and-no-play girl."

"That was always to balance you, the quintessential all-play girl. Anyway, I'm a one-third owner of Pretenses. I believe in protecting my investments." She scowled at the ground, kicked it. "Hell, there's not even a bottle cap to give us a little beep and thrill here."

"Are you feeling all right?" Margo's eyes narrowed, looked closer. "You look a little washed out." And frail, she realized. Frail and edgy. "If I didn't know better I'd say you were the one who was pregnant."

"That would be a good trick since I haven't had sex in what feels like the last millennium."

"Which could be why you seem edgy and washed out." But she didn't grin. "Really, Kate, what's going on?"

She wanted to say it, spill out all of it. Knew if she did she would find comfort, support, loyalty—whatever she needed. My problem, she reminded herself.

"Nothing." Kate made herself look down her nose disdainfully. "Except I'm the one doing all the work and my arms are falling off while you sit on your rock and pose for a *Glamorous Mothers-to-Be* photo shoot." She rotated her shoulders. "I need a break."

Margo studied her friend for another moment, tapping her fingers on her knee. "Fine. I'm hungry anyway. Let's see what Mum packed." Opening the nearby hamper, Margo let out a long, heartfelt moan. "Oh, God, fried chicken."

Kate peeked in the hamper. Five minutes more, she decided, then she was digging in. Mrs. Williamson's chicken was bound to erase the nagging hunger pains. "Is Josh back from London?"

"Hmm." Margo swallowed gamely. "Tomorrow. Templeton London did a little remodeling, so he's going to bring back some stock for the shop. And I asked him to check with some of my contacts there, so we may have a nice new supply. It would save me a buying trip."

22

"I remember when you couldn't wait to get on a plane."

"That was then," Margo said smugly. "This is now." She bit into the drumstick again, then remembered something and waved a hand. "Umm, forgot. Party next Saturday night. Cocktails, buffet. Be there."

Kate winced. "Do I have to dress up?"

"Yes. Lots of our customers." She swallowed again. "Some of the hotel brass. Byron De Witt."

Pouting, Kate turned off the machine and grabbed a chicken thigh out of the hamper. "I don't like him."

"Of course not," Margo said dryly. "He's gorgeous, charming, intelligent, world-traveled. Absolutely hateful."

"He knows he's gorgeous."

"And that takes a lot of nerve. I don't really give a damn whether you like him or not. He's taken a lot of the weight off Josh here at the California hotels, recovered a lot of the ground Peter Ridgeway lost for us."

She caught herself and glanced over toward Laura. Peter was Laura's ex-husband, the girls' father, and whatever she thought of him, she wouldn't criticize him in front of Ali and Kayla.

"Just be civil."

"I'm always civil. Hey, guys," Kate called out and watched Ali and Kayla's pretty blond heads pop up. "We've got Mrs. Williamson's fried chicken over here, and Margo's eating it all."

With shouts and scrambling feet, the girls dashed up to join the picnic. Laura came after them and sat cross-legged at Margo's feet. She watched her daughters squabble over one particular piece of chicken. Ali won, of course. She was the older of the two and in recent months the more demanding.

Divorce, Laura reminded herself as Ali smugly nibbled her chicken, was very, very hard on a ten-year-old girl. "Ali, pour Kayla a glass of lemonade too."

Ali hesitated, considered refusing. It seemed, Laura thought as she kept cool, calm eyes on her daughter's mutinous ones, that Ali considered refusing everything these days. In the end,

Ali shrugged and poured a second glass for her sister.

"We didn't find anything," Ali complained, choosing to forget the fun she'd had giggling and digging in the dirt. "It's boring."

"Really?" Margo selected a cube of cheese from a plastic container. "For me, just being here and looking is half the fun."

"Well . . ." Whatever Margo said was, to Ali, gospel. Margo was glamorous and different; Margo had run away to Hollywood at eighteen, had lived in Europe and had been involved in wonderful, exciting scandals. Nothing ordinary and awful like marriage and divorce. "I guess it's kinda fun. But I wish we'd find more coins."

"Persistence." Kate flipped a finger from Ali's chin to her nose. "Pays. What would have happened if Alexander Graham Bell had given up before he put that first call through? If Indiana Jones hadn't gone on that last crusade?"

"If Armani hadn't sewed that first seam?" Margo put in and earned a fresh giggle.

"If *Star Trek* hadn't gone where no one had gone before," Laura finished, and had the pleasure of seeing her daughter flash a smile.

"Well, maybe. Can we see the coin again, Aunt Margo?"

Margo reached in her pocket. She'd fallen into the habit of carrying the old Spanish gold coin with her. Ali took it gingerly, and because she was awed, as always, held it so that Kayla could coo over it too.

"It's so shiny." Kayla touched it reverently. "Can I pick some flowers for Seraphina?"

"Sure." Leaning over, Laura kissed the top of her head. "But don't go near the edge to throw them over without me."

"I won't. We always do it together."

"I guess I'll help her." Ali handed Margo the coin. But when she stood up, her pretty mouth went thin. "Seraphina was stupid to jump. Just because she wasn't going to be able to marry Felipe. Marriage is no good anyway." Then she remembered Margo and blushed.

"Sometimes," Laura said quietly, "marriage is wonderful and kind and strong. And other times it isn't wonderful enough, or kind enough or strong enough. But you're right, Ali, Seraphina shouldn't have jumped. When she did that, she ended everything she could have become, threw away all those possibilities. It makes me feel very sorry for her." She watched her daughter, head drooping, shoulders hunched, walk away. "She's so hurt. She's so angry."

"She'll get through this." Kate gave Laura's hand a bracing squeeze. "You're doing everything right."

"It's been three months since they've seen Peter. He hasn't even bothered to call them."

"You're doing everything right," Kate repeated. "You're not responsible for the asshole. She knows you're not to blame—inside she knows that."

"I hope so." Laura shrugged and picked at a piece of chicken. "Kayla just bounces and Ali broods. Well, I guess we're a textbook example that kids can grow up in the same house and be raised by the same people and turn out differently."

Kate's stomach wrenched.

"True." Margo had a low-grade urge for a cigarette, quashed it. "But we're all so fabulous. Well . . ." She smiled sweetly at Kate. "Most of us."

"Just for that, I'm eating the last piece of chicken." Kate popped a couple of Tums first. Medication helped her to eat when she had no desire for food. Nervous heartburn, she thought of the low burn just under her breastbone. Insisted on thinking of it that way. "I was telling Margo that I'd be able to pitch in at the shop on Saturdays."

"We could use the help." Laura shifted so she could continue the conversation and keep an eye on her daughters. "Last Saturday was a madhouse, and I could only give Margo four hours."

"I can put in a full day."

"Wonderful." Margo plucked some glossy grapes from a

bunch. "You'll be hunkered over the computer the whole time, trying to find mistakes."

"If you didn't make them, I wouldn't have to find them. But . . ." She held up a hand, not so much to avoid the argument as to make a point. "I'll stay at the counter, and I have twenty bucks that says I make more sales than you by the time we close."

"In your dreams, Powell."

On Monday morning, Kate wasn't thinking about dreams or treasure hunts. At nine sharp, with her third cup of coffee at her elbow, her computer booted, she was behind her desk in her office at Bittle and Associates. Following her daily routine, she had already removed her navy pin-striped jacket, draped it behind her chair, and rolled up the sleeves of her starched white shirt.

The sleeves would be rolled back down and the jacket neatly buttoned into place for her eleven o'clock meeting with a client, but for now it was just Kate and numbers.

And that was how she liked it best.

The challenge of making numbers dance and shuffle and fall neatly into place had always fascinated her. There was a beauty in the ebb and flow of interest rates, T-bills, mutual funds. And a power, she could privately admit, in understanding, even admiring, the caprice of finance, and confidently advising clients how best to protect their hard-earned money.

Not that it was always hard-earned, she thought with a snort as she studied the account on her screen. A good many of her clients had earned their money the old-fashioned way.

They'd inherited it.

Even as the thought crossed her mind, she cringed. Was that her father in her, sneering at those who had inherited wealth? Taking a deep breath, she rubbed a hand over the tense spot in the back of her neck. She had to stop this, seeing ghosts around every thought in her head.

It was her job to advise and protect and to ensure that any account she handled through Bittle was served well. Not only was she not envious of her clients' portfolios, she worked hand in glove with lawyers, bookkeepers, brokers, agents, and estate planners to provide each and every one of them the very best in short- and long-term financial advice.

That, she reminded herself, was who she was.

What she reveled in was the numbers, their stoic and dependable consistency. For Kate two and two always and forever equaled four.

To realign herself, she skimmed through a spreadsheet for Ever Spring Nursery and Gardens. In the eighteen months since she had taken over that account, she'd watched it slowly, cautiously expand. She believed strongly in the slow and the cautious, and this client had taken her direction well. True, the payroll had swelled, but the business justified it. Outlay for the health plan and employee benefits was high and nipped at the profit margin, but as a woman raised by the Templetons, she also firmly believed in sharing success with the people who helped you earn it.

"A good year for bougainvillea," she muttered, and made a note to suggest that her client ease some of the last quarter's profits into tax-free bonds.

Render unto Caesar, sure, she thought, but not one damn penny more than necessary.

"You look beautiful when you're plotting."

Kate glanced up, her fingers automatically hitting the keys to store her data and bring up her screen saver. "Hello, Roger."

He leaned against the doorjamb. Posed, was Kate's unflattering thought. Roger Thornhill was tall, dark, and handsome, with classic features reminiscent of Cary Grant in his prime. Broad shoulders fit beautifully under a tailored gray suit jacket. He had a quick, brilliant smile, dark-blue eyes that zeroed in flatteringly on a woman's face, and a smooth baritone that flowed like melted honey.

Perhaps it was for all of those reasons that Kate couldn't abide him. It was only coincidence that they were on the same fast track for partnership. That, she assured herself often, had nothing to do with why he annoyed her.

Or just a very little to do with it.

"Your door was open," he pointed out and strolled in without invitation. "I figured you weren't very busy."

"I like my door open."

He flashed that wide, toothy smile and eased a hip onto the corner of her desk. "I just got back from Nevis. A couple of weeks in the West Indies sure clears out the system after the tax crunch." His gaze roamed over her face. "You should have come with me."

"Roger, when I won't even have dinner with you, why would you think I'd spend two weeks frolicking with you in the sand and surf?"

"Hope springs eternal?" He took one of the pencils, sharpened like swords, from her Lucite holder, slid it idly through his fingers. Her pencils were always sharpened and always kept in the same place. There was nothing in her office that didn't have a proper slot. He knew all of them. An ambitious man, Roger made use of what he knew.

He also made use of charm, keeping his eyes on hers, smiling. "I'd just like us to get to know each other again, outside the office. Hell, Kate, it's been almost two years."

Deliberately, she raised an eyebrow. "Since?"

"Okay, since I messed things up." He put the pencil down. "I'm sorry. I don't know how else to say it."

"Sorry?" Voice mild, she rose to refill her coffee, though the third cup wasn't sitting well. She sat again, watching him as she sipped. "Sorry that you were sleeping with me and one of my clients at the same time? Or that you were sleeping with me in order to get to my client? Or that you seduced said client into moving her account from my hands to yours? Which of those are you apologizing for, Roger?"

"All of them." Because it invariably worked with females, he tried the smile again. "Look, I've already apologized countless times, but I'm willing to do it again. I had no business seeing Bess, ah, Mrs. Turner, much less sleeping with

28

her, while you and I were involved. There's no excuse for it.''

"We agree. Good-bye.''

"Kate.'' His eyes stayed on hers, his voice flowing, just the way she remembered it had when she had moved under him, climbing toward climax. "I want to make things right with you. At least make peace with you.''

She cocked her head, considered. There was right and there was wrong. There were ethics and there was the lack of them. "No.''

"Damn it.'' With his first sign of temper, he stood up from the desk, the movement jerky and abrupt. "I was a son of a bitch. I let sex and ambition get in the way of what was a good, satisfying relationship.''

"You're absolutely right,'' she agreed. "And you didn't know me well the first time around if you have any hope that I'd let you repeat the performance.''

"I stopped seeing Bess months ago, on a personal level.''

"Oh, well, then.'' Leaning back in her chair, Kate enjoyed a good, rolling laugh. "Jesus Christ, you're a case, Roger. You think because you've cleared the field, I'm going to suit up and jump into the game? We're associates,'' she told him, "and that's all. I'm never going to make the mistake of getting involved with someone at work again, and I'm never—repeat, never—going to give you another shot.''

His mouth thinned. "You're afraid to see me outside the office. Afraid because you'd remember how good we were together.''

She had to sigh. "Roger, we weren't that good. My appraisal would put us at adequate. Let's just close the books on this one.'' In the interest of sanity, she rose, held out her hand. "You want to put it behind us, let's. No hard feelings.''

Intrigued, he studied her hand, then her face. "No hard feelings?''

No feelings at all, she thought, but decided not to say it. "Fresh sheet,'' she said. "We're colleagues, marginally friendly. And you'll stop pestering me about having dinner or taking trips to the West Indies.''

He took her hand. "I've missed you, Kate. Missed touching you. All right," he said quickly when he saw her eyes narrow, "if that's the best I can do, I'll take it. I appreciate your accepting my apology."

"Fine." Struggling to be patient, she tugged her hand away. "Now I've got work to do."

"I'm glad we worked this out." He was smiling again as he walked to the door.

"Yeah, right," she muttered. She didn't slam the door behind him. That would have indicated too much emotion. She didn't want Roger the slime Thornhill, to get the idea there was any emotion inside her where he was concerned.

But she did close the door, quietly, purposefully, before sitting back down at her desk. She took out a bottle of Mylanta, sighed a little, and chugged.

He had hurt her. It was demoralizing to remember just how much he had hurt her. She hadn't been in love with him, but with a little more time, a little more effort, she could have been. They had had the common ground of their work, which she believed could have served as a strong foundation for more.

She had cared for him, and trusted him, and enjoyed him.

And he had used her ruthlessly to steal one of her biggest clients. That was almost worse than discovering he'd been jumping from her bed to her client's bed and back again.

Kate took another swig from the bottle before recapping it. She had, at the time, considered going to Larry Bittle with a formal complaint. But her pride had outweighed whatever satisfaction she might have gleaned from that.

The client was satisfied, and that was the bottom line at Bittle. Roger would have lost some ground, certainly, if she'd filed a complaint. Others in the office would have distrusted him, pulled back from him.

And she would have looked like the whining, betrayed female, sniveling because she had mixed sex and business and had lost.

Better that she'd kept it to herself, Kate decided and put the

Mylanta back in her drawer. Better that she'd been able to say, straight to his face, that she had put the whole incident behind her.

Even if it was a lie, even if she would detest him for the rest of her life.

With a shrug, she recalled her data. Better by far to avoid slick, smart, gorgeous men with more ambition than heart. Better, much better, to stay in the fast lane on the career track and avoid any and all distractions. Partnership was waiting, with all the success it entailed.

When she had that partnership, had climbed to that next rung, she would have earned it. And maybe, she thought, just maybe, when she reached that level of success, she would be able to prove to herself that she was not her father's daughter.

She smiled a little as she began to run figures. Stick with numbers, pal, she reminded herself. They never lie.

Chapter Three

The minute Kate walked into Pretenses, Margo scowled. "You look like death."

"Thanks. I want coffee." And a moment alone. She headed up the curving stairs to the second floor, found the pot already brewing.

She knew she hadn't slept more than three hours, not after poring over every detail in the report from the detective back east. And every detail had confirmed that she was the daughter of a thief.

It was all there—the evidence, the charges, the statements. And reading through those papers had killed the faint hope she'd hidden even from herself that it had all been some sort of mistake.

Instead, she had learned that her father had been out on bail at the time of the accident and had instructed his lawyer to accept the plea bargain he'd been offered. If he hadn't been killed that night on that icy stretch of road, he would have been in prison within the week.

Telling herself to accept it, to get on with her life, she drank her coffee hot and black. She needed to go back down, get to work. And face a friend who knew her too well to miss signs of stress.

Well, she thought, carrying her cup with her, she had other excuses for a poor night's sleep. And there was nothing to be gained by obsessing over facts that couldn't be changed. From this moment, Kate promised herself, she would cease to think about it.

"What's going on?" Margo demanded when Kate wound her way down the stairs. "I want an answer this time. You've been jumpy and out of sorts for weeks. And I swear you're losing weight with every breath. This has just gone on long enough, Kate."

"I'm fine. Tired." She shrugged. "A couple of accounts are giving me some problems. On top of that it's been a weird week." Kate opened the cash register, counted out the bills and coins for morning change. "Monday, that scum Thornhill came slinking into my office."

Margo turned from setting up the teapot. "I hope you kicked his ass right out again."

"I let him think we've made up. It was easier," she said before Margo could comment. "He's more likely to leave me alone now."

"You're not going to tell me that's what's keeping you up at night."

"It gave me some bad moments, okay?"

"Okay." Margo smiled in sympathy. "Men are pigs, and that one is a blue ribbon hog. Don't waste your beauty sleep on him, honey."

"Thanks. Anyway, that was only the first weird thing."

"The wacky life of a CPA."

"Wednesday, I got tossed this new account. Freeland. It's a petting zoo, kiddie park, museum. Very strange. I'm learning all about how much it costs to feed a baby llama."

Margo paused. "You lead such a fascinating life."

"You're telling me. Then yesterday, the partners all huddled together for most of the afternoon. Even the secretaries were barred. Nobody has a clue, but the rumor is somebody's about to be canned or promoted.'' Kate shrugged and closed the cash register. "I've never seen them powwow like that. They had to make their own coffee.''

"Stop the presses.''

"Look, my little world has just as much intrigue and drama as anyone else's.'' She stepped back as Margo advanced on her. "What?''

"Just hold still.'' Grabbing Kate's lapel, Margo pinned on a crescent-shaped brooch dangling with drops of amber. "Advertise the merchandise.''

"It's got dead bugs in it.''

Margo didn't bother to sigh. "Put some lipstick on, for God's sake. We open in ten minutes.''

"I don't have any with me. And I'll tell you right now, I'm not going to work with you all day if you're going to be picking on me. I can sell, ring up, and box just fine without painting my face.''

"Fine.'' Before Kate could evade her, Margo picked up an atomizer and spritzed her with perfume. "Advertise the merchandise,'' she repeated. "If anyone asks what you're wearing, it's Bella Donna's Savage.''

Kate had just worked up a snarl when Laura burst in. "I thought I was going to be late. Ali had a hair emergency. I was afraid one of us would kill the other before it was over.''

"She's getting more like Margo every day.'' Wishing it were coffee, Kate strolled over to pour herself tea and used it to wash down a palm full of pills she didn't want either of her friends to see. "I meant that in the worst possible way,'' she added.

"A young girl becoming interested in appearance and grooming is natural,'' Margo shot back. "You were the changeling in the family. Still are, as you constantly prove, by going around like a scarecrow dressed in navy blue serge.''

Unoffended, Kate sipped at her tea. "Navy serge is classic because it's serviceable. There is only a very small percentage

35

of the population who feel honor bound to fart through silk.''

"Jesus, you're crude," Margo managed over a laugh. "I don't even want to argue with you."

"That's a relief." Hoping to keep it that way, Laura hurried over to turn the Open sign around. "I'm still cross-eyed from arguing with Allison. If Annie hadn't intervened, it would have been hairbrushes at ten paces."

"Mum always could defuse a good fight," Margo commented. "Okay, ladies, remember, we're pushing Mother's Day. And in case it slipped both of your minds, expectant mothers also warrant gifts."

Kate braced for the onslaught and struggled to ignore the viselike clamp on her temples that was usually the sign of a migraine on the boil.

Within an hour Pretenses was busy enough to keep all three of them occupied. Kate boxed up a Hermès bag of dark-green leather, wondering what anyone needed with a green leather purse. But the slick slide of the credit card machine kept her cheerful. She was, by her calculations, neck and neck with Margo on sales.

It was a fine feeling, she thought as she wrapped the gold and silver box in elegant floral paper, watching the business progress. And the combo of competition and medication had eased the headache that had been threatening.

She had to give Margo full credit for it. Pretenses had been a dream rising like smoke from the ashes of Margo's life.

Just over a year ago, Margo's career as a popular model in Europe, her exposure and financial rewards as the Bella Donna Woman, had been rudely cut off. Not that Margo was blameless, Kate thought, smiling as she handed the purchase to her customer. She'd been reckless, foolish, headstrong. But she hadn't deserved to lose everything.

She'd come back from Milan broken and nearly bankrupt, but in a matter of months, through her own grit, she had turned her life around.

Opening a shop and selling her possessions in it had been Josh Templeton's idea originally. His idea, Kate mused, to keep Margo from sinking, since he was blindly in love with her. But Margo had expanded the idea, nurtured it, polished it.

Then Laura, reeling from her husband's deceit, betrayal, and greed, had taken the bulk of what he'd left of her money and helped Margo buy the building for Pretenses.

When Kate had insisted on acquiring a one-third interest, thus making herself a partner, it had been because she believed in the investment, because she believed in Margo. And because she didn't want to be left out of the fun.

Of all of them, she understood the risks best. Nearly forty percent of new businesses failed within a year, and almost eighty percent went under within five.

And Kate worried over it, gnawed on it at night when she couldn't sleep. But Pretenses, Margo's conception of an elegant, exclusive, and unique secondhand shop that offered everything from designer gowns to teaspoons, was holding its own.

Kate's part in it might have been small, and her reasons for getting involved certainly straddled the practical and the emotional, but she was enjoying herself. When she wasn't obsessing.

Here was proof, after all, that life could be what you made of it. She badly needed to hang on to that idea.

"Is there something I can show you?" The man she smiled at was thirtyish, attractive in a rugged, lived-in manner. She appreciated the worn jeans, the faded shirt, the dashing reddish moustache.

"Ah, well, maybe. This necklace here."

She looked down into the display, zeroed in on his choice. "It's pretty, isn't it? Pearls are so classic."

Not regular pearls, she thought as she lifted the necklace out. What the hell were they called? She continued to search through her mind as she draped the necklace over a velvet form.

"Seed pearls," she remembered and beamed at him. He really was awfully cute. "It's called a lariat," she added.

She'd gotten that off the tag. "Three strands, and the clasp, or the slide thing has a . . ." Give me a minute. "A mabe pearl set in gold. Tradition with a flair," she added, enjoying the ad lib.

"I wondered how much . . ." Hesitating, he flipped the tiny, discreet price tag over. To his credit, he winced only slightly. "Well," he smiled a little, "it hits the top of my price range."

"It's something she'll wear for years. Is it for Mother's Day?"

"Yeah." He shifted his feet, running a calloused finger over the strands. "She'd go nuts over it."

She melted toward him. Any man who would take such time and trouble for a gift for his mother earned top points from Kate Powell. Especially when he looked just a little bit like Kevin Costner. "We have several other really nice pieces that aren't quite so expensive."

"No, I think . . . maybe . . . Could you put it on so I could get a better picture?"

"Sure." Happy to oblige, she fastened it around her neck. "What do you think? Is it great?" She angled the counter mirror so that she could judge for herself and added, laughing, "If you don't buy it, I might have to snap it up myself."

"It looks awfully pretty on you," he said with a shy, quiet smile that made her want to scoop him up and bundle him into the back room. "She's got dark hair like you. Wears it longer, but the pearls look good with dark hair. I guess I'll have to take it. Along with that box over there, the silver one with all the fancy scrolling."

Still wearing the necklace, Kate scooted out from behind the counter to get the trinket box he'd pointed to. "Two presents." She reached up to undo the necklace clasp. "Your mother must be a very special woman."

"Oh, she's great. She's going to like this box. She sort of collects them. The necklace is for my wife, though," he added. "I'm getting all my Mother's Day shopping done at one time."

"Your wife." Kate forced herself to keep her lips cheerily

curved at the corners. "I guarantee she'll love it. But if she or your mother prefers something else, we have a thirty-day exchange and return policy." With what she considered admirable restraint, Kate laid the necklace down. "Now, will that be cash or charge?"

Ten minutes later she watched him saunter out. "The cute ones," she muttered to Laura, "the nice ones, the ones who love their mothers are all married."

"There, there." Laura patted Kate's arm before reaching under the counter to select the proper box. "It looked like a very good sale."

"Puts me at least two hundred up on Margo. And the day's young."

"That's the spirit. But I should warn you, she's got one back in the wardrobe room now, and she's definitely leaning toward Versace."

"Shit." Kate turned to scan the main showroom for prey. "I'm going for the blue-haired lady with the Gucci bag. She's mine."

"Reel her in, tiger."

Kate didn't break for lunch and told herself it was because she wanted to keep up her momentum, not because her stomach was acting up again. She had tremendous success in the second-floor ladies' boudoir and racked up two peignoirs, a stained-glass accent lamp, and a tasseled footstool.

Maybe she did sneak into the back room a couple of times to boot up the computer and check Margo's bookkeeping. But only when her lead was comfortable. She corrected the expected mistakes, rolled her eyes over a few unexpected ones, and tidied up the files.

She was forced to admit, in the end, that accountant's lapse was what cost her the victory. When she came back, smug, already preparing the lecture she intended to deliver to Margo on the cost of careless accounting, her rival was closing a sale.

A whopper.

Kate knew antiques. A child didn't grow up at Templeton House and not learn to recognize and appreciate them. Her heart sank even as dollar signs revolved in her head when she recognized the piece Margo was cooing over.

Louis XVI, Kate recited in her head. A *secrétaire-à-abattant*, probably near 1775. The marquetry panels, typical of that era, included vases and garlands of flowers, musical instruments and drapery.

Oh, it was a stunner, Kate thought, and one of the remaining pieces from Margo's original stock.

"I'm sorry to lose it," Margo was telling the dapper white-haired gentleman who leaned on a gold-headed cane and studied the *secretaire* and the woman who described it with equal admiration. "I bought it in Paris several years ago."

"You have a wonderful eye. In fact, you have two wonderful eyes."

"Oh, Mr. Stiener, that's so sweet of you." In her shameless style, Margo trailed a finger down his arm. "I do hope you'll think of me, now and again, when you're enjoying this."

"I can promise you I will. Now, as to shipping?"

"Just come over to the counter and I'll take all the necessary information." Margo crossed the room, hips swinging, and shot Kate a triumphant look.

"I think that crushes you for the day, ace," she said when her customer strolled out.

"The day's not over," Kate insisted. "We still have two hours until closing. So until the fat lady sings—which will be you in a few months—don't count your chickens."

"Such a sore loser." Margo clucked her tongue and was ready to pounce when the door jangled. It wasn't a customer, but she pounced anyway. "Josh!"

He caught her, kissed her, then pulled her to a chair. "Off your feet." He kept one hand on her shoulder and turned to glare at Kate. "You're supposed to be keeping an eye on her, making sure she doesn't overdo."

"Don't hang this on me. Besides, Margo doesn't stand when she can sit and doesn't sit when she can lie down. And I made her drink a glass of milk an hour ago."

Josh narrowed his eyes. "A whole glass?"

"What she didn't spit at me." Because it amused and touched her to see her big brother worry and fuss, Kate decided to forgive him. She stepped over and kissed him. "Welcome home."

"Thanks." He stroked a hand over her hair. "Where's Laura?"

"Upstairs with a couple of customers."

"And there's another one in the wardrobe room," Margo began, "so—"

"Sit," Josh ordered. "Kate can handle it. You're looking pale."

Margo pouted. "I am not."

"You're going home and taking a nap," he decided. "No way you're going to work all day, then run around giving a party. Kate and Laura can finish out here."

"Sure we can." Kate shot Margo a smug look. "A couple of hours should do it."

"Keep dreaming, Powell. I've already won."

"Won?" Always interested in a bet, Josh looked from woman to woman. "Won what?"

"Just a friendly wager that I could outsell her."

"Which she's already lost," Margo pointed out. "And I'm feeling generous. You can have the two-hour handicap, Kate." Taking Josh's hand, she rubbed it against her cheek. "And when you've lost, officially, you wear the Ungaro slip dress, the red, to the party tonight."

"The thing that looks like a nightgown? You might as well be naked."

"Really?" Josh wiggled his eyebrows. "No offense, Kate, hope you lose. Come on, duchess, home, bed."

"I'm not wearing a red slip to any party," Kate insisted.

"Then don't lose," Margo said with a careless shrug as she walked with Josh to the door. "But when you do, have Laura pick out the accessories."

She wore a hammered-gold collar and triangular earrings that danced below her lobes. Her complaints that she looked

41

like a slave girl captured by the Klingons fell on deaf ears. Even the shoes had been forced on her. Red satin skyscrapers that had her teetering at three and a half inches over her normal five seven.

She sipped champagne and felt like a fool.

It didn't help matters that some of her clients were there. Margo and Josh's acquaintances ran toward the rich, the famous, and the privileged. And she wondered how she was going to maintain her image as a clearheaded, precise, and dedicated accountant when she was dressed like a bimbo.

But a bet was a bet.

"Stop fidgeting," Laura ordered when she joined Kate on the terrace. "You look stunning."

"This from a woman tastefully garbed in an elegant suit that covers her extremities. What I look," she said after another gulp of champagne, "is desperate. I might as well be wearing a sign. 'Single Woman, HIV negative, apply in person.'"

Laura laughed. "As long as you're hiding out here, I don't think you have to worry about it." With a sigh, she leaned back on the decorative banister. "God, it's a beautiful night. Half-moon, starlight, the sound of the sea. A sky like that, it doesn't seem like anything bad could ever happen under it. This is a good house. Can you feel that, Kate? Margo and Josh's house. It's good."

"Excellent investment, prime location, excellent view." She smiled at Laura's bland stare. "Okay, yeah, I can feel it. It's a good house. It has heart and character. I like thinking of them here, together. Of them raising a family here."

Relaxed now, she leaned back with Laura. There was music drifting through the open doors and windows, the friendly sound of conversation, the tinkle of laughter. She could smell flowers, the sea, a mix of feminine perfumes, exotic tidbits being passed around on silver trays. And she could, simply by standing there, feel the permanence and the promise.

Like Templeton House, she mused, where she had spent so much of her life. Maybe that was why she had never been driven to make a home of her own, why an apartment convenient to work was all she'd wanted. Because, she thought with a faint smile, she could always go home to Templeton House. And now she could always come here as well.

"Oh, hello, Byron. I didn't know you were here."

At Laura's easy greeting Kate's pretty mood popped. She opened her eyes, straightened up from the banister and squared her shoulders. Something about Byron De Witt always made her feel confrontational.

"I just got here. I had some business that ran over. You look lovely, as always." He squeezed Laura's offered hand lightly before turning his gaze to Kate. The shadows were deep enough that she didn't notice his deep-green eyes widen slightly. But she did catch the quick, amused grin. "Nice to see you. Can I get either of you a fresh drink?"

"No, I have to get back inside." Laura stepped toward the terrace doors. "I promised Josh I'd charm Mr. and Mrs. Ito. We're in hot competition for their banquet business in Tokyo."

She was gone too quickly for Kate to scowl at her.

"Would you like another glass of champagne?"

Kate scowled down into her glass instead. It was still half full. "No, I'm fine."

Byron contented himself by lighting a thin cigar. He knew Kate's pride wouldn't permit her to bolt. Normally, he wouldn't have stayed with her any longer than manners dictated, but at the moment he was a little tired of people and understood that ten minutes with her would be more interesting than an hour with the party crowd. Especially if he could irritate her, as he seemed so skilled at doing.

"That's quite a dress, Katherine."

She bristled, as he'd expected, at his use of her full name. Grinning around the cigar, he leaned back and prepared to enjoy the diversion.

"I lost a bet," she said between her teeth.

"Really?" He reached out to toy with and tug up the thin strap that had slid off her shoulder. "Some bet."

"Hands off," she snapped.

"Fine." Deliberately he moved the strap down again so that she was forced to pull it up. "You've got a good eye for real estate," he commented and nodded at the surroundings when she frowned at him. "You steered Josh and Margo to this place, didn't you?"

"Yeah." She watched him, waited, but he seemed content to puff on his cigar and study the view.

He was just the type she'd decided to dislike. Poster-boy gorgeous, she termed it derisively. Thick brown hair that showed hints and streaks of gold waved with careless attraction around a heart-stopping face. What would have been charming dimples in his youth had deepened to creases in his cheeks that were now designed to incite a woman's sexual fantasies. The firm, hero's chin, the straight, aristocrat's nose, and those dark, dark green eyes that could, at his whim, slide over you as if you were invisible or pin you shuddering to the wall.

Six two, she judged, with the long limbs and strong shoulders of a long-distance runner. And of course, that voice, with its faint, misty drawl that hinted of hot summer nights and southern comfort.

Men like him, Kate had decided, were not ever to be trusted.

"That's new," he murmured.

Caught staring and appraising as his sharp green eyes shifted to hers, Kate looked quickly away. "What?"

"That scent you're wearing. It suits you better than the soap and talc you seem so fond of. Straight up sexy," he continued, smiling when she gaped at him. "No games, no illusions."

She'd known him for months, ever since he had transferred from Atlanta to Monterey to take over Peter Ridgeway's position at Templeton. He was, by all accounts, a savvy, experienced, and creative hotelier, one who had worked his way to the top of the Templeton organization over a period of fourteen years.

She knew he came from money, polite southern wealth, steeped in tradition and chivalry.

44

She had disliked him on sight and had been confident, despite his unflagging manners, that her feelings were reciprocated.

"Are you coming on to me?"

His eyes, still on hers, filled with humor. "I was commenting on your perfume, Katherine. If I were coming on to you, you wouldn't have to clarify."

She tossed back the rest of her wine. A mistake, she knew, with a migraine lurking. "Don't call me Katherine."

"That always seems to slip my mind."

"Like hell."

"Exactly. And if I were to tell you you're looking particularly attractive tonight, that would be an observation, not an overture. Anyway . . . Kate. We were discussing real estate."

She continued to scowl. Even Margo's favored Cristal champagne didn't sit well on a nervous stomach. "We were?"

"Or were about to. I'm considering buying a home in the area. Since my six-month trial period is almost over—"

"You had a trial period?" It cheered her considerably to picture him on probation at Templeton California.

"I had six months to decide if I wanted to be based here permanently or go back to Atlanta." Reading her mind easily, he grinned. "I like it here—the sea, the cliffs, the forests. I like the people I work with. But I don't intend to continue to live in a hotel, however well run and lovely it may be."

She shrugged, irritated by the way the wine seemed to be sitting like lead under her breastbone. "Your business, De Witt, not mine."

He would not, he told himself patiently, allow her prickly nature to divert him from his objective. "You know the area, you have contacts and a good eye for quality and value. I thought you could let me know if you hear about any interesting property, particularly in the Seventeen Mile Drive area."

"I'm not a realtor," she muttered.

"Good. That means I don't have to worry about your commission."

Because she appreciated that, she bent. "There is a place—might be a little big for your needs."

"I like big."

"Figures. It's near Pebble Beach. Four or five bedrooms, I can't remember. But it's back off the road, a lot of cypress trees and a nice established yard. Decks," she continued, squinting her eyes as she tried to remember. "Front and back. Wood—cedar, I think. Lots of glass. It's been on the market about six months and hasn't moved. There's probably a reason for that."

"Might be it was waiting for the right buyer. Do you know the realtor?"

"Sure, they're a client. Monterey Bay Real Estate. Ask for Arlene. She shoots straight."

"I appreciate it. If it works out, I'll have to buy you dinner."

"No, thanks. Just consider it a—" She broke off as pain stabbed into her stomach, then, like a sick echo, erupted in her head. The glass slipped out of her hand and shattered on the tile even as he grabbed her.

"Hold on." He picked her up, had a moment to notice she was little more than bones and nerves, before he eased her onto the cushions of a chair. "Jesus Christ, Kate, you're dead white. I'll get someone."

"No." Biting back on the pain, she grabbed at his arm. "It's nothing. Just a twinge. Sometimes alcohol—wine on an empty stomach," she managed, regulating her breathing. "I should know better."

His brow knit, his voice thrummed with impatience. "When did you eat last?"

"I was kind of swamped today."

"Idiot." He straightened. "There's enough food around here for three hundred starving sailors. I'll get you a damn plate."

"No, I—" Ordinarily that vicious look wouldn't have quelled her, but at the moment she was feeling shaky. "Okay, thanks, but don't say anything. It'll only worry them, and

46

they've got all these people here. Just don't say anything," she repeated, then watched him, after one last, smoldering look, stride off.

Her hand trembled a bit as she opened her bag and swigged from a small medicine bottle. All right, she promised herself, she would take better care of herself. She'd start trying those yoga exercises Margo had shown her. She'd stop drinking so much damn coffee.

She would stop thinking.

By the time he came back she was feeling steadier. One look at the plate he carried and she let out a laugh. "How many of those starving sailors do you intend to feed?"

"Just eat," he ordered and popped a small, succulent shrimp into her mouth himself.

After a moment's deliberation, she scooted over on the cushion. A distraction, even in the form of Byron De Witt, was what she needed. "I guess I have to ask you to sit down and share."

"You're always so gracious."

She chose a tiny spinach quiche. "I just don't like you, De Witt."

"Fair enough." He dipped into some crab soufflé. "I don't like you either, but I was taught to be polite to a lady."

Yet he thought of her. Odder still, he dreamed of her, a fog-drenched, erotic dream he couldn't quite remember in the morning. Something about the cliffs and the crash of waves, the feel of soft skin and a slim body under his hands, those big, dark, Italian eyes staring into his.

It left him uncomfortably amused with himself.

Byron De Witt was sure of many things. The national debt would never be paid, women in thin cotton dresses were the best reason for summer, rock and roll was here to stay, and Katherine Powell was not his type.

Skinny, abrasive women with more attitude than charm didn't appeal to him. He liked them soft, and smart, and sexy. He admired them simply for being women and delighted in

47

the bonuses of quiet conversation, hardheaded debate, outrageous laughter, and hot, mindless sex.

He considered himself as much of an expert on the female mystique as any man could be. After all, he'd grown up surrounded by them, the lone son in a household with three daughters. Byron knew women, and knew them well. And he knew what he liked.

No, he wasn't remotely attracted to Kate.

Still, the dream nagged at him as he prepared for the day. It followed him into the executive weight room, tugged at the back of his mind as he pushed himself through reps and sets and pyramids. It lingered while he finished off his routine with twenty minutes of the *Wall Street Journal* and the treadmill.

He struggled to think of something else. The house he intended to buy. Something close to the beach so that he could run on the sand, in the sun instead of on a mechanical loop. Rooms of his own, he mused, done to his own taste. A place where he could mow his grass, turn his music up to earsplitting levels, entertain company, or enjoy a quiet, private evening.

There had been few quiet, private evenings in his childhood. Not that he regretted the noise, the crowds he had grown up with. He adored his sisters, had tolerated their ever-increasing hordes of friends. He loved his parents and had always considered their busy social and family life normal.

Indeed, it had been the uncertainty as to whether he could bear to be so far away from his childhood home and family that had made him put the six-month-trial-period clause into his agreement with Josh.

Though he did miss them, he'd realized he could be happy in California. He was nearly thirty-five, and he wanted his own place. He was the first De Witt to move out of Georgia in two generations. He was determined to make it the right move.

If nothing else, it would stop the not-so-subtle family pressure for him to settle down, marry, start a family. The distance would certainly make it difficult for his sisters to continually shove women they considered perfect for him under his nose.

48

He had yet to meet a woman who was perfect for him.

As he stepped into the shower back in his penthouse office suite, he thought of Kate again. She was definitely wrong.

If he'd dreamed about her, it was only because she'd been on his mind. Annoyed that she continued to be, Byron turned up the radio affixed to the tiles until Bonnie Raitt bellowed out the challenge to give them something to talk about.

He was merely concerned about her, he decided. She'd gone so pale, become so quickly and unexpectedly vulnerable. He'd always been a sucker for a damsel in distress.

Of course, she was an idiot for not taking care of herself. Health and fitness weren't an option in Byron's mind but a duty. The woman needed to learn to eat properly, cut back on the caffeine, exercise, build up some flesh, and jettison some of those jangling nerves.

She wasn't half bad when she lost the attitude, he decided, stepping out of the shower with Bonnie still blasting. She'd given him a decent lead on the kind of property he was interested in, and they'd even managed to have a reasonable conversation over a shared plate.

And she had looked . . . interesting in that excuse for a dress she'd been wearing. Not that he was interested, Byron assured himself as he lathered up to shave. But she had a certain gamine appeal when she wasn't scowling. Almost Audrey Hepburn-ish.

He swore when he nicked his chin with the razor, put the blame for his inattention directly on Kate's head. He didn't have time to analyze some bony, unfriendly numbers cruncher with a chip on her shoulder. He had hotels to run.

Chapter Four

Kate knew it was a mistake even when she set up the appointment. It was, she admitted, like picking at a scab, ensuring that a wound would never heal cleanly. Her father's friend, Steven Tydings, was more than willing to meet her for lunch. She was, after all, his new CPA, and he'd told her he was a man who liked to keep his finger on the pulse of his finances.

She was sure she could work with him, do her job. Yet every time Kate had opened his file, she'd fought off a sick feeling in her stomach, flashback memories of her father. Bitter complaints about bills, about just missing that big break.

She had forgotten all of that, forged her memories of her parents more out of need, she realized now, than reality. Hers had not been a happy home, nor had it been a stable one. Though she had woven it as such in her dreams.

Now that it was impossible to pretend otherwise, she realized it was equally impossible not to probe, not to poke. Not to know.

She had nearly balked when Tydings insisted on meeting at

Templeton Monterey. The dining room there was the best in the area, the view of the bay superb. None of the excuses that she came up with had changed his mind. So at twelve-thirty sharp, she sat across from him at a window seat with a chef's salad in front of her.

It didn't matter where she was, Kate told herself as she picked at her meal. Laura was working at Pretenses. If anyone recognized her and mentioned it, it would be a simple matter to tell Laura she'd been lunching with a client. It was, after all, true.

For the first half hour, Kate guided the conversation to business. Strictly business. Whatever the circumstances, his account was entitled to and would receive her best. And he was pleased, telling her so often as she constantly eased her dry throat by sipping Templeton mineral water.

"Your dad had a way with numbers too," Tydings told her. He was a toughly built, compact man in his middle fifties who beamed at her out of dark-brown eyes. Success sat as stylishly on him as his suit.

"Did he?" Kate murmured, staring down at Tydings's hands. Well-manicured, businessman's hands. No flash, but a simple gold band on his finger. Her father had liked flash— heavy gold watches, the small diamond ring he wore on his pinky. Why should she remember that now? "I don't remember."

"Well, you were just a little thing. But I'll tell you, Linc had a gift for numbers. He could run figures in his head. You'd have thought he had a calculator in there."

It was her opening, and she had to take it. "I don't understand how someone that good with numbers could make such an enormous mistake."

"He just wanted bigger things, Katie." Tydings sighed, eased back in his chair. "He had a run of bad luck."

"Bad luck?"

"Bad luck, and bad judgment," Tydings qualified. "The ball got away from him."

"Mr. Tydings, he embezzled funds. He was going to

prison." She took a deep breath, braced herself. "Was money so important to him that he would steal, that he would risk everything he risked just to have it?"

"You have to see the whole picture, understand the frustrations, the ambitions . . . well, the dreams, Katie. Linc always felt he was overshadowed, outclassed by the Templeton branch of the family. No matter what he did, how hard he tried, he could never measure up. That was a hard pill for a man like him to swallow."

"Just what kind of a man was he that he would be so envious of someone else's success?"

"It wasn't like that, exactly." Obviously uncomfortable, Tydings shifted in his seat. "Linc had a powerful need to succeed, to be the best."

"Yes." She struggled against a shudder. Tydings might have been describing the daughter rather than the father. "I understand that."

"He just felt that if he could catch a break, just one break, he could build on it. Make something. He had the potential, the brains. He was a smart, hardworking man. A good friend. With a weakness for wanting more than he had. He wanted the best for you."

Tydings's smile spread again. "I remember the day you were born, Katie, how he stood there looking at you through the glass and making all these big plans for you. He wanted to give you everything, and it was hard for him to always settle for less."

She hadn't needed everything, Kate thought later when she sat alone at the table. She had only needed parents who loved her and loved each other. Now she would have to live knowing that what her father had loved most was his own ambition.

"Something wrong with your lunch?"

She glanced over, and the hand she had pressed protectively against her stomach fisted as Byron slid into the chair that Tydings had vacated. "Are you on dining room detail? I thought the brass stayed up in the lofty regions of the penthouse."

53

"Oh, we mingle with the lower floors occasionally." He signaled to a waitress. He'd been watching Kate for ten minutes. She had sat completely still, staring out of the window, her meal untouched, her eyes dark and miserable. "The chicken bisque," he ordered. "Two."

"I don't want anything."

"I hate to eat alone," he said smoothly, as the waitress cleared the dishes. "You can always play with it like you did your salad. If you're not feeling well, the bisque should perk you up."

"I'm fine. I had a business lunch." Under the table she pleated her napkin in her lap. She wasn't ready to get up, wasn't sure her legs were strong enough. "Who eats at business lunches?"

"Everyone." Leaning forward, he poured two glasses of mineral water. "You look unhappy."

"I have a client with an imbalance of passive income. That always makes me unhappy. What do you want, De Witt?"

"A bowl of soup, a little conversation. You know, I developed this hobby of conversation as a child. I've never been able to break it. Thank you, Lorna," he said when the waitress set a basket of warm rolls between them. "I've noticed that you often have a bit of trouble in that area. I'd be happy to help you, as I'm sort of a buff."

"I don't like small talk."

"There you are. I do." He held out a roll he'd broken apart and buttered. "In fact, I'm interested in all manner of talk. Large, small, meaningless, profound. Why don't we start this particular session with me telling you that I've got an appointment to view that house you recommended."

"Good for you." Since the bread was in her hand now, she nibbled.

"The realtor speaks highly of you." When Kate only grunted, then scowled down at the bowl of soup that was slipped under her nose, Byron smothered a grin. Damned if she wasn't too much of a challenge to resist. "I may just solicit your services myself, as I'll be staying in Monterey. Hardly practical to keep my accountant back in Georgia."

"It's not necessary to have an accountant in the same location. If you're satisfied with his or her work, there's no need to change."

"That's the way to drum up business, kid. I also have a habit of eating," he continued. "If you need help along those lines, I can tell you that you start by dipping your spoon into the soup."

"I'm not hungry."

"Think of it as medicine. It might put some color back in your cheeks. You not only look unhappy, Kate, you look tired, beaten down, and closing in on ill."

Hoping it would shut him up, she spooned up some soup. "Boy, now I'm all perked up. It's a miracle."

When he only smiled at her, she sighed. Why did he have to sit there, acting so damn nice and making her feel like sludge?

"I'm sorry. I'm lousy company."

"Was your business meeting difficult?"

"Yes, as a matter of fact." Because it was soothing, she sampled the bisque again. "I'll deal with it."

"Why don't you tell me what you do when you're not dealing with difficult business problems?"

The headache at the edges of her consciousness wasn't backing off, but it wasn't creeping closer. "I deal with simple business problems."

"And when you're not dealing with business?"

She studied him narrowly, the mild, polite eyes, the easy smile. "You *are* coming on to me."

"No, I'm considering coming on to you, which is entirely different. That's why we're having a basic conversation over a bowl of soup." His smile widened, flirted. "It also gives you equal opportunity to consider whether or not you'd like to come on to me."

Her lips twitched before she could stop them. "I do appreciate a man who believes in gender equality." She also had to appreciate that for a few minutes he'd taken her mind off her troubles. That he knew it, yet didn't push the point.

"I think I'm beginning to like you, Kate. You are, I believe, an acquired taste, and I've always enjoyed odd flavors."

"That's quite a statement. My heart's going pitty-pat."

He laughed, a quick, full-throated, masculine sound that appealed, however much she would have preferred otherwise.

"Yeah, it's definite. I like you. Why don't we expand this conversation thing over a full meal? Say, dinner. Tonight?"

She was tempted to agree, for the simple reason that being around him made her think about something other than herself. But . . . She set her napkin beside her bowl. She thought it would be best to err on the side of caution with a man like Byron De Witt. "I don't want to form habits too quickly. I have to get back to the office."

She rose, amused when he automatically got to his feet. Gender equality or not, she decided, he was southern gentleman through and through. "Thanks for the soup."

"You're welcome." He took her hand, held it lightly and enjoyed the faint line that popped up between her brows. "Thanks for the conversation. We will have to do it again."

"Hmm," was her best response as she slid the strap of her briefcase over her shoulder and walked away.

He watched her go and wondered what problem, business or otherwise, had made her look so devastated. And so alone.

The rumor mill was working overtime at Bittle and Associates. Every tiny, underripe fruit plucked from the grapevine was chewed lavishly at the water cooler, the copy room, the storage closet.

Larry Bittle and his sons, Lawrence Junior and Martin—just call me Marty—continued their closed-door meetings with the other partners every morning. Copies of accounts were delivered to the group by Bittle Senior's tight-lipped, sharp-eyed executive assistant regularly.

If she knew anything, went the wisdom of the water cooler, she wasn't saying.

"They're working their way through every account," Roger

told Kate. He'd hunted her down in the stockroom when she went to replenish her supply of computer paper. "Marcie in Accounts Receivable said they're even going over internal ledgers. And Beth, the Dragon Lady's assistant, says they've been on the hot line with the lawyers."

Lips pursed, Kate grabbed a handful of Ticonderoga number 2's. "Are all your sources female?"

He grinned. "No, but Mike in the mail room is coming up dry. What's your take?"

"Gotta figure internal audit."

"Yeah, that's mine. But here's the question, Kate. Why?"

In truth, that very question had been on her mind for days. She considered. Smart, ambitious, ruthless people had the best gossip. Since Roger fit all the requirements, she decided to share her thoughts in hopes of priming his pump.

"Okay, we've had a couple of really good years. In the past five we've increased our client base by fifteen percent. Bittle's growing, so I'm thinking expansion, maybe a new branch. They'd put Lawrence in charge, add more associates, and give some of us the option of relocating. A big step like that would take a lot of thought and planning, and the partners would want to focus hard on the bottom line."

"Could be. There's been noises before about opening in the L.A. area, snagging more media accounts. But I've been hearing other grumblings, too." He leaned closer, lowered his voice, and his eyes were bright with excitement. "Larry's been thinking about passing the torch. Retiring."

"Why would he?" Kate whispered in response. They sounded like conspirators. "He's only sixty."

"Sixty-two." Roger glanced over his shoulder. "And you know how his wife likes those cruises. She's always bugging him to take one to Europe, around the Med, that sort of thing."

"How do you know that?"

"Beth. Assistant to the assistant. She got brochures for the old man. The Bittles' fortieth anniversary is coming up this year. If he retires early, there's going to be a partnership slot up for grabs."

"A new partner." It made sense. Perfect sense. All the meetings, the account checks. The current partners would have to weigh and judge, debate and discuss who would be most qualified to move up. She barely stopped herself from dancing a jig. She had to remember who it was she was talking to. Roger was her toughest competitor.

"Maybe." She shrugged, though inside, glee was spreading like a lovely pink balloon. "But I don't see Larry sailing off into the sunset yet. No matter how much his wife nags him."

"We'll see." Roger kept a sly smile on his face. "But something's going to happen, and it's going to happen soon."

Kate walked sedately back to her office, closed the door, put her supplies neatly away. Then she danced her jig.

She didn't want to get ahead of herself, didn't want to start projecting. The hell she didn't. Dropping into her chair, she spun herself around once, twice, and a giddy third time.

She had an MBA from Harvard, had graduated in the top ten percent of her class. In the five years she'd worked for Bittle, she had brought in twelve new accounts through client recommendations. And had lost only one. To that jerk Roger.

But even that hadn't gone out of house. She personally generated over two hundred thousand a year in billing. So did Roger, she admitted. She kept an eye on him. But when Marty had awarded her a raise last year, he'd told her she was considered the cream of Bittle's associates. Larry Bittle called her by her first name, and his wife and daughters-in-law had been known to drop by Pretenses to shop.

A partnership. At twenty-eight, she would be the youngest partner ever at Bittle. She would have exceeded by years her own rigid expectations of herself.

And wouldn't it, in some way, erase this taint she felt? This secret she had buried inside. If she was a success, it would overshadow all the rest.

She allowed herself to dream about it—the new office, the new salary, the new prestige. She would be consulted on policy, her opinion would be weighed and respected. Giggling, she leaned back in the chair and spun again. She would have a private secretary.

She would have everything she'd ever wanted.

Kate imagined picking up the phone, calling the Templetons in Cannes. They'd be so happy for her, so proud of her. Finally, she would be able to believe that everything they'd done for her was deserved.

She'd have a celebration with Margo and Laura. Oh, that would be sweet. At long last Kate Powell had come into her own, had done something important and solid. Years and years of work and study, of aching shoulders, tired eyes, and a burning stomach would have paid off.

All she had to do was wait.

Forcing herself to push the dream to the back of her mind, she swiveled to her computer and got to work.

She hummed as she ran figures, calculated expenditures, logged tax deductions, clucked over capital gains, and figured depreciation. As usual, she tuned in to the work and lost track of time. Kate came up blinking when the beep from her watch told her it was five o'clock.

Another fifteen minutes to close the file, she decided, then glanced up in mild annoyance at the knock on her door. "Yes?"

"Ms. Powell." Lucinda Newman—or the Dragon Lady, as she was unaffectionately called among the rank and file— stood imposingly in the doorway. "You're wanted in the main conference room."

"Oh." Kate's heart gave a wild, joyful leap, but she kept her face composed. "Thanks, Ms. Newman. I'll be right there."

Well aware that her hands were trembling with anticipation, Kate pressed them together in her lap. She had to be cool and professional. Bittle wasn't going to offer a partnership to a giddy, giggling woman.

She had to be what she always was, what they expected her to be. Practical, levelheaded. And, oh, she was going to savor the moment, remember every detail. Later, when she was out of sight and earshot, she would scream all the way to Templeton House.

Kate rolled down her sleeves, shrugged into her jacket, and smoothed it into place. She hesitated over taking her briefcase, then decided it only made her look more dedicated to the job.

With measured steps she took the stairs to the next floor, walked past the partners' offices toward the executive conference room. No one who chanced to see her in the quiet corridor would have realized her feet weren't touching the tasteful tan carpet. She thumbed an antacid out of the roll in her pocket, knowing it would do little to calm her jittery stomach.

She wondered if a bride on her wedding night could feel any more nervous and thrilled than she did as she raised a hand to knock politely on the thick paneled door.

"Come in."

She lifted her chin, put a polite smile on her face as she turned the knob. They were all there, and her heart gave another skipping leap. All the partners, the five powers of the firm, were seated around the long, glossy table. Large tumblers of water stood by each place.

She skimmed her gaze over each of them, wanting to remember this moment. Fusty Calvin Meyers with his usual suspenders and red bow tie. Elegant and terrifying Amanda Devin, looking stern and beautiful. Marty, of course, sweet and homely and rumpled. Lawrence Junior, steady, balding, and cool.

And of course, the senior Bittle. She had always thought he looked like Spencer Tracy—that lived-in face, the sweep of white hair, the stocky, powerful little body.

Her pulse bumped, aware that all eyes were on her.

"You wanted to see me?"

"Sit down, Kate." From his seat at the head of the table, Bittle gestured to one at the foot.

"Yes, sir."

He cleared his throat as she took her chair, settled. "We thought it best to meet at the end of the workday. You're aware, I'm sure, that we've been involved for the past several days in a check of our accounts.''

"Yes, sir." She smiled. "Speculation's been racing down the corridors." When he didn't smile back, she felt a nervous tickle at the back of her throat. "It's hard not to get on the rumor train, sir.''

"Yes." He let out a breath, folded his hands. "A discrepancy in an income tax payment came to Mr. Bittle Junior's attention last week."

"A discrepancy?" Her gaze shifted to Lawrence.

"In the Sunstream account," he clarified.

"That's one of mine." The nervous tickle at the back of her throat changed to a nervous dread in her stomach. Had she made some sort of stupid error in the chaos of the tax crunch? "What kind of discrepancy?"

"The client's copy of the tax form indicates a federal payment due of seven thousand six hundred and forty-eight dollars." Lawrence opened a file, took out a thick stack of papers. "Is this your work, Ms. Powell?"

He was the only Bittle who called her Ms. Powell. Everyone in the firm was accustomed to his formality. But it was the clipped manner of his speech that put her on alert. Carefully she took out her glasses and slipped them on as the papers were passed down to her.

"Yes," she said after a quick glance. "It's my account, I did the tax work. This is my signature."

"And as with several of our clients, the firm cuts the checks for tax payments for this one."

"Some prefer it." She dropped her hands into her lap. "It distances them, a bit, from the sting. And it's more convenient."

"Convenient," Amanda commented and drew Kate's eye. "For whom?"

This was trouble, was all Kate could think. But from what and where? "Many clients prefer to come into the office, discuss the tax situation and the results—argue and vent." They all knew this, she thought, scanning the table again. Why did

61

she have to explain? "The client will sign the necessary forms and the account exec will issue the check out of escrow."

"Ms. Powell." Lawrence took another stack of papers from his file. "Can you explain this?"

As smoothly as possible, Kate wiped her damp palms on her skirt, then studied the forms passed to her. Her mind went momentarily blank. She blinked, focused, swallowed hard.

"I'm not sure I understand. This is another copy of the 1040 filed for Sunstream, but the tax due amount is different."

"Twenty-two hundred dollars less," Amanda pointed out. "This is the form and the payment made on April fifteenth of this year to the IRS. The check drawn out of escrow was for this amount."

"I don't understand when or how the other copy was generated," Kate began. "All work sheets are filed, of course, but any excess forms are shredded."

"Kate." Bittle drew her attention with one quiet word. "The excess money was transferred via computer out of the client's escrow account in cash."

"In cash," she repeated, blank.

"Since this came to our attention, we initiated a check on all accounts." Bittle's face was grave as he watched her. "Since late March of this year, amounts that total seventy-five thousand dollars have been withdrawn from escrow accounts, seventy-five thousand in excess of tax payments. Computer withdrawals, in cash, from your accounts."

"From my clients?" She felt the blood drain out of her face, couldn't stop it.

"It's the same pattern." Calvin Meyers spoke for the first time, tugging on his bright red tie. "Two copies of the 1040s, small adjustments on various forms, to total excess on the client's copy in amounts ranging from twelve hundred to thirty-one hundred dollars." He puffed out his cheeks. "We might not have caught it, but I golf with Sid Sun. He's a whiner about taxes and kept after me to look over his form and be certain there was nothing else he could use to cut his payment."

Embezzlement. Were they accusing her of embezzlement? Was this some awful nightmare? They knew about her father and thought . . . no, no, that was impossible. While her hand flexed nervously in her lap, she kept her voice even.

"You examined one of my accounts?"

Calvin lifted an eyebrow. The last thing he'd expected from steady-as-she-goes Kate Powell was blank-eyed panic. "I did so to get him off my back, and in examining his copy, I found several small errors. I thought it best to look further and pulled out our file copy of his latest return."

She couldn't feel anything. Even her fingertips had gone numb. "You think I stole seventy-five thousand dollars from my clients. From this firm."

"Kate, if you could just explain how you think this might have happened," Marty began. "We're all here to listen."

No, her father had stolen from clients. Her father. Not her. "How could you think it?" Her voice shook, shamed her.

"We haven't come to any firm conclusion," Amanda countered. "The facts, the numbers, however, are here, in black and white."

Black and white, she thought as the print blurred, as it overlapped with visions of newspaper articles from twenty years past. "No, I—" She had to lift a hand, rub her eyes to clear them. "It's not. I didn't."

Amanda tapped one scarlet nail on the tabletop. She'd expected outrage, had counted on the outrage of the innocent. Instead, what she saw was the trembling of the guilty.

"If Marty hadn't gone to bat for you, if he hadn't insisted we search for some rational explanation, even incompetence on your part, we would have had this meeting days ago."

"Amanda," Bittle said quietly, but she shook her head.

"Larry, this is embezzlement, and over and above the legal ramifications, client trust and confidence have to be considered. We need to clear this matter up quickly."

"I've never taken a penny, not a penny from any client." Though terrified that her legs would buckle, Kate shot to her feet. She would not be sick, she told herself, though her stomach was heaving into her throat. "I couldn't." It seemed to be all she could say. "I couldn't."

Lawrence frowned at his hands. "Ms. Powell, money is easily hidden, laundered, spent. You've assisted a number of clients in investments, accounts in the Caymans, in Switzerland."

Investments. Bad investments. She pressed a hand to her throbbing temple. No, that had been her father. "That's my job. I do my job."

"You recently opened a business," Calvin pointed out.

"I'm a one-third partner in a secondhand boutique." Grief and fear and nausea swirled inside her, made her hands shake. She had to be coherent, she ordered herself. Shaking and weeping only made her look guilty. "It took almost all my savings to do it."

She drew in a breath that burned, stared straight into Bittle's eyes. "Mr. Bittle—" But her voice broke, and she had to begin again. "Mr. Bittle, I've worked for you for five years. You hired me a week out of graduate school. I've never given this firm anything but my complete loyalty and dedication, and I've never given a client anything but my best. I'm not a thief."

"I find it difficult to believe you are, Kate. I've known you since you were a child and always considered my decision to hire you one of my best judgment calls. I know your family."

He paused, waiting for her to rebound, to express her fury at being used. To demand to assist the firm in finding the answers. When she did nothing but stare blindly, he had no choice.

"However," he said slowly, "this matter can't be ignored. We'll continue to investigate, internally for now. It may become necessary to go outside the firm with this."

"To the police." The thought of it dissolved her legs so that she had to brace herself with a hand on the table. Her vision grayed and wavered. "You're going to the police."

"If it becomes necessary," Bittle told her. "We hope to resolve the matter quietly. Bittle and Associates is responsible, at this point, for adjusting the escrow accounts.'' Bittle studied the woman standing at the end of the table, shook his head. ''The partners have agreed that it is in the firm's best interest for you to take a leave of absence until this is cleared up.''

''You're suspending me because you think I'm a thief.''

''Kate, we need to look into this carefully. And we have to do whatever is in the best interest of our clients.''

''A suspected embezzler can't handle accounts.'' The tears were going to come, but not yet. She could hold them back just a little longer. ''You're firing me.''

''A leave of absence,'' Bittle repeated.

''It's the same thing.'' Accusations, disgrace. ''You don't believe me. You think I've stolen from my own clients and you want me out of the office.''

He saw no other choice. ''At this time, yes. Any personal items in your office will be sent to you. I'm sorry, Kate. Marty will escort you out of the building.''

She let out a shuddering breath. ''I haven't done anything but my best.'' Picking up her briefcase, she turned stiffly and walked to the door.

''I'm sorry. Christ, Kate.'' With his lumbering stride, Marty caught up with her. ''What a mess, what a disaster.'' He started huffing when she took the stairs down to the main level. ''I couldn't turn them around.''

She stopped, ignoring the pain in her stomach, the throbbing in her head. ''Do you believe me? Marty, do you believe me?''

She saw the flicker of doubt in his earnest, myopic eyes before he answered. ''I know there's an explanation.'' He touched her gently on the shoulder.

''It's all right.'' She made herself push through the glass doors on the lobby level, walk outside.

''Kate, if there's anything I can do for you, any way I can help . . .'' He trailed off lamely, standing by the door as she all but ran to her car.

''Nothing,'' she said to herself. ''There's just nothing.''

*   *   *

At the last minute she stopped herself from running to Templeton House. To Laura, to Annie, to anyone who would fold her in comforting arms and take her side. She swung her car to the side of the road rather than up the steep, winding drive. She got out and walked to the cliffs.

She could stand alone, she promised herself. She had had shocks, survived tragedies before. She'd lost her parents, and there was nothing more devastating than that.

There had been boys she'd dreamed over in high school who had never dreamed back. She'd gotten over it. Her first lover, in college, had grown bored with her, broken her heart and moved on. She hadn't crumbled.

Once, years before, she had fantasized about finding Seraphina's dowry all alone, of bearing it proudly home to her aunt and uncle. She had learned to live without that triumph.

She was afraid. She was so afraid.

Like father, like daughter. Oh, dear God, would it come out now? Would it all come out? And how much more damning then? What would this do to the people who loved her, who had had such hopes for her?

What was it people said? Blood will tell. Had she done something, made some ridiculous mistake? Christ, how could she think clearly now when her life had been turned upside down and shattered at her feet?

She had to wrap her arms tight around her body against the spring breeze, which now seemed frigid.

She'd committed no crime, she reminded herself. She'd done nothing wrong. All she'd done was lose a job. Just a job.

It had nothing to do with the past, nothing to do with blood, nothing to do with where she had come from.

With a whimper, she eased down onto a rock. Who was she trying to fool? Somehow it had to do with everything. How could it not? She'd lost what she had taught herself to value most next to family. Success and reputation.

Now she was exactly what she'd always been afraid she was. A failure.

How could she face them, any of them, with the fact that

she'd been fired, was under suspicion of embezzling? That she had, as she always advised her clients not to, put all of her eggs in one basket, only to see it smashed.

But she would have to face them. She had to tell her family before someone else did. Oh, and someone would. It wouldn't take long. She didn't have the luxury of digging a hole and hiding in it. Everything she was and did was attached to the Templetons.

What would her aunt and uncle think? They would have to see the parallel. If they doubted her . . . She could stand anything, anything at all except their doubt and disappointment.

She reached in her pocket, chewed viciously on a Tums, and wished for a bottle of aspirin—or some of the handy tranqs Margo had once used. To think she'd once been so disdainful of those little crutches. To think she had once considered Seraphina a fool and a coward for choosing to leap rather than stay and face her loss.

She looked out to sea, then rose and walked closer to the edge. The rocks below were mean. That was what she'd always liked best about them, those jagged, unforgiving spears standing up defiantly to the constant, violent crash of water.

She had to be like the rocks now, she thought. She had to stand and face whatever happened next.

Her father hadn't been strong. He hadn't stood, he hadn't faced it. And now, in some twisted way, she was paying the price.

Byron studied her from the side of the road. He'd seen her car whiz past as he was leaving Josh's house. He wasn't sure what impulse had pushed him to follow her, still wasn't sure what was making him stay.

There was something about the way she looked, standing there at the edge of the cliff, so alone. It made him nervous, and a little annoyed. That vulnerability again, he supposed, a quiet neediness that called to his protective side.

He wouldn't have pegged her as the type to walk the cliffs or stare out to sea.

He nearly got back into his car and drove off. But he shrugged and decided that since he was here, he'd might as well enjoy the view.

"Hell of a spot," he said as he walked up to her. It gave him perverse pleasure to see her jolt.

"I was enjoying it," she muttered and kept her back to him.

"Plenty of view for two to enjoy. I saw your car, and . . ." When he got a look at her, he saw that her eyes were damp. He'd always been compelled to dry a woman's tears. "Bad day?" he murmured and offered her a handkerchief.

"It's just windy."

"Not that windy."

"I wish you'd go away."

"Ordinarily I try to comply with women's requests. Since I'm not going to in your case, why don't you sit down, tell me about it?" He took her arm, thinking the tension in it was edgy enough to cut glass. "Think of me as a priest," he suggested, dragging her with him. "I wanted to be one once."

"To use some clever phrasing, bullshit."

"No, really." He pulled her down on a rock with him. "I was eleven. Then puberty hit, and the rest is history."

She tried and failed to tug free and rise. "Did it ever occur to you that I don't want to talk to you? That I want to be alone?"

To soothe, because her voice was catching helplessly, he stroked a hand over her hair. "It crossed my mind, but I rejected it. People who feel sorry for themselves always want to talk about it. That, next to sex, was the main reason I decided against the seminary. And dancing. Priests don't get lots of opportunity to dance with pretty women—which, I suppose, is the same thing as sex. Well, enough about me."

He put a determined hand under her chin and lifted it. She was pale, those long, spiky lashes were wet and those deep, doe's eyes damp. But . . .

"Your eyes aren't red enough for you to have had a good cry yet."

"I'm not a sniveler."

"Listen, kid, my sister highly recommends a good cry, and she'd deck you for calling her a sniveler." Gently, he rubbed his thumb over Kate's chin. "Screaming's good, too, and throwing breakables. There was a lot of that in my house."

"There's no point—"

"Venting," he interrupted smoothly. "Purging. There aren't any breakables around here, but you could let out a good scream."

Emotions welling up inside her threatened to choke her. Furiously she jerked her face free of his hand. "I don't need you or anyone to charm me out of a mood. I can handle my own problems just fine. If I need a friend, all I have to do is go up to the house. Up to the house," she repeated as her gaze focused on the towering structure of stone and wood and glass that held everything precious to her.

Covering her face with her hands, she broke.

"That's a girl," he murmured, relieved by the natural flow of tears. "Come here now." He drew her close, stroking her hair, her back. "Get it all out."

She couldn't stop. It didn't matter who he was, his arms were strong, his voice understanding. With her face buried against his chest, she sobbed out the frustration, the grief, the fear, let herself for one liberating moment be coddled.

He rested his cheek on her hair, held her lightly. Lightly because she seemed so small, so fragile. A good grip might shatter those thin bones. Tears soaked through his shirt, cooled from hot to cold on his skin.

"I'm sorry. Damn it." She would have pulled away, but he continued to hold her. Humiliated, she squeezed her aching eyes shut. "I never would have done that if you'd left me alone."

"You're better off this way. It's not healthy to hold everything in." Automatically, he kissed the top of her head before easing her back to study her face.

Why it should have charmed him, wet, blotchy, streaked with mascara as it was, he couldn't have said. But he had a terrible urge to shift her onto his lap, to kiss that soft, sad mouth, to stroke her again, not quite so consolingly.

Bad move, he cautioned himself, and wondered how any man faced with such sexy distress could think like a priest.

"Not that you look better." He took the handkerchief she'd balled up in her fist and mopped at her face. "But you should feel better enough to tell me why you're so upset."

"It has nothing to do with you."

"So what?"

She could feel another sob bubbling in her chest and blurted out the words before it could escape. "I got fired."

He continued calmly cleaning and drying her face. "Why?"

"They think—" Her voice hitched. "They think I—"

"Take a breath," he advised, "and say it fast."

"They think I stole money out of client escrow. Embezzled. Seventy-five thousand."

Watching her face, he stuck the ruined linen back in his pocket. "Why?"

"Because—because there are duplicate 1040s, and money missing. And they're my clients."

And my father—my father. But she couldn't say that, not out loud.

In fits and starts she babbled out the gist of her meeting with the partners. A great deal of it was incoherent, details crisscrossing and overlapping, but he continued to nod. And listen.

"I didn't take any money." She let out a long, unsteady breath. "I don't expect you to believe me, but—"

"Of course I believe you."

It was her turn to gather her wits. "Why?"

Leaning back a little, he took out a cigar, shielding the flame on his lighter with a cupped hand. "In my line of work, you get a handle on people quickly. You've been around the hotel business most of your life. You know how it is. There are plenty of times with a guest, or staff, that you have to make a snap judgment. You'd better be accurate." Puffing out smoke, he studied her. "My take on you, Katherine, in the first five minutes, was—well, among other things—that you're

70

the type of woman who would choke on her integrity before she loosened it to breathe.''

Her breath came out shaky, but some of the panic eased. ''I appreciate it. I think.''

''I'd have to say you worked for a bunch of shortsighted idiots.''

She sniffled. ''They're accountants.''

''There you go.'' He smiled, ran a finger down her cheek when she glared. ''A flash there in those big brown eyes. That's better. So, are you going to take it lying down?''

Rising, she straightened her shoulders. ''I can't think about how or what I can take now. I only know I wouldn't work at Bittle again if they came crawling on their hands and knees through broken glass.''

''That's not what I meant. I meant someone's embezzling and pointing the finger at you. What are you going to do about it?''

''I don't care.''

''You don't care?'' He shook his head. ''I find that hard to believe. The Katherine Powell I've seen is a scrapper.''

''I said I don't care.'' And her voice hitched again. If she fought, looked too close, demanded too much, they might uncover what her father had done. Then it would be worse. ''There's nothing I can do.''

''You've got a brain,'' he corrected.

''It doesn't feel like it at the moment.'' She put a hand to her head. Everything inside was mushy and aching. ''They can't do anything else to me because I don't have the money, and they'd never be able to prove I do. As far as I'm concerned right now, finding who's skimming is Bittle's problem. I just want to be left alone.''

Surprised at her, he stood up. ''I'd want their ass.''

''Right now, I just want to be able to get through the next few hours. I have to tell my family.'' She closed her eyes. ''Earlier today, I actually thought, hoped, that I was going to be called in and offered a partnership. Signs indicated,'' she said bitterly. ''I couldn't wait to tell them.''

71

"Brag?" But he said it gently, with hardly any sting.

"I suppose. 'Look at what I did. Be proud of me because . . . ' Well, that's done. Now I have to tell them that I lost it all, that the prospects of getting another position or finessing any clients are nil for the foreseeable future."

"They're family." He stepped toward her and laid his hands on her shoulders. "Families stand by each other."

"I know that." For a moment, she wanted to take his hand. He had such big, competent hands. She wanted to take it and press it to her cheek. Instead she stepped back, turned away. "That makes it worse. I can't begin to tell you how much worse. Now, I'm feeling sorry for myself all over again."

"It comes and goes, Kate." Well aware that they were doing a little dance and dodge of physical contact, he draped an arm around her shoulders. "Do you want me to go up with you?"

"No." She was appalled, because for an instant she'd wanted to say yes. To lean her head against that broad shoulder, close her eyes, and let him lead. "No, I have to do it." She slipped away from him again, but faced him. "This was awfully nice of you. Really. Nice."

He smiled, his dimples deepening. "That wouldn't have been insulting if you hadn't sounded quite so surprised."

"I didn't mean to be insulting." She managed a smile of her own. "I meant to be grateful. I am grateful . . . Father De Witt."

Testing, he lifted a hand, skimmed his fingers through her short cap of hair. "I decided I don't want you to think of me as a priest after all." His hand slid down the back of her neck. "It's that sex thing again."

She felt it herself—inconvenient little hormonal tugs. "Hmm." It seemed as good a response as any. And certainly safe. "I'd better go get this done." Eyes warily on his, she backed up. "I'll see you around."

"Apparently you will." He stepped forward, she backed up again.

"What are you doing?"

Amused at both of them, he raised his eyebrows. "Going to my car. I'm parked behind you."

"Oh. Well." As casually as possible, she turned and walked to the car as he fell into step beside her. "I, ah, have you seen the house yet, the one on Seventeen Mile?"

"I have an appointment to view it tonight, as it happens."

"Good. That's good." She jangled her keys in her pocket before pulling them out. "Well, I hope you like it."

"I'll let you know." He closed a hand over hers on the door handle. When her gaze flew suspiciously to his, he smiled. "My daddy taught me to open doors for ladies. Consider it a southern thing."

She shrugged, slid into the car. "Well, 'bye."

"I'll be in touch."

She wanted to ask what that was supposed to mean, but he was already walking toward his own car. Besides, she had a pretty good idea.

Chapter Five

"It's outrageous. It's insulting."

In a rare show of temper, Laura stormed around the solarium. Thirty minutes before, Kate had interrupted homework time, and Laura had shifted from solving the mysteries of punctuation and multiplication tables with her daughters to the shock of hearing Kate's story.

Watching her friend, Kate was glad she'd had the presence of mind to ask to speak to Laura privately. The flash in the gray eyes, the angry flush staining those cool ivory cheeks, and the wild gestures might have frightened the children.

"I don't want you to be upset," Kate began.

"You don't want me to be upset?" Laura rounded on her, the curling swing of chin-length bronze hair flying, the soft, pretty mouth pulled back into a snarl. "Then what exactly should I be when my sister gets plugged between the eyes?"

Oh, yeah, Kate thought, this definitely would have given the girls a jolt. If she hadn't been so miserable, she would have laughed. Laura the Cool had metamorphosed into Laura the Enraged. Despite being five two, she looked capable of going ten rounds with the champ.

"Don't want me to be upset!" Laura repeated, her small, almost fairylike frame revving high as she stalked around the lush glass-walled room. "Well, I'm not upset. I'm past upset and heading beyond pissed. How dare they? How dare those pinheaded idiots think for one minute, for one instant, that you'd steal money?"

She slapped at the swaying fronds of a potted palm. "When I think how many times the Bittles have been guests in this house, it makes my blood boil. Treating you like a common criminal. Escorting you out of the building. I'm surprised they didn't bring out the cuffs and the SWAT team." Sun pouring through the glass walls glinted fiercely in her eyes. "Bastards, idiot bastards."

She pounced, all five feet two inches of raging fury, on the slim white phone beside the padded chaise. "We're calling Josh. We're suing them."

"Hold it. No, hold it, Laura." Torn between tears and laughter, Kate slapped a hand over her friend's. For the life of her, Kate couldn't remember why she'd hesitated to come here, to Templeton House. This was exactly what she'd needed to snap her back. "I can't tell you how much I appreciate the tirade, but—"

"You haven't begun to see a tirade."

"I've got nothing to sue them about. The evidence—"

"I don't give a fuck about evidence." At Kate's bubble of laughter, her eyes narrowed. "Just what the hell are you laughing at?"

"I'll never get used to hearing you say 'fuck.' It's just not natural." But she swallowed because the laugh had come perilously close to hysteria. "And seeing you storm around this elegant room with all the hibiscus and ferns is quite a show." She caught her breath. "I didn't come here to send you on a rampage, though it's doing wonders for my bruised ego."

"This isn't about ego." Laura struggled to get a grip on her temper. She lost it rarely because it was a powerful thing,

76

a dangerous thing. "It's about defamation of character, loss of income. We're not going to let them get away with this, Kate. We've got a lawyer in the family, and we're going to use him."

There was no use in pointing out that Josh wasn't a litigator. She certainly wouldn't have told Laura that the very thought of pursuing the matter, particularly through the legal system, had her feeling nauseated again. Instead, she struggled to keep it light.

"Maybe we could have him tack on loss of consortium, just for kicks. I always liked that one."

"How can you joke?"

"Because you've made me feel so much better." Suddenly she felt like crying again, and hugged Laura tight instead. "I knew in my heart you'd stand behind me, but in my head, in my gut . . . I was just so shattered. Oh, God." She eased away to press a hand to her stomach. "I'm going to start again."

"Oh, Kate. Oh, honey, I'm so sorry." Gently now, Laura slipped a hand around her waist. "Let's sit down. We'll get some tea, some wine, some chocolate, and figure this out."

Kate sniffed back the tears, nodded. "Tea's good. Alcohol hasn't been agreeing with me lately." She managed a smile. "Chocolate never fails."

"Okay. Just sit right here." Normally she would have gone to the kitchen herself, but she didn't want to leave Kate alone. Instead she crossed the glossy fieldstone floor to the intercom by the doorway—the system Peter had insisted they install to summon the servants. After a few murmured instructions, she came back to Kate and sat down.

"I feel so useless," Kate said. "So stripped. I don't think I appreciated, really, how Margo must have felt last year when she had the rug pulled out from under her."

"You were there for her. Just like Margo and I, and everyone, will be here for you. Anyone who knows you won't believe you did anything wrong."

"Even one who doesn't," she murmured, thinking of Byron. "Still, plenty will believe it. It's going to get out, I can promise you that. I'm used to defending myself," she continued. "Skinny girls with more brains than charm tend to hide through high school, or fight through it."

"And you always fought."

"I'm out of practice." She closed her eyes and leaned back. The room smelled like a garden, she thought. Peaceful, calm. She badly needed to find calm again. "I don't know what I'm going to do, Laura. It's probably the first time in my life I don't have a plan." She opened her eyes again, met the concern in Laura's. "I know it's going to sound foolish, but everything I am and wanted to be was tied up in my career. I was good at it. More than good. I needed to be. I chose Bittle because it was an old, established firm, there was plenty of room and opportunity for advancement, because it was close to home. I liked the people there—and I don't like that many people. I felt comfortable and appreciated."

"You'd feel comfortable and appreciated at Templeton," Laura said quietly and took her hand. "You know there's no question that you could have a position there tomorrow. Mom and Dad wanted you in the organization."

With a taint on her, she thought, that stretched back a generation. No, that she would not ask. "They've done enough for me."

"Kate, that's ridiculous."

"Not to me. I can't go crawling to them now. I'd hate myself." It was the only thing she felt capable of standing firm on. Maybe it was pride, but it was all she had left. "It's going to be hard enough to call them and tell them about this."

"You know exactly what their reaction will be, but I'll do it if you like."

Would they remember? Kate wondered. Just for an instant, remember? And doubt. That she had to face as well. Alone. "No, I'll call them in the morning." She ran a hand over her slim navy skirt and tried to be practical. "I've got a little time to weigh my options. Money isn't an immediate problem. I've got some set aside, and there's the income, meager though it

78

is, from the shop." Her hand jerked. "Oh, God. Oh, my God, is this going to affect the shop?"

"Of course not. Don't worry."

"Don't worry?" Kate sprang up. Her stomach began doing flip-flops again. " 'Pretenses' third partner suspected of embezzlement.' 'CPA skimming client accounts.' 'Former Templeton ward under investigation.' "

She squeezed her eyes shut, terrified of what that investigation might uncover. Blood will tell. Think of now, she ordered herself. One step at a time.

"Jesus, Laura, it never occurred to me until this second. I could ruin it. A lot of my clients shop there."

"Just stop it. You're innocent. I wouldn't be surprised if a great many of your clients dismiss this whole business as nonsense."

"People have a funny attitude about their money, Laura, and about the people they hire to handle it for them."

"That may be, but you're going to start handling mine. Don't even think about arguing," Laura said before Kate could open her mouth. "I don't have a lot to work with since Peter scalped me in the divorce, but I expect you to fix that. And it's about time you started pulling your weight at the shop. Margo and I are adequate bookkeepers, but—"

"That's a matter of opinion."

Pleased, Laura cocked a brow. "Well, then, you'd better get busy protecting our investment. You were too busy before, but now you've got time on your hands."

"So it seems."

"And by putting in some time behind the counter as well, you can take some of the pressure off Margo and me."

Kate's mouth fell open. "You expect me to clerk? Regularly? Damn it, Laura, I'm not a saleswoman."

"Neither was Margo," Laura said placidly. "And neither was I. Circumstances change. Bend or break, Kate."

She wanted to remind Laura that she had an MBA from Harvard. She'd graduated with honors a full year early. She'd been within a breath of a partnership at one of the most respected firms in the area, had handled millions of dollars a year in accounts.

She closed her mouth again because none of it was worth a damn at the moment. "I don't know an Armani from ... anything."

"You'll learn."

It was self-indulgent, but she pouted anyway. "I don't even like jewelry."

"The customers do."

"I don't understand why people need to clutter up their house with dust catchers."

Laura smiled. If Kate was arguing, she thought, she was coming around. "That's easy. To keep us in business."

"Good point," Kate conceded. "I haven't done too badly the few Saturdays I've been able to help out. It's just dealing with people, day after day."

"You'll learn to live with it. We really need you on the books. We didn't push it before because we didn't want to pressure you. Actually Margo did, but I talked her out of it."

One of the many wounds she'd been planning to lick healed over. "Really?"

"No offense, Kate, but we've been open about ten months. Margo and I decided after about ten days that we really hate accounting. We hate spreadsheets. We hate percentages. We hate figuring the sales tax we have to send off every month."

Laura let out a sigh, lowered her voice. "I shouldn't tell you, she asked me not to, but ..."

"What?"

"Well, Margo ... We didn't think we could add to our overhead with a full-time bookkeeper, not yet anyway. So Margo's been looking into taking classes."

"Classes." Kate blinked. "Accounting classes? Margo? Jesus Christ."

"And business management, and computers." Laura winced. "Now, with the baby coming along, it seems like a lot to handle. I'm fairly computer-literate," she added, hoping to press her point. "I have to be, working conventions and special events at the hotel. But retail's a different matter entirely." Knowing the value of timing, she waited a beat, let it sink in. "I just don't see how I could squeeze any classes in myself, between working at Templeton, the shop, the girls."

"Of course not. You should have told me you were having that rough a time. I'd have picked up the ball."

"You've been cross-eyed with work for six months. It didn't seem fair."

"Fair? Hell, it's business. I'll come in first thing in the morning and take a good look at the books."

Laura managed to keep her smile pleasant rather than smug as Ann Sullivan wheeled in a tea cart. "The girls have finished their homework," Ann began. "I brought extra cups and plates so they could join you. I thought you might enjoy a little tea party."

"Thank you, Annie."

"Miss Kate, it's good to see—" Her smile of greeting faded the minute she looked into Kate's swollen, red-rimmed eyes. "What's the matter, darling?"

"Oh, Annie." Kate caught the hand Ann had lifted to her cheek, soothed herself with it. "My life's a mess."

"I'll get the girls," Laura said, rising. "And another cup," she added, nodding at Ann. "We'll have our tea party, and work on straightening it out."

Because Kate had always been the awkward one, and the feisty one, she held a special place in Ann's heart. After pouring two cups, selecting two chocolate-frosted cakes, Ann sat down and draped an arm around Kate's shoulder.

"Now, you drink your tea and eat some sweets and tell Annie all about it."

Sighing, Kate burrowed. Dorothy from Kansas was right, she decided. There really was no place like home.

"I don't like the way she keeps talking about software." Behind the counter of Pretenses, Margo muttered into Laura's ear. "The only software I want to know about is cashmere."

"We don't have to know," Laura muttered right back. "Be-

81

cause she knows. Think about all the Sunday evenings we sweated over the books.''

''Right.'' But Margo pouted. ''Actually, I thought I was getting pretty good at it. The way she talks, it's like I was brain-dead.''

''Want to go into the back room and help her out?''

''No.'' That was definite. Margo scanned a browsing customer, calculated nine more seconds before the next subtle sales pitch. ''But I don't like the way she's taking this whole mess. No way our Kate walks away from a fight.''

''She's hurt, shaken.'' Though Laura was worried over it herself. ''This is just recovery time.''

''It better be. I'm not going to be able to hold Josh back from storming into Bittle much longer.'' A martial light glowed in her Mediterranean blue eyes. ''I'm not going to be able to hold myself back, for that matter. Creeps, jerks.''

She continued to mutter as she approached the customer, but her face underwent a metamorphosis. Easy, sophisticated beauty. ''That's a gorgeous lamp, isn't it? It belonged to Christie Brinkley.'' Margo trailed a finger down the mother-of-pearl shade. ''Confidentially, it was a gift from Billy, and she didn't want to keep it around any longer.''

Truth or fiction? Laura wondered, muffling a laugh. The ownership was fact, but the little sidebar was probably fantasy.

''Laura.'' With the long-suffering look she'd worn after the first hour with the books, Kate stepped out of the back office. ''Do you realize how much money you're wasting by short-ordering boxes? The more you order at a time, the less each costs. The way we go through them—''

''Ah, yes, you're right.'' Out of defense and necessity, Laura looked at her watch. ''Oops, piano lessons. Gotta go.''

''You're buying tape at the dime store rather than through a wholesaler,'' Kate added, dogging Laura to the door.

''I should be shot. 'Bye.'' And she escaped.

Her foot tapping, Kate turned, with the intent of nagging Margo. But her partner was busy fussing with a customer over some silly little lamp that didn't look as if it could light a closet, much less a room.

It helped to nag. It felt good to take charge. Even if it was over boxes and tape.

"Miss. Oh, miss." Another woman came out of the wardrobe room carrying a pair of white spangled pumps. "Do you have these in an eight narrow?"

Kate looked at the shoes, looked at the woman, and wondered why anyone would want a pair of shoes covered with iridescent sequins. "Everything's out that's in stock."

"But these are too small." She all but wailed it, thrusting the shoes at Kate. "They're perfect with the dress I've chosen. I have to have them."

"Look," Kate began, then ground her teeth together as Margo caught her eye with a fiery warning look. She remembered the routine Margo had drummed into her head. Hated it, but remembered. "Pretenses is almost exclusively one of a kind. But I'm sure we can find something that works for you." Already missing her computer, she guided the customer back into the wardrobe room.

It took a great deal of control not to yelp. Shoes were tumbled everywhere, rather than neatly arranged on the shelves. Half a dozen cocktail dresses were tossed haphazardly over a chair. Others had slipped to the neat little Aubusson.

"Been busy, haven't we?" Kate said with a frozen smile.

The woman let out a trill of laughter that cut right through the top of Kate's skull. "Oh, I'm just in love with everything, but I'm very decisive once I've made up my mind."

That was a statement for the books. "Okay, which dress have you become decisive about?"

It took twenty minutes, twenty hemming and hawing, oohing and ahing minutes, before the customer settled on a pair of white slingbacks with satin bows.

Kate struggled to arrange the yards of white tulle in the skirt of the dress the woman couldn't live without. Tulle, Kate thought as she finally zipped it into a bag, that would certainly make the woman resemble an oversized wedding cake.

Her work complete, Kate handed over dress, shoes, and sales receipt and even managed a smile. "Thanks so much for shopping at Pretenses."

"Oh, I love it here. I just have to see these earrings."

"Earrings?" Kate's heart sank.

"These. I think they'd be wonderful with the dress, don't you? Could you just take it out of the bag again so I could see?"

"You want me to take the dress out of the bag." With a fierce smile, Kate leaned over the counter. "Why don't you—"

"Oh, the Austrian crystals just make those earrings, don't they?" Dashing around the counter, Margo gave Kate a shove that knocked her a full foot sideways. "I have a bracelet that's just made to go with them. Kate, why don't you take the dress back out while I unlock the case?"

"I'll take the damn dress back out," Kate muttered with her back turned. "But I'm not putting it in again. No one can make me." Spoiling for a fight, she scowled as the door jingled open. Her scowl only deepened at Byron's quick smile.

"Hello, ladies. I'll just browse until you're free."

"You're free," Margo said meaningfully to Kate. "I'll finish up here."

One devil was the same as another, Kate supposed and walked reluctantly out from behind the counter. "Looking for something?"

"Mother's Day. I bought my mother's birthday present in here a couple of months ago, and it made me a hero. I figured I'd stick with a winner." He reached out, skimmed a knuckle along her jaw. "How are you feeling?"

"Fine." Embarrassed at the memory of sobbing in his arms, she turned stiffly away. "Did you have anything specific in mind?"

In answer, he put a hand on her shoulder, turned her around. "I thought we'd parted on semi-friendly terms at least."

"We did." She reeled herself in. There was no point in

blaming him, though it was more satisfying. "I'm just a little wired. I nearly punched that customer."

Lifting an eyebrow, Byron glanced over Kate's head at the woman currently sighing over a bracelet. "Because?"

"She wanted to see earrings," Kate said between her teeth.

"Good God, what is the world coming to? If you promise not to hit me, I swear I won't even look at a pair of earrings in here. I may never look at a pair anywhere again."

She supposed that deserved at least a smile. "Sorry. It's a long story. So, what does your mother like?"

"Earrings. Sorry." He let out a rumbling chuckle. "Hard to resist. She's an internist with nerves of steel, a wicked temper, and a sentimental streak for anything that has to do with her children. I'm thinking hearts and flowers. Anything that falls into that basic symbolism."

"That's nice." She did smile. She was a sucker for a man who not only loved his mama but understood her. "I don't know the stock very well. It's my first week on the job."

She looked neat as a pin, he mused, in her tidy little gray suit with a Windsor-knotted striped tie. The sensible shoes shouldn't have led him to speculate on her legs. Surprised that that was exactly what he was doing, he cleared his throat.

"How's it going?"

She glanced back at Margo. "I think my coworkers are plotting my demise. Other than that, good enough. Thanks." But when he continued to study her, she shifted. "You did come in for a gift, right—not to check up on me or anything?"

"I can do both."

"I'd rather you—" The door opened again, heralding the entrance of three laughing, chattering women. Kate grabbed Byron's arm in a steely grip. "Okay, I'm with you. You need my undivided attention. I'll give you ten percent off if you take up all my time until they leave."

"A real people person, aren't you, Katherine?"

"I'm a desperate woman. Don't screw with me." She kept her hand firmly on his arm as she steered him to a corner of the shop.

"Your scent's different again," he commented, indulging himself with a sniff close to her hair. "Subtle, yet passionate."

"Something Margo squirted on me when I was distracted," she said absently. This was her new life, she reminded herself. The old was gone, and she was going to make the best of what she had left. "She likes us to push the merchandise. She'd have hung jewelry all over me if I hadn't escaped." From her safe distance, she glanced back and made a face at her partner. "Look, she made me wear this pin."

He glanced down at the simple gold crescent adorning her lapel. "It's very nice." And drew the eye to the soft swell of her breasts. "Simple, classic, subdued."

"Yeah, right. What do pins do but put holes in your clothes? Okay, back to business. It so happens, there's this music box that might make you a hero again."

"Music box." He brought himself back to the business at hand. "Could work."

"I remember it because Margo just picked it up at an estate sale in San Francisco. She'd know the circa this and the design that. I can tell you it's lovely."

She lifted it, a glossy mahogany box large enough for jewelry or love letters. On its domed lid was a painting of a young couple in medieval dress, a unicorn, and a circle of flowers. The lid opened to deep-blue velvet and the charming strains of "Für Elise."

"There's a problem," he began.

"Why?" Her back went up. "It's beautiful, it's practical, it's romantic."

"Well." He rubbed his chin. "How am I going to take up all your time when you've shown me the perfect gift first thing?"

"Oh." Kate glanced over her shoulder again. The three fresh customers were in the wardrobe room making a lot of female-on-the-hunt noises. Trying not to feel guilty, she looked over at Margo, who was expertly rebagging the tulle. "Want to buy something else? It's never too early to shop for Christmas."

86

He angled his head. "You've got to learn to gauge your clientele, kid. Here's a man coming in to buy a Mother's Day gift three days before the mark. A gift that he will now have to have shipped overnight to Atlanta. That type doesn't shop for Christmas until sometime after December twenty-first."

"That's very impractical."

"I like to use up my practicality at work. Life is different."

When he smiled at her, the creases in his face deepened. She liked the look of them, caught herself wondering how it would feel to trace her finger along those charming dents. Surprised at herself, she blew out a breath. Steady, girl.

"Then maybe you should look at something else, to like, compare."

"No, this is it." It intrigued him to see that he was making her uncomfortable, and that the discomfort was sexual. Deliberately, he put his hands over hers so that they held the box together. "Why don't I dawdle over the wrapping paper?"

That, she decided, was definitely a come-on. She'd have to think about whether or not she liked it later. "Okay, that'll work." She sent Margo a beaming smile as they crossed paths, then set the music box carefully on the counter.

Margo closed the door behind her now-satisfied customer and aimed an automatically flirtatious smile at Byron. "Hello, Byron. It's wonderful to see you."

"Margo." He caught her hand, brought it to his lips. The gesture was as automatic as her smile. "You look incredible, as always."

She laughed. "We just don't get enough men in here, particularly handsome, gallant ones. Have you found something you like?"

"Kate saved my life with a Mother's Day gift."

"Did she?" As Kate studiously boxed Byron's selection, Margo leaned over the counter, caught Kate by her red-and-blue-striped tie, and tugged viciously. "I'm going to kill you later. Excuse me, Byron. I have customers."

Kate kept her hot eyes on Margo's retreating back. "See, I told you. She wants me dead."

"One definition of family is a constant state of adjustment."

Kate lifted a brow. "From Webster's?"

"From De Witt's. Let's try the paper with the little violets. Margo's a remarkable woman."

"I've never known a man who didn't think so. No, that's wrong," she said as she measured wrapping paper. "Laura's ex-husband couldn't stand her. Of course, that was because she's the housekeeper's daughter, and he's a puss-faced snob. And I think it was because he wanted her. Men do. And it irritated him."

Intrigued by the brisk way she worked, the almost mathematical manner in which she aligned the box and folded corners on the gift wrap, he leaned on the counter. Her hands were really quite lovely, he noted. Narrow, competent, unadorned.

"How did he feel about you?"

"Oh, he hated me, too, but that didn't have anything to do with sexual fantasy. I'm the poor relation who has the nerve to say what she thinks." When her stomach jittered, she glanced up and frowned. "I don't know why I told you all that."

"Could be repressed conversation urges. You don't talk to people for long periods, then you get caught in a conversation and forget you don't like to talk to people. I told you, it can be a pleasant hobby."

"I don't like to talk to people," she muttered. "Most people. You want purple ribbon or white?"

"Purple. You interest me, Kate."

Wary, she looked up again. "I don't think that's necessary."

"Just an observation. I assumed you were cold, prim, rude, annoying, and self-involved. I'm not ordinarily that far wrong with people."

She jerked the ribbon into a knot, snipped off the ends. "You're not this time, either. Except for the prim."

"No, the rude and annoying probably stick, but I've been reevaluating the rest."

She chose a large, elaborate bow. "I don't want an evaluation."

"I didn't ask. It's another hobby of mine. Gift card?"

Frowning again, she found the one to match the paper and slapped it on the counter in front of him. "We can overnight it."

"I'm counting on it." He handed her his credit card, then took out a pen to write on the card. "Oh, by the way, I made an offer on the house you recommended. Like the music box, it's exactly what I was looking for."

"Good for you." After a brief search, she found the shipping form, set it down beside the box. She suppressed the urge to ask him about it, the house, what had appealed to him, the terms. Damn conversation.

"If you'll fill in the name and address where you want it shipped, we'll have FedEx pick it up in the morning. She'll get it with twenty-four hours to spare and save you a whining phone call."

His head lifted. "My mother doesn't whine."

"I was referring to you." Her smug smile faltered when two more customers came in.

"Isn't that handy?" Byron dashed off his mother's name and address. "We're all done, just in time for you to help some new customers."

"Listen, De Witt. Byron—"

"No, no, don't bother to grovel. You're on your own." He pocketed his card, the receipt, then tore off his copy of the shipping form himself. "See you around, kid."

He strolled toward the door. The sound of "Miss, could you show me these earrings?" was music to his soul.

Chapter Six

Byron didn't like to interfere with his department heads, but he knew—and wanted them to know—that at Templeton problems rose to the top. His interest in hotels and all their crosshatched inner workings had begun during a summer stint at Atlanta's Doubletree. Three months as a bellman had taught him more than the proper way to handle a guest's luggage and had earned him more than enough cash to buy his first vintage car.

He'd learned there were dramas and tragedies playing out daily, not just behind the closed doors of rooms and suites, but behind the front desk, in sales and marketing, in housekeeping and engineering. In fact, everywhere within the buzzing hive of a busy hotel.

It had fascinated him, had pushed him toward sampling other aspects, from desk clerk to concierge. His curiosity about people, who they were, what they expected, what they dreamed of, had given him a career.

He wasn't the doctor his parents had not so secretly hoped

he would be. Nor had he been the travel-weary trust-fund kid his circumstances could have made him. He had a career he enjoyed, and the constant variety of life in a big hotel continually intrigued him.

He was a problem solver, one who considered the individual as well as the big picture. His choice of moving into the Templeton organization had been a simple one. He'd spent a great deal of time studying hotels—the luxurious, the opulent, the small and tidy, the chains with their brisk pace, the old Europeans with their quiet charm, the Las Vegas ones with their flash and gaudiness.

Templeton had appealed to him because it was family-run, traditional without being stodgy, efficient without sacrificing charm, and above all, personable.

He didn't have to make it his business to know the names of the people who worked with and under him. It was simply a part of his makeup to take an interest, to retain information. So when he smiled at the woman currently checking in a guest, called out a casual, "Good morning, Linda," he wasn't aware that her pulse picked up several beats or that her fingers fumbled on the keyboard as she watched him pass through on his way to the offices.

Another section of the beehive was here. Ringing phones, clicking faxes, humming copiers, the clack of keyboards. He passed stacks of boxes, crowded desks. He exchanged a few greetings as he went, causing several pairs of shoulders to straighten and more than a few female employees to wish they'd checked their lipstick.

The door to his destination was open, and he found Laura Templeton with a phone to her ear. She offered him a harried smile and gestured to a chair.

"I'm sure we can arrange that. Mr. Hubble in Catering . . . Yes, yes, I understand how important it is. Mr. Hubble—" She broke off, rolled her eyes at Byron. "How many extra chairs would you like, Ms. Bingham?" She listened patiently, a small smile playing at the corners of her mouth. "No, of course not. And I'm sure you'll have plenty of room if you make use of the terrace. No, I don't believe it's calling for rain. It should be a lovely evening, and I'm sure your reception will be elegant. Mr. Hubble—'' Now she gritted her teeth. ''Why don't I talk to Mr. Hubble for you and get back to you? Yes, by noon. I will. Absolutely. You're welcome, Ms. Bingham.'' She hung up. ''Ms. Bingham is insane.''

''Is she the orthodontist convention or the interior decorating?''

''Decorating. She has decided, at the last minute, that she simply must give a reception tonight for sixty of her closest friends and associates. For reasons I can't explain, she doesn't trust Bob Hubble to pull it off.''

''Templeton,'' Byron said and smiled at her. ''The trouble is, your name is Templeton. Which puts you in a lofty position.''

You wouldn't know it from her office, he thought. It was tiny, cramped and windowless. He knew she'd chosen the position and the work space herself when she had decided to squeeze out time for a part-time job at the hotel.

Byron didn't know how she managed—her family and home, the shop, the hotel. But she seemed to him to be the soul of serenity and quiet efficiency. Until you looked close enough, at the eyes. There, shadowed in their lake-gray depths, were doubt and worry and grief. Remnants, he thought, of a shattered marriage.

''You didn't have to come down here, Byron.'' She finished scribbling notes to herself as she spoke. ''I would have made it up to your office this morning.''

''It's all right. Problem with the tooth soldiers?''

''You'd think orthodontists would have a little decorum, wouldn't you?'' With a sigh, she pulled papers out of a file. ''We've had complaints from both bars, but that's nothing I can't handle.''

''I've yet to come across anything you can't handle.''

''I appreciate that. But there's a delicate situation. One of the doctors apparently was having a, let's say, intimate moment with one of the other doctors when her husband decided to pay an unannounced surprise visit.''

"God, I love this job." Byron settled back. "It's like a long-running soap opera.''

"Easy for you to say. I spent an hour this morning dealing with the penitent woman. She sat where you are, spilling out tears and the whole sordid story of her marriage, her affairs, her therapy.''

Weary with the memory, Laura pressed her fingers to the inside corner of her eye, almost relieving the tension that was living there. "This is her third husband, and she claims to be addicted to adultery.''

"She should go on *Oprah*. Women who are addicted to adultery, and the men who love them. Do you want me to talk to her?''

"No, I think I sent her off steady enough. Our problem is, the husband wasn't too thrilled to find his wife and his''— she winced—"his brother-in-law wrapped in matching Templeton robes.''

"It just gets better. Don't stop now.''

"The husband popped his brother-in-law—who, I should add for clarification, is married to our heroine's sister—in the mouth. Knocked out several thousand dollars' worth of caps and so forth. There was some damage to the room, nothing major. A couple of lamps and crockery.'' She waved that away. "But our problem is that the guy with the broken mouth is threatening to sue the hotel.''

"Another victim.'' If he hadn't been so amused with the scenario, he would have sighed. "What's his rationale?''

"That the hotel is responsible for letting the husband in. He—the husband—called room service from a house phone, ordered champagne and strawberries for his wife's room. He had a dozen roses with him,'' she added. "Then he waited until the wine arrived, slipped into the room behind the waiter, and—well, the rest is history.''

"I don't think we've got any real problem here, but I'll take the file.''

"I appreciate it." Relieved, Laura passed the torch. "I'd talk to the man myself, but I get the impression he's not too keen on women in authority. And, to be honest, I'm swamped. The orthodontists have their banquet tonight, and the cosmetic people are coming in tomorrow."

"And, of course, Ms. Bingham."

"Right." She checked her watch and rose. "I'd better get down to Catering. There was one other little thing."

Standing up himself, he raised an eyebrow. "The decorators are wrestling in the atrium?"

"Not yet." Because she appreciated him, she smiled. It was second nature to Laura to hide nerves. "It was an idea I had for the shop, but since it involves the hotel, I wanted to run it by you."

"Laura, it's your hotel."

"No, at the moment I work here, and you're the boss." She picked up her clipboard and passed it from one of her hands to the other. "Last fall we put on a reception and charity auction at the shop. We intend to do it every year. But I was thinking we could plan another event. Straight advertising, really. A fashion show, using clothes and accessories from the shop, during the holiday season. The White Ballroom would be ideal, and it's not booked for the first Saturday in December. I thought we could feature gala attire, formals, ballgowns, in addition to accessories, all from the shop. We'd advertise it in both the hotel and the resort, with percentage-off certificates issued to Templeton employees and guests."

"You've got marketing in the blood. Listen, Laura, you work conventions and special events." He put an arm around her shoulders as they left the office. "You don't need my go-ahead."

"I like to dot my i's, so to speak. After I've talked it over with Margo and Kate, I'll work up a proposal."

"Fine." She'd given him the opening he'd been hoping for. "So how is Kate?"

"She's holding up. Of course, she occasionally drives Margo and me crazy. A born salesman Kate isn't," Laura said with feeling. "But she's competitive enough to make it work." Her smile softened, spread. "And if Margo or I so much as breathes on the books, she hisses. So that's a blessing. Still . . ."

"Still?"

"They damaged something inside her. I don't know how seriously yet, but she's too together, too controlled. She won't talk about it, won't even discuss what should be done. Just closes up when any of us try to draw her out. Kate used to be a champion tantrum thrower."

Now her fingers fidgeted restlessly, tapping a pencil, plucking at papers on her clipboard. "She's taking this without a fight. When Margo's career blew up and she lost her spot as the spokeswoman for Bella Donna, Kate wanted to organize a protest. She actually talked about going down to L.A. and picketing on Rodeo Drive."

Remembering put a smile back on Laura's face. "I never told Margo, because I managed to talk Kate out of it, but that's the way she is. She spits and claws and slaps when she's up against a personal problem. But not this time. This time she's pulled in, and I don't understand it."

"You're really worried about her," Byron realized.

"Yes, I am. So's Margo, or she would have strangled Kate half a dozen times by now. She wants us to fill out a sheet in something called a columnar pad every day."

"Once an accountant," he said.

"She carries one of those electronic memo pads in her pocket all the time. She's starting to talk about co-linking and getting on-line. It's terrifying." When he laughed, Laura caught herself and shook her head. "Ask a simple question . . ." she began. "Does everybody dump on you this way?"

"You didn't dump. I asked."

"Josh said you were the only man he wanted in this job. It's easy to see why. You're so different from Peter—" This time she didn't just catch herself, she clenched her teeth. "No, I'm not getting started on that. I'm already behind schedule and Ms. Bingham's waiting. Thanks for taking the orthodontists off my hands."

"My pleasure. You might not hear it very often, but you're an asset to Templeton."

"I'm trying to be."

As she walked away, Byron turned in the opposite direction, studying her careful and precise report as he went.

At the end of the day he met with Josh at Templeton Resort. The office there was a sprawling room on the executive level, with windows offering a view of one of the resort's two lagoonlike pools, surrounded by hibiscus in riotous bloom and a patio with redwood tables under candy-pink umbrellas.

Inside, it was built for comfort as well as business with deeply cushioned leather chairs, Deco lamps, and a stylish watercolor street scene of Milan.

"Want a beer?"

At the offer Byron merely sighed low and deep. He accepted the bottle from Josh, tipped it back. "Sorry to hit you at the end of the day. It's the first I could get away."

"There is no end of the day in the hotel business," Josh said.

"Your mother said that." Byron grinned. Susan Templeton was one of his favorite people. "You know if your father would just step aside like a gentleman, I'd beg her to marry me." He drank again, then nodded at the file he'd put on Josh's desk. "I started to fax this business over, then thought I'd just swing by personally."

Instead of going behind the desk, Josh picked up the file and stretched out in the chair opposite Byron. He skimmed the reports with varying reactions. A chuckle, a groan, a sigh, an oath.

"That sums up my feelings," Byron concurred. "I had a talk with Dr. Holdermen myself a few hours ago. He's still a guest. He's got temporary caps on and a real beaut of a black eye. My take is he doesn't have a case, but he's pissed off enough, and embarrassed enough, to pursue it."

Josh nodded, came to his own conclusions. "And your recommendation?"

"Let him."

"Agreed." Josh tossed the file onto his desk. "I'll pass it along to Legal with that recommendation. Now . . ." Josh settled back, the beer bottle cupped loosely in his hand, his eyes curious. "Why don't you tell me why you're really here? You can handle this kind of nuisance in your sleep."

Byron rubbed his chin. "We know each other too well."

"Ten years on and off should be enough. What's on your mind, By?"

"Kate Powell."

Josh's brows shot up. "Really?"

"Not in that context," Byron said, a bit too quickly. "It was something Laura said today that got me thinking about the whole situation. Bittle made some serious allegations against her, yet they haven't pursued it. And neither has she. It's going on three weeks now."

"I'm going to get pissed off again." Feeling his temper bubbling, Josh rose and paced it off. "My father used to play golf with Larry Bittle. I don't know how many times he's been over to the house. He's known Kate since she was a kid."

"Have you talked to him?"

"Kate almost took my head off when I threatened to." Scowling, Josh gulped down his beer. "That was okay, but then she just shut down. She seemed so shaky over the whole thing, I didn't push. Hell, I've been so wrapped up in Margo and the baby, I let it slide. We did this heartbeat thing at the doctor's today. It was so cool. You could just hear it, beating away, this quick little bopping." He stopped when he caught Byron's grin. "Kate," he began again.

"That's okay, you can indulge in obsessive expectant fatherhood for a minute."

"There's more. It's not an excuse for letting my sister dangle." He sat again, with a muscle in his cheek twitching. "We've decided to settle with Ridgeway. Goddamn bastard cheats on Laura, scalps her, ignores his children, alienates half the staff at the hotel, and we end up cutting him a check for a quarter million just to avoid a premature termination suit.''

"It's rough," Byron agreed. "But he'll be gone."

"He better stay gone."

"You could always break his nose again," Byron suggested.

"There is that." Willing himself to relax, Josh rolled his shoulders. "You could say I've been a little distracted the last few weeks. And Kate, she's always been so self-reliant. You begin to take it for granted."

"Laura's worried about her."

"Laura worries about everyone but Laura." Josh brooded for a minute. "I haven't been able to get through to Kate. She won't talk about it, at least not to me. I hadn't considered going over her head to Bittle. Is that what you're getting at?"

"It's none of my business. The thing is . . ." Byron studied his beer for a moment, then lifted those calm, clear eyes to Josh. He'd thought it through, as he did any problem, and had come to one conclusion. "If Bittle does decide to pursue a case against her, wouldn't she be better off to take the offensive now?"

"The threat of a nice fat libel suit, an unjustified suspension, loss of income, emotional distress."

Byron smiled and finished off his beer. "Well, you're the lawyer."

It took him the best part of a week, but Josh was hotly pleased when he strolled into Pretenses. He'd just come from a meeting with the partners of Bittle and Associates.

He caught his wife around the waist and kissed her thrillingly, to the delight of the customers milling about the shop.

"Hi."

"Hi, yourself. And what are you doing in my parlor in the middle of the day?"

"I didn't come for you." He kissed her again and barely restrained himself from laying a hand on her stubbornly flat stomach. He couldn't wait for it to grow. "I need to talk to Kate."

"Captain Queeg is in the office, rolling marbles and talking about strawberries."

Josh winced. "I thought you were calling her Captain Bligh these days."

"He wasn't insane enough. She's redoing the filing system. Color-coded."

"Good God. What's next?"

Margo narrowed her eyes. "She put up a bulletin board."

"She must be stopped. I'll go in." He drew a deep breath. "If I'm not out in twenty minutes, remember, I've always loved you."

"Very funny," she muttered, and managed to hold the smile back until he'd slipped into the rear office.

Josh found Kate mumbling over files. Her hair stood up in spikes, and the first two fingers of her right hand were covered with rubber tips.

"Less than a year," she said without turning around, "and you and Laura have managed to misfile half of everything. Why the hell is a fire insurance invoice in the umbrella file?"

"Someone should be flogged."

Unamused, she turned, eyed him. "I don't have time for you, Josh. Your wife's making my life a living hell."

"Funny, she says the same thing about you." Despite her ferocious glare, he walked over and kissed the tip of her nose. "I hear you're color-coding the files."

"Somebody has to. The software I installed keeps clean records, but you're better off backing up with hard copy in retail. I told Margo to do this months ago, but she's more interested in selling trinkets."

"God knows how you can expect to keep a retail business running by selling things!"

She drew in a breath, refusing to hear how foolish she sounded. "My point is you can hardly keep any business successful if you don't concern yourself with the details. She's been logging shoes under wardrobe instead of accessories."

"She needs to be punished." He grabbed Kate's shoulders. "Let me do it."

Chuckling, she shoved him back. "Go away. I don't have time to laugh right now."

"I didn't come by for laughs. I need to talk to you." He pointed to a chair. "So sit."

"Can't this wait? I have to be back in the showroom in an hour. I want to get the files in shape first."

"Sit," he repeated and gave her a brotherly nudge. "I just had a meeting at Bittle."

The impatience drained out of her eyes, leaving them cold and blank. "Excuse me?"

"Don't take that tone with me, Kate. It's past time this was dealt with."

She continued to take that tone, quiet and icy, as fear clawed at her insides. "And you decided you were the one to deal with it?"

"That's right. As your attorney—"

"You're not my attorney," she shot back.

"Who went to court to get you out of that speeding ticket three years ago?"

"You, but—"

"And who looked over your lease for your apartment before you signed it?"

"Yes, but—"

"Who wrote your will?"

Her face turned mutinous. "I don't see that that has anything to do with it."

"I see." Idly, he studied his manicure. "Just because I've handled all the pesky little legal details of your life doesn't make me your lawyer."

"It doesn't give you the right to go behind my back and talk to Bittle. Particularly since I asked you to leave it alone."

"Fine, it doesn't. Being your brother does."

Bringing up family loyalty was, in Kate's opinion, hitting below the belt. She sprang to her feet. "I'm not the inadequate, incapable little sister, and I won't be treated like one. I'm handling this."

"How?" Primed to fight, he got to his feet as well. "By color-coding the files in here?"

"Yes." Since he was shouting now, Kate matched her voice to his. "By making the best of the situation. By getting on with my life. By not whining and crying."

"By backing down and doing nothing." He poked his finger against her shoulder. "By going into denial. Well, it's gone on long enough. Bittle and company know that they're facing legal action."

"Legal action?" The blood drained out of her face. She could feel every drop flow. "You told them I was going to sue? Oh, my God." Dizzy, she leaned on the desk.

"Hey!" He grabbed her in alarm. "Sit down. Catch your breath."

"Leave me alone. Leave me the hell alone. What have you done?"

"What needed to be done. Now come on, honey, sit down."

"Jesus Christ." She exploded, and rather than a poke on his shoulder, she landed a punch on it. "How dare you?" Her color was back, flaming. "How dare you threaten legal action?"

"I didn't tell them you were going to sue. I merely left them chewing over that impression."

"I told you to leave it. This is my business. Mine." She threw up her arms, spun around. "What gave you this brainstorm, Joshua? I'm going to kill Margo."

"Margo didn't have anything to do with it, though if you would open your beady eyes for five minutes, you'd see how worried she is about you. How worried everyone is."

Because he might poke her again, he decided his hands were safer in his pockets. "I shouldn't have let it go this long, but I've had things on my mind. If By hadn't dropped by and given me a push, it would have taken me longer, but I'd have gotten to it."

102

"Stop." Breathing hard, she held up a hand. "Playback. Byron De Witt talked to you about me?"

Realizing his misstep, Josh tried a quick retreat. "Your name came up in conversation, that's all. And it started me—"

"My name came up." Now she was breathing between clenched teeth—teeth that matched the fists ready at her sides. Anger was better, she realized, than panic. "Oh, I just bet it did. That son of a bitch. I should have known he couldn't keep his mouth shut."

"About what?"

"Don't try to cover up. And get out of my way." Her shove was fierce enough and unexpected enough to knock him back. Before he could make the grab, she was sailing past him.

"Just a damn minute. I haven't finished."

"You go to hell," she shot back over her shoulder, causing several customers to glance around nervously as she stormed out of the office. She sent Margo one seething glare before slamming the front door behind her.

"Well." Struggling with a smile, Margo handed a bagged purchase to a wide-eyed customer. "That's thirty-eight fifty-three out of forty." Still smiling, she handed over the change. "And the show was free. Please come again."

With the wariness of a man who understood trouble when it stared at him from sultry blue eyes, Josh approached the counter. "Sorry about that."

"We'll deal with sorry later," she said under her breath. "What did you do to upset her?"

Just like a woman, he thought, to take the woman's side. "I tried to help her."

"You know how she hates that. Why, instead of taking your head off, did she storm out of here looking like she was going to take someone else's head off?"

He sighed, scratched his chin, shuffled his feet. "She'd finished taking my head off. Now she's going for Byron's. He sort of suggested that I help her."

Margo tapped coral-tipped nails on the glass counter. "I see."

"I really ought to call him, give him some advance warning." But when Josh reached for the phone on the counter, Margo laid a firm hand over his.

"Oh, no. I don't think so. We wouldn't want to spoil Kate's advantage."

"Margo, it's only fair."

"Fair has nothing to do with it. And you're going to be too busy waiting on customers to make personal calls."

Now he stuck his hands in his pockets. "Duchess, I've got a meeting in a couple of hours. I don't have time to help you out around here."

"Thanks to you, I'm shorthanded." Knowing that that wouldn't get her very far, she let her shoulders slump. "And I'm feeling a little tired."

"Tired?" Panic came on wings. "You should get off your feet."

"You're probably right." Though she felt strong as a horse, she scooted a stool over to the cash register and perched on it. "I'll just sit here and ring up sales for the next hour. Oh, Josh, darling, be sure to offer the customers champagne."

Enjoying herself, she slipped off her shoes and prepared to watch her adorable husband handle a storeful of customers.

The only show she would have preferred to witness was the one that would be starting shortly in the penthouse office of Templeton Monterey.

The first analogy that came to Byron's mind was that of a wild, possibly rabid, deer charging.

Kate cut through his shocked, protesting assistant like a sharp knife through quivery jelly, snarled like a feral she-wolf, and might very well have delivered the knockout punch of a flyweight champ if Byron hadn't signaled his assistant to retreat.

"Well, Katherine." He barely missed a beat when she slammed the door with a resounding *crack*. "What an unexpected pleasure."

"I'm going to kill you. I'm going to rip off your meddling nose and stuff it in your flapping mouth."

"As much fun as I'm sure that'll be, would you like a drink first? Some water? You're a bit flushed."

"Who the hell do you think you are?" She sprang toward the desk, smashed her palms down on its polished, and just now crowded, surface. "What possible right do you have to mix in my business? Do I strike you as some weak-willed, empty-headed woman who needs a man to defend her?"

"Which one of those questions would you like me to answer first? Why don't I take them in order?" he said before she could shout again. "You know exactly who I am. I didn't mix in your business any more than any tentative and concerned friend would, and no, no indeed, I don't see you as weak-willed or empty-headed. I see you as stubborn, rude, and potentially dangerous."

"You haven't got a clue how dangerous, pal."

"That threat might have more weight if you'd take off those filing tips. They spoil the image."

A strangled sound erupted from her throat as she looked down and discovered the brown rubber tips still on her fingers. Smooth and quick, she ripped them off and threw them at him. Just as smooth, just as quick, he caught them both before they hit his face.

"Good arm," he commented. "I bet you played ball in school."

"I thought I could trust you." For reasons she didn't want to analyze, thinking of that made her eyes sting. "I even, for one brief, foolish moment, thought I could learn to like you. Now I see that my first impression of you as an arrogant, self-important, sexist jerk was totally on the mark." Her sense of betrayal was every bit as keen as her fury. "I was reeling when you found me on the cliffs, I was vulnerable. Everything I said there I said to you in confidence. You had no right to run to Josh with it."

He set the rubber tips on his desk. "I didn't say anything to Josh about that day on the cliffs."

"I don't believe you. You went to him—"

"I don't lie," he said sharply. She glimpsed the steel beneath the polish. "Yes, I went to him. Sometimes it takes someone outside the family to put things on the table. And your family is torn up about what happened to you, Kate. More worried about the way you're behaving."

"My behavior isn't—"

"Any of my business," he finished for her. "Odd that something as harmless as my speaking with Josh sends you into a tailspin of revenge and retribution, but being questioned about embezzlement makes you curl up in the fetal position and suck your thumb."

"You don't know what I'm doing, what I'm feeling. And you have no right to pass judgment."

"No, that's all quite true. If you weren't so self-involved, you'd see that no one's passing judgment. But as an outsider I can tell you that your family is hurting for you."

Her flush died until her cheeks were bone-white. "Don't lecture me about my family. Don't you dare. They're the most important people in the world to me. I'm handling this my way because of my family."

He cocked his head. "Which means?"

"Which means that, too, is none of your business." She pressed her fingers to her eyes, fighting for control. "Nothing and no one is more on my mind than my family."

He believed that without hesitation, and only felt more sorry for her. "Your way of handling this situation isn't working."

"How the hell do you know?"

"Because people talk to me." His voice was gentle now, and the edge of temper had smoothed out of it. "Margo, Laura, Josh. Because I know how worried and angry I'd be if it was my sister."

"Well, it isn't your sister." The anger snapped back into her voice, but her cheeks stayed white. "I'm capable of dealing with this. Josh has enough on his plate without being guilted into taking this on."

"Do you really think guilt has anything to do with it?"

She fumbled, recovered. "Don't twist my words around, De Witt."

"Those were your words, Powell. Now, if you've finished with your tantrum, we can discuss this."

"Tantrum—"

"I'd heard you were good at them, but now that I've had a firsthand demonstration, I see the reports were understated."

He'd never thought that dark, glossy brown could turn to fire until he watched it happen in her eyes. "I'll show you a tantrum." With one swipe she sent most of the papers on his desk flying, then raised her fist. "Come out from behind that desk."

"Oh, you tempt me." His voice was ominously quiet, his eyes dangerously cool. "I've never hit a woman in my life. And never have I found it necessary to make that statement before. But you tempt me, Katherine, to break all kinds of records. Now either sit down or get out."

"I'm not sitting down, and I'm not getting out until we—" She broke off, strangling a cry as she pressed a hand under her breasts.

Now he did come around the desk, cursing all the way. "Damn it. Damn it! What are you doing to yourself?"

"Don't touch me." The burning pressure made her eyes water, but she struggled when he led her to a chair.

"You're going to sit down. You're going to try to relax. And if you don't have your color back in thirty seconds, I'm hauling your skinny butt to the hospital."

"Just leave me alone." She fumbled out her antacids, knowing it was like trying to put out a forest fire with a water pistol. "I'll be fine in a minute."

"How often does this happen?"

"None of your business." She yelped in pain and shock when he pressed two fingers to her abdomen.

"Do you have your appendix?"

"Keep your hands off me, Dr. Feelgood."

He only continued to frown and moved his fingertips to the inside of her wrist. "Been skipping meals again?" Before she

107

could evade, he caught her face in his hands and took a long, objective look. Her color was seeping back, slowly, and her eyes were filled with temper again rather than pain. But he saw other things. "You're not sleeping. You're tired, overstressed and undernourished. Is that how you're handling this?"

Her stomach quivered, an echo of pain and nerves. "I want you to leave me alone."

"You don't always get what you want. You're exhausted, Kate, and until you start taking better care of yourself, someone else will have to do it for you. Be still," he ordered in an absent murmur, holding a hand on her shoulder as he checked his watch. "I'm tied up here until after six. I'll pick you up at seven. Will you be at the shop or at home?"

"What the hell are you talking about? I'm not going anywhere with you."

"I realize I'm annoyed with myself for handling this matter badly. You do seem to bring out the worst in me," he added, mostly to himself. "So, you're going to get a decent meal and the opportunity to discuss these gripes of yours in a civilized manner."

It was frightening her, the casual manner he assumed, the glint of heat in his eye that warned he could shift out of casual mode at any moment.

"I don't want to have dinner with you, and I'm not feeling civilized."

Considering, he rocked back on his heels, so that their eyes were level. "Let's try it this way. You go along with this or I pick up the phone and call Laura. It should take her about two minutes to get up here, and when she does, I'll tell her that twice now I've seen you go white and double over."

"You have no right."

"No, Kate, what I have here is the hammer. That beats the hell out of rights." He checked his watch again. "I have a conference call coming through in about five minutes, or we'd finish more of this now. Since the reasonable thing for you to do is go home and get some rest, I assume you'll go back to the shop. I'll pick you up at seven.''

Trapped, she nudged him aside and got to her feet. "We close at six.''

"Then you'll have to wait, won't you? And don't slam the door on your way out.''

Of course she did, and he found he had to smile. But the smile faded when he picked up the phone and hurriedly punched in a number. "Dr. Margaret De Witt, please. It's her son." Another look at his watch brought out a mild oath. "No, I can't wait. Would you ask her to call me when she's free? The office before six, at home after seven. Thanks.''

He hung up, then began to put in order the papers Kate had scattered. Almost amused, he pocketed the filing tips she'd left behind. He doubted that Kate would appreciate him calling his mother the internist for an over-the-phone diagnosis of her symptoms.

But somebody had to look out for her. Whether she wanted it or not.

Chapter Seven

She was going to be calm. Kate promised herself that. She'd made a fool of herself, barging into Byron's office, shouting and raging. She wouldn't have minded that so much—if it had worked. There was nothing worse than having a good temper fit snuffed out by reason, patience, and control.

It was more than humiliating.

She didn't much care for taking orders either. Frowning, she looked around the shop she'd just closed. She could simply walk out, she considered, drumming her fingers on the counter. She could just stroll right out, go anywhere she wanted. Home, for a drive, to Templeton House for dinner. That might be the best option, she thought, rubbing a hand absently over the grinding ache in her stomach. She was hungry, that was all. A good meal at Templeton House, an evening with Laura and the girls would soothe all the pangs and nerves.

It would serve Byron right if she wasn't there when he came gunning for her. For that, she was sure, was his intention.

Soothe the victim with reason, with promises of calm discussions, then, *pow*, shoot her between the eyes.

And that, she knew, was the reason she was staying put. Kate Powell never walked away from a challenge.

Let him come, she told herself grimly as she began to wander about the shop. She could handle Byron De Witt in her sleep. Men like him were so used to getting their own way with a quick smile, a murmured word, they didn't know how to act with a woman who stood firmly on her own feet.

Besides, now that her finances were a little strained, she acknowledged the advantage of a free meal.

The grinding came back, like a sneering echo. Nerves, she thought again. Of course she was nervous. She knew better than anyone that Pretenses could barely support three incomes and stay afloat. They were lucky to have made it through the first year. But the odds were still against them.

She frowned down at a stylish glass rhinoceros in pale gold. How long, she wondered, were they going to be able to sell things quite that foolish? The price tag made her laugh. Nine hundred dollars? Who in their right mind would plunk down nearly a thousand dollars for something so ridiculous?

Margo, she decided, and her lips curved up again. Margo had a keen eye for the expensive, the ridiculous, and the salable.

If Pretenses went down the toilet, Margo would be fine. She had Josh now, a baby on the way, a beautiful home. A far cry from her circumstances a year ago, Kate mused, and was glad for her.

But there was Laura to worry about, and the girls. They wouldn't starve, Kate knew. The Templetons wouldn't allow it. They would live in Templeton House, which would give them far more than a roof over their heads. It would give them a home. Since Laura was too proud to touch the income from her Templeton stocks, she could work at the hotel and earn a living, a good one. But how badly would her ego be bruised if the business she started herself failed?

Kate had discovered a great deal about the difficulties of functioning with a scraped ego.

They had to make the shop work. It was Margo's dream, and it had become Laura's. It was all Kate had to hold on to. All her neat little plans were ruined. There would be no partnership at Bittle, no possibility of striking out with her own firm at some future date. No pretty brass plaque on her office door. No office, she thought, and sat down on a painted wooden bench.

Right now she had sleepless nights, headaches that never quite faded, a stomach that refused to behave, and Pretenses.

Pretenses, she thought with a thin smile. Margo had named it well. The three owners were just full of them.

The knock on the door made her jolt, then swear, then straighten her shoulders as she rose and went to unlock it. She nudged Byron aside, stepped out onto the little flower-decked veranda, and locked up again.

Pedestrian and street traffic churned past with all the noise and bustle that usually accompanied it. Tourists, she thought absently, searching for just the right spot to enjoy a vacation dinner. Members of the workforce heading home after a long day. Couples out on dates.

Just where did Kate Powell fit in?

"I'm not going because you told me I was going," she said without preliminary. "I'm going because I want the opportunity to speak calmly and clearly about the situation, and because I'm hungry."

"Fine." He cupped a hand under her elbow. "We'll take my car. I managed to find a space in the lot across the street. It's a busy area."

"It's a good location," she began as he led her to the curb. "A stone's throw from Fisherman's Wharf and the water. Tourists are a big part of our business, but a lot of the locals come here to shop too."

Two young boys on a rented tandem bike whizzed by behind her, laughing like hyenas. It was a beautiful evening, full of soft light and soft scents. A night for beach walking, she mused, or for tossing hunks of bread to the gulls as the couple by the water was doing just now. A night, she thought, for couples. Kate nibbled her lip as Byron guided her across the street.

"I can follow you. There are a dozen restaurants within walking distance, for that matter."

"We'll take my car," he repeated, gently and firmly maneuvering through the crowded parking lot. "And I'll bring you back to yours when we're finished."

"It would save time and be more efficient if—"

"Kate." He turned and looked at her, really looked, and scotched the annoyed remark hovering on his tongue. The woman was exhausted. "Why don't you try something new? Go with the flow."

He opened the passenger door of his vintage Mustang and waited with some amusement for her bad-tempered shrug. He wasn't disappointed.

She watched him round the hood. He'd ditched his tie and jacket, she noted, opened his collar. The casual, easy look suited those lineman's shoulders, she supposed, the beachcomber hair. She decided to realign her strategy and wait until they were at dinner before beginning the lecture she'd been planning.

She could, when necessary, manage small talk with the best of them.

"So, you're into classic cars."

He settled behind the wheel. The minute he turned the key the radio exploded with Marvin Gaye. Byron turned it down to a murmur before cruising through the lot.

"Sixty-five Mustang with a 289 V-8. A car like this isn't just a mode of transportation. It's a commitment."

"Really?" She liked the creamy white bucket seats, the trained-panther ride, but couldn't think of anything more impractical than owning a car older than she was. "Don't you have to spend a lot of time babying it, finding parts?"

"That's the commitment. Runs like a dream," he added

with an affectionate stroke to the dash as he merged into traffic. "She was my first."

"First what? First car?"

"That's right." He grinned at her baffled stare. "Bought her when I was seventeen. She's got over two hundred thousand miles on her and still purrs like a kitten."

Kate would have said it was more "roars like a lion," but that wasn't her problem. "Nobody keeps their first car. It's like your first lover."

"Exactly." He downshifted, eased around a turn. "As it happens, I had my first lover in the backseat, one sweet summer night. Pretty Lisa Montgomery." He sighed reminiscently. "She opened a window to paradise for me, God bless her."

"A window to paradise." Unable to resist, Kate craned her neck and studied the pristine backseat. It wasn't very difficult to imagine two young bodies groping. "All that in the back of an old Mustang."

"Classic Mustang," he corrected. "Just like Lisa Montgomery."

"But you didn't keep her."

"You can't keep everything, except memories. Remember your first time?"

"In my college dorm room. I was a slow starter." Marvin Gaye had given way to Wilson Pickett. Kate's foot began to keep time. "He was captain of the debate team and seduced me with his argument that sex, next to birth and death, was the ultimate human experience."

"Good one. I'll have to try it sometime."

She slanted a look at his profile. Hero perfect, she judged, with just a hint of rugged. "I don't imagine you need lines."

"It never hurts to keep a few in reserve. So what happened to the captain of the debate team?"

"He was used to getting his point across inside of three minutes. That ability bled over into the ultimate human experience."

"Oh." Byron fought back a grin. "Too bad."

"Not really. It taught me not to build up unrealistic expectations and not to depend on someone else to fulfill basic needs." Kate scanned the scenery. Her foot stopped tapping as she tensed up again. "Why are we on Seventeen Mile?"

"It's a pretty drive. I enjoy taking it every day. Did I mention that I was able to arrange renting the house I'm buying until we settle?"

"No, you didn't." But she was getting the drift. "You said we were going to have dinner and a civilized discussion."

"And we are. You can take a look at the favor you did for me at the same time."

Even as she formulated several arguments against, Byron turned into a driveway and pulled up behind a dramatically glossy black Corvette.

"It's a '63, first year the Stingray rolled out of Detroit," he said with a nod toward the car. "Three hundred sixty horsepower, fuel-injected. An absolute beauty. Not that the original 'Vette wasn't a honey before the redesign. They don't make bodies like that anymore."

"Why do you need two cars?"

"Need isn't the issue. Anyway, I have four cars. The other two are back in Atlanta."

"Four," she murmured, and found this little quirk of his amusing.

"Fifty-seven Chevy, 283-cubic-inch V-8. Baby blue, white sidewalls, all original equipment." There was affection in his voice. Kate thought the southern heat of it flowed over the words like a man describing a lover. "Every bit as classy as the songs they wrote about her."

"Billie Jo Spears." Kate knew her music trivia. "Fifty-seven Chevrolet.' "

"That's the best." Surprised and impressed, he grinned at her. "Keeping her company is a '67 GTO."

" 'Three deuces and a four speed'?"

"Right." His grin widened. "And a 389."

She grinned back. "Just what the hell are three deuces, automotively speaking?"

"If you don't know already, it would take a little time to explain. Just let me know if you ever want a serious lesson."

Then he put a hand over Kate's and shifted his gaze to the house. She was relaxed enough not to pull away. "It's great, isn't it?"

"It's nice." All wood and glass, she mused, bilevel decks, flowers already blooming riotously, that wonderful cypress bent and magical. "I've seen it before."

"From the outside." Knowing she'd never wait for him to come around to her door, he leaned across her to open it. And inhaled the simple scent of soap. Enjoying it, he let his gaze wander lazily from her mouth to her eyes. "You'll be another first."

"Excuse me?"

God, was he losing his mind or was he actually starting to look forward to that edgy tone? "My first guest." He got out of the car, retrieved his briefcase and jacket. As they started up the walk, he took her hand in a friendly gesture. "You can hear the sea," he pointed out. "It's just close enough. I've caught a couple of glimpses of seals, too."

It was charming—almost too charming, she thought. The setting, the sounds, the scent of roses and night-blooming jasmine. What was left of the setting sun spread vivid, heartbreaking color across the western sky. The twisted shadows from the trees were long and deep.

"A lot of tourists drive along here," she said, fighting the spell. "Isn't that going to bother you?"

"No. The house is set back from the road, and the bedrooms face the water." He turned the key in the lock. "There's just one problem."

She was glad to hear it. Perfection made her nervous. "What?"

"I don't have much in the way of furniture." He opened the door and proved his point.

It shouldn't have delighted her. Bare floors, bare walls, bare space. Yet she found it delightful, the way the entranceway flowed into a room. The simplest of welcomes. The wide glass doors on the facing wall exploded with that stunning sunset, almost demanded to be opened wide to it.

The yellow pine floors gleamed under her feet as she stepped inside, crossed over them. There was no rug, as yet, to tame that ocean flood of shine.

He would get one, she imagined. It was practical, sensible. But, she thought, it would also be a shame.

From her outside survey of the house, she hadn't guessed that the ceilings were so high or that the stairs leading to the next level were open, as open as the carved pickets in the ornate railing that skirted the second story.

She could see how cleverly, how simply one room became another, so that the house appeared to be one large living space. White walls, golden floors, and the beautiful bleeding light from the west.

"Great view," she managed and wondered why her palms were damp. Casually she wandered to a crate on which stood an elaborate stereo system. The only piece of furniture was a ratty recliner with duct tape holding the arms together. "You've got the essentials, I see."

"No point in living without music. I picked up the chair at a yard sale. It's so awful it's wonderful. Want a drink?"

"Just some club soda, or water." Alcohol was off the list for a couple of reasons, and he was one of them.

"I've got some Templeton mineral water."

She smiled. "Then you've got the best."

"I'll take you on a tour after I've gotten dinner started. Come in the kitchen and keep me company."

"You know how to cook?" It was the shock of it that made her follow him.

"Actually, I do. You like grits and chitlins, right?" He waited a beat, turned, and wasn't disappointed with the look of sheer horror on her face. "Just kidding. How about seafood?"

"Not those crawfish things."

"I make a hell of a crawfish étouffée, but we'll save that for when we're better acquainted. If the rest of the house hadn't already sold me, this would have done it.''

The kitchen was done in dramatic maroon and white tiles, with a center island that gleamed like an iceberg. A built-in banquette curved in front of a wide window that looked out on blooming flowers and the deep-green lawn.

"Subzero," Byron commented, running a loving hand over the stainless-steel front of a wide refrigerator. "Convection oven, Jenn-Air range, teak cabinets."

There was a big blue bowl of fresh, glossy fruit on the counter. The grinding in Kate's stomach told her if she didn't eat soon, she'd die. "You like to cook?"

"It relaxes me."

"Okay, why don't you relax? I'll watch."

She had to admit it was an impressive show. She sipped chilled water while he sliced an array of colorful vegetables. His movements were brisk and, as far as she could tell, professional. Intrigued, she moved closer, watched his hands.

Very nice hands, now that she took a good look. Long fingers, wide palms, with a neat manicure that didn't take away from the basic masculinity.

"Did you, like, take a course or something?"

"Or something. We had this cook. Maurice." Byron turned a red bell pepper into long, neat strips. "He told me he'd teach me how to box. I was tall and skinny, regularly got the shit beat out of me at school."

Kate stepped back, did a slow survey. Broad shoulders, trim waist, narrow hips. Long limbs, certainly. And with his sleeves rolled up for cooking, she could see forearms that looked just a bit dangerous. "What happened? Steroids?"

He chuckled and went briskly to work on an onion. "I grew into my arms and legs after a while, started working out, but I was about twelve and pathetically awkward."

"Yeah." Kate sipped, remembering her own adolescence. The trouble was, she'd never grown into anything. Still the runt of the litter, she mused. "It's a rough age."

"So Maurice said he'd teach me to defend myself, but I had to learn to cook. It was, according to him, just one more

119

way to become self-sufficient.'' Byron drizzled oil into a large cast-iron pan already heating on the stove. ''In about six months I whipped Curt Bodine's bad ass—he was the bane of my existence at the time.''

''I had Candy Dorall, now Litchfield,'' Kate put in conversationally. ''She was always my bane.''

''The terminally pert Candace Litchfield? Redhead, smug, foxy face, annoying little giggle?''

Anyone who described Candy so accurately deserved a smile. ''I think I might like you after all.''

''Did you ever punch Candy in her sassy nose?''

''It's not her nose. She had rhinoplasty.'' Kate snacked on a strip of pepper. ''And no, but we did stuff her naked into a locker. Twice.''

''Not bad, but that's girl stuff. Me, I just beat the hell out of Curt, salvaged masculine pride while earning the appropriate macho rep. And I could produce a chocolate soufflé to die for.''

When she laughed, he paused and turned to face her. ''Do that again.'' When she didn't respond, he shook his head. ''You really ought to laugh more, Katherine. It's a fascinating sound. Surprisingly full and rich. Like something you'd expect to hear floating out of the window of a New Orleans brothel.''

''I'm sure that's a compliment.'' She lifted her water glass again, made herself keep her eyes level with his. ''But I rarely laugh on an empty stomach.''

''We'll fix that.'' He tossed minced garlic into the hot oil. The scent was immediate and wonderful. The onion went in next, and she began to salivate.

He pried the lid off a covered bowl, slid shelled shrimp and scallops into the pan. She thought it was a bit like watching a mad scientist at work. A glug of white wine, a pinch of salt, a slight grating of what he told her was ginger. Quick stirs and shakes to mix all those pretty strips of vegetables.

In less time than it might have taken her to peruse a menu, she was sitting down to a full plate.

"It's good," she said after her first bite. "It's really good. Why aren't you in food services?"

"Cooking's a hobby."

"Like conversation and old cars."

"Vintage cars." It pleased him to see her eat. He'd decided on the menu because he'd wanted to get something healthy into her. He imagined her snatching junk food when she remembered to eat at all, snacking on antacids. No wonder she was too thin. "I could teach you."

"Teach me what?"

"To cook."

She speared a shrimp. "I didn't say I couldn't cook."

"Can you?"

"No, but I didn't say I couldn't. And I don't need to as long as there's takeout and microwave ovens."

Because she'd refused his offer of wine, he stuck with water himself. "I bet there's a place reserved for you at McDonald's drive-through window."

"So? It's quick, it's easy, and it's filling."

"Nothing wrong with the occasional french fry, but when it's a dietary staple—"

"Don't start with me, Byron. This is why I'm here in the first place." Remembering her plan, she got down to business. "I don't like people, particularly people I barely know, interfering in my life."

"We have to get to know each other better."

"No, we don't." It was weird, she realized, how easily she'd become distracted, and interested, and at ease. Time had slipped by when all she'd meant to do was give him the sharpest edge of one piece of her mind. "Your intentions might have been good, but you had no business going to Josh."

"Your eyes are fabulous," he said and watched them narrow with suspicion. "I don't know if it's because they're so big, so dark, or because your face is narrow, but they really pack a punch."

"Is that one of your reserved lines?"

"No, it's an observation. I happen to be looking at your

121

face, and it occurs to me that it has all these contrasts. The snooty New England cheekbones, the wide, sexy mouth, angular nose, the big, doe eyes. It shouldn't work, but it does. It works better when you're not pale and tired, but that adds a rather disconcerting fragile quality.''

She shifted. ''I'm not fragile. I'm not tired. And my face has nothing to do with the subject under discussion.''

''But I like it. I liked it right away, even when I didn't like you. Now I wonder, Kate,'' he continued, laying a hand over hers, twining fingers. ''Why did you put so much effort into making sure I didn't look twice in your direction?''

''I didn't have to put any effort into that. I'm not your type any more than you're mine.''

''No, you're not,'' he agreed. ''Still, I occasionally enjoy sampling something . . . different.''

''I'm not a new recipe.'' She pulled her hand free, pushed her plate aside. ''And I came here to have, as you termed it, a civilized discussion.''

''This seems civilized to me.''

''Don't pull out that reasonable tone.'' She had to squeeze her eyes shut and count to ten. She made it to five. ''I hate that reasonable tone. I agreed to go to dinner with you so that I could make myself clear, so that I could do so without losing my temper the way I did earlier today.''

For emphasis, she leaned forward a little, was distracted by discovering that there was a thin gold halo around his pupils. ''I don't want you meddling in my life. I don't know how to make it any more plain than that.''

''That's plain.'' Since they seemed to have finished the meal, he picked up the plates and carried them to the counter. Sitting again, he took a cigar from his pocket, lit it. ''But there's a problem. I've developed an interest in you.''

''Yeah, right.''

''You find that difficult to believe?'' He puffed out smoke, considered. ''So did I initially. Then I realized what kicked it off. I'm driven to solve problems and puzzles. Answers and solutions are essential to me. Do you want coffee?''

"No, I don't want coffee." Didn't he know it drove her crazy the way he could slide from one topic to the next in that slow, southern drawl of his. Of course he did. "And I'm not a problem or a puzzle."

"But you are. Look at you, Kate. You white-knuckle your way through life." He reached out, deliberately uncurled her fist. "I can almost see whatever fuel you bother to put inside you being sucked away by nerves. You have a loving family, a solid base, an excellent mind, but you pick at details as if they were knotted threads. You never consider just snipping one off. Yet when you're faced with the injustice, the insult of being fired from a job that was a huge part of your life, you sit back and do nothing."

It grated and hurt and shamed. And because she couldn't explain to him, or to those who cared for her, it festered. "I'm doing what works for me. And I didn't come here for an analysis."

"I haven't finished," he said mildly. "You're afraid to be vulnerable, even ashamed of it. You're a practical woman, yet you're aware you're physically run-down and you're doing nothing about that either. You're an honest woman, but you're putting all of your energy into denying there might be even a mild hint of attraction between us. So you interest me." He took a last drag on his cigar, tamped it out. "The puzzle of you interests me."

She got to her feet slowly to prove to both of them she was still in control. "I realize it might be difficult—no, next to impossible—for you to realize that I'm not interested in you. I'm not vulnerable, I'm not ill, and I'm not even mildly attracted."

"Well." He unfolded himself and rose. "We can put at least one of those statements to the test." His eyes stayed watchful on hers as he cupped a hand behind her neck. "Unless you're afraid you're wrong."

"I'm not wrong. And I don't want—"

He decided it was simpler not to let her finish. The woman could argue with the dead. He covered her mouth with his quietly, with barely a whisper of pressure and promise. When her hands jerked up to his chest, he scooped an arm around her waist and brought her gently closer.

For his own pleasure, he skimmed his tongue over her lips, then dipped inside when they parted. He thought, foolishly, that he could hear a new window to a new paradise begin to creak open.

Then she trembled, and he forgot to be amused at both of them. When he eased back he saw that she was still pale, her eyes dark and clouded. Testing, he pressed light kisses on either side of her mouth and watched her lashes flutter.

"I don't—I can't—God." The hand pressed against his chest balled into a fist. "I don't have the time or the inclination for this."

"Why?"

Because her head was spinning, her pulse was pounding, and her juices were running in a way they hadn't in—ever. "You're not my type."

That clever mouth curved. "You're not mine either. Go figure."

"Men who look like you are always scum." She knew better, absolutely knew better, but she couldn't stop her hands from streaking up his chest and grabbing all that wonderful gold-tipped hair. "It's like the law."

His lips curved. "Whose law?"

She could have had a snappy comeback for that, if she'd just been able to concentrate. "Oh, the hell with it," she muttered and dragged his mouth back to hers.

Nerves and needs seemed to pulse from her in fast, greedy waves. He couldn't stand against them, could barely stand at all once her mouth started its assault. He should have known she wouldn't believe in the slow and the gradual, or the easy sweetness of a lazy seduction. But he hadn't considered that the fire-drenched demands of that mobile mouth would undermine his innate sense of reason.

In the space of a heartbeat he went from enjoying her to devouring her.

His arms banded around her, forgot about her long, fragile bones and soft, spare flesh. He used his teeth because that mouth, that wide, sultry mouth seemed to have been made for him to ravish. The scent of soap was absurdly sexy. He could almost taste it as he ran hot, wild kisses down her throat.

"It's only because I haven't had sex in so long." She gasped out the rationale even as her eyes crossed.

"Okay. Whatever." He curled his hands around her tiny, tight butt and muffled a moan against her throat.

"A year," she managed. "Okay, it's been nearly two, but after the first few months you hardly . . . Jesus, touch me. I'm going to scream if you don't touch me."

Where? He nearly panicked. He was unable to tell one part of her from another. He was steeped in all of her. Instinct had him tugging her crisp white shirt out of the waistband of her skirt, fumbling with buttons.

"Upstairs." He swore ripely as the buttons refused to yield. He didn't have enough sanity left to be appalled at how his fingers shook. "We should go upstairs. I've got a bed."

Desperate, she grabbed his hand and pressed it to her breast herself. "You've got a floor right here."

He managed a laugh. "I'm beginning to love practical women."

"You haven't seen anything—" Then it hit her. The first wave of pain was followed so swiftly by a second she barely managed a choked gasp.

"What? What is it? Did I hurt you?"

"No, it's nothing." He was trying to straighten her up as she doubled over. "It's just a twinge. It's—" But the burning was spreading like wildfire, and the fear burst through with it as she felt her skin break out in a cold, clammy sweat. "Just give me a minute." Blindly she reached out for something to balance her and would have fallen if he hadn't scooped her up.

"The hell with this." The words exploded between gritted teeth. "The hell with it. I'm taking you to the hospital."

"No. Stop it." Desperate for relief, she hooked an arm un-

125

der her breasts and pressed. "Just take me home."

"In a pig's eye." Like a warrior hoisting his conquest, he carried her out of the house. "Save your breath and yell at me later. Right now you're doing what you're told."

"I said take me home." She didn't bother to fight him when he strapped her into the car. All of her energy had to focus on dealing with the pain.

He backed out of the drive, saying nothing as she tore Tums out of the roll habitually in her pocket. Instead, he snatched up the car phone and punched in a number. "Mom." He drove fast, whipping the car around curves, and interrupted his mother's apology for not returning his call. "It's okay. Listen, I've got a friend, a woman, five sevenish, maybe a hundred and five pounds, mid-twenties." He swore lightly, cradling the phone on his shoulder as he shifted gears. "It's not that," he said at the inevitable chuckle. "I'm taking her to the hospital right now. She's got abdominal pain. It seems to be habitual."

"It's just stress," Kate managed between shallow breaths. "And your lousy cooking."

"Yes, that's her. She can talk, and she's lucid. I don't know." He glanced briefly at Kate. "Any abdominal surgery, Kate?"

"No. Don't talk to me."

"Yeah, I'd say she lives with a lot of stress, brings most of it on herself. We'd eaten about forty-five, fifty minutes before," he said in response to his mother's brisk questions. "No, no alcohol, no caffeine. But she lives on goddamn coffee and eats Tums like chocolate drops. Yeah? Is there a burning sensation?" he demanded of Kate.

"It's just indigestion," she muttered. The pain was backing off. Wasn't it? Please, wasn't it?

"Yes." He listened again, nodded. He was grimly aware of where his mother's questions were heading. "How often do you get that gnawing ache, under the breastbone?"

"None of your business."

"You don't want to piss me off right now, Kate. You really don't. How often?"

"A lot. So what? You're not taking me to any hospital."

"And the grinding in the stomach?"

Because he was describing her symptoms with pinpoint accuracy, she closed her eyes and ignored him.

He spoke to his mother another moment, punched up the gas. "Thanks, that's what I figured. I'm going to take care of it. Yeah, I'll let you know. I will. 'Bye." He hung up, kept his eyes firmly on the road. "Congratulations, you idiot. You've got yourself a nice little ulcer."

Chapter Eight

No way did she have an ulcer. Kate comforted herself with that thought, and the image of how foolish Byron was going to look for rushing her to the hospital with a case of nervous heartburn.

Ulcers were for repressed wimps who didn't know how to express their emotions, who were afraid to face what was inside them. Kate figured she expressed her emotions just fine, and at every opportunity.

She was simply dealing with more stress than usual. Who wouldn't have a jittery stomach after the two months she'd just had? But she was handling it, she told herself, shutting her eyes tight against the incessant burning pressure. She was handling it her way.

The minute Byron stopped the car, she would explain yet again, calmly, that Kate Powell took care of Kate Powell.

She would have, too. If she could have caught her breath. But he jerked to a halt in front of the emergency room, slammed out of the car, and plucked her out of her seat before she could so much as squeak.

Then it was worse, because she was inside, with all the sounds and scents of a hospital. Emergency rooms were all the same, everywhere. The air inside was thick with despair and fear and fresh blood. Antiseptics, alcohol, sweat. The slap of crepe-soled shoes and the whisper of wheels on linoleum. It paralyzed her. It was all she could do to keep herself from curling into a ball in the hard plastic chair where he'd dumped her.

"Stay," he ordered curtly before marching over to the admitting nurse.

She didn't even hear him.

Flashes of memory assaulted her. She could hear the high, desperate scream of sirens, see the red lights pulsing and spinning. She was eight years old again, and the dull throb deep inside her ached like a wound. And blood—she could smell it.

Not hers. Or very little of her blood. She'd barely had a scratch. Contusions, they had called them. Minor lacerations. A mild concussion. Nothing life-threatening. Nothing life-altering.

But they had wheeled her parents away, even while she'd screamed for her mother. And they had never come back.

"It's your lucky night," Byron said when he came back to her. "Not much going on. They're going to take a look at you now."

"I can't be here," she murmured. "I can't be in a hospital."

"That's the breaks, kid. This is where the doctors are." He lifted her to her feet, surprised when she went along like an obedient puppy. He passed her off to a nurse, then settled down to wait.

Kate told herself the more she cooperated, the quicker they would let her go. And they had to let her go. She wasn't a child now who had no choice. She stepped into the narrow examining area, shuddering once at the sound of the curtain being drawn closed behind her.

"Let's see what we've got here."

The doctor on duty was young and pretty. A round face, narrow eyes behind wire-framed glasses, dark hair scooped back at the side with simple bobby pins.

It had been a man before, Kate remembered. He'd been young, too, but his eyes had been exhausted and old. Mechanically, Kate answered the standard questions. No, she didn't have any allergies, she'd had no surgery, she was taking no medication.

"Why don't you lie back, Ms. Powell? I'm Dr. Hudd. I'm going to check you out. Are you having pain now?"

"No, not really."

The doctor lifted an eyebrow. "No or not really?"

Kate closed her eyes and struggled to steep herself in the here and now. "Some."

"Tell me when it increases."

Soft hands, Kate thought as they began to probe her. Doctors always seemed to have soft hands. Then she hissed as the doctor applied pressure under her breastbone.

"That's the spot, huh? How often does this happen?"

"It happens."

"Do you find the discomfort occurs after a meal, say, an hour or so after a meal?"

"Sometimes." She sighed. "Yes."

"And when you drink alcohol?"

"Yes."

"Is there any vomiting?"

"No." Kate swiped a hand over her clammy face. "No."

"Dizziness?"

"No. Well, not really."

Dr. Hudd's unpainted mouth pursed as she pressed her fingers to Kate's wrist. "Your pulse is a little fast."

"I don't want to be here," Kate said flatly. "I hate hospitals."

"Yeah, I know the feeling." The doctor continued as she made notations on a chart, "Describe the pain for me."

Kate stared up at the ceiling, pretended she was talking

131

aloud to herself. "It's a burning in the torso, or an aching."
She wouldn't stay here, she reminded herself calmly. On this
table, behind these curtains. "More like sharp hunger pains in
my stomach. They can get pretty intense."

"I bet. How have you been dealing with it?"

"My heartburn," Kate said dully. "Mylanta."

The doctor chuckled, patted Kate's hand. "Are you under
a lot of stress, Ms. Powell?"

My father was a thief, I've lost my job, and the cops could
be knocking on my door any minute. There's nothing I can
do about it, nothing, that won't make it worse.

"Who isn't?" She tried not to jerk when the doctor lifted
her eyelid and shined a light to check her pupils.

"How long have you been having these symptoms?"

"Somewhere around forever. I don't know. They've gotten
worse in the last couple of months."

"Sleeping well?"

"No."

"Taking anything for that?"

"No."

"How about headaches?"

"No, thanks. I have plenty of them. Nuprin," she said, anticipating the question. "Excedrin. I switch off."

"Mm-hmm. When was your last physical?" When Kate
didn't answer, the doctor eased back, pursed her lips again.
"That long ago, huh? Who's your regular doctor?"

"I go see Minelli once a year for a pap. I don't get sick."

"You're doing a good imitation of it now. I'll follow that
up with my imitation of an exam. Let's check your blood
pressure."

Kate submitted to it. She was calmer now, certain that the
ordeal was almost over. She imagined the doctor would dash
off a prescription and be done with it.

"Blood pressure's a little high, heart's strong. You're un-
derweight, Ms. Powell. Dieting?"

"No. I never diet."

"Lucky you," Hudd said, with a considering look in her

132

eye. It was a look Kate recognized, one that made her sigh.

"I don't have an eating disorder, doctor. I'm not bulimic, not anorexic. No binging, no purging, no pills. I've always been thin."

"So you haven't lost any weight lately?"

"A few pounds, maybe," Kate admitted. "My appetite's been kind of sporadic. Look, I've had some problems at work and it's stressed me out. That's all. Believe me, if I had a choice, I'd rather have curves than angles."

"Well, when we solve this problem, you should put them back on. After we run a few tests—"

Kate's hand shot out, curled around the doctor's wrist. "Tests? What kind of tests?"

"Nothing that involves torture chambers, I promise. We need some X-rays, a barium certainly. And I recommend an upper G.I. These are to pinpoint and to eliminate."

"I don't want any tests. Give me a pill and let me out of here."

"Ms. Powell, it's not quite that simple. We'll get you in and out of X-ray as quickly as possible. I'll try to schedule the G.I. for first thing in the morning. Once we get you admitted—"

Panic was white, Kate realized. White rooms and women in white uniforms. "You're not keeping me here."

"Just overnight," the doctor soothed. "It's not that I don't respect your boyfriend's diagnosis . . ."

"He's not my boyfriend."

"Well, I'd work on that if I were you, but in any case, he's not a doctor."

"His mother is. He talked to his mother on the way over. Ask him. I want you to get him back here. I want you to get him."

"All right. Try to calm down. I'll go talk to him. Just lie down here and try to relax." The doctor eased Kate's shoulders back.

Once she was alone, Kate struggled to breathe deeply, evenly. But terror was circling.

"Still arguing," Byron began when he stepped into the room.

Kate popped up like a spring. "I can't stay here." She snatched at his shirt front with trembling hands. "You have to get me out."

"Now, listen, Kate—"

"I can't stay here overnight. I can't spend the night in a hospital. I can't." Her voice lowered to a broken whisper. "My parents."

Confusion came first. Did she expect him to call the Templetons in France to back her up? Then he remembered—her own parents were dead. Had been killed in an accident. Hospital.

And he saw that what he had taken for pain and bad temper in her eyes was sheer terror.

"Okay, baby." To soothe her, he pressed his lips to her brow. "Don't worry. You're not going to stay."

"I can't." She felt her breath hitch, felt the simmering hysteria start its greasy rise.

"You won't. I promise." He cupped her face until her swimming eyes met his. "I promise, Kate. I'm going to talk to the doctor now, then I'll take you home."

Hysteria receded, replaced by trust. "All right. Okay." She closed her eyes. "All right."

"Just give me a minute." He stepped to the other side of the curtain with the doctor. "She's got a phobia. I didn't realize it."

"Look, Mr. De Witt, most people don't like spending time in hospitals. There are times I don't like it myself."

"I'm not talking about ordinary resistance." Frustrated, he dragged a hand through his hair. "That's all I thought it was. But it's a lot more. Listen, her parents were killed in some sort of accident when she was a kid. I don't know the details, but there must have been some hospital time. She's panicked at staying here, and she isn't the panicking type."

"She needs these tests," the doctor insisted.

134

"Dr. . . . Hudd, is it? Dr. Hudd, she's got an ulcer. Textbook symptoms. We both know it."

"Because your mother said so?"

"My mother's chief of internal medicine at Atlanta General."

Hudd's brows shot up. "Dr. Margaret De Witt?" She sighed again. "Impressive. I've read a number of her papers. Though I tend to agree with her diagnosis, I'm sure she'd agree with my procedure. Signs point to a duodenum ulcer, but I can't discard other possibilities. These tests are standard."

"And if the patient is so distressed, emotionally wrecked, that the idea of the tests aggravates the preexisting condition?" He waited a beat. "Neither one of us is going to be able to force her to have them. She'll just walk out of here, go on popping Tums until she's got a hole in her stomach you could sink a putt through."

"No, I can't force her to have the tests," Hudd said irritably. "And I can give her medication, in exchange for a promise that she comes back as an outpatient for a barium X-ray if symptoms recur."

"I'll see that she does."

"You'd better. Her blood pressure's up, her weight's down. She's hoarding stress. I'd say she's got a breakdown on the boil."

"I'll take care of her."

Dr. Hudd hesitated a moment, measuring him. Then nodded. "I'm sure you will." She reached for the curtain, glanced back. "Is your father Dr. Brian De Witt?"

"Thoracic surgery."

"And you're—"

"In hotels." He smiled charmingly. "But my sisters are doctors. All three of them."

"There's one in every family."

"I'm sorry," Kate murmured. She kept her head back, resting it against the car's seat. Kept her eyes closed.

"Just follow doctor's orders. Take your medicine, get your rest. Cut back on the jalapeños."

She knew he said it to make her smile, and tried to oblige him. "And I was just craving some. I didn't want to ask until I was sure we'd managed the great escape, but how did you talk her out of admitting me?"

"Reason, charm, compromise. And by invoking my mother's name. She's a big deal."

"Oh."

"And a promise," he added, "that if it happens again, you go in for X-rays—as an outpatient." He laid a hand over hers, squeezed. "This isn't something you can ignore, Kate. You have to take care of this, and yourself."

She fell silent again. It was all too embarrassing. And there were still little hot licks of panic flickering in her stomach.

When she opened her eyes again, she saw the moon-kissed sweep of Big Sur, the rise of cliffs, the flash of forests, the wild curve of the road with thin mists of fog hovering. Tears stung her eyes. She'd asked him to take her home, and he'd understood. Home was Templeton House.

The lights were glowing against the windows. Glowing in a warmth and welcome that was as dependable as sunrise. She could smell the flowers, hear the sea. Even before he had fully stopped the car at the top of the drive, the door swung open. Laura raced out.

"Oh, honey, are you all right?" Her robe swirling around her legs, Laura wrenched open the car door and all but absorbed Kate into her arms. "I've been so worried!"

"It's all right. It's so silly. I—" Then she spotted Ann hurrying out and nearly broke.

"There, darling girl." Crooning, Ann tucked an arm around Kate's waist. "Let's get you inside now."

"I—" But it was too easy to just let her head rest on Ann's shoulder. Here were memories of warm cookies and sweet tea. Of soft sheets and cool hands.

"Byron." Laura cast a distracted look back at him. "I'm so grateful you called. I—" She looked toward Kate, already halfway to the house with Ann. "Please come in. Let me get you some coffee."

"No, I'll head on home." It was obvious that Laura was oblivious to everyone but Kate. "I'll come by later and see how she is. Go ahead."

"Thank you. Thank you so much." She dashed away.

He watched her catch up and flank Kate on the other side. The three of them slipped into the house as one.

She slept for twelve hours and awakened rested and dazed. She was in the room of her middle childhood. The wallpaper was the same, the subtle pastel stripes. The blinds of her late adolescence had been replaced by lace curtains that swayed at the open windows. They had been Kate's grandmother's. Had hung in her own mother's bedroom. Aunt Susie had thought they would bring her comfort when she had first settled in Templeton House, and she'd been right.

They brought her comfort now.

There had been many a morning Kate had lain in the big, soft four-poster and watched those curtains flutter. And felt her parents close.

If she could just talk to them now, she thought. Just try to understand why her father had done what he had done. But what comfort would there be in that? What excuse could possibly justify it?

She had to concentrate on the now. Had to find a way to live in the now. And yet how could she not drift back?

It was the house, most of all, she supposed. It held so many memories. There was history here, eras, people, ghosts. Like the cliffs, the forests, those wildly shaped cypress trees, it held magic.

She turned her face into the pillow, encased in Irish linen. Ann always saw to it that the bed linen was scented lightly with lemon. There were flowers on the night table, a Waterford vase filled with sweet-smelling freesia. A note was propped against it. Recognizing Laura's handwriting, she stirred herself to reach out.

Kate, I didn't want to wake you when I left. Margo and I are at the shop this morning. We don't want to see you there. Annie has agreed to lock you in your room if necessary. You're to take your next dose at eleven sharp, unless you sleep through it. One of us will come home at lunchtime. You're expected to stay in bed. If you ever scare us like this again . . . I'll threaten you in person. I love you, Laura.

Just like her, Kate mused, and set the note aside. But she couldn't very well stay in bed all day. Too much thinking time in bed. No, she decided to call it by its name: brooding time. So she would find something to keep her from brooding. Her briefcase had to be somewhere, she decided. She'd just—

"And what do you think you're about, young lady?" Ann Sullivan stood in the doorway with a tray in her hand and a hard light in her eyes.

"I was going to . . . go to the bathroom. That's all." Cautiously Kate finished climbing out of bed and ducked into the adjoining bath.

Smiling, Ann set down the tray and moved to fluff the pillows. All her girls thought they could lie when the chips were down, she mused. And only Margo was any good at it. She waited, her back soldier straight, until Kate came back in. Then Ann merely pointed at the bed.

"Now, I'm going to see to it that you eat, take your medicine, and behave yourself." With smooth efficiency, Ann fit the tray over Kate's lap. "An ulcer, is it? Well, we're not putting up with that. No, indeed. Now Mrs. Williamson has fixed you some nice soft scrambled eggs and toast. And there's herb tea. She says chamomile will soothe your innards. You'll eat the fruit too. The melon's very mild."

"Yes, ma'am." She felt as though she could eat for hours. "Annie, I'm sorry."

"For what? For being knotheaded? Well, you should be." But she sat on the edge of the bed and, in the time-honored fashion, laid her hand over Kate's brow to test for fever. "Working yourself up until you're sick. And look at you, Miss

Kate, nothing but a bag of bones. Eat every bite of those eggs.''

"I thought it was heartburn," she murmured, then bit her lip. "Or cancer."

"What is this nonsense?" Appalled, Ann snagged Kate's chin in her hand. "You were worrying you had cancer and did nothing about it?"

"Well, I figured if it was heartburn I could live with it. And if it was cancer, I'd just die anyway." She grimaced at the violent glare. "I feel like such a fool."

"I'm glad to hear it, for you are." Clucking her tongue, Annie poured Kate's tea. "Miss Kate, I love you, but never in my life have I been more angry with anyone. No, you don't. Don't you dare tear up while I'm yelling at you."

Kate sniffled, took the tissue Ann held out, and blew her nose fiercely. "I'm sorry," she said again.

"Be sorry, then." Exasperated, she handed over another tissue. "I thought Margo was the only one of you who could make me crazy. You may have waited twenty years to do it, my girl, but you've matched her. Did you once tell your family you were feeling poorly? Did you once think what it would mean to us if you ended up in the hospital?"

"I thought I could handle it."

"Well, you couldn't, could you?"

"No."

"Eat those eggs before they're cold. There's Mrs. Williamson down in the kitchen, fretting over you. And old Joe the gardener cutting his precious freesia so you could wake to them. That's to say nothing of Margo, who kept me on the phone thirty minutes or more this morning, so worked up over you, she is. And Mr. Josh, who came by and looked in on you before he would go on to his work. And do you think Miss Laura got a wink of sleep last night?"

As she lectured, Ann piled toast with raspberry preserves and handed it to Kate. "That's to say nothing of how the Templetons are going to feel when they hear."

"Oh, Annie, please don't—"

"Don't tell them?" Ann said, with a fierce look at Kate. "Is that what you were going to say, missy? Don't tell the people who loved and cared for you, who gave you a home and a family?"

No one, Kate thought miserably, piled on jam or shame like Ann Sullivan. "No. I'll call them myself. Today."

"That's better. And when you're feeling more yourself, you're going to go and thank Mr. De Witt in person for taking care of you."

"I . . ." Foreseeing fresh humiliation, Kate toyed with her eggs. "I did thank him."

"And you'll thank him again." She glanced up as a maid knocked quietly on the open door.

"Excuse me. These just arrived for Miss Powell." She carried in a long white florist's box and set it on the foot of the bed.

"Thank you, Jenny. Wait just a moment and we'll see what vase we'll use. No, you finish eating," Ann continued. "I'll open this."

She undid the bow, opened the lid, and the room was filled with the scent of roses. Two dozen long-stemmed yellows bloomed against a bed of glossy green. She allowed herself one quiet, feminine sigh.

"Fetch the Baccarat, will you, Jenny? The tall one in the library breakfront."

"Yes, ma'am."

"Now I know I'm sick." Cheered, Kate plucked up the envelope. "Imagine Margo sending me a bunch of flowers." But when she tore out the card, her jaw dropped.

"Not from Margo, I take it." With the privilege of time and affection, Ann slipped the card out of Kate's fingers and read, " 'Relax, Byron.' Well, well, well."

"It's nothing to 'well' about. He's just feeling sorry for me."

"Two dozen yellow roses are something aside from sympathy, girl. That's moving toward romance."

"Hardly."

"Seduction, anyway."

Kate remembered the wild embrace in his kitchen. Hot, intense, rudely interrupted. "Maybe. Sort of. If I was the seducing type."

"We all are. Thank you, Jenny. I'll take it from here."

Ann took the vase from the maid and went into the bathroom to fill it. She wasn't surprised, and not just a little pleased, to see Kate sniffing thoughtfully at one of the blooms when she came back.

"Drink your tea now while I arrange these. It's a relaxing thing, arranging flowers."

She took a pair of scissors from the old kneehole desk, spread the tissue that had covered the flowers on the dresser, and got to work. "Something you take your time about, enjoy. Plunking them by the handful into a handy vase doesn't bring any joy."

Kate dragged her thoughts away from detailing a list of Byron De Witt's qualities. Confident, kind, interfering, sexy, meddlesome. Sexy. "It gets the job done."

"If that's all you're after. In my opinion, Miss Kate, you've always been in a hurry to get the job done, whatever it may be. You've forgotten the pleasure of doing. Rushing through something to get to the next something might be productive, but it's not fun."

"I have fun," Kate muttered.

"Do you now? From what I've seen, you've even turned your weekly treasure hunts into a scheduled chore. Let me ask you this. If you were, by some wild chance in your quest for efficiency, to stumble over Seraphina's dowry, what would you do with it?"

"Do with it?"

"That's what I asked. Would you take the riches and sail around the world, lie on some lazy beach, buy a fancy car? Or would you invest it in mutual funds and tax-free bonds?"

"Properly invested, money makes money."

Ann slipped a stem gently into the vase. "And for what? So it can pile up neatly in some vault? Is that the only means

141

to the end, or end to the means? Not that you haven't done a tidy job with helping me build up a fine nest egg, darling, but you've got to have dreams. And sometimes they have to be beyond your immediate reach.''

''I have plans.''

''I didn't say plans. I said dreams.'' Wasn't it odd, Ann mused. Her own daughter had always dreamed too much. Miss Laura had dreamed simple dreams that had broken her heart. And little Miss Kate had never let herself dream enough. ''What are you waiting for, darling? To be as old as me before you indulge yourself, enjoy yourself?''

''You're not old, Annie,'' Kate said softly. ''You'll never be old.''

''Tell that to the lines that crop up on my face daily.'' But she smiled as she turned. ''What are you waiting for, Katie?''

''I don't know. Exactly.'' Her gaze shifted to the crystal vase behind Ann, filled to bursting with yellow flowers that glowed like sunlight. She could, if she bothered to, count on one hand the number of times a man had sent her roses. ''I haven't really thought about it.''

''Then it's time you did. Top of the list is what makes Kate happy. You're good at list making, God knows,'' she said briskly, then went to the closet for the robe Kate always left in her room at Templeton House. ''Now you can sit out on the terrace in the sun for a while. You sit there and do nothing but dream for a bit.''

Chapter Nine

A week of pampering was excellent medicine. For Kate it was also nearly an overdose. Yet anytime she made noises about going home and getting back to work, everyone within earshot ganged up on her.

Telling herself she would turn over a new leaf if it killed her, she struggled to let it ride, to go with the flow, to take life as it came.

And wondered how anyone could live that way.

She reminded herself that it was a gorgeous evening. That she was sitting in the garden with a child snuggled in her lap, another at her feet. Her ulcer—if it was an ulcer—hadn't given her any real trouble in days.

And she had found there, in the home of her childhood, a peace that had been missing.

"I wish you could live with us forever and ever, Aunt Kate." Kayla looked up, her gray eyes soft in her angel's face. "We'd never let you get sick or worry too much."

"Aunt Margo says you're a professional nitpicker." Ali

giggled at the term and carefully brushed pink polish on Kate's toenails. "What's a nit?"

"Aunt Margo." Wasn't it bad enough, Kate thought, that she was going to have hot-pink toenails, without adding insult to injury? "Good thing for her I happen to like nits."

"If you didn't go back to your apartment, we could play with you every day." For Kayla, this was the ultimate bribe. "And you and Mama could have tea parties like Annie said you used to when you were little."

"We can all have tea parties when I come visit," Kate reminded her. "That's more special."

"But if you lived here, you wouldn't have to pay rent." Ali capped the polish and looked entirely too wise for a ten year old. "Until you regain your financial feet."

A fresh smile flitted around Kate's mouth. "Where'd you get that?"

"You're always saying stuff like that." Ali smiled and pressed her cheek against Kate's knee. "And Mama's working a lot now and nothing's the way it used to be. It's better with you here."

"I like being with you, too."

Touched and torn, Kate stroked Ali's curly hair. A sunshine-yellow butterfly flitted through the air and landed gracefully in the cup of a red petunia. For a moment, Kate caressed the child and watched the butterfly's wings gently open and close as it fed.

How hard would it be, she wondered, to simply stay here, like this, forever? Just drift. Forget everything. Not hard at all, she realized. And wasn't that part of the reason it wasn't possible for her?

"I have to go back to my own place. That doesn't mean I won't spend lots of time with you. Every Sunday for sure, so we can find all of Seraphina's gold."

She looked up in relief at the sound of footsteps. If this kept up, she'd be ready to agree to anything her nieces wanted. "There's the nit now."

Margo only raised an elegant eyebrow as the girls giggled.

"I'll consider that a private joke. I'm too jazzed to be annoyed with you. Look!" After tugging up her sleek linen tunic, she pulled out the elastic waist of her slacks. "I couldn't get my skirt zipped this morning. I'm starting to show." Her face glowing, she turned to the side. "Can you tell?"

"You look like a beached whale," Kate said dryly, but Kayla bounced up and rushed over to press an ear against Margo's tummy.

"I can't hear him yet," she complained. "Are you sure he's in there?"

"Absolutely sure, but I can't guarantee the *he* part." Abruptly her lips trembled, her eyes filled. "Kate, it moved. This afternoon I was helping a customer decide between an Armani and a Donna Karan, and I felt this, this fluttering. I felt the baby move. I felt—I felt—" She broke off and burst into wild tears.

"Oh, Jesus." Jolting up, Kate gathered the goggle-eyed girls and nudged them toward the flagstone path. "This is a good thing," she assured them. "She's crying because she's happy. Tell Mrs. Williamson we want a whole jug of lemonade, the kind she makes that fizzes."

Whirling back to Margo, she hugged her close. "I was only kidding before. You're not fat."

"I want to be fat," Margo sobbed. "I want to waddle. I want to stop being able to sleep on my stomach."

"Okay." Torn between amusement and concern, Kate patted her. "Okay, honey, you will. In fact, I think you're already starting to waddle. A little."

"Really?" Margo sniffed, caught herself. "Oh, shit, listen to me. I'm crazy. I'm doing this kind of thing all the time these days. I felt the baby move, Kate. I'm going to have a baby. I don't know anything about being a mother. I'm so scared. I'm so happy. Hell, I've wrecked my mascara."

"Thank God, she's coming back." A little shaky herself, she eased Margo into a chair. "What does Josh do when you have one of these crying jags?"

"Passes the tissues."

"Great." Without much hope, Kate searched her pockets. "I don't have any."

"I do." Margo sniffed and blew and sighed. "Wacky hormones." She used a fresh tissue to dab, then ran an expert hand over her fancy French braid. "I came out here to see how you were feeling."

"Unlike you, there doesn't seem to be anything going on in my stomach. It's fine. I think that ulcer business was just bullshit."

Recovered, Margo lifted a brow. "Oh, do you? Do you really?"

Because she recognized that tone, Kate braced for a fight. "Don't start on me."

"I've waited for days to start on you. But you're feeling fine now. So I can tell you, you're an insensitive, selfish idiot. You sent everyone who has the poor judgment to care about you into a tailspin of worry."

"Oh, and it would have been sensitive and selfless of me to whine and complain—which you're an expert at—and—"

"Take care of yourself," Margo finished. "See a doctor. No, not you, you're too smart for that, too busy for that."

"Get off my back."

"Pal, I've just climbed on, and I'm staying there like that monkey in the story. You've had a week of everyone patting your head and stroking you. Now you can take your dose of reality. Mr. and Mrs. T are on their way back here."

Guilt heaped on Kate's head. "Why? There's no need for them to come all this way. It's just a stupid ulcer."

"Ah, now you admit it's an ulcer." Margo popped up again, whirled around the chair. "If this was a twelve-step program, you'd have made it to step one. They'd have been on the first plane the minute Laura called them, but she and Josh convinced them everything was under control and to finish up their business first. But nothing would stop them from seeing for themselves that their Kate was well."

"I talked to them myself. I told them it was nothing major."

"No, no, nothing major. You get suspended under suspicion

of embezzlement, end up in the ER. Nothing for them to worry about.'' She propped her hands on her hips. ''Who the hell do you think you are?''

''I—''

''Josh is furious, blaming it all on Bittle, and beating himself up because he didn't jump on them the minute they axed you.''

''That has nothing to do with it.'' Kate sprang up as well, her shouts matching Margo's decibel for decibel. ''Josh has nothing to do with it.''

''That's just like you. That's just perfectly like you. Nobody has anything to do with anything when it applies to you. That's why Laura's been blaming herself for not paying attention to how you were feeling, what you were doing. That doesn't mean a damn to you.''

With fizzing lemonade sloshing in a glass pitcher, Laura all but ran toward the sounds of battle. ''What's going on here? Margo, stop yelling at her.''

''Shut up,'' Margo and Kate shouted in unison as they faced off.

''I could hear you all the way in the kitchen.'' Struggling not to slam glass on glass, Laura set the pitcher down on the table. Wide-eyed and fascinated, her daughters watched the three-way bout.

''I have to yell,'' Margo insisted. ''To get the sound through that thick head of hers. You're too busy feeling sorry for her to yell.''

''Don't drag Laura into this.'' But even as she said it, Kate whirled on Laura. ''And you have no business blaming yourself for my problems. You are not responsible for me.''

''If you took better care of yourself,'' Laura snapped back, ''no one would have to be responsible for you.''

''Ladies.'' Not sure whether he should be amused or wary, Josh stepped behind his nieces, took the glasses they carried out of their hands. ''Is this any way to throw a party?''

''Stay out of this.'' Kate's voice vibrated with fury. ''All

147

of you stay out of my life. I don't need to be watched over and worried over. I'm perfectly capable—"

"Of making yourself sick," Margo finished.

"Everybody gets sick," Kate roared. "Everybody has pain."

"And those who are capable, seek help." Laura put her hands on Kate's shoulders and firmly shoved her into a chair. "If you'd had any sense, you'd have gone to the doctor, gone into the hospital for tests. Instead, you act like an idiot and send the entire family into an uproar."

"I couldn't go to the hospital. You know I can't . . . I can't."

Remembering, Laura rubbed her hands over her face. This is where temper got you, she thought. Sniping at a hurting friend. "Okay." Her voice gentle now, she eased onto the arm of Kate's chair. When her eyes met Margo's, she saw that Margo had also remembered Kate's shuddering childhood fear. "That's done now. You have to start taking care so it doesn't happen again."

"Which means you have to start practicing to be human," Margo said, but there wasn't any sting in it.

"Are they still mad?" Kayla whispered, still clutching Josh's trouser leg with one hand.

"Maybe a little, but I think it's safe now."

"Mama never yells." Unsettled, uneasy, Ali chewed on her nails. "She never yells."

"She used to yell at me. It takes a lot to make her yell. It has to really, really matter. And once she hit me right in the nose," Josh said.

Fascinated, Kayla reached up and rubbed her fingers over Josh's nose as he bent down. "Did it bleed and everything?"

"And everything. Kate and Margo had to pull her off me. Then she felt really bad." Then he grinned. "Even though I started it. What do you say we have some of that lemonade?"

Ali walked behind her uncle and studied her mother with a curious and considering eye.

*　　*　　*

148

It had to be done, Kate reminded herself. It was Sunday morning. Her aunt and uncle were expected by mid-afternoon. Before she faced them, she had to face Byron.

It was her new plan for a healthy life. Deal with your personal and emotional problems as carefully as you dealt with the practical ones. Why, she wondered, was it so much harder?

She'd secretly hoped he wouldn't be home. A lot of people went to brunch on Sunday mornings, or to the beach. Somewhere. But both of his cars were in the drive. Even parked behind them, she could hear the music pounding out of the windows. Creedence Clearwater Revival. She spent a moment listening to John Fogerty's fervent warning about a bad moon on the rise.

She hoped it wasn't an omen.

It was difficult to reconcile a man with his looks—smooth, elegant—and his obvious preference for down-and-dirty rock and edgy Motown. Well, she wasn't here to analyze his musical tastes. She was here to thank him and then turn the page on this awkward chapter in her life.

Prompting herself as she went, Kate got out of the car, started toward the house. She would be casual, brief, friendly, cheerful. She would turn the whole matter into a joke on herself, show the proper appreciation for his consideration and concern. And get out.

She drew a breath, rubbed her hands over the thighs of her jeans, then knocked. And laughed at herself. Superman wouldn't have heard a knock over the blast of CCR. She pressed the doorbell hard. At the tinny notes of "Hail, Hail, the Gang's All Here" she gaped in shock, then shook with laughter. Enjoying the absurdity, she pressed it again, then a third time.

He came to the door, sweaty and incredibly sexy in tattered shorts and a sweatshirt with the sleeves torn off. "The doorbell tune isn't mine," he said immediately. "I can't change it until after the settlement."

"I bet that's what you tell everyone." She indulged herself

149

with a long, thorough look. "Did I interrupt a wrestling match?"

"Weight lifting." He stepped back. "Come on in."

"Look, I can come back when you're not busy pumping iron." Christ, he had amazing muscles. Everywhere. How had she missed that?

"I was nearly finished anyway. Gatorade?" He held up the bottle in his hand, and when she shook her head, glugged from it himself. "How are you feeling?"

"Fine. That's why I dropped by. To—" He leaned close, closed the door behind her, and made her jump. "To tell you I was fine. And to thank you for . . . things. The flowers. They were nice."

"Any flare-ups?"

"No. It's not a big deal. Really." Nervous, she shrugged her shoulders, rubbed her palms together. "One out of ten people ends up with a peptic ulcer. All socioeconomic levels, too. There's no clear evidence that they hit on, you know, people with a lot of stress and harried schedules."

"Been researching, have we?" A smile flirted around his mouth.

"Well, it seemed the logical thing to do. All in all."

"Uh-huh. And did your research also reveal that people with chronic anxiety tend to be more susceptible and to aggravate the condition?"

She dipped her restless hands in her pockets. "Maybe."

"Sit down." He gestured to the single chair before he walked over to turn down the music.

"I can't stay. My aunt and uncle are coming in today."

"Their flight's not due until two-thirty."

He'd know, of course. She caught herself twisting her fingers together, and made herself stop. "Yes, but I have things to do, and so do you. So, I'll just . . ."

She was saved by a scrabbling sound and the surprising sight of two running balls of yellow fur. "Oh, God." Automatically, she went down on her knees and caught the deliriously happy puppies in her arms. "Oh, you're so cute. Aren't you sweet? Aren't you wonderful?"

In unanimous agreement, they bathed her face with eager tongues, yipped and wiggled, crawling over each other to get closer.

"That's Nip and Tuck," Byron informed her as he got down on the floor with them.

"Which is which?"

He sent one puppy into slant-eyed ecstasy by scratching a furry belly. "I don't know. I figured we'd work it out with time. I've only had them a couple of days."

Kate picked one up to nuzzle and forgot she'd been anxious to get in and out. "What are they?"

"A little of this and a little of that. Some golden retriever, some Lab."

Before the second puppy could desert her, she kissed his nose. "Followed you home, right?"

"I adopted them from the animal shelter. They're eight weeks old." Byron found the remnants of a well-chewed rawhide bone on the floor and skidded it over the polished wood for the pups to chase.

"Mind if I ask what you're going to do with two puppies when you're at work?"

"Take them with me—for a while. I figure I can fence in part of the backyard, and they'll have each other for company when I'm not here." They came barreling back, jumped him. "I was only going to get one, but then . . . well, they're brothers and it seemed only fair." He glanced over, found her smiling at him. "What?"

"You wouldn't know it to look at you."

"Wouldn't know what?"

"You're a sucker."

He shrugged, tossed the bone again. "I'd think a practical woman like you would see the value of taking both. A backup dog is a sensible plan."

"Yeah, right."

"Jesus, Kate, have you ever been in one of those shelters?

151

They break your heart.'' He tolerated wet, sloppy kisses from the rebounding puppies. ''They're doing a great job—don't get me wrong—but all those cats and dogs, just waiting for somebody to come along and take them. Or . . .''

''Yeah. Or.'' She reached over, rubbing her hand over the dog in his lap. ''You saved them.'' Her gaze came back to his. ''You're good at that.''

He reached out, curled a hand around her calf and slid her over until their knees bumped. ''I tend to get attached to things I save. You look good.'' Anticipating her, he kept his hand on her leg and kept her from scooting back. ''Rested.''

''I didn't do much more than rest all week. And eat.'' She smiled a little. ''I gained three pounds.''

''Well, strike up the band.''

''It may not seem like much to you, ace, but I've spent most of my life trying to develop something resembling a figure. I tried everything you read about in the back of magazines and Sunday supplements.''

He had to grin. ''Get out of here.''

''No, really. There I was, faced with Margo—who I think was born built—and Laura's feminine little body. I always looked like their undernourished younger brother.''

''You don't look like anyone's younger brother, Kate. Believe me.''

Feeling foolishly flattered, she shrugged. ''Anyway—''

''Despite the amazing weight gain and the lack of symptoms,'' he interrupted, ''you are going to see your regular doctor.''

''I don't have much choice. My family's ganged up on me.''

''That's what family's for. You gave us a scare.''

''I know. I've been lectured by experts on my careless, selfish ways.''

He smiled and patted her legs. ''Sting?''

''Big-time. I'm thinking about just having 'I'm sorry' tattooed on my forehead so I don't have to keep repeating myself. And speaking of apologies.'' She blew out a breath, fluttered her bangs. "I was going to try to get out of here without bringing this up, but I'm trying to reform."

Her brows knit, as they did whenever she had to face a thorny problem or unsettling task. This qualified for both. "The other night, before I had my little . . . attack, we were . . ."

"On our way to the floor, as I remember." He reached over the puppy that had fallen asleep in his lap, brushed at the hair above her ear. "Looks like we got there after all."

"What I want to say is that things got out of hand. My fault as much as yours," she added.

"Fault's assigned when there's a mistake."

"That's my point." She should have known it wouldn't be simple. Nip or Tuck was draped across her thigh, snoring. She busied herself with stroking his head. "We don't—*I* don't jump into bed with men I hardly know."

"It was going to be the floor," he reminded her. He still had a hard time going into his own kitchen without imagining what might have been. "And I never assumed you did. Otherwise, it wouldn't be two years since you've had sex."

Her mouth dropped open. "Where did you get an idea like that?"

"You mentioned it," he said easily, "when I was trying to get your clothes off."

She closed her mouth, let air out her nose. "Oh. Well, that only strengthens my point." Uneasy, she watched him gently lift the puppy from his lap and set it aside, where it curled deeper into sleep. "What happened was just a moment." He repeated the procedure with the second puppy. Kate's heart began to thud. "A hormone burst."

"Uh-huh." He didn't even touch her, just leaned forward until his mouth slid expertly over hers.

Kate could almost feel her mind tilt and her brains flow out. Well, she needed a distraction, didn't she? An outlet for all this tension. It seemed like the most sensible thing in the world to unfold her legs, wrap them around his waist and dive in.

"This only proves it," she murmured. She threaded her

153

hands through his hair and gripped. "Proves I'm right."

"Shut up, Kate."

"Okay."

It was wonderfully, brutally hot. She hadn't known until that instant how cold she had been. Until his unshaven cheeks rubbed roughly over her skin, she hadn't known how soft she could be. Or how gratifying it could be to be the soft one.

She let out a long, grateful moan when his hands streaked under her T-shirt to stroke her back, slid around to cup and squeeze her tingling breasts. The flick of his thumbs over her nipples shot a bolt of heat through her center that vibrated achingly in her crotch. Arching back, she pulled his head down until his mouth replaced his hands.

He suckled through cotton, tormenting himself with fantasies of what her flesh would feel like, taste like, sliding under his tongue. She was so . . . slight. That neat, almost boyish torso should never have appealed to him. There was no womanly flare of hip, and her breasts were small.

And firm, and warm.

The way she moved against him, that edgy eagerness of a woman already teetering on the edge, was viciously arousing. He wanted, needed, to shove her back, rip aside that denim and drive himself inside her until they were both screaming.

Instead he dragged his mouth back to hers, slid a hand between their bodies and sent her free-falling over the edge. He shuddered himself when she convulsed, ordered himself to breathe when her head dropped limply on his shoulder.

Well, he thought, that should hold one of us.

It took her a moment to realize that he'd stopped, was just holding her. "What?" she managed. "Why?"

The dazed questions nearly made him smile. "I decided I didn't want it to be a hormone burst. For either of us." He eased her back, studied her flushed face, the heavy, glazed eyes. "Better now?"

"I don't think—" Couldn't think. "I don't know—Don't you want to—?"

He crushed his mouth to hers in a kiss that tasted of dark

154

and swirling frustration. "Does that answer your question?" Taking her by the shoulders, he gave her a quick, satisfying shake.

"You're trying to confuse me." Part of her brain was starting to regenerate, and with it, temper. "This is some kinky version of *Gaslight*."

This time he did smile. "God, you're a pain in the ass. Listen to me, Katherine, I want you. I haven't the smallest clue why, but I just want the hell out of you. If I'd followed my first instinct, you'd be flat on your back, naked, and I'd be feeling a lot better than I do right now. But I'll be goddamned if you're going to pick yourself up afterward and claim I just helped you end your sexual drought."

Her eyes snapped back into focus. "That's a hideous thing to say."

"Yeah, it is. And that's just how you'd have rationalized it. I'm not giving you the chance. What I am doing is giving you the chance to get used to the idea of having me as a lover."

"Of all the—"

"Just keep quiet for once," he said mildly. "We're going to take this slow, go out together in public, have a few reasonable conversations, take some time to figure each other out."

"In other words, it's going to be all your way."

He angled his head, nodded. "Yeah, that sums it up." When she tried to wriggle free, he simply sighed and held her in place. "Honey, I'm as stubborn as you are, and a hell of a lot stronger. That puts me one up."

"You're not going to keep me here when I don't want to be here."

He gave her a friendly kiss on the nose. "You may be a scrapper, but you've got toothpick arms. We can work on that," he added, ignoring the strangled sounds she made. "In fact, there's no time like the present."

She thought she'd had all the shocks she could handle for one morning, but she got a fresh one when he hauled her up and slung her over his shoulder. "Are you insane? Put me down, you muscle-bound son of a bitch. I'll have you hauled in for assault."

"It's muscles we're going to deal with," he said mildly, as he carted her into an adjoining room. "Believe me, there's nothing like a good workout to relieve tension. Considering your ulcer and your desire to gain weight, this is something you should add to your daily routine." He set her down, caught the fist she swung at him in his hand, gave it an affectionate squeeze. "You want to be able to put some power behind that punch. We'll work on your biceps."

"This isn't happening," she said and closed her eyes. "I'm not even here."

"We need to work on diet and nutrition, too, but we'll get to that." They were going to get to a lot of things, he thought, as soon as she didn't look as if he could knock her flat with one exhale. "Right now, I think you should start off with three-pounders." He took two metal dumbbells from a rack. "You'll work up to five. You're going to want to go buy yourself some girl weights."

She opened her eyes again. "Did you say girl weights?"

"No offense. They make these nice plastic-coated sets of free weights in colors." He put a weight into each of her hands, curled her fingers around them. The only thing that stopped her from dropping them on his feet was curiosity.

"Why are you doing this?"

"You mean besides because I find myself oddly attracted to you?" He smiled into her eyes as he positioned her elbows at her waist. "I think I'm starting to like you. Now pretend you're lifting and lowering these through mud. Concentrate on your biceps and keep your elbows in place."

"I don't want to lift weights." Hadn't this man just minutes ago taken her to rough and blistering orgasm? "I want to hit you."

"Just think about how much harder you'll be able to hit me once you've got some muscle." He guided her arms down, then up. "Just like that, but resist both ways."

156

"These are too light. It's silly."

"They won't feel so light after a few sets. You're going to work up a nice sweat before I'm finished with you."

She sent him a sweet smile. "Yeah, that's what I thought before." Pleased with herself, she lowered the weights, lifted them. Then her brain flashed. "Goddamn you, Byron, are you saving me again?"

He stepped behind her, positioned her shoulders. "Just pump iron, kid. We'll work out the details later."

Chapter Ten

It was always good to have Aunt Susan and Uncle Tommy home. Kate had worried that something would show in her face—or worse, that there would be something in theirs. The knowledge of crimes past, the doubt of her own innocence. But there had been only concern, and acceptance.

Their visit also meant extending her stay at Templeton House. It was difficult seeing them every day with the questions she tried to ignore drumming in the back of her mind. Questions she couldn't bring herself to ask.

She used the routine to carve out the path she intended to follow. Days at the shop—work to challenge the brain and keep it busy. Evenings with her family to soothe the heart. The occasional date with Byron to keep her on her toes.

He was a new element. Seeing him, wondering about him helped keep her from brooding about the turn her life had taken. She'd decided to think of him as a kind of experiment. Kate preferred that term to "relationship." And it wasn't an altogether unpleasant experiment. A few dinners, a movie now and again, perhaps a walk on the cliffs.

Then there were those long, stirring kisses he apparently loved to indulge in. Kisses that had her heart flopping in her chest like a landed trout, sent her senses cartwheeling into each other. Then ended, leaving her aching and baffled. And itchy.

The entire relationship—no, *experiment*, she corrected—left him far too much in control. Now that she was feeling a little steadier—all right, healthier—she was going to work on balancing the power.

"That's good to see." Susan Templeton stood at the doorway, her arm tucked through her husband's. "Our Kate never did enough daydreaming, did she, Tommy?"

"Not our sensible girl." He closed the door to the office behind them. He and his wife had worked out the logistics of this maneuver, and following their plan, they flanked the small desk where Kate had been pretending to work.

"I was trying to calculate our advertising budget for the next quarter." She flipped the screen saver onto her monitor. "If you're smart, you two will hide in here before Margo can put you to work."

"I promised her a couple of hours." Thomas winked. "She thinks she charmed me into it, but I get a kick out of working that old cash register."

"Maybe you'll give me some tips on salesmanship. I can't quite get the knack of it."

"Love what you sell, Katie girl, even if you hate it." He cast an experienced eye around the office, noted the tidy shelves, the organized work space. "Somebody's been streamlining in here."

"Nobody puts things, and people, in their place better than Kate." Susan laid a hand over Kate's, kept her soft blue eyes level. "Why haven't you put Bittle in his?"

Kate shook her head. Because she'd been waiting for days for one of them to bring it up, she didn't panic. She had her rationale ready. "It's not important." But Susan's eyes stayed on hers, calm, patient, waiting. "It was too important," she

160

corrected. "I'm not going to let it matter to me."

"Now you listen here, girl—"

"Tommy," Susan murmured.

"No." He cut his wife off with a snap of sizzling temper. In contrast to Susan, his slate-gray eyes were sizzling. "I know you wanted to soft-pedal this business, Susie, but damned if I will."

He loomed over the desk, a tall man, powerfully built, well used to taking control, be it in business or family. "I expected better of you, Kate. Letting yourself get run roughshod over, giving up without a fight. Turning your back on something you worked for your whole life. Worse, getting yourself sick over it instead of standing up to it. I'm ashamed of you."

Those were words he'd never said to her before. Words she'd worked her entire life to keep him from saying. Now they struck her like a backhanded slap. "I—I never took any money."

"Of course you didn't take any money."

"I did the best I could. I know I let you down. I'm sorry."

"We're not talking about me," he shot back. "We're talking about you. You've let yourself down."

"No, I—" Ashamed of her. He was ashamed of her. And angry. "I put everything I had into my job. I tried to—I thought I was on the fast track to partner, and then you'd—"

"So the first time you take a knock, you crumble?" He leaned forward, poking his finger at her. "Is that your answer?"

"No." Unable to face him, she stared at her hands. "No. They had evidence. I don't know how, because I swear to you I never took any money."

"Give us some credit, Katherine," Susan said quietly.

"But they had the forms, my signature." The breath was backing up in her lungs. "If I'd pushed, they might have filed charges. It might have gone to court. I'd have to . . . You'd have to . . . I know people are whispering about it, and that's embarrassing for you. But if we just leave it alone, it'll pass. It'll just pass."

This time Susan held up a hand before her husband could interrupt. She, too, was accustomed to control. "You're concerned that we're embarrassed."

"It all reflects. It's all of a piece, isn't it?" She squeezed her eyes tightly shut. "I know that what I do reflects on you. If I can just wait it out, build something here with the shop. I know I owe you."

"What bullshit is this?" Thomas exploded.

"Hush, Tommy." Susan sat back, folded her hands. "I'd like Kate to finish. What do you owe us, Kate?"

"Everything." She looked up then, eyes swimming. "Everything. Everything. I hate disappointing you, knowing I've disappointed you. I had no way to stop it, to prepare for it. If I could fix it, if I could go back and fix—"

She broke off, shuddering as she realized she was mixing past and present. "I know how much you've given me, and I wanted to pay you back. Once I'd made partner . . ."

"It would have been a proper return on our investment," Susan concluded. She got slowly to her feet because every muscle in her body was tingling. "That is insulting, arrogant, and cruel."

"Aunt Susie—"

"Be quiet. Do you actually believe we expect payment for loving you? How dare you think such a thing?"

"But I meant—"

"I know what you meant." All but shaking with fury, she clutched her husband's shoulder. "You think we took you into our home, into our lives, because we felt pity for the poor orphaned child? Do you think it was charity—worse, the kind of charity that comes with strings and expectations? Oh, yes," she continued, fired up now. "The Templetons are known for their charitable works. I assume we fed you, clothed you, educated you because we wanted the community to witness our largesse. And we loved you, comforted you, admired you, disciplined you because we expected you to grow into a successful woman who would then pay us back for our time and effort with the importance of her position."

162

Rather than interrupt what he couldn't have said better himself, Thomas handed Kate a handkerchief so she could wipe her streaming eyes.

Susan leaned over the desk. Her voice was low, had remained low even in anger. "Yes, we pitied the little girl who had lost her parents so tragically, so brutally, so unfairly. Our hearts ached for the child who looked so lost and so brave. But I'll tell you something, Katherine Louise Powell, the minute you stepped through the door of Templeton House you became ours. Ours. You were my child then, and you still are. And the only things any of my children owe me or their father is love and respect. Don't you ever, *ever* throw my love in my face again."

She turned on her heel, sailed out of the room, and let the door click quietly behind her.

Thomas huffed out a long breath. His wife's tirades were few and far between, but they were brilliant. "Put your foot in it, didn't you, Katie girl?"

"Oh, Uncle Tommy." She could see the world she'd tried to piece back together shattered in her hands. "I don't know what to do."

"Start by coming over here." When she'd crawled into his lap and buried her face in his chest, he rocked her. "Never knew such a bright child could be so stupid."

"I'm screwing everything up. I don't know what to do. I just don't know how to fix it. What's wrong with me?"

"Plenty, I'd say, but nothing that can't be mended."

"She was so angry with me."

"Well, that can be mended too. You know one of your problems, Kate? You've focused on figures so long you think everything has to add up and be equal. It's just not true with people and feelings."

"I never wanted to bring either of you into this. To hurt you, remind you—" She broke off, shook her head fiercely. "I always wanted to be the best for you. The best in school, in sports. Everything."

"And we admired your competitive spirit, but not when it eats a hole in your gut."

Exhausted from tears, she laid her head against his shoulder. It was cowardice, she thought, that had eaten that hole in her gut. Now she had to face it all, what had been, what was, and what would come.

"I'm going to fix things, Uncle Tommy."

"Take my advice and give Susie a little time to cool off. She gets hard of hearing when her temper's on boil."

"Okay." Kate drew a deep breath and sat up. "Then I guess I'll start with Bittle."

His face broke into a huge grin. "Now that's my Kate."

In the parking lot of Bittle and Associates, Kate flipped down her rearview mirror to take one last critical look at her face. Margo had performed a little miracle. She'd dragged Kate upstairs and with cold compresses, eyedrops, lotions, and makeup had erased all traces of damage. Kate decided she no longer looked as though she had spent twenty minutes bawling like a scolded child. She looked efficient, composed, and determined.

That was perfect.

She told herself it didn't bother her that conversations stopped when she sailed into the first-floor lobby. She didn't mind the stares and murmurs, the strained smiles and curiosity-laced greetings. They were, in fact, an eye-opener.

The few people who greeted her warmly, who detoured to stop her on her march to the second floor and offer support, showed her that she'd made more friends at Bittle than she'd realized.

It took only one twist of the corridor to bring Kate face to face with the dragon. Newman raised a brow, gave Kate one brief, chilly stare. "Ms. Powell. May I help you?"

"I'm on my way to see Marty."

"Do you have an appointment?"

Kate angled her chin. The fingers gripping the handle of her briefcase tightened. "I'll take that up with Marty and his secretary. Why don't you go tell Mr. Bittle Senior that the disgraced associate has invaded the hallowed halls?''

Like a Swiss guard protecting royalty, Newman shifted her stance. ''I see no reason for you to—''

''Kate.'' Roger poked his head out of his office, rolled his eyes behind Newman's back, and beamed a smile. ''Good to see you. I was hoping you'd make it by. Oh, Ms. Newman, I've got that report Mr. Bittle Senior needed.'' Like a magician pulling a rabbit out of his hat, Roger produced a sheaf of papers. ''He was anxious to see it.''

''Very well.'' She shot Kate one last warning glance, then hurried down the hallway.

''Thanks,'' Kate murmured. ''I think we might have come to blows.''

''My money was on you.'' He put a supportive hand on her shoulder. ''This situation really sucks. I'd have called you, but I didn't know what to say.'' He dropped his hand, stuck it in his pocket. ''How to act.''

''It doesn't matter. I didn't have anything to say myself.'' Until now. Now, she had plenty to say.

''Listen.'' He nudged her toward his office door but didn't, Kate noted wryly, invite her inside. ''I don't know how much pressure your lawyer's putting on.''

''My lawyer?''

''Templeton. The partners went into a powwow after he came in and stirred them up. Maybe that's a good thing, I don't know. You've got to handle it the way you think best. I can tell you that it looks like the partners are divided over whether or not to pursue and prosecute.''

His brow creased and his voice, like a conspirator's, was low and dramatic. ''Amanda's leading the charge, and Bittle Junior's behind her. My take is that Calvin and Senior are on the fence, with Marty solidly against.''

''It's always good to know who's in your corner and who's going for your throat,'' Kate murmured.

''All this craziness over a lousy seventy-five K,'' Roger said in disgust. ''It's not like you killed anyone.''

Kate stepped back, studied his face. "Stealing is stealing, seventy-five cents or seventy-five K. And I didn't take any money."

"I didn't say you did. I didn't mean it that way." But there was doubt in his voice even as he took her hand to squeeze it. "I meant everybody overreacted. I get the impression that if you came up with the money, it would all go away."

Slowly, firmly, she drew her hand free. "Would it?"

"I know it's a lousy deal either way, but hell, Kate, the Templetons sneeze that much money away every day. It would offset the chance of you being charged, ruining your whole damn life. Sometimes you've got to choose between the rock and the hard place."

"And sometimes you've got to stick. Thanks for the advice."

"Kate." He took a step after her, but she didn't stop or look back. With a shrug, he went back into his office.

Word was already out. Marty came to his door personally to meet her. He offered his hand, shook hers in a friendly, professional manner. "Kate, I'm glad you came by. Come inside."

"I should have come before," she began as she followed him past his secretary, who was doing her best to look busy and disinterested.

"I thought you would. Want anything? Coffee?"

"No." It was the same old Marty, she thought as she took her seat. From the wrinkled shirtsleeves to the affable smile. "I'm cutting back. I want to say first that I appreciate you seeing me like this."

"I know you didn't skim any funds, Kate."

The quiet statement stopped the neat little opening speech she'd prepared. "If you know that, why . . . Well, why?"

"I know it," he said, "because I know you. The signatures, the forms indicated otherwise, but I'm sure as I'm sitting here that there's another explanation." He wagged a finger, signaling her that he wasn't finished but was formulating his thoughts. The gesture nearly made her smile, it was so famil-

166

iar. So Marty. "Certain people, ah, believe that I feel so strongly in this matter because I'm . . . attracted to you."

"Well, that's just silly."

"Actually I am—was. Am." Stopping himself, he rubbed his hands over his rapidly coloring face. "Kate, I love my wife. I would never . . . that is, other than the occasional thought, which I would never act on, I would never . . . Never," he finished, leaving her quite literally speechless.

"Um," was all she could think of in response.

"I'm not bringing that up to embarrass either one of us. Though it seems to have done just that." He cleared his throat as he rose, and with nervous hands poured two mugs of coffee. As he handed her one, he remembered. "Sorry, you said you didn't want any."

"I'll take it." What was a little afterburn in comparison with staggered shock? "Thanks."

"I only mentioned that because people who know me well have sort of noticed that I— Not that you've done anything to encourage, or that I would have done anything even if you had."

"I get the picture, Marty." She allowed a breath to ease quietly through her lips, studied his wide, harmless, homely face. "I'm flattered."

"It muddies the waters, so to speak. I'm sorry for that. But I feel your record with this firm stands for itself. I'll continue to do everything I can to prevent formal charges being filed and to get to the bottom of this situation."

"I don't think I appreciated you enough when I worked here." She set her mug aside and rose. "Marty, I want to talk to the partners. All of them. I think it's time I took a stand."

He nodded as though he'd merely been waiting for her to say so. "I'll see if I can arrange it."

It didn't take him long. He might have been considered the puppy dog of Bittle, but he knew what buttons to push. Within thirty minutes, Kate was again seated at the long, polished table in the conference room.

In keeping with the strategy she'd outlined on the drive

over, she made eye contact with each partner, then settled her gaze firmly on Bittle Senior. "I've come here today, without my lawyer, in an effort to keep this meeting informal. Even personal. I realize your time is valuable, and I appreciate each of you taking that time to listen to what I have to say."

She paused, once again glanced at the faces around the table, once again addressed herself to the senior partner and founder. "I worked for this firm for nearly six years. I dedicated my professional, and a good deal of my personal, life to it. My goals were not selfless. I worked very hard to bring in accounts, to keep accounts assigned to me satisfied and viable in order to increase Bittle's revenue and reputation, with the ultimate aim of sitting at this table as a partner. Not once during my employment here did I ever take one penny from an account. I was raised, as you know, Mr. Bittle, by people who value integrity."

"It is your accounts that remain in question, Ms. Powell," Amanda put in briskly. "Your signature. If you've come here today with an explanation, we are prepared to hear it."

"I haven't come here for explanations. I haven't come to answer questions or to ask them. I've come here to make a statement. I have never done anything illegal or unethical. If there is a discrepancy in the accounts, I am not responsible for it. I'm prepared to make this same statement, if necessary, to each client involved. Just as I am prepared to go to court and defend myself against these charges."

Her hands were beginning to shake, so she gripped them tightly together under the table. "If charges are not brought, and this matter is not satisfactorily resolved within thirty days, I will advise my attorney to file suit against Bittle and Associates for unjustified termination and slander."

"You would dare to threaten this firm." Though his voice was quiet and clipped, Lawrence fisted a hand on the table.

"It's not a threat," she said coolly, even as her stomach jittered and churned. "My career has been sabotaged, my reputation impugned. If you believe I would sit idly by and do nothing about that, then I'm not surprised that you believe I would embezzle from my accounts. Because you don't know me at all."

Bittle leaned back in his chair. He steepled his hands, considered. "It's taken you some time to come around to this position, Kate."

"Yes, it has. This job meant everything to me. I'm starting to believe that everything is just too much. I couldn't have stolen from you, Mr. Bittle. You of all people know me well enough to be sure of that."

She waited a moment, wanting him to remember her, personally. "If you want a question to ponder," she continued, "ask yourselves this: Why would I have pilfered a measly seventy-five thousand when if I had needed or wanted money, I would only have had to go to my family? Why would I have worked my butt off for this firm all these years when I could have taken a top position in the Templeton organization at any time?"

"We have asked ourselves those questions, Kate," Bittle told her. "And those questions are the very reason this matter hasn't been resolved."

She rose, slowly. "Then I'll give you the answer. I'm not sure it's an attractive one, but I know the answer is pride. I'm too goddamn proud to have taken a dollar from this firm that wasn't mine. And I'm too proud to do nothing when I'm accused of embezzlement. Ms. Devin, gentlemen, thank you for your time." She shifted her gaze, smiled. "Thanks, Marty."

Not a single murmur followed her out the door.

She stopped shaking when she hit Highway 1 and realized where her instincts were taking her. Even before she pulled her car to the shoulder, got out to walk toward the cliffs, she was calm again.

There were fences to mend, work to do, responsibilities to handle. But for a moment, there was just Kate and the soothing roar of the sea. Today it was sapphire, that perfect blue that called to lovers and poets and pirates. The foam, far below the lapped shale and rock was like the froth of lace on the hem of a woman's velvet skirt.

She climbed down a ways, enjoying the swirl of wind, the taste of salt and sea that flavored it. Wild grasses and flowers defied the elements and grew, fighting their way out of thin soil and cracks in stone. Gulls wheeled overhead, their breasts as white as moonlight, the golden sun flashing off their spread wings.

Diamonds glittered on the water, and further out, whitecaps rode the sea like fine horses. The music never stopped, she thought. The ebb and flow, the crash and thunder, the eerily female screams of the gulls. How often had she come here to sit, to watch, to think? She couldn't count the number of hours.

Sometimes she was pulled here simply to be, other times to sit in solitude and work out some thorny problem. In her early years at Templeton House she had come here, to these cliffs, above this sea, under this sky, to quietly grieve for what she had lost. And to struggle with guilt over being happy in her new life.

She didn't dream here, had always told herself to wait for that until next year, or the next. The present had always taken priority. What to do now.

She stood on the comfortably wide ledge and asked herself what to do now.

Should she call Josh and tell him to go ahead with preparation for a suit against Bittle? She thought she had to. As difficult and potentially dangerous as such an action was, she could no longer ignore—or pretend to ignore—what had been done to her life. She hadn't been born a coward, nor had she been raised as one. It was time she dealt with that part of herself that was constantly in fear of failure.

In a way, she supposed, she had acted like Seraphina, metaphorically tossing her life over a cliff rather than working with the hand she'd been dealt.

That was over now. A little late, she admitted, but she had done the right thing. The Templeton thing, she thought with a smile as she picked her way down a rough and crooked incline. Uncle Tommy had always said that you couldn't be stabbed in the back if you faced your attackers.

The first step she needed to take was to face her aunt. Somehow she had to make things right there again. Kate looked back, and though she was too far down the slope to see the house, she could picture it.

Always there, she mused, tall and strong and waiting. Offering shelter. Hadn't it been there for Margo when her life had smashed around her? For Laura, and her girls, during the most difficult period of their lives?

It had been there for her, Kate thought, when she had been lost and afraid and numb with grief. Just as it was there now.

Yes, she'd done the right thing, Kate thought again as she looked back out to sea. She hadn't given up. She'd finally remembered that a good noisy fight was better than a quiet, dignified surrender.

She laughed a little and drew a deep breath. The hell with surrender, she decided. It was no more palatable than a cowardly plunge off the cliffs. The loss of a job, a goal, a man wasn't an ending. It was just another beginning.

Byron De Witt was another step she needed to take, she decided. Time for another beginning there. The man was driving her crazy with his patience, and it was past time for her to take control again. Maybe she would just ride over there later and jump him.

The thought of that had her laughing loud and long. Imagine his reaction, she mused, clutching her stomach. What did a proper Southern gentleman do when a woman threw him down and tore off his clothes? And wouldn't it be fascinating to find out?

She wanted to be held and touched and taken, she realized as the laughter in her stomach melted into warm, liquid need. But not by just anyone. By someone who could look at her the way he did, the way he looked deep, as though he could see places inside her that she hadn't dared to explore yet.

She wanted the mystery of that, wanted to match herself against a man strong enough to wait for what he wanted.

Hell, she admitted, she wanted him.

If she was strong enough to screw up her courage and face the partners at Bittle, if she had enough left inside her to deal with the damage she'd done to the aunt she adored, then she damn well had enough grit to handle Byron De Witt.

It was time she stopped planning and started doing.

Turning, she started back up the narrow path.

It was right there, as if it had been waiting. At first she simply stared, sure that she was imagining things. Hadn't she just come that way? Hadn't she and Laura and Margo combed every inch of this section of the cliffs over the past months?

Slowly, as if her bones were old and fragile, she bent down. The coin was warm from the sun, glinting like the gold it surely was. She felt the texture, the smooth face of the long-dead Spanish monarch. She turned it over in her palm twice, each time reading the date as if she expected it to change. Or simply vanish like a waking dream.

1845.

Seraphina's treasure, that small piece of it, had been tossed at her feet.

Chapter Eleven

Kate broke records on the drive back to Pretenses. Even the state trooper who stopped her to issue a lecture on traffic laws and a speeding ticket didn't dampen her spirits—or slow her down. She made it into Monterey in under twenty minutes.

Too wired to cruise for a legal parking space, she zipped through traffic, double-parked, and raced through the strolling wall of tourists.

She spun to the left, narrowly avoiding a collision with a kid on a skateboard, and all but stumbled through the door of the shop.

Her eyes were more than a little wild.

"I started to call from the car." Gasping, she pressed both hands to her thudding heart as Margo gaped at her. "I'm winded," she realized. "I'm going to have to take those workouts Byron's come up with more seriously."

"You had an accident." Margo bolted from the customer she'd been waiting on and made it to Kate seconds before

Thomas got there. He was calling for Susan as he hurried over to take Kate's arm.

"Are you hurt? You'd better sit down." He halfway carried her to a chair.

"I'm not hurt. There wasn't an accident." Her adrenaline was so high, she was surprised everyone couldn't see it bouncing off the walls. "Well, there was the skateboard incident, but we both escaped unharmed. I didn't call because it wouldn't have seemed dramatic enough over the phone."

Then she began to laugh, so hard and so deep she was forced to clutch her ribs. Margo's hand snaked out and pushed Kate's head between her knees.

"Get your breath back," Margo ordered. "Maybe she had a flare-up. Maybe we should call the doctor."

"No, no, no." Still laughing, Kate dug into her pocket and held up the coin like a trophy. "Look."

"Damn it, Kate, how'd you get my coin?"

"It's not yours." Kate nipped it back before Margo could make the grab. "This one's mine." She bolted up and kissed Margo hard on the mouth. "Mine. I found it on the cliffs. It was just lying there, out in the open. Look, it didn't even have any sand or salt on it. It was just there."

After deciding the glowing flush on Kate's face didn't jibe with an ulcer attack, Margo exchanged a quiet look with Thomas. "Sit down, Kate, catch your breath. Let me finish up here."

"She doesn't believe me." Kate grinned hugely as Margo moved off to her customer. "She thinks I snatched hers and went crazy. It's all the stress I'm under." Letting her head fall back, she laughed like a loon. "Stress is a killer."

"Maybe some water," Thomas murmured, and looked up in relief as his wife hurried down the stairs. "Kate seems to be a little hysterical."

Calmly efficient, Susan took the bottle of champagne from the ice bucket and poured half a glass. "Drink," she ordered. "Then breathe."

"Okay." Kate obeyed, but she couldn't stop snickering.

"You're all looking at me as if I'd grown another head. I haven't snapped, Uncle Tommy. I promise. I just found part of Seraphina's dowry. I was walking on the cliffs and it was right there. Bright as a penny and a lot more valuable."

"Just sitting there," Margo hissed as she walked by carrying a Limoges box in the shape of a sun hat. "Like hell. Take her upstairs, will you, Mrs. T? I'll be up as soon as I can."

"Good idea," Kate agreed. "There's more champagne up there. We're going to need a lot of it." She tucked the coin back in her pocket, toyed with it as she climbed the winding stairs. First things first, she ordered herself, and turned as she stepped into the kitchen. "I need to talk to you, Aunt Susie."

"Hmm." Her back stiff, Susan crossed to the stove and put a kettle on to boil. The pretty little eyebrow windows were open to the breeze and all the bells and whistles that were summer on Cannery Row. But Susan said nothing.

"You're still angry with me." Kate sucked in both breath and triumph. "I deserve it. I don't know how to apologize, but I hate knowing that I hurt you."

"I hate knowing you feel the way you do."

Kate shifted her feet. Staring at the pretty footed glass bowl filled with fresh fruit that sat on the counter, she tried to find the right words.

"You never gave anything to me with strings attached. I put them there."

Susan turned, met Kate's eyes. "Why?"

"I'm no good at explaining things that don't add neatly up. I'm better with facts than with feelings."

"But I already know the facts, don't I?" Susan said quietly. "You'll have to make an attempt at explaining your feelings if we're going to settle this, Kate."

"I know. I love you so much, Aunt Susie."

The words, and the simple emotion in them neatly sliced away a layer of Susan's anger. But the bafflement was still there, and under it, the hurt. "I've never doubted that, Kate. I wonder why you should doubt how very much I love you."

"I don't. It's just . . ." Knowing she was already fumbling

175

it, Kate slid onto a stool, folded her hands on the counter. "When I came to you, you were already a unit. Whole. Templeton House, you and Uncle Tommy, all so open and perfect. Like a fantasy. A family."

Her words stumbled over each other in their hurry to get out. "There was Josh, the crown prince, the heir apparent, the clever, golden son. Laura, the princess, sweet and lovely and kind. Margo, the little queen. Stunning, dazzling really, and so sure of her place. Then me, bruised and skinny and awkward. I was the ugly duckling. That makes you angry," she said when Susan's eyes fired. "I don't know how else to describe it."

Deliberately, she made herself slow down, choose her words with more care. "You were all so good to me. I don't mean just the house, the clothes, the food. I don't mean the things, Aunt Susie, though they were staggering to a child who'd come from my barely middle-class background."

"Do you think we would have treated you differently if we hadn't had certain advantages?"

"No." Kate shook her head briskly. "Absolutely not. And that was only more staggering." Pausing, she stared down at her hands. When she lifted her eyes again, they were glossy with threatening tears. "All the more staggering," she repeated, "now, because . . . I found out about my father."

Susan simply continued to stare, her head angled attentively. "Found out?"

"About what he did. About the charges against him." Sick and terrified, Kate watched her aunt's brow crease, then slowly clear.

"Oh." She let out a long, long sigh. "God, I'd forgotten."

"You—you'd forgotten?" Stunned, Kate ran a hand through her hair. "You'd forgotten he was a thief? You'd forgotten that he stole, was charged, that you paid off his debts and took his daughter into your home? The daughter of a—"

"Stop it." It was a sharp order rather than the sympathy Susan would have preferred. But she knew her Kate. "You're in no position to judge what a man did twenty years ago, what was in his mind or heart."

"He stole," Kate insisted. "He embezzled funds. You knew all of it when you took me in. You knew what he'd done, what he was. Now I'm under suspicion for essentially the same thing."

"And it becomes clear why you sat back and took it, and made yourself ill. Oh, you poor, foolish child." Susan stepped forward, cupped Kate's face in her hands. "Why didn't you tell us? Why didn't you let us know what you were thinking, feeling? We would have helped you through it."

"Why didn't you tell me? Why didn't you tell me what he had done?"

"To what purpose? A grief-stricken child has burden enough. He made a mistake, and he would have paid for it."

"You paid for it." She tried to swallow, couldn't. "You took your own money and made restitution for him. For me."

"Do you think that matters, that Tommy or I gave that part of it even a moment's thought? You mattered, Kate. Only you mattered." She smoothed back Kate's hair. "How did you find out?"

"A man, a client who came in. He was a friend of my father's. He thought I knew."

"I'm sorry you found out that way." Susan dropped her hands, stepped back. "Maybe we should have told you when you were older, but after a while, it just passed away. What timing," she murmured, heartsick. "You found this out shortly before the business at Bittle?"

"A couple of months before. I looked into it, found articles from newspapers, hired a detective."

"Kate." Susan wearily pressed her fingers to her eyes. "Why? If you'd needed to know, to understand, we would have explained. You had only to ask."

"If you'd wanted to talk about it, you would have."

After a moment Susan nodded. "All right. All right, that's true."

"I just needed to know, for certain. Then I tried to put it

177

aside. I tried, Aunt Susie, to forget it, to bury it. Maybe I could have, I don't know. But then, all of a sudden, I was in the middle of this. The discrepancy of funds from my clients' accounts, what was my explanation, internal investigations, suspension.'' Her voice broke like glass, but she made herself go on. ''It was a nightmare, like an echo of what must have happened to my father. I just couldn't seem to function or fight back or even think. I've been so afraid.''

Kate pressed her lips together. ''I didn't think I could tell you. I was ashamed to tell you, and afraid that you might think—even for just a second you might think that I could have done it. Because he'd done it. I could stand anything but that.''

''I can't be angry with you again, even for such foolishness. You've had a rough time of it, Kate.'' Susan gathered her close.

''It'll come out,'' Kate murmured. ''I know it will, and people will talk. Some will assume I took money because my father took money. I didn't think I could stand that. But I can.'' She sat back, scrubbed away her tears. ''I can stand it, but I'm sorry. I'm so sorry it touches you.''

''I raised my children to stand on their own feet and to understand that family stands together. I think you forgot the second part of that for a while.''

''Maybe. Aunt Susie . . .'' She had to finish, finish all of it. ''You never made me feel like an outsider, not from the first moment you brought me home. You never treated me like a debt or an obligation. But I felt the debt, the obligation, and wanted, always, to be the best. I never wanted you to question whether you'd done the right thing by taking me, by loving me.''

With her own heart still aching, Susan folded her arms. ''Do you think we measure our love by the accomplishments of the people we care for?''

''No. But I did—do. It's my failing, Aunt Susie, not yours. At first, I'd go to bed at night wondering if you'd change your mind about me in the morning, send me away.''

"Oh, Kate."

"Then I knew you wouldn't. I knew you wouldn't," she repeated. "You'd made me part of the unit, part of the whole. And I'm sorry if it makes you angry or hurts you, but I owe you for that. I owe you and Uncle Tommy for being who and what you are. I'd have been lost without you."

"Did you ever consider, Kate, what you did to complete our lives?"

"I considered what I could do to make you proud of me. I couldn't be as beautiful as Margo, as innately kind as Laura, but I could be smart. I could work hard, plan things out, be sensible and successful. That's what I wanted for myself, and for you. And . . . there's something else you should know."

Susan turned to switch off the spurting kettle, but didn't pour the hot water over the waiting tea. "What, Kate?"

"I was so happy at Templeton House, and I would think that I wouldn't be there with you, with everyone, if the roads hadn't been icy that night, if we hadn't gone out, and the car hadn't skidded and crashed. If my parents hadn't died."

She lifted her eyes to Susan's. "And I wanted to be there, and as the years passed, I loved you so much more than I could remember loving them. And it seemed horrible to be glad I was with you instead of them."

"And you've nurtured that ugly little seed all these years." Susan shook her head. She wondered if parents and their children ever really understood each other. "You were a child, barely eight years old. You had nightmares for months, and you grieved more than any child should have to. Why should you go on paying for something over which you had no control? Kate." Her fingers stroked gently over Kate's temples. "Why shouldn't you have been happy? Would you have been better off clinging to the pain and the grief and the misery?"

"No."

"So you chose guilt instead?"

"It seemed that the best thing that had ever happened in my life had grown out of the worst. I could never make sense of it. It was as if my life began the night they died. I knew if

179

a miracle had happened and my parents had come to the door of Templeton House, I would have run to you and begged you to keep me."

"Kate." Susan shook her head, smoothed Kate's hair back from her face. "If God Almighty had come to the door, I'd have fought Him tooth and nail to keep you with me. And I don't feel the least bit guilty about it. What happened wasn't your fault or mine. It doesn't make sense. It just is."

Nearly believing it, Kate nodded. "Please say you'll forgive me."

Susan stepped back, eyed her. Her child, she thought. A gift given to her out of tragedy. So complicated, so layered. So precious. "If you feel you have to owe me for—how did you put it—making you part of the unit, the payment is that you accept who you are, what you've made yourself. We'll be even then."

"I'll work on it, but in the meantime . . ."

"You're forgiven. But," she continued as Kate sniffled, "we're going to work on the rest of this together. Together, Kate. When Bittle deals with one Templeton, he'll deal with all of them."

"Okay." Kate knuckled a tear away. "I feel better."

"I'm sure you do." Susan's lips curved. "So do I."

Eyes wide and a little wild, Margo burst into the kitchen. "Let me see that coin," she demanded, and thrust a hand into Kate's pocket before Kate could move.

"Hey!"

"Oh, my God." Margo goggled at it, then goggled at the matching doubloon she held in her other hand. "I checked my purse. I really thought you were playing some sort of idiotic joke on me. They're the same."

And the world somehow settled neatly back into place. "I was trying to tell you," Kate began, then grunted when Margo grabbed her and squeezed.

"They're the same!" Margo shouted and held the coins in front of Susan's face. "Look, Mrs. T! Seraphina."

"They're certainly from the right place and the right time."

Struggling to switch gears, Susan frowned over the coins. "You just found this one, Kate."

"No, this one." In a proprietary move, Kate snatched the coin from Margo's left hand. "Mine," she stated.

"I can't believe it. All these months since I found the first one. All these months we've been searching and scraping and hauling that silly metal detector around. And you just stumble over it."

"It was just there."

"Exactly." Margo crowed in triumph. "Just like the first one was just there. It's a sign."

Kate rolled her eyes. "It's not magic, Margo. It's luck. There's a difference. I just happened to be there after the coin got kicked up or washed up or whatever."

"Hah," was all Margo had to say to that. "We've got to tell Laura. Oh, who the hell can remember where she is with that insane schedule of hers?"

"If you'd bother to look at the weekly schedule I've posted in the office, you'd know exactly where she is." Feeling superior, Kate glanced at her watch. "If memory serves, she's at the hotel for the next thirty minutes, then she has a meeting with Ali's teacher. After that—"

"We don't need after that. We'll just—" Margo stopped short. "Hell, we can't just close the shop in the middle of the afternoon."

"Go ahead," Susan told her. "Tommy and I can mind the store for an hour."

"Really?" Margo beamed at her. "I wouldn't ask, but this is so exciting, and we're in it together."

"You've always been in it together," Susan said.

"It perked her up." Margo loitered in the lobby after their brief contact with Laura. "It's frustrating to have to wait until Sunday to go back and look, but with her schedule we're lucky to manage that."

"Don't you think she's taken on an awful lot?"

Kate scanned the sweeping lobby with its elaborate potted

181

plants, half hoping to see Byron breeze by on some executive mission. Instead she saw wandering guests, bustling bellmen, a group of women standing near the revolving doors with shopping bags heaped at their feet and a look of happy exhaustion on their faces.

"I know she likes to fill her time," Kate continued. "And it probably helps keep her mind off . . . things. But she barely has a minute in the day just for herself."

"Ah, you finally noticed." Then Margo shook her head and sighed. "I can't nag her about it anymore. When I suggested that the shop could probably swing a part-time clerk and that she could cut back there, she almost took my head off." Absently she rubbed a soothing hand over her belly as the baby kicked. "I know the bulk of her salary here at the hotel is earmarked for the kids' tuition."

"That bastard Peter." Kate's teeth began to grind even as she thought of it. "He was a slimy creep for taking Laura's money, but taking his own children's . . . that makes him whatever's lower than slime. She could have fried his sorry ass in court."

"That's what I'd have done," Margo agreed. Amused, she noted that two men in one of the lobby's plush seating areas were trying to catch her eye. "What you'd have done. Laura has to handle this her own way."

"And her way is to hold down two jobs, raise two children on her own, support a full staff because she's too softhearted to lay anyone off. She can't keep working twenty out of twenty-four hours, Margo."

"You try telling her." Out of long habit, she sent the hopeful men a quick, flirtatious smile.

"Stop playing with those insurance salesmen," Kate ordered.

"Is that what they are?" Carelessly, Margo scooped her long hair back. "Anyway, Josh and I have pushed Laura as far as we can push. She's not budging. Nobody could tell you to take a vacation, could they? To see a doctor?"

"Okay, okay." That was the last thing Kate wanted to hash

over. "I had reasons, and I'll explain it to you when we have a little more time. I should have told you before."

"What?"

"We'll talk about it," she promised, then baffled her friend by leaning in and kissing her. "I love you, Margo."

"Okay, what have you screwed up?"

"Nothing. Well, everything, but I'm starting to fix it. Now, back to Laura. We'll just have to do more to pick up the slack. Maybe take the girls off her hands a few hours every week. Or run some of the errands she's always got a million of. And worrying about this is spoiling my mood." She pulled the coin out of her pocket, watched it glint. "Once we find Seraphina's dowry, the rest will be irrelevant."

"Once we do, I'm going to open a new branch of Pretenses. In Carmel, I think."

Surprised, Kate swept her gaze up to Margo's face. "I'd have figured you for a cruise around the world, or a new haute couture wardrobe."

"People change." Margo shrugged. "But I might add in a short cruise and a swing down Rodeo Drive."

"It's a relief to know people don't change too much." But maybe they could, Kate mused. Maybe they should. "Look, there's something I want to do. Can you handle the shop until closing?"

"With Mr. and Mrs. T there, I don't have to go back myself." With a chuckle, Margo dug out her car keys. "If I could keep them in the shop for a month, we'd double our profits. Oh, say hi to Byron for me."

"I didn't say I was seeing Byron."

Margo sent a sly smile over her shoulder as she walked away. "Sure you did, pal."

It was demoralizing to realize she was so obvious. Demoralizing enough that Kate nearly talked herself out of going up to the penthouse. She was still arguing with herself when she stepped out of the elevator. When she was told Mr. De Witt was in conference, she decided it was for the best.

At loose ends, she rode back down, but rather than heading

183

to her car, she wandered out to the pool. Leaning on the stone wall that skirted it, she watched the play of the courtyard fountain, the people who sat at the pretty glass tables sipping colorful drinks under festive umbrellas. She spotted name tags pinned to lapels that identified conventioneers taking a break from seminars.

In striped lounge chairs around the curving tiled pool lounged bodies slicked with sunscreen. Magazines and bestsellers were being read, headphones were in place. Waitpeople in cool pastel uniforms delivered drinks and snacks from the poolside bar and grill. Other guests splashed and played in the water, or simply floated, dreaming.

They knew how to relax, Kate thought. Why had she never acquired this simple skill? If she were to stretch out in one of those lounge chairs, she'd be asleep in five minutes. That was how her body was trained. Or if sleep refused to come, restlessness would have her up and gone, with her mind ordering her not to waste time.

Since this appeared to be a red-letter day in the life of Kate Powell, she decided to give wasting time a try. She slid onto a seat at the bar and ordered something with the promising name of Monterey Sunset. She lingered over it for nearly half an hour, watching people come and go, catching snatches of conversation. Then she ordered another.

It wasn't so bad, this time wasting, she decided. Especially when she felt so hollowed out inside. A good feeling, she realized. As if she'd purged herself of something that had been gnawing at her too long.

It was time to repair those rents in her life, or perhaps to ignore some of them and move on. There was promise in this hollow feeling, in the possibilities of how to fill it.

Carrying her drink, she wandered through the hotel gardens, reminding herself to enjoy the scents of camellia, jasmine, to appreciate the vivid shades of the tumbling bougainvillea. She sat on a stone bench near a pair of cypress and wondered how people managed to do nothing and not go insane.

It was probably best to try it in stages, she decided. Like

exercise, an hour the first time out was probably overdoing. She rose, with the idea of going back to the shop and checking inventory, then she heard his voice.

"Be sure to cross-check the details with Ms. Templeton tomorrow. She'll need to be aware of these changes."

"Yes, sir, but it will require more staff—at least two more waitpeople and an extra bartender."

"Three more waitpeople. We want this smooth. I think Ms. Templeton will agree that this is the best position for the third bar setup. We don't want staff running through the guests with ice buckets, do we? Now, Lydia, Ms. Templeton has her finger on this particular pulse."

"Yes, sir, but these people keep changing their minds."

"That's their prerogative. It's our problem to accommodate them. What I wanted to discuss with you, Lydia, is the complimentary coffee setup on the east terrace every morning. We refined that a bit at the resort a couple of weeks ago, and it's working out well."

He came around the path as he spoke, caught sight of Kate sitting on the stone bench with a pretty drink in her hand and a quiet smile on her lips. And lost his train of thought.

"Mr. De Witt?" Lydia prompted. "The coffee setup?"

"Ah, right. Check with my assistant for the memo. It's all laid out. Let me know what you think." He didn't precisely push her along, but the intent was there. "We'll go over all of this with Ms. Templeton in the morning."

Once Lydia was on her way, he stopped at the bench, looked down at Kate. "Hi."

"Hi. I'm practicing."

"Practicing what?"

"Doing nothing."

He thought it was like coming across a fawn in an enchanted garden—those dark, deep, oddly slanted eyes, the warm and humid scent of flowers. "How's it going?"

"It's not as easy as it looks. I was about to give up."

"Let's give it another minute," he suggested and sat beside her.

"I didn't think the brass worried about little things like complimentary coffee setups."

"Every detail is a piece, every piece makes up the whole. And speaking of details"—he turned her face toward his, touched his lips to hers—"you look wonderful. Really. I'd say revived."

"I feel revived. It's a long story."

He grinned. "I'd like to hear it."

"I think I might like to tell you." She thought he was someone she could tell. No, she realized, she knew he was. "I came by to tell Laura a portion of it, then decided to hang around and try the nothing experiment."

He struggled with disappointment. The way he'd found her, sitting there, it had been as though she'd been waiting for him. "Want to go into the details, over dinner?"

"I'd love to." She rose, held out a hand. "If you're cooking."

He hesitated. He'd been very careful to avoid being completely alone with her. When he was alone with her he seemed to forget little things like timing and finesse. Now she was standing there, holding out her hand, with her lips curved in a way that let him know she understood his dilemma. And was enjoying it.

"Fine. It'll give me a chance to try out the barbecue grill I picked up a couple days ago."

"Tell you what, I'll bring dessert and meet you there."

"Sounds like a plan."

Testing both of them, she stretched onto her toes and closed her mouth softly, lingeringly over his. "I'm a terrific planner."

He stood where he was, his hands firmly tucked in his pockets, while she walked away. He decided one of them was about to have their plans tumbled. It would certainly be interesting to see which one it was.

Flaky, creamy, decadent chocolate eclairs had seemed the perfect choice. Kate set the bakery box on the table in his

186

kitchen and watched him through the window. He'd left the door unlocked, in invitation. She'd accepted it, had come in to a blast of searing Bruce Springsteen, noted he'd added a couple of pieces of furniture to complement the ratty recliner.

The low coffee table with the checkerboard inlay looked expensive and unique, as did the stained-glass lamp and the thick geometric-patterned area rug. She admitted she was dying to see the rest of the house, but she made herself go into the kitchen.

And there he was in the backyard, wrestling the puppies over a sock. He looked as at home in jeans and a T-shirt as he had earlier in his tailored suit and silk tie. It made her wish she'd taken the time to swing by home and change into . . . anything, she thought, but this tidy pin-striped suit and sensible shoes. In compromise, she took off her jacket and undid the top button of her shirt before she went out to join him.

She stepped onto the redwood deck. A deck, she noticed, that he'd made his own with the simple addition of pottery planters filled with geraniums and pansies and trailing vines. A complex and somewhat terrifying gas grill stood shiny and new near the double glass doors, and a pair of redwood chairs, deeply cushioned in navy, were positioned to offer a view of the lawn leading down to the sea.

He'd had the yard fenced in, she noted, with wooden pickets to keep his precious pets in but still leave it all open to the view. A gate stood by the beach steps, offering easy access to the sea.

He'd planted something at regular intervals along the fencing. She could see tender young plants and the carefully packed mulch around them. She imagined he'd done the digging there himself. Some sort of trailing flowering vine, she supposed, that would, in time, grow and tumble color over the fence.

A patient man, Byron De Witt, she mused. One who would enjoy watching those vines grow and bloom and tangle year after year.

And she knew he would experience a quiet satisfaction

when the first bud blossomed. Then he would tend it. The man enjoyed tending things.

Puppies yapped, the sea murmured, and the wind trailed lightly through the fluttering cypress leaves. As the sky deepened from blue to indigo splashed with scarlet, she felt a quick flutter around her heart. There were, she supposed, perfect spots in the world. It seemed Byron had found one of them and claimed it.

And so did he look perfect, she realized, with the wind in his hair, puppies at his feet. That long, mouthwatering, muscular build was tucked snug and sexy into denim and cotton. Her reaction to it, to him, completely unprecedented, was to grab hold and tear in with fingers and teeth. She wanted to taste and take. She wanted to be taken.

She wanted.

With legs less than steady, she descended the short flight of steps to the yard. The puppies dashed up to her, yipping and leaping. Even as she crouched to welcome them, she kept her eyes on Byron.

"What did you plant along the fence?"

"Wisteria. It'll take a little while to establish." He looked over to the fence line. "But it'll be worth the wait. There was always some growing on a trellis outside my bedroom back in Georgia. It's a scent that stays with you."

"You've already done a terrific job with the place. It's gorgeous out here. Must take a lot of time to add all these touches."

"When you find what you're looking for, you take care of it." He crossed to her. "We can take a walk down to the beach after dinner if you like." He stroked a hand over her hair, much as he had done to the dogs' fur. Then he stepped back. "Catch this." He snapped his fingers twice. "Sit."

Butts wiggling frantically, both dogs sat. He had them offer their paws, and after some confusion, lie down. Though their bodies quivered with suppressed excitement.

"Very impressive," Kate commented. "Does everyone do what you tell them?"

"It's just a matter of asking often enough in the right way." He pulled two dog biscuits out of his back pocket. "And bribery usually works." The dogs took the treats and raced away to feast. "I've got a nice red Bordeaux breathing. Why don't I get it, and you can tell me about this interesting day of yours?"

She lifted a hand, laid it on his chest. Felt the heat, the rhythm. "There's something I think I want to say to you."

"All right. Let's go inside." He thought it was best to get into the brightly lit kitchen, away from the sumptuous sunset and seductive night air.

But she kept her hand on his chest and stepped closer. It must have been their color, Byron thought, that made her eyes glow so erotically through the twilight shadows.

"I was going to avoid men like you, on a personal level," she began. "It was to be a kind of principle, a rule of thumb. I'm very fond of rules and principles."

He arched a brow. "And generalities?"

"Yes, and generalities, because they usually have some basis in fact, or they wouldn't have gotten to be generalities. I'd decided after a couple of unfortunate experiences that when something, or someone, looked too good, it was probably bad for me. You may be bad for me, Byron."

"Have you been working on this theory long?"

"Actually I have, but it may need some further adjustments. In any case, I didn't like you when I first met you."

"Now there's a surprise."

She smiled and disconcerted him by moving closer. "I didn't like you because I started wanting you the first minute. That was uncomfortable for me. You see, I prefer wanting things that are tangible and that can be acquired through time, planning, and effort. I don't like being uncomfortable, or wanting someone I don't understand, who is in all probability bad for me, and who doesn't fit my requirements."

"You have requirements too?" He didn't care for the sensation of being annoyed and aroused at the same time.

"Absolutely. One of the main requirements is a lack of

demand. I don't think you're an undemanding man, and that's, undoubtedly, going to be my biggest mistake. One of the other things I really, really hate to do is make mistakes. But I'm working on being more tolerant of myself.''

''Is that something else you're practicing, like doing nothing?''

''Exactly.''

''I see. Well, now that we've established that this fledgling relationship with me is practice for your personal tolerance, I'll start dinner.''

She laughed and put her other hand on his chest. ''I irritate you. I don't know why I find that so funny.''

''It doesn't surprise me, Katherine. You have an abrasive, contrary nature and like nothing better than stirring things up.''

''You're right, absolutely right. It's terrifying how easily you understand me. And the more patient you are, the more compelled I am to poke at you. We are so completely wrong for each other, Byron.''

''Who's arguing?'' He curled his fingers around her wrists, intent on pushing her hands aside.

''Take me to bed,'' she said simply, and slid her hands through his loosened grip to his shoulders. ''Now.''

Chapter Twelve

He wasn't easily shocked. But her simple demand rocked him back as efficiently as a short left jab. He'd been sure she was ending what had barely begun between them. He'd been prepared to be coldly furious, but to school himself into not giving a damn.

Because it was undoubtedly unwise to touch her, he kept his arms at his sides. "You want me to take you to bed, now, because it's a mistake, because you've theorized that I'm bad for you, and because we're completely wrong for each other."

"Yes. And because I want to see you naked."

He managed a laugh, and would have stepped back, but she locked her hands at the back of his neck. "I think I need a drink," he muttered.

"Byron, don't make me get rough with you." She moved in, her body bumping his, her arms tightening. "I've been working out. Sort of. I think I could take you if I had to."

Telling himself to be amused, he pinched her biceps gently.

The tiny muscle gave like putty. "Yeah, you're a regular Amazon, honey."

"You want me." She nipped her way up his throat. "If you don't, I'll have to kill you."

The little blood left in his head shot straight to his loins. "I think my life's safe. Kate—" Her hands raced busily to the snap of his jeans. "Don't—Christ!" And tugged at his zipper. "Hell," he muttered, and gave in to the animal long enough to savage her mouth with his.

She made a sound in her throat like a cat purring over prey.

"Hold on." He grabbed her shoulders and pushed her back. "Just hold on one damn minute." He panted out a breath, then another. "You know the trouble with flings?"

"No, what's the trouble with them?"

"I'm trying to remember." He wanted to rub his hands over his face, but he didn't dare release her. "Okay, I've got it. However momentarily satisfying they are, you end up dissatisfied. That's not the way it's going to be here. This isn't going to be a fling. You're going to have to accept that."

What was wrong with him? she wondered. Men weren't supposed to complicate sex. "Fine, we'll call it something else."

"There are strings, Kate." His hands still on her shoulders, he began slowly backing her toward the house. He could already see her naked and gleaming. "Trust. Honesty. Affection. Once I touch you, no one touches you but me."

"They're not exactly lined up around the block waiting to get their hands on me." Her feet bumped into the steps. Automatically, she stepped up, back again. He was looking at her in that way that made her both nervous and eager. As if he were looking beyond, to what no one else had seen, even herself. "I don't sleep around."

"Neither do I. I consider intimacy a serious business. And I'll have intimacy from you, Kate, in bed and out. That's bottom line."

"Look—" Her throat was burning dry, her hormones bouncing. "This isn't a business contract."

192

"No." He backed her easily through the kitchen. "It's a personal one. That's much more involved, much more important. You put the deal on the table." He swept her into his arms. "I'm defining the terms."

"I— Maybe I have terms of my own."

"Better put them out here then. This deal's about to close."

"We need to keep this simple."

"Not an option." At the top of the stairs, he turned left, carried her through a doorway and into a room washed with the last vivid light of the western sky.

"We're healthy, unattached adults," she began, talking fast now. "This is a mutual physical relationship."

"There's more to sex than the physical." He smiled as he laid her on the bed. "I guess I'll have to show you."

He kissed her, a long, slow, lazy meeting of lips that lingered until every nerve in her body was vibrating like the strings of a plucked harp. Eager for more, she dragged him closer so that all the heat swirling through her seemed to center on their mouths.

He could have taken her in one greedy gulp. Knowing it, he eased back. "Honey, where I come from, we pace ourselves." He linked his fingers with hers so that she couldn't tear down his defenses with those narrow, nervous hands. "Now relax." He lowered his head to trail nibbling kisses along her jawline. "And enjoy." Down her throat. "We've got all the time in the world."

She thought he would kill her with patience, rip her to shreds with gentleness. His lips were soft, smooth, deliciously, devastatingly slow as they cruised over her face. Each time they met hers, he took the kiss just a degree deeper, just a whisper warmer. Her muscles went from hot wires to soft wax.

The change aroused him mercilessly. The sound of her breathing, low and deep and slow, the thrill when a breath ended on a moan, a sigh. Her quivering impatience slipped into mindless pliancy. When he unbuttoned her shirt, revealing the simple white camisole beneath, she did nothing more than murmur her pleasure.

Fascinated by the simplicity of her form, he traced his fingertips over the soft cotton, then up over softer flesh. The most subtle of curves, he mused as her breath began to quicken again at his feathering touch. Linking fingers again, he nuzzled the cotton aside, flicked his tongue over her nipple.

She arched in response, biting back a groan. So small, he thought, so firm. So sensitive. He swept his tongue under the cotton, moistening her other breast, and felt her quake beneath him.

So he suckled slowly, gently, darkly pleased with the way she writhed under him, with the quick, helpless whimpers that sounded in her throat as he increased pressure and speed.

When he felt as if he might die if he didn't plunge into her, when her hips were pistoning as if she would explode if he didn't fill her, he drew back and slipped out of bed.

"What? What?" Dazed, desperate, she sat up.

"The light's going," he said quietly. "I can't see you. I want to see you." There was the abrasive scratch of a match striking, the flare of light that softened as flame was touched to the wick of a candle, then a second, a third. And the room was suddenly rich and romantic with wavering light.

She pressed a hand to her breast, shocked to realize that the hot, quivering nerves inside belonged to her. What was he doing to her? She wanted to ask, but was afraid of the answer.

Then he tugged the T-shirt over his head, tossed it aside. She let out a breath of relief. Now—it would be now. And all these twisting sensations would smooth out into the understandable.

He stepped out of his shoes. She was only mildly surprised when he slipped hers off as well, slid his hand up her leg to just under the hem of her rucked-up skirt.

"Would you take your top off?"

All but hypnotized, she blinked at him. "What? Oh."

"Slowly," he said, laying a hand on hers before she could yank it free. "No rush."

She did as he asked because her limbs were so heavy. His gaze took a lazy journey from her face, down her torso and back again, before he took the thin cotton from her, set it aside. His eyes stayed on hers as he eased her back.

"You keep looking at me," she murmured. Her skin trembled when he slid his hands further under her skirt, when he curled his fingers around the waistband of her panty hose and began to draw them down. "I don't know what you expect."

"Neither do I. I thought we'd find out together." He lowered his head and pressed his lips to her inner thigh. "Now I know why you always walk as if you were ten minutes late for a five-minute appointment. It's all this leg. All this long leg."

"Byron." She was burning up. Good God, couldn't he feel it? "I can't take this."

But she would, he thought, and unhooked her skirt. "I haven't even started yet." He slipped the skirt off and quivered himself at the sight of that slim, angular body in his bed. Resting a bent knee on the bed, he cupped her. She bowed back, pressing desperately against him.

His eyes darkened dangerously as he watched her face, the play of sensations and light, the helpless trembling of lashes and lips. Then the utter surrender to self and to him when the orgasm rippled through her.

Wanting more as wildly as she, he closed his mouth over her breast and built her relentlessly toward peak again.

"I can't." Nearly terrified at what he'd pulled out of her, of what he seemed to create inside her, she dragged at his hair. "I'm not—"

"Sure you can." He gasped out the words before his mouth fused with hers. Heat was pouring out of her, all but pumping out of her pores. He'd never known a woman to be so responsive and so resistant at once. The need, the drive to show her he was the one, the only one who could bring that response and break that resistance made him hold off that final pleasure for the tortured maze of sensations between.

It seemed he owned her body. She had no control, and had lost the will to find any. His hands, his lips were everywhere, and each time she thought he would rush to finish it, he would cause her to erupt again, then move patiently on.

She was painfully aware of her body, and his, the melding and the contrasts, the race of pulses. Candlelight flickered over his face, those sleek, slick muscles, making it all almost too beautiful to bear. The taste of him was potent, like some dark, slow-acting drug that had already seeped into her blood to addict her.

He braced himself over her, waiting for her eyes to open and focus on his. "I didn't want you," he said in a voice strained to the edge of control. "Then I wanted nothing else. Understand that."

"For God's sake, Byron. Now!"

"Now," he echoed and plunged into her. "But not just now."

The warm red haze over her mind cooled slowly. She became aware of the world outside of her own body. The candlelight continued to flicker against her closed lids in soft, surreal patterns. The night wind had risen, causing the curtains at the windows to whisper. She could hear the music again, the low throb of bass from the stereo downstairs, the answering wail of a tenor sax. The smell of hot, pooling wax, and sweat, and sex.

She had the taste of him in her mouth, and the good, solid feel of him beneath her. He'd rolled her over so that she lay sprawled across him. Concerned, she supposed, that he would crush her. Always the gentleman.

Just how did she play this? she wondered. How did she handle the aftermath of such wild, spectacular sex? Initiating it was one thing, participating was clearly, and fabulously, another. But she felt certain that these first few moments of the after would set the precedent for how they would go on.

"I can actually hear your mind clicking back in gear," he murmured. There was a hint of amusement in his voice as he smoothed down her messy cap of hair. "It's fascinating. I don't know that I've ever been quite so attracted to a woman's brain before." When she started to shift, he ran his hands down her back, gave her butt a friendly squeeze. "No, don't move yet. Your head's ahead of me."

She took a chance, raised her head to look at him. Those gorgeous green eyes of his were at half-mast. The mouth that had so recently sent her system into overdrive was softened with a faint smile. He was, she decided, the perfect picture of the fully satisfied male animal.

"Is this going to be awkward?" she wondered aloud.

"Doesn't have to be. It seems to me that we've been heading here since the first minute we met. Whether we knew it or not."

"Which poses the next question."

Ah, that tidy, practical, ordered mind, he thought. "Which is, what direction do we take from here? We'll have to talk about that." He rolled her over and, before she could speak again, took her mouth in a long, deep, mind-hazing kiss. "But first, the practicalities."

He scooped her off the bed, into his arms. Her system gave a fresh jerk. It was so odd, being carried this way, experiencing the arousing vulnerability of being physically outmatched. "I'm not sure I like the way you do this."

"Let me know when you make up your mind. Meanwhile, I vote for a shower and dinner. I'm starving."

No, it wasn't going to be awkward, she concluded. In fact, it was amazingly pleasant to be wearing one of his faded T-shirts, listening to Bob Seger's sandpaper vocals grinding out rock. Byron had trusted her to put a salad together while he grilled the steaks. She was finding the process enjoyable—the colors and textures of the vegetables he'd set out for her. The summer-garden scent of them. She couldn't remember being quite so aware of food before. She liked to eat, Kate thought, but taste had always been the main stimulus. Now she decided there was more to it than that. There was the feel of the food, the way different ingredients played off each other, harmonized or clashed.

The moist, feathery layers of an artichoke heart, the firm

snap of a carrot, the subtle bite of cucumber, the delicacy of salad greens.

She set down the chef's knife and blinked. What the hell was she doing? Romanticizing a salad? Good God. Carefully, she poured herself half a glass of the wine he'd set on the counter to breathe. Though she hadn't had any recent flareups, she was still leery of alcohol. She sipped the wine gingerly.

She could see him through the glass doors, talking to the dogs as he turned the steaks. Flame and smoke billowed.

They were cooking together, she thought. She was wearing his shirt. Dogs were begging for scraps, and music was playing.

It was all so quietly domestic. Terrifying.

"Honey—" Byron slid open the doors. "You want to pour me a glass of that? These steaks are about done."

"Sure." Easy, girl, she warned herself. This was just a nice, pleasant evening between two consenting adults. Nothing to get jittery over.

"Thanks." Byron took the glass she brought to him, swirled the wine before drinking. "You want to eat out here? It's a nice night."

"Okay." And more romantic, she thought as they carried out the dinnerware. Why shouldn't she enjoy a little starlight and wine with the man who'd just become her lover? There was nothing wrong with that.

"You've got that line between your eyebrows," he commented, sampling and approving her mixed salad. "The one you get when you're trying to calculate your bottom line."

"I was calculating how much of this steak I can eat without exploding." Eyes on her plate, she cut another bite. "It's wonderful."

"While I find it surprisingly satisfying to feed you, the food isn't what's bouncing around in your mind like a pinball." He started to ask her to look at him, then took the more direct route. He laid a hand on her bare thigh and watched her gaze shoot to his. "Why don't I make it easy for you? I want you to stay with me tonight."

She picked up her wineglass, fiddled with the stem. "I don't have any clothes."

"So we'll get up early, give you enough time to swing by your place and change before work." He reached out, ran a fingertip down her throat. Such a long, slim throat. "I want to make love with you again. I want to sleep with you. Is that simple enough?"

Because it should have been, she nodded. "I'll stay, but I don't want any complaints when the alarm goes off at six."

He only smiled. It was a rare day for him not to be up already and jogging along the beach by six. "Whatever you say. Now, there's more. I said there were strings. I meant it."

That was what she'd been trying to keep neatly locked in the back of her mind. Wanting to choose her words with care, she continued to eat. "I'm not involved with anyone," she began.

"Yes, you are. You're involved with me."

A quick chill of warning ran down her spine. "I meant I'm not involved with anyone else. I don't intend to see anyone else while we're . . . involved. However it may seem by the way I came here tonight, sex isn't casual for me."

"Nothing's casual for you." He topped off his wine, then hers. "But sex is the easy part. It doesn't take a lot of thought, instinct kicks in, the body takes over."

His gaze rested on her face. Her eyes were wary, he noted, like those of a doe that had unexpectedly come across a stag in the woods. Or a hunter. "I have feelings for you."

Her heart bumped. She used knife and fork to cut meat as if the precise size and shape of it were paramount. "I think we've established that."

"Not just desires, Katherine. Feelings. I'd planned on sorting them out before we found ourselves at this stage. But . . ." He shrugged, ate, let her absorb the words. "I like maps."

Her already baffled brain clicked over into complete confusion. "Maps."

"Points of interest. Routes from one place to the next. I like plotting them out. One of the reasons I'm interested in hotels is because they're like a world. Self-contained, full of movement and places and people."

As he spoke, he cut the bone from what was left of his meal, then did the same with Kate's. He gave each of the wide-eyed dogs a feast.

"Hotels are never really stationary. Just the building is. But inside there are births, deaths, politics, passions, celebrations, and tragedies. Like any world, it runs more or less a certain way, along a certain route. But the detours, the surprises, the problems, are always there. You explore them, enjoy them, solve them. I fucking love it."

She pondered as he sat back, lit one of his cigars. She had no earthly idea how they had shifted from a discussion on their relationship to his work, but it was fine with her. Relaxed again, she picked up her wine.

"That's why you're so good at your job. My aunt and uncle consider you the best, and they're very picky."

"We generally do our best with something we enjoy." He watched her through a haze of smoke. "I enjoy you."

Her smile spread slowly as she edged toward him. "Well, then."

"You're a detour," he murmured, taking her hand before it could become too busy, bringing it to his lips. "When I map out the particular world I'm moving in, I always anticipate a few detours."

"I'm a detour." She was insulted enough to tug her hand free. "That's flattering."

"It was meant to be." He grinned at her. "While I'm on this intriguing and very attractive alternate route, I don't intend to worry how long it will take to navigate it."

"And I'm along for the ride? Is that it?"

"I'd prefer saying we're in this together. Where we end up depends on both of us. But I know this. I want you with me. I haven't completely figured out why, but I can't get past the wanting part. When I look at you, it's enough."

No one had ever made her feel more desired. He'd used no soft, alluring words, composed no odes to her eyes, and yet she felt vital and alive and very much wanted. "I'm not sure whether I'm confused or seduced, but it seems to be enough for me, too."

"Good." Most of the tension he'd been holding in seeped away as he brought her hand to his lips again. "Now that you're relaxed, why don't you tell me about this fascinating day of yours?"

"My day?" Absolutely blank, she stared at him. Then her eyes cleared, went bright. "Oh, Jesus, my day. I'd completely forgotten."

"I can't tell you how gratifying that is." He laid a hand on her thigh again, slid it slowly up. "If you'd like to forget about it for a while longer . . ."

"No." As she pushed his hand firmly away, she chuckled. "I was bursting to talk about it, and then I started thinking about getting you into bed, and it slipped down a couple of notches on the priority list."

"How about I let you get me in bed again, and we talk later?"

"Nope." She scooted out of reach. "I've already had you, pal. The encore can wait."

"That sound you hear is my ego deflating." He sat back with his cigar, his wine, gestured with the glass. "Okay, kid, spill it."

She wondered how it would feel to simply say it aloud. "In March I found out that my father had embezzled funds from the ad agency he worked for before he was killed." She let out a breath, pressed a hand to her stomach. "God."

It was, he thought, the piece he'd been sure was missing, falling into place. "In March," Byron repeated, studying her face. "You hadn't known about it before?"

"No, nothing. I keep expecting people to be shocked. Why aren't you shocked?"

"People make mistakes." And his voice softened when he

calculated just how much she'd suffered. "Cut you off at the knees, didn't it?"

"I didn't cope very well. I thought I was. I thought I could bury it, just push it in. Didn't work."

"You didn't talk to anyone?"

"I couldn't. Margo found out she was pregnant, and Laura, she's handling so much and . . . I was ashamed. That's what it comes down to. I couldn't face it."

And had made herself ill, he thought, with worry and stress and guilt. "Then you got hit at Bittle."

"It didn't seem that it could really be happening. Some sort of cosmic joke. It paralyzed me, Byron. I've never been so afraid of anything, or felt so helpless. Ignoring it seemed the only solution. It would go away, somehow just go away. I'd just keep myself busy with other things, not think about it, not react, and it would get better."

"Some snap," he murmured, "some collapse, and some dig their trenches."

"And I pulled the covers over my head. Well, that's done." In a half-toast to herself, she lifted her glass. "I talked to my aunt and uncle. Instead of making it better, that made it worse. I hurt them. I was trying to explain why I was grateful to her and Uncle Tommy, and I said things wrong. Or I was wrong, and it came out badly. She was so angry with me. I don't remember her ever being that angry with me."

"She loves you, Kate. You'll square this with her."

"She's already forgiven me. Or mostly. But it made me realize I had to face it. All of it. I went to Bittle today."

"Now you're digging the trenches."

She let out a shaky breath at his response. "It's past time I did."

"Now are you going to beat yourself up because you weren't iron woman, because you needed time to pull your resources together?"

The corner of her mouth twitched. She'd been tempted to do just that. Apparently he knew her very, very well. "No, I'm going to concentrate on dealing with now."

202

"You didn't have to go to Bittle alone."

She looked down at the hand that had covered hers. What made him offer support so easily? she wondered. And what was making her count so heavily on the offer?

"No, I did have to go alone. To prove to myself and everyone at Bittle that I could. I used to play baseball, in school. I was a good clutch hitter. Two out, a run behind, put Kate in the box. I'd concentrate on the feel of the bat in my hands because my stomach would be churning and my knees shaking. If I concentrated on the feel of the ash solid in my hands and kept my eyes dead on the eyes of the pitcher, I'd still be terrified, but nobody would know it."

"Trust you to turn a game into life or death."

"Baseball is life or death, especially in the bottom of the ninth." She smiled a little. "That's how I felt when I walked into Bittle. Two out, bottom of the ninth, and they'd already winged two strikes past me while I stood there with the bat on my shoulder."

"So you figured if you were going to go down, you'd go down swinging."

"Yeah, now you get it."

"Honey, I was a starting pitcher all the way through college. Went All-State. I ate clutch hitters like you for breakfast."

When she laughed, some of his worry eased. She took a moment to sip her wine, study the star-strewn sky. "It felt good. It felt right. Even being scared felt right because I was doing something about it. I demanded a partners' meeting, and there I was, back in the conference room, just like the day they fired me. Only this time I fired back."

She took a deep breath before launching into a play-by-play of what had happened inside the conference room. He listened, admiring the way her voice strengthened, her eyes hardened. Perhaps her vulnerability pulled at him, but this confident, determined woman was no less appealing.

"And you're prepared to deal with the fallout if they press formal charges?"

"I'm prepared to fight and to face all the fallout. And I'm prepared to do some serious thinking about who set me up. Because somebody did. Either because they were focused on me or because I was convenient. But someone used me to cheat the firm and the clients, and they're not going to get away with it."

"I can help you." He held up a hand before she could object. "I've got a feel for people. And I've spent my entire adult life dealing with the intrigues and petty pilfering of a large organization. You're the expert with figures, I'm better with personalities, motivations."

He could see her turning it over in her mind, weighing the possibilities. He smiled. "Let's use baseball again. You're the batter, I'm the pitcher. You swing away. I finesse."

"You don't even know any of the people involved."

He would make it his business to, he thought grimly, but he kept his voice mild. "So, you'll tell me about them. You're practical enough to admit there's an advantage to a fresh viewpoint."

"I suppose it wouldn't hurt. Thanks."

"We can start working on the bios tomorrow. I can see why you were wired. You've had quite a day."

"It took some doing to bring myself down after the business at Bittle. Then I knew I had to face Aunt Susie. I took a breather at the cliffs, and—"

She jumped up from her chair. "Jesus, I forgot! I can't believe I actually forgot! God, what did I do with it?" Foolishly, she patted her hips, then remembered she was wearing nothing but an oversized T-shirt. "My pocket. I'll be right back. Stay here."

She streaked inside like a bullet, leaving Byron shaking his head after her. The woman was a mass of contradictions, he decided as he rose to clear the table. It was no use reminding himself that he preferred the quiet, soothing, and sophisticated type. The Laura type, he supposed. Well-mannered, well-read, well-bred.

Yet he'd never felt this bright, hot need with Laura. Or with anyone, for that matter.

Instead, it was Kate, this bumpy and often inconvenient detour, who continually fascinated him.

Just how would his complicated and turbulent Kate react if he told her he was beginning to believe he was falling in love with her?

"Hah!" Triumphant, she bolted back into the kitchen, prepared to bask in his astonishment. She smiled smugly as he stared at her, eyes dark and intense. "I found it."

She was flushed and rumpled. Her short hair stood in spikes, those long, slim legs pale gold beneath the hem of his shirt. She had no figure to speak of, was more bone than curve. The little mascara she'd bothered with was smudged under her eyes. Her nose was crooked. Had he noticed that before? The nose was just slightly off center, and her mouth was certainly too wide for that narrow face.

"You're not beautiful," he said in a quiet statement that made her brow knit. "Why do you look beautiful when you're not?"

"How much of that wine did you drink, De Witt?"

"Your face is wrong." As if to prove it to himself, he came around the counter for a closer look. "It's like whoever put it together used a couple of spare parts from someone else's."

"This is all very fascinating," she said impatiently. "But—"

"At first glance your body looks like it belongs to a teenage boy, all arms and legs."

"Thank you very much, Mr. Universe. Have you finished your unsolicited critique of my looks?"

"Almost." His lips curved a little as he skimmed a hand along her jaw. "I love the way you look. I can't figure out why, but I love the way you look, the way you move." He slipped his arms around her, drew her in. "The way you smell."

"This is a novel way to seduce me."

"The way you taste," he continued and skimmed his lips up her throat.

205

"And it's surprisingly effective," she managed between shivers. "But I really wanted you to look at this."

He plucked her up, set her down on the counter, then slid his hand around to cup her bare bottom. "I'm going to make love with you here." He closed his teeth over the nipple that strained against the thin cotton. "Is that all right with you?"

"Yes. Good." Her head fell back. "Wherever."

Satisfied with that, he rubbed his lips over hers. "What do you want me to see?"

"Nothing. Just this."

He caught the coin that slipped through her fingers and puzzled over it. "Spanish? A doubloon, I suppose. Isn't this Margo's?"

"No. Mine. I found it." She drew in a long, shuddering breath, let it out. "God, how do you do that? It's like turning off a switch in my head. I found it," she repeated, struggling to separate her sense from her senses. "Today, on the cliffs. It was just lying there. Seraphina's dowry. You've heard the legend."

"Sure." Intrigued, he turned the coin over in his hand. "The star-crossed lovers. The young Spanish girl left behind in Monterey when the boy she loves goes off to fight the Americans. She hears he's been killed, and in despair she jumps off the cliffs."

He lifted his gaze from the gold to her eyes. "The cliffs, it's said, across from Templeton House."

"She had a dowry," Kate added.

"Right. A chest filled with her bride gift, bestowed by a loving, indulgent father. One variation says she hid it to protect it from the invaders until her lover returned. Another says she took it into the sea with her."

"Well." Kate picked the coin out of his palm. "I go with the first."

"Haven't you and Laura and Margo been combing those cliffs for months?"

"So? Margo found a coin last year, now I've found one."

"At this rate, you'll be rich beyond your wildest dreams

about the middle of the next millennium. You believe in legends?''

"What of it?" Ready to pout, she shifted. "Seraphina existed. There's documentation, and—''

"No." He kissed her gently. "Don't spoil it. It's nice to know you can just believe. It's even nicer to know you want me to believe.''

She studied his face. "Well, do you?''

He took the coin from her and set it down where it gleamed like a promise beside them. "Of course," he said simply.

Chapter Thirteen

Storms blew in, pelting the coast with driving rain, sweeping it with raging winds. Relief that the dangerously dry season might be averted with the unrelenting wet warred with worry over flooding and mudslides.

Kate tried not to take the nasty weather personally. But there was no doubt that it prevented her from intensifying the treasure hunts. Even as the rains abated, the cliffs were too wet for safety.

So they would wait.

There was certainly enough to occupy her. Pretenses' summer season was in full swing. Tourists crammed Cannery Row, jammed the wharf, queued up for a trip through the aquarium. Arcades clattered with the sounds of games and jingling tokens, and families strolled the sidewalks licking ice cream from sugar cones.

The busy carnival atmosphere out in the streets meant business.

Some came to feed the gulls and watch the boats. Some

came to gaze upon the street that Steinbeck had immortalized. Some came to bask in the eternal spring that Monterey offered, or take the sweeping drive along the coast.

Many, many were lured by Margo's clever display windows to come in and browse. And those who browsed often bought.

"I see dollar signs in your eyes again," Laura murmured.

"We're up ten percent from this period last year." Kate turned from her desk and looked at Laura. "By my calculations, Margo should be able to pay off all of her debts by the end of the next quarter. When the holiday shopping season hits, we're actually going to be in the black."

Eyes narrowed, Laura came farther into the room. "I thought we were already in the black."

"Not technically." As she spoke, she continued to crunch figures. "We take a minimum percentage in lieu of salary. We have our pool for resupplying. Then there's operating expenses."

She worked one-handed as she reached for her cup of tea—and tried to pretend it was coffee. "Initially the bulk of our stock was Margo's property, and she took the lion's share of those profits in order to square with her creditors. We're gradually moving into new stock, which is acquired by—"

"Kate, just skip all the details. Are we operating at a loss?"

"We have been, but—"

"I've been taking money every month."

"Of course you have. You have to live. We have to live," Kate amended quickly, seeing the guilt cloud Laura's eyes.

Seeing that it would be necessary to explain and reassure, she set the cup down, resisted the keyboard. "This is how it works, Laura. We take what we need—what we're entitled to, and plow the rest back into the business. Each of us has personal expenses in addition to the shop overhead. Once those are seen to, we reinvest the profit. If there is any."

"And if there isn't, we're in the red, and that means—"

"That means reality. There's nothing unusual in operating at a loss in a new business." Kate bit back a sigh and wondered why she hadn't begun the discussion a different way.

"Forget all the ledgers for a minute. What I'm telling you is good news. We're going to end this calendar year not just eking out a minimal living and paying off old debts. We're going to make a profit. A real profit. That's rare in a business that's barely into its second year. By my projections, we'll have a net gain in the mid five figures."

"So we're okay?" Laura said cautiously.

"Yeah, we're okay." Smiling, Kate ran her fingers over the keys of her computer as if they were adored children. "If the charity auction goes as well as last year, we'll be cooking."

"That's what I came in to talk to you about." Laura hesitated, frowned at the figures on the screen. "We're really all right?"

"If you can't trust your accountant, who can you trust?"

"Right." She had to believe it. "Well, then, you won't have any problem cutting a few checks."

"You've come to the right place." Humming, Kate took the invoices from Laura, and then choked. "What the hell are these?"

"Refreshments." Laura offered a bright, hopeful smile. "Entertainment. Oh, and advertising. All auction-related."

"Christ, we're paying this for mind-numbing chamber music from a bunch of nerds? Why can't we just plug in a CD? I told Margo—"

"Kate, it's a matter of image. And this trio isn't a bunch of nerds. They're very talented." She patted Kate's shoulder, well aware why Margo had suggested that she be the one to pass along the bills. "It's union scale, just like the waitpeople."

Grumbling, Kate flipped open the checkbook. "Margo has to do everything in an ornate and showy fashion."

"That's why we love her. Just think how the cash register's going to sing the week after the auction. All those rich, materialistic customers with large disposable incomes."

"You're trying to sweet-talk me."

"Is it working?"

"Say 'large disposable incomes' again."

211

"Large disposable incomes."

"Okay, I feel better."

"Really? Good." Laura winced, held her breath. "About the fashion show we've set up for December? You agree that's still a good idea?"

"It's a great idea. A well-executed special event will more than pay for itself, and it has the potential of generating new clientele."

"Exactly my thought. Okay, here's my preliminary budget." She kept her eyes squeezed shut as she dropped the figures in Kate's lap. She heard the yelp, and when she opened her eyes, she saw Kate plucking at the back of her shirt.

"What are you doing?"

"I'm trying to pull out the knife you just stuck in my back. Jesus Christ, Laura, we've got the clothes, you've tapped your committees for the models. Why do you need all this money?"

"Decorations, advertising, refreshments. It's all listed. It's negotiable," she said, backing out. "Consider it a wish list. Gotta get back on the floor."

Making noises in her throat, Kate scowled at the door. The trouble was, she decided, both of her partners were too used to being rich to fully appreciate that they no longer were. Or that Pretenses wasn't, she corrected.

Margo had married for love, but she'd married a Templeton, and Templeton meant money.

Laura was a Templeton, and despite being hosed by her exhusband, she would always have access to millions. She just wouldn't take it.

It was up to good old practical Kate, she decided, to keep things on an even keel.

When the door opened again, she didn't bother to turn around. "Don't hassle me, Laura. I swear I'll cut this wish list of yours down until you won't be able to serve anything but Popsicles and club soda"

"Kate." Laura's voice was quiet enough that Kate whipped around in her chair.

"What's wrong? What—"

212

She broke off at the sight of the man standing beside Laura. Fiftyish, she judged, with a hairline beyond what could legitimately be called receding. He had the beginnings of jowls, and bland brown eyes. His suit was neat and inexpensive. Somewhere along the line, he'd punched extra holes in his brown leather belt to accommodate his paunch.

But it was his shoes that tipped her off. She couldn't have said why those shiny black shoes with the double-knotted laces shouted cop.

"Kate, this is Detective Kusack. He wants to talk to you."

She wasn't certain how she managed to get to her feet when she'd stopped feeling her legs. But she was facing him, surprised somehow that their eyes were on a level. "Am I under arrest?"

"No, ma'am. I have a few questions regarding an incident at Bittle and Associates."

He had a voice like gravel bouncing on sandpaper. It reminded her foolishly of Bob Seger's gritty rock and roll. "I think I'd like to call my lawyer."

"Margo's already calling Josh." Laura moved to her side.

"That's your option, Ms. Powell." Kusack poked out his bottom lip as he considered her. "Maybe it would be best all round if he met us at the precinct. If you'll come along with me, I'll try not to take up too much of your time. I can see you're busy."

"It's all right." Kate put a hand on Laura's arm before Laura could step forward. "It's all right. Don't worry. I'll call you."

"I'm coming with you."

"No." With icy fingers, Kate picked up her purse. "I'll call you as soon as I can."

She was taken to an interview room designed to intimidate. Intellectually, she knew that. The plain walls, the scarred center table and uncomfortable chairs, the wide mirror that was obviously two-way glass were all part of a setup to aid the police in getting information from suspects. No matter how

Kate's practical side ordered her not to be affected, her skin crawled.

Because *she* was the suspect.

She had Josh beside her, looking particularly lawyerly in a tailored gray suit and muted striped tie. Kusack folded his hands on the table. Big hands, Kate noted distractedly, adorned with a single thin gold wedding band. He was a nail-biter, she thought, staring with dull fascination at his ragged, painfully short fingernails.

For the space of several heartbeats, there was nothing but humming silence, like the hushed anticipation just before the curtain rose on the first act of a major play. A bubble of hysterical laughter nearly fizzed out of her throat at the image.

Act one, scene one, and she had the starring role.

"Can I get you something, Ms. Powell?" Kusack watched her muscles jerk in reaction to his voice as her gaze flew from his hands to his face. "Coffee? A Coke?"

"No. Nothing."

"Detective Kusack, my client is here, at your request, in the spirit of cooperation." His cultured voice chilly and hard, Josh gave Kate's tense hand a comforting squeeze under the table. "No one wants this matter cleared up more. Ms. Powell is willing to make a statement."

"I appreciate that, Mr. Templeton. Ms. Powell, I'd like it if you'd answer a few questions, so I can get this all straight in my mind." He gave her a kindly, avuncular smile that made her insides quiver. "I'm going to read you your rights. Now that's just procedure, just the way we have to do things."

He recited the words that anyone who had ever watched an episode of a police drama from *Kojak* to *NYPD Blue* knew by rote. She stared at the tape recorder, silently documenting every word, every inflection.

"You understand these rights, Ms. Powell?"

She shifted her eyes, stared into his. The curtain was up, she thought. Damned if she was going to blow it. "Yes, I understand."

"You worked for the accounting firm of Bittle and Associates from . . ." He flipped pages in a small dog-eared note-book, read off dates.

"Yes, they hired me straight out of graduate school."

"Harvard, right? You got to have a lot of smarts to get into Harvard. I see you graduated as a Baker Scholar, too."

"I worked for it."

"Bet you did," he said easily. "What kind of stuff did you do at Bittle?"

"Tax preparation, financial and estate planning. Investment advice. I might work in tandem with a client's broker to build or enhance a portfolio."

Josh lifted a finger. "I want it on record that during my client's employment at this firm she increased business by bringing in accounts. Her record there was not only unblemished, it was superior."

"Uh-huh. How do you go about bringing in accounts, Ms. Powell?"

"Contacts, networking. Recommendations from current accounts."

He took her through the day-to-day business of her work, the questions slowly paced, quietly asked until she began to relax.

He scratched his head, shaking it. "Me, I can't make a damn bit of sense out of all those forms Uncle Sam wants us to fill out. Used to sit down with them every year, all spread out on the kitchen table. With a bottle of Jack to ease the pain." He grinned winningly. "The wife finally had enough of that. Now I take everything up to H & R Block in April and dump it on them."

"That makes you very typical, Detective Kusack."

"They're always changing the rules, aren't they?" He smiled again. "Somebody like you would have to understand rules. And how to get around them."

When Josh objected to the tone of the question, Kate shook her head. "No, I can respond to that. I understand the rules, Detective Kusack. It's my job to recognize what's black and white, and where the shades of gray are. A good accountant uses the system to circumvent the system when possible.''

"It's kind of a game, isn't it?"

"Yes, in a way. But the game has rules, too. I wouldn't have lasted a month at a firm with Bittle's structure and reputation if I hadn't played by those rules. An accountant who doctors tax forms, or cheats the IRS endangers herself and her client. I wasn't raised to cheat.''

"You were raised right here in Monterey, weren't you? You were the ward of Thomas and Susan Templeton.''

"My parents were killed when I was eight. I—''

"Your father had a bit of a financial problem before his death,'' Kusack commented and watched Kate's face go sheet-white.

"Charges brought and never resolved concerning my client's father twenty years ago have no bearing here,'' Josh stated.

"Just background, counselor. And an interesting coincidence.''

"I wasn't aware of my father's problems until recently,'' Kate managed. How had he found out so quickly? she wondered. Why had he looked? "As I said, both my parents were killed when I was a child. I grew up in Templeton House in the Big Sur area.'' She took a quiet breath. "The Templetons didn't consider or treat me as a ward but as a daughter.''

"You know, I'd have figured they'd have taken you into the Templeton organization. A woman with your skills, and they've got all those hotels, the factories.''

"I didn't choose to join the Templeton organization.''

"Now why was that?''

"Because I didn't want to take anything else from them. I wanted to go out on my own. They respected my decision.''

"And the door remained open,'' Josh put in. "Anytime Kate wanted to walk through. Detective, I don't see what this line of questioning has to do with the matter at hand.''

"Just laying a foundation.'' Despite the recorder, he continued to make little notations in his tattered notebook. "Ms.

Powell, what was your salary at Bittle at the time of your termination?''

"A base of fifty-two-five, plus bonus."

"Fifty-two thousand." Nodding, he flipped through his book as if checking facts. "That's quite a come-down for someone who had the run of a place like Templeton House."

"I earned it, and it was enough for my needs." She felt a line of cold sweat drip down her back. "I know how to make money from money. And in an average year, I would add twenty thousand to that base in bonuses."

"Last year you opened a business."

"With my sisters. With Margo and Laura Templeton," Kate qualified.

"It's risky, starting a business." Those bland eyes stayed on hers. "And expensive."

"I can give you all the statistics, all the figures."

"You like to gamble, Ms. Powell."

"No, I don't. Not in the standard sense of Vegas or the track. The odds always favor the house. But I appreciate an intelligent, and cautious, investment risk. And I consider Pretenses to be just that."

"Some businesses need to be fed a lot. Something like this shop of yours, keeping stock, all that overhead."

"My books are clean. You can—"

"Kate." Josh put a hand on her arm in warning.

"No." Furious now, she shook it off. "He's implying that I would take the easy way, because my father did. That I embezzled from Bittle to keep Pretenses afloat, and I'm not having it. We've worked too hard to make the shop run. Especially Margo. I'm not having it, Josh. He's not going to say that the shop's involved." She seared Kusack with one hot glare. "You pick up the books at the shop anytime. You go over them line by line."

"I appreciate the offer, Ms. Powell," Kusack said mildly. He opened a folder, slid papers out. "Do you recognize these forms?"

217

"Of course. That's the 1040 I completed for Sid Sun, and that other one is the altered duplicate."

"That's your signature?"

"Yes, on both copies. And no, I can't explain it."

"And these printouts for computer-generated withdrawals from Bittle's escrow accounts?"

"It's my name, my code."

"Who had access to your office computer?"

"Everyone."

"And to your security code?"

"No one but me, as far as I know."

"You gave it to no one?"

"No."

"You kept it in your head."

"Of course."

Kusack kept his eyes on hers as he leaned forward. "Must be some trick, keeping all kinds of numbers in your head."

"I'm good at it. Most people keep numbers in their heads. Social security, PIN numbers, telephone numbers, dates."

"Me, I have to write everything down. Otherwise I mix it all up. I guess you don't worry about that."

"I don't—"

"Kate." Josh interrupted again, met her impatient glance with a quiet look. "Where do you record the numbers?"

"In my head," she said wearily. "I don't forget. I haven't had to look up the security code in years."

Lips pursed, Kusack examined his ragged nails. "Where would you look it up, if you had to?"

"In my Filofax, but . . ." Her voice trailed off as the impact hit home. "In my Filofax," she repeated. "I have everything in it."

She grabbed her purse, fumbled through it, and took out the thick, leather-bound book. "For backup," she said, opening the book. "Backup's the first rule. Here." She located the page, nearly laughed. "My life in numbers."

Kusack scratched his chin. "You keep that with you."

"I just said it's my life. That's literally true. It's always in my bag."

"Where do you keep your bag—say, during office hours?"

"In my office."

"And you'd carry it around with you. I know my wife never takes two steps without her pocketbook."

"Only if I was leaving the building. Josh." She clutched his hand. "Only if I was leaving the building. Anybody in the firm could have taken the code. Christ, anybody at all." She squeezed her eyes tight. "I should have thought of it before. I just wasn't thinking at all."

"That's still your signature on the forms, Ms. Powell," Kusack reminded her.

"It's a forgery," she snapped and rose to her feet. "You listen to me. Do you think I'd risk everything I worked for, everything I was given, for a lousy seventy-five K? If money was what was important to me, I could have picked up the phone, called my aunt and uncle, called Josh, and they would have given me twice that without a single question. I'm not a thief, and if I were, I sure as hell would cover my tracks better than this. What idiot would use her own code, her own name, leave such a pathetically obvious paper trail?"

"You know, Ms. Powell"—Kusack folded his hands on the table again—"I asked myself that same question. I'll tell you what my take is. The person had to be one of three things: stupid, desperate, or very, very smart."

"I'm very smart."

"That you are, Ms. Powell," Kusack said with a slow nod. "That you are. You're smart enough to know that seventy-five large isn't peanuts. Smart enough to be able to hide it where it couldn't easily be found."

"Detective, my client denies any knowledge of the money in question. The evidence is not just circumstantial but highly questionable. We both know you can't make a case with this, and you've taken up enough of our time."

"I appreciate your cooperation." Kusack tidied the papers and put them back in his file. "Ms. Powell," he continued, as

Josh led her to the door, "one more thing. How'd you break your nose?"

"Excuse me?"

"Your nose," he said with an easy smile. "How'd you break it?"

Baffled, she lifted a hand and rubbed it, felt the familiar angle. "Bottom of the ninth, stretching a double into a three-bagger in a bad imitation of Pete Rose. I cracked it against the fielder's knee."

His teeth flashed. "Safe or out?"

"Safe."

He watched her go, then flipped the file open again and studied the signatures on the forms. Stupid, desperate, or very, very smart, he thought.

Chapter Fourteen

"He doesn't believe me." Reaction set in the minute the door closed behind her. All the anger and righteousness jittered away into fear.

"I'm not so sure of that," Josh murmured and navigated her out of the interviewing area. He could feel her body vibrate through the hand he held to her back. "But what matters is they don't have a case. There isn't enough to take to the DA, and Kusack knows it."

"It does matter." She pressed a hand to her churning stomach. Not the ulcer this time, she hoped. But that was little comfort when the alternative diagnosis was shame and fear. "It matters what he thinks, what Bittle thinks, what everyone thinks. However much I don't want it to, it matters."

"Listen to me." He turned her in the corridor to face him, kept his hands on her shoulders. "You did fine in there. Better than fine. It might not have been the exact route I would have recommended as your attorney, but it was effective. The records in your Filofax open up a whole new area of investigation. Now consider who led you to that."

"You did." When he shook his head, she drew her brows together. Because Josh expected it, she ordered herself to think clearly. "He did. Kusack did. He wanted me to tell him I had the code written down somewhere."

"Somewhere where it could be accessed." Josh's hands gentled on her shoulders. "Now I want you to put this aside. I mean it, Kate," he continued even as she opened her mouth to protest. "Let Kusack do his job, let me do mine. You have people behind you. That's something I don't want you to forget again."

"I'm scared." She pressed her lips together, wanting her voice to be level even in the admission. "The only time I wasn't scared was when he made me mad. Now I'm scared all over again. Why did he bring up my father, Josh? How did he know about it? What reason would he have for looking that far into my background?"

"I don't know. I'm going to find out."

"They have to know at Bittle." Despair was a stone sinking in her gut. "If Kusack knows, so do the partners. Maybe they knew about it before, and that's why—"

"Kate, stop."

"But what if they never find out who did it? If they don't find out, then I'm always going to—"

"I said stop. We will find out. That's a promise—not from your lawyer but from your big brother." He drew her close, kissed the top of her head, then spotted Byron striding down the hall. He recognized barely controlled fury when he saw it and decided it was just what Kate needed to take her mind off the interview.

"By, good timing. You'll run Kate home, won't you?"

She spun around, confused and embarrassed. "What are you doing here?"

"Laura tracked me down." He shot a look at Josh that clearly stated they would talk later and began to usher Kate down the hall. "Let's get out of here."

222

"I need to go back to the shop. Margo's alone."

"Margo can handle herself." He towed her down the steps, past the desk, and outside, where the sun was blinding bright. "Are you all right?"

"Yeah. A little turned around inside, but okay."

He'd driven his 'Vette, the sleek, streamlined two-seater in muscle-car black. Settling inside a thirty-year-old car only made the entire day all the more surreal.

"You didn't have to come all the way down here."

"Obviously." Despising the impotency, he gunned the engine viciously. "You'd have called if you'd wanted my help. Now you're stuck with it."

"There wasn't anything you could do," she began and winced at the molten look he shot her before he cruised out of the parking lot. "They didn't charge me with anything."

"Well, it's our lucky day, isn't it?" He wanted to drive. He wanted to drive fast to dissipate some of the bubbling anger before it boiled over and burned them both. To cancel any possibility of conversation, he flicked up the volume on the car stereo, and Eric Clapton's angry guitar licks scorched the air.

Perfect, Kate thought, and shut her eyes. Mean music, a muscle car and southern-fried temper. She told herself the migraine brewing and the highly possible visit by her old pal Mr. Ulcer were enough to worry about.

She found her sunglasses in her purse and put them on before dry-swallowing medication. Through the tinted lenses, the light seemed calmer, kinder. The wind whipped, cooling her hot cheeks. She had only to lay her head back, raise her face, to see the sky.

Byron said nothing, but sent the car slashing up Highway 1 like a bright black sword cleaving through sea and rock. It tore through a low-lying cloud, burst out of the thin vapor, and roared back into the flash of sun.

He'd been battling feelings of impotence and hot fury since Laura's call. *The police took Kate in for questioning. We don't know what they're going to do. A detective came to the shop, and he took her.*

The jingle of fear in Laura's usually calm voice had set off a violent chain reaction in him. The fear had been fueled by hurt. Kate hadn't called him.

He'd imagined her alone—it hadn't mattered that Laura had assured him Josh was with her. He'd envisioned her alone, frightened, at the mercy of accusations. His overworked imagination had pictured her handcuffed and led off in chains.

And there was nothing he could do but wait.

Now she was sitting beside him, her eyes shielded by dark glasses that made her skin all the more pale in contrast. Her hands were clasped in her lap, deceptively still until you noted the knuckles were white. And she had told him there was no need for him.

He didn't question the impulse, but swung to the side of the road. At the Templeton House cliffs where she had once wept on his shoulder.

She opened her eyes. It didn't surprise her in the least that he had stopped there, there at a spot of both peace and drama. Before she could reach for the door handle, he was leaning across her to jerk open the door himself.

An old habit, she decided. With all that temper swirling around in him, the gesture couldn't be considered courtly.

In silence they walked to the cliffs.

"Why didn't you call me?" He hadn't meant to ask that first, but it popped out of his mouth.

"I didn't think of it."

He whirled on her so quickly, so unexpectedly, that she stumbled back a step, crushed a scattering of tiny white wildflowers underfoot. "No, you wouldn't. Just where the hell am I on that agenda of yours, Katherine?"

"I don't know what you mean. I didn't think of it because—"

"Because you don't need anyone but Kate," he shot back. "Because you don't want to need anyone who might upset

224

that profit-and-loss ledger in your head. I wouldn't have been of any practical use, so why bother?''

''That's not true.''

How could she deal with an argument now? she wondered. How could she handle that brilliant fury in his eyes? She had a terrible urge to simply press her hands to her ears, squeeze her eyes shut so that she could neither see nor hear. So she could just be alone in the dark.

''I don't understand why you're so angry with me, but I just don't have the energy to fight with you now.''

He gripped her arm before she could turn away. ''Good. Then you can just listen. Try to imagine what it was like to be told by someone else that the police had taken you in. To visualize what might be happening to you, what you were going through, and to be powerless to change it.''

''That's just it. There wasn't anything you could do.''

''I could have been there.'' He shouted over the wind that raked through his hair like wild fingers. ''I could have been there for you. You could have known there was someone who cared there for you. But you didn't even think of it.''

''Damn it, Byron, I couldn't think at all.'' She jerked away, walked along the cliff path. Even a few steps would distance her from the upheaval of emotion, the avalanche, the flood of it, before she broke into pieces. ''It was like being shut down, or frozen up. I was too scared to think. It wasn't personal.''

''I take it very personally. We have a relationship, Kate.'' He waited while she slowly turned around, watching him through eyes guarded by dark glasses. With some effort, he drew in his temper and spoke with measured calm. ''I thought I made it clear what that entails for me. If you can't accept the basic terms of a relationship with me, then we're wasting our time.''

She hadn't thought anything could squeeze past the pain in her head, the ache in her stomach, the sizzle of shame in her blood. But she hadn't counted on despair. Somehow despair always made room for itself.

Her eyes burned as she looked at him, standing in the sun

and wind. "Well, you dumping me certainly puts a cap on the day."

She started past him with some idea of running up to Templeton House, getting inside and shutting everything else out.

"Goddamn it." He spun her around, crushing his mouth to hers in a kiss that tasted of bitter frustration. "How can you be so hardheaded?" He shook her, then kissed her again until she wondered why her overtaxed brain didn't simply implode. "Can't you see anything unless it's in a straight line?"

"I'm tired." She hated, resented, the shakiness of her voice. "I'm humiliated. I'm scared. Just leave me alone."

"I'd like nothing better than to be able to leave you alone. Just walk away and chalk it up to a bad bet."

He pulled off her sunglasses, stuck them in his pocket. He'd wanted to see her eyes, and now he recognized swirling in them the same anger and hurt that twisted in him. "Do you think I need the turmoil and complications you've brought into my life? Do you actually think I'd tolerate all that because we're good in bed?"

"You don't have to tolerate it." She fisted her hands on his chest. "You don't have to tolerate any of it."

"Damn right I don't. But I am tolerating it because I think I'm in love with you."

She'd have been less surprised if he'd simply hauled her up and tossed her over the cliff. In an attempt to keep her reeling head in place, she pressed a hand to her temple.

"Hard to come up with a response?" His voice was as sharp and smooth as a newly oiled sword. "That's not surprising. Emotions don't add up in neat columns, do they?"

"I don't know what I'm supposed to say to you. This isn't fair."

"It's not about fair. And at the moment I don't like the situation any more than you do. You're a far cry from the girl of my dreams, Katherine."

That had her eyes clearing. "Now I know what to say. Go to hell."

"Unimaginative," he decided. "Now get this into that computer-chip brain of yours." He pulled her up onto her toes until their eyes were level. "I don't like to make mistakes any more than you do, so I'm going to take the time to figure out exactly how I feel about you. If I decide you're what I want, then you're what I'll have."

Her eyes narrowed, glinting with dangerous lights. "How incredibly romantic."

His lips curved in quick and genuine humor. "I'll give you romance, Kate, and plenty of it."

"You can take your warped concept of romance and—"

He cut her off with a soft, quiet kiss. "I was worried about you," he murmured. "I was afraid for you. And you hurt me because you didn't turn to me."

"I didn't mean to—" She snapped back before her bones could melt. "You're twisting this around. You're trying to confuse me." Surrendering to pain, she shut her eyes. "Oh, God, my head aches."

"I know. I can see it." As a parent might soothe a child, he touched his lips to her left temple, then her right. "Let's sit down." He eased her down onto a rock, then stood behind her to massage the tense muscles of her neck and shoulders. "I want to take care of you, Kate."

"I don't want to be taken care of."

"I know." Over her head he watched the sea gleam as the sun burned through a cloud and streamed down. She couldn't help that, he supposed, any more than he could help his own need to protect and defend. "We'll have to find an area of compromise there. You matter to me."

"I know. You matter to me, too, but—"

"That's a nice place to stop," he told her. "I'm asking you to think of me. And to accept that you can turn to me. For the little things—and for the big ones. Can you handle that much?"

"I can try." She wanted to believe it was the medication finally kicking in that was making the pain slide away. But a part of her, the part she'd long considered foolish, thought it was the sea and the cliffs. And him. "Byron, I didn't mean to hurt you. I hate hurting people I care about. It's the worst thing for me."

"I know." He pressed his thumbs to the base of her neck, searching out stubborn knots of tension. And smiled when she leaned back against him.

"When I saw you in the police station, I was embarrassed."

"I know that too."

"Well, it's nice to be so transparent."

"I know where to look in you. It seems to be some kind of innate skill. It's one of the reasons I think I may be in love with you." He felt the tension leap back into her muscles. "Relax," he suggested. "We may both learn to live with it."

"My life is, to put it mildly, in upheaval."

She stared straight ahead to the horizon. The sky always met the sea, she mused, no matter how distant. But people didn't always, couldn't always find that joining point.

"I also know my own limitations," she continued. "I'm not ready for that kind of leap."

"I'm not sure I am myself. But if I take it, I'm pulling you with me." He came around the rock to sit beside her. "I'm very good at handling complications, Kate. I'll handle you." When she opened her mouth, he pressed his fingers to it. "No you don't. You'll tense up again. You're just going to say you won't be handled, then I'll have to say something about how if you let someone take part of the control now and again you wouldn't have so many headaches. Then we'd just go around until one of us gets pissed off again."

She frowned at him. "I don't like the way you fight."

"It always drove my sisters crazy. Suellen used to say I used logic like a left jab."

"You've got a sister named Suellen?"

He raised an eyebrow. "From *Gone With the Wind*. My mother chose all our names from literature. Got a problem with that?"

"No." She plucked at a speck of lint on her skirt. "It just sounds so southern."

He chuckled, wondering if she realized she made the South

sound like another planet. "Honey, we *are* southern. Suellen, Charlotte as in Brontë, Meg from *Little Women*."

"And Byron, as in Lord."

"Exactly."

"You don't have the poetic pallor or the clubfoot, but you do sort of have the dreamy good looks."

"Flattery." He kissed her lightly in response. "I guess you're feeling better."

"I guess I am."

"So." He draped an arm over her shoulders. "How was your day?"

With a weak laugh, she turned her face, nuzzled it against the curve of his neck. "It sucked. It really, really sucked."

"Want to talk about it?"

"Maybe." It wasn't really so hard to lean against a strong shoulder, she decided, if she just concentrated. "I should call Laura. I told her I would."

"Josh will tell her you're with me. She won't worry."

"She'll worry whether I call or not. Laura worries about everyone." Kate let the silence soothe a moment, then began with Kusack's appearance at the shop.

Byron didn't interrupt, but listened, assessed, and considered.

"I don't think he believed me. The way he kept watching me, with this kind of cat patience, you know? When he mentioned my father, my brain just froze up. I knew I should have been prepared for it. Right from the start of this I knew that would be the worst and I should have been prepared. But I wasn't."

"It hurt you," Byron murmured. "More than any of the rest."

"Yes." She reached back, gripped his hand, baffled and relieved that he would understand so easily. "It hurt that this stranger, this cop, should damage the man I'm trying to remember. The one who used to spin ridiculous dreams for me, who I'm trying to believe only wanted the best for me. And

I can't defend him, Byron, because what he did is against everything I believe in.''

"That doesn't mean you didn't love your father and aren't entitled to remember the best parts of him."

"I'm working on that," she murmured. "The problem is I have to stay focused on what's happening now. It's harder than I imagined. When Kusack brought out the forms, I couldn't explain why they both had my signature. But Josh seemed to think it went well, especially that business with the security code."

"Electronic thievery rolled in right along with the microchip. You said the siphoning off started about a year and a half ago. Who's had access to your computer during that time period?"

"Dozens of people." Isn't that why it's all so hopeless? she thought. "There's not a big turnover at Bittle. It's a good firm."

"So who needs money, who's smart, and who would point the finger at you?"

"Who doesn't need money?" she countered, irritated because her mind was refusing to travel a logical path. "Bittle hires smart, and I don't know anyone in the firm who has it in for me personally."

"Maybe it wasn't personal so much as convenient. A cautious amount of money," he murmured. "Like a test—or a way to offset small, annoying debts. And the timing, Kate, haven't you considered the timing?"

"I can't follow you."

"Why now, why you? Is it just a coincidence that you should find out about your father at essentially the same time this skimming was noticed?"

"What else could it be?"

"Maybe someone else found out and used it."

"I didn't tell anyone."

"What did you do? The day you found out, what did you do?"

"I sat there at my desk, reeling. I didn't want to believe it, so I checked."

He would have banked on it. "How?"

"I accessed the library back in New Hampshire, ordered faxes of newspaper articles, contacted the lawyer who handled the details. I hired a detective."

He considered. Every one of those steps generated data. Phone records, computer records, paper trail. "And noted the data in your Filofax."

"Well, yes, the names and phone numbers, but—"

"And the transmissions to and from New Hampshire were on your computer?"

"I—" She began to see, began to feel ill all over again. "Yes. The records of faxes sent and received. If someone wanted to look. But still, they'd have to have my password, and—"

"Which is noted in your Filofax," he finished. "Who would be the last person questioned coming out of your office if you weren't there?"

"Any one of the partners, I suppose. One of the executive assistants." She shrugged, unsurprised to find that her shoulders were tightening up again. "Hell, any of the other accountants on that floor. No one would think twice about seeing an associate breeze out of another associate's office."

"Then we'll concentrate on those. The third Bittle you talked about. Who is it . . . Marty?"

"Marty wouldn't embezzle from his own company. That's ludicrous."

"We'll see. Meanwhile, how do you think he'd react if you asked him to get you copies of the forms in question?"

"I don't know."

"Why don't we find out?"

An hour later, Kate hung up the phone in Byron's kitchen. "I should have known he'd come through. He'll make copies as soon as he's able to and bring them to you at the hotel." She worked up a smile. "It's like a little intrigue. I'm surprised he didn't ask for passwords. He's actually enjoying it."

"Our man on the inside."

"I should have thought of this angle right from the beginning. Now I can add feeling stupid to the rest of it."

"Emotions tend to cloud logic," he told her. "Otherwise I might have hit on it earlier myself."

"Well . . ." She wasn't sure she was ready to deal with that line of thought just now. "Anyway, Marty told me that they decided to turn it over to the police after my showdown the other day. His father's not happy about it, but the vote carried."

"Do you regret facing up to them?"

"No, but there's going to be gossip now. Plenty of it." Trying to keep it light, she smiled at him. "How do you feel about having an alleged embezzler of dubious lineage for a lover?"

"I think that requires a test." He gathered her close, skimming his hands up her back and into her hair in the way she'd come to anticipate.

Her mouth lifted to his, opened for his. "I guess this means you're not going back to work this afternoon."

"Good guess." His mouth stayed busy as he circled her out of the kitchen.

"Where are we going? Haven't I already mentioned all this floor you have around here?"

He chuckled against her throat. "I haven't shown you my new sofa."

"Oh." She let him ease her back on the generous cushions. "It's very nice," she murmured as his weight pressed her deeper into them. "Long." His fingers parted her blouse, exposing her as she arched to his touch. "Soft."

"We so rarely make it to the bedroom." He lowered his head, nipped lightly at her breasts. "I wanted something . . . accommodating . . . on the main level."

"Very considerate of you." She gasped when his mouth closed over her, sucked her in.

It was so easy to let the heat take her, to spin her mind

232

away, to follow the demands of her own body. For pleasure. For sensation. For tastes and textures. She tugged his tie loose when his mouth sought hers again, loosened the buttons that prevented flesh from meeting flesh.

But he wouldn't let her hurry, and her impatience drained away until she was steeped and savoring.

Strong, broad shoulders, hair glorious gold at the tips, the subtle creases in his cheeks. That long, rippled torso. She luxuriated in the feel of those smooth hands gliding over her, lingering here, pressing there, then skillfully bringing her to a long, shimmering orgasm that poured through her system like warmed wine.

He thought it stunning to watch her, the flickers of pleasure and tension and release that played over her face. Arousal had blood rising to her cheeks, caused her eyes to darken and glow like rich, aged brandy. The body beneath his arched and flowed, quivered and grew erotically damp.

The taste of soap and salt between her breasts enchanted him. The feel of those narrow, restless hands enjoying his own flesh delighted him, darkly. The need to be in her, to join body to body and bury himself deep was overpowering.

He filled her, shuddering when those exotically female muscles clutched around him. Yet it wasn't enough.

He pulled her up until her arms were wrapped around his neck, her legs around his waist. With his mouth he swallowed each of the moans that trembled from her throat, then raced his lips over that long white column where a pulse beat like fury.

She panted out his name, blinded by the single primal urge to reach the summit. Her hips pumped, jackhammer quick, as the craving grew maddening, the pleasure unbearable. She was willing to beg, if only the words would come, but instead she sank her teeth into his shoulder.

It flashed through her like an overstoked furnace, hot and violent. Stunned and helpless, she clung, then felt the magic pulse between them as he poured himself into her.

*　　*　　*

233

The phone awakened her an hour later. Disoriented, Kate fumbled for the receiver before she remembered she wasn't home. "Yes, hello."

"Oh. I'm sorry. I must have the wrong number. I'm calling Byron De Witt's residence."

Dazed, Kate stared around the room. The antique oak chest of drawers, the warm green walls and white curtains, the clever watercolor seascapes. A thriving ornamental lemon tree in a glazed pot in front of the window. And the lulling, ceaseless sound of the sea.

Byron's bedroom.

"Ah . . ." She sat up, rubbing a hand over her face. Cool ivory sheets slipped down to her waist. "This is Mr. De Witt's residence."

"Oh, I didn't realize he'd gotten a housekeeper already. I expect he's at work. I was just going to leave a message on the machine for him. Tell him Lottie called, won't you, honey? He can reach me anytime this evening. He's got the number. 'Bye now.''

Before Kate was fully awake, she was staring at the receiver and listening to the rude buzz of a dial tone.

Housekeeper? Lottie? He's got the number? Well, fuck.

She slammed down the phone and scrambled up. The scent of him was still on her skin, and he was getting calls from some bimbo named Lottie. Typical, she decided, and looked around for her clothes. Which were, she recalled, downstairs where he'd left them when he carried her up to bed. Ordered her to take a nap. And she'd been so softened by lovemaking that she meekly obeyed.

Hadn't she told herself from the start that men like him were all the same? The better-looking they were, the more charming they were, the bigger scum they were. Men who looked like Byron had women crawling all over them every day of the week.

And he'd said he thought he loved her. What a crock. Energized with righteous fury, she marched downstairs and snatched up her clothes. Scum. Swine. Slime. Ignoring her hose, she struggled into skirt and blouse, fumbling with her buttons as he came through the deck door with the dogs at his heels.

"Thought you'd still be sleeping."

She eyed him narrowly. "I bet you did."

"I took the dogs for a run on the beach. We should go down later. The storm's brought some nice shells in." He walked into the kitchen as he spoke. Swaggering like a gunslinger, she followed. "Want a beer?" He twisted the cap off one, guzzled. As he lowered the bottle, he caught the glint of steel in her eyes. "Problem?"

"Problem? No, no problem at all." Before she could stop herself she'd bunched up her fist and plowed it into his belly. It was like hitting rock. "Be sure when you see Lottie you tell her I'm not your goddamn housekeeper."

He rubbed his belly more in surprise than discomfort. "Huh?"

"Oh, brilliant. You always have such a sharp riposte, De Witt. How dare you? How dare you say the things you said to me, do the things you did, and have some . . . some tramp named Lottie on the side?"

It wasn't quite clear, but he thought he was starting to catch up. "Lottie called?" he ventured.

She made the same sound in her throat that he'd heard once or twice before. As much for her sake as his own, he held up a hand and backed off. "You're going to hurt yourself if you hit me again."

Her gaze shifted, lingered on the kitchen block filled with black-handled knives. He didn't believe it, not for an instant. But he stepped between her and the sharp implements.

"Now, I'm going to guess that the phone woke you up, and it was Lottie. And Lottie, by the way, is not a tramp."

"I say she is, and either way, you're still a lying, two-timing scum. How long did you expect to get away with telling her I was your housekeeper? And just what were you going to tell me she was?"

He studied his beer for a moment, tried to keep the gleam

out of his eyes when they met hers. "My sister."

"Oh, very original. I'm out of here."

"Not so fast." It wasn't much of a challenge to grab her one-armed around the waist and haul her to a chair. She was kicking, swinging, but he managed it easily. "Lottie," he said as he shoved her in place again, "*is* my sister."

"You don't have a sister named Lottie," she fired back. "You idiot, you told me your sisters' names just a few hours ago. Suellen, Meg, and—"

"Charlotte," he finished, and didn't bother to conceal the smugness. "Lottie. She's a pediatrician, married, three kids. And she has just the kind of warped sense of humor that might make her appreciate having my lover call her a tramp." He watched the embarrassed blush stain Kate's cheek. "Want that beer now?"

"No." Voice strained, pride forfeited, she got to her feet. "I apologize. I don't normally jump to conclusions. It's been a difficult and emotional day."

"Uh-huh."

Damn him. "I was asleep when she called, and she never gave me a chance to say anything."

"That's Lottie."

"And I just assumed. I was asleep," she said, furious. "Disoriented. I was—"

"Jealous," he finished and backed her up against the refrigerator. "That's okay. I like it—to a point."

"I don't like it, to any point. I'm sorry I hit you."

"You're going to have to work on those arms if you want to have any impact." He put a hand under her chin to lift it. "You wouldn't have gone for the knives, would you?"

"Of course not." She slanted her gaze toward them, shrugged. "Probably not."

He let his hand drop, took another swig of beer. "Honey, you terrify me."

"I'm sorry, really. There's no excuse for behaving that way. It was knee-jerk." She pressed her hands together. Confession

236

always hurt. "I was involved with someone a couple of years ago. I don't get involved easily, and he wasn't what you could term the faithful type."

"Did you love him?"

"No, but I trusted him."

He nodded, set the beer aside. "And trust is more fragile than love." He cupped her face in his hands. "You can trust me, Kate." He pressed his lips to her brow, then eased back with a grin on his face. "I would never risk having you slice off any important appendages with a chef's knife."

Feeling both soothed and foolish, she settled into his arms. "I would never have used it." Her lips curved against his. "Probably."

Chapter Fifteen

"This is so incredibly dumb." Naked, Kate fidgeted and blew the bangs out of her eyes. "I feel like an idiot."

"Leave your hair alone," Margo ordered. "I worked too hard on it to have you screw it up. And stop gnawing on your lip."

"I hate wearing lipstick. Why won't you let me see my face?" Kate craned her neck, but Margo had draped the mirror in the wardrobe room. "I look like a clown, don't I? You made me look like a clown."

"Actually, it's more like a twenty-dollar hooker, but it's such a nice look for you. Hold still, damn it, so I can get you into this thing."

Suffering mightily, Kate lifted her arms as Margo hooked her into what seemed to be some instrument of medieval torture. "Why are you doing this to me, Margo? I cut the check for your dippy string trio, didn't I? I went along with the truffles—even though they're snuffed out by pigs and hideously expensive."

239

Her face set like a general leading troops into battle, Margo adjusted the bustier. "You agreed to follow my guidance for your image tonight. The Annual Reception and Charity Auction is Pretenses' most important event. Now stop bitching."

"Stop playing with my tits."

"Oh, but I love them so. There." Margo stepped back, then nodded in satisfaction. "I didn't have much to work with, but . . ."

"Keep it up, Miss D Cup," Kate grumbled, then looked down and goggled. "Jesus, where did they come from?"

"Amazing, isn't it? In the right harness, those puppies just rise."

"I have breasts." Stunned, Kate patted the swell rising above black satin and lace. "And cleavage."

"It's all a matter of proper positioning and making the most of what we have. Even when it's next to nothing."

"Shut up." Grinning, Kate slicked her hands down her torso. "Look, Ma. I'm a girl."

"You ain't seen nothing yet. Put this on." Margo tossed her a thin swatch of stretchy lace.

Kate studied the garter belt, tugged it, snorted. "You're kidding."

"I'm not putting it on for you." Margo patted the bulge under her sparkling silver tunic. "At seven months and counting, bending over isn't as easy as it used to be."

"I feel like I'm in dress rehearsal for a porn flick." But after a struggle, Kate snapped the garter belt into place. "It's a little hard to breathe."

"Hose," Margo ordered. "You'd better sit down to put them on." With her hands on her hips, Margo supervised the production. "Not so fast, you'll snag. Those aren't your industrial-strength panty hose."

Brows beetled, Kate flicked up a glance. "Do you have to watch me?"

"Yes. Where's Laura?" Margo wondered and began to pace. "She should be here. And if the musicians don't show

240

up in the next ten minutes, they won't have time to set up before the guests start to arrive.''

''Everything'll be fine.'' Stalling, Kate smoothed her hose up her legs. ''You know, Margo, I really do think it would be best if I kept sort of a low profile tonight. With this cloud over my head, it makes things awkward.''

''Chicken.''

Kate's head shot up. ''I am not a chicken. I'm a scandal.''

''And last year I was the scandal.'' Margo shrugged her shoulders. ''Maybe we can work something out so that Laura can fill the role next year.''

''It's not funny.''

''Nobody understands that better than I do.'' Margo laid a hand on Kate's flushed cheek. ''Nobody understands how scared you are right now better than I do.''

''I guess not.'' Comforted, Kate turned her face to Margo's palm. ''It's just that it's dragging on for so long. I keep expecting that Kusack character to show up and cart me off in chains. It's not enough that they can't prove I did it if I can't prove I didn't.''

''I'm not going to say you'll get through it. That's not enough either. But no one who knows you believes it. And didn't you say Byron had some sort of angle to work on?''

''He didn't really explain.'' She moved her shoulder, tugged at the elastic strap on the lacy belt. ''Just mumbled the equivalent of me not worrying my pretty head over it. I really hate that.''

''Men like to play white knight, Kate. It doesn't hurt to let them do that now and again.''

''It's been weeks since Marty got the copies to us. I've gone over them all, line by line, but . . .'' She trailed off. ''Well, we've all been pretty busy, and I haven't been jolted out of sleep by the sound of bullhorns telling me they've got me surrounded.''

''Don't worry. When that happens we won't let them take you alive. If they raid the shop tonight, we'll have Byron help you escape in one of his macho cars.''

"If he makes it at all. He had to fly down to L.A. this morning. I thought I told you."

"He'll be back in time."

"He couldn't say for sure." And Kate refused to pout over it. "It doesn't matter."

"You're crazy about him."

"I am not. We have a very mature, mutually satisfying relationship." Distracted, she tugged on the strap again. "How do these silly things work?"

"God. Let me." Huffing, Margo knelt down and demonstrated how to hook the hose.

"I beg your pardon." Laura paused at the doorway, stuck her tongue in her cheek. "I seem to be *de trop*. Perhaps there's something you two would like to share with me."

"Another comedienne." Kate looked down at the top of Margo's head and giggled. "Christ, now here's a scandal. Pregnant former sex symbol and suspected embezzler celebrate their alternative lifestyle."

"Could I just go get my camera?" Laura asked.

"Done." Margo proclaimed, then held up a hand. "Stop snickering, Laura, and help me up."

"Sorry." As she hauled Margo to her feet, Laura's gaze fell on Kate. Her friend was sitting in an elegant Queen Anne chair wearing a black bustier with matching lacy garter belt and sheer black stockings. "Why, Kate, you look so . . . different."

"I have tits," she stated and rose. "Margo gave them to me."

"What are friends for? You might want to finish dressing, unless that's your outfit for this evening. The musicians pulled up behind me."

"Terrific. Laura, it's the off-the-shoulder floor-length bronze." Margo gestured vaguely as she started into the main showroom. "I'll be back."

"Why does she think I need to be dressed? I've been dressing myself for several years now."

"Let her fuss." Laura took down the gown Margo had chosen. "It helps keep her from being nervous about tonight. And . . ." Laura pursed her lips as she studied the dress. "She's got a hell of an eye. This is going to look great on you."

"I hate all this." Sighing lustily, Kate stepped into the gown. "I mean, it's okay for her, she loves it. And you— you'd look elegant in tinfoil. I'd never be able to wear what you've got on. What is that, anyway?"

"Ancient," Laura said, dismissing her smartly tailored copper-toned evening suit. "I'm getting one last wear out of it before I put it into stock. There, all hooked in. Stand back, let me see."

"I don't look stupid, do I? My arms aren't bad now. I mean, my biceps are sort of happening. I've been working on the delts, too. Bony shoulders aren't very attractive."

"You look beautiful."

"I don't really care, but I don't like looking stupid."

"Okay, we're right on schedule," Margo announced as she hurried back in. With one hand she supported her belly and tried to ignore the fact that the baby seemed determined to settle directly on her bladder. She tilted her head, took a long, narrowed-eyed study of her creation, and nodded. "Good, really good. Now a few finishing touches."

"Oh, listen."

"Oh, Mommy, do I have to wear that exquisite jeweled collar?" Margo whined as she lifted it from the box. "Oh, please, not those gorgeous earrings too."

Kate rolled her eyes as Margo decorated her. "Can you imagine what she's going to do to that kid? The minute it pops out she's going to have it swaddled in Armani and accessorized."

"Ungrateful brat." Margo took a purse atomizer out of her pocket and spritzed before Kate could evade.

"You know I hate that."

"Why else would I do it? Turn around and—drum roll, please." With a flourish, Margo tugged the draping off the mirror.

"Holy shit." Her mouth agape, Kate stared at the reflection. There was enough of Kate to recognize, she thought, dazed. But where had those exotic eyes come from, and that unquestionably erotic mouth? The figure, an actual figure, draped in shimmering bronze that made all that exposed skin seem polished.

She cleared her throat, turned, turned again. "I look good," she managed.

"A grilled cheese sandwich looks good," Margo corrected. "Baby, you look dangerous."

"I kind of do." Kate grinned and watched that siren's mouth move smugly. "Damn, I hope Byron gets here. Wait till he gets a load of me."

He was doing his best to get there. The trip to L.A. had been inconvenient but necessary. Under normal circumstances, he would have arranged to make a full swing of it, spot-checking the hotels and resorts in Santa Barbara, San Diego, San Francisco. It was important, he knew, for the staff at every Templeton hotel to feel that personal connection with the home base.

Josh handled the factories, the vineyards and orchards, the plants, and continued to spot-check the international branches. But California was Byron's responsibility. He never took responsibility lightly.

And there were still ruffled feathers to be smoothed from Peter Ridgeway's reign, which by all accounts had been as cold as it had been efficient.

He knew what was expected of him—the personal touch that Templeton was founded and thrived on. The memory for names and faces and details.

Even as he jetted back, Byron dictated a raft of memos to his assistant, fired off countless faxes, and completed one final meeting via air phone.

Now he was home, and late, but he'd anticipated that. With the finesse of long habit, he quickly fastened the studs on his tuxedo shirt. Maybe he should call Kate at the shop and tell her he was on his way. A glance at his watch told him the reception was into its second hour. She'd be busy.

Would she miss him?

He wanted her to. He wanted to imagine her looking toward the door whenever it opened. And hoping. He wanted her to be thinking of him, wishing he were there so they could share some comment or observation about the other guests. The way couples always did.

He looked forward to seeing that speculation in her eyes when she studied him. That look of hers that so clearly said, *What are you doing here, De Witt? What's going on between us? And why?*

She would continually march along looking for the practical answer, the rational one. And he would cruise on the emotional.

It made, he decided as he adjusted his black tie, for a good mix.

He was willing to wait for her to come to the same conclusion. At least for a little while. She needed to resolve this crisis, put the whole ugly business behind her. He intended to help her. And he could wait for that before looking toward the future.

When the phone beside the bed rang, he considered letting the machine take it. Family or work, he supposed, and either of those could do without him for a couple of hours. Then again, Suellen was expecting her first grandchild, and . . .

"Hell." He snapped up the phone. "De Witt."

He listened, questioned, verified. And with a grim smile on his face, hung up. It appeared he had a stop to make before the party.

Kusack was still at his desk. It was his wife's bridge night and her turn to host the evening. He preferred the sloppy meatball sandwich and lukewarm cream soda at his desk to the tiny lady treats being served at Chez Kusack. He definitely preferred the smell of stale coffee, the headachy ringing of phones, and the incessant bickering and complaining of his colleagues to the cloying perfumes, the giggles and gossip of the ladies' bridge club.

There was always paperwork to see to. Though it would have earned him sneers to admit it, he enjoyed paperwork and plowed through it like a St. Bernard through a blizzard. Slow and steady.

He liked the tangibility of it, even the foolish convoluted policespeak so necessary to any official report. He'd made the adjustment to computers more smoothly than many cops his age. To Kusack a keyboard was a keyboard, and he had used what he called the Bible method of typing—seek and ye shall find—all of his professional life.

It never failed him.

He was tapping on keys, grinning to himself as the letters popped onto his screen when a man in a tuxedo interrupted him.

"Detective Kusack?"

"Yeah." Kusack sat back, skimmed his cop's eyes over the suit. No rental job, he deduced. Tailor-made and very pricey. "It ain't prom night, and you're too old anyhow. What can I do for you?"

"I'm Byron De Witt. I'm here regarding Katherine Powell."

Kusack grunted, picked up his can of soda. "I thought her lawyer's name was Templeton."

"I'm not her lawyer, I'm her . . . friend."

"Uh-huh. Well, friend, I can't discuss Ms. Powell's business with anybody who walks in here. No matter how nice they dress."

"Kate didn't mention how gracious you were. May I?"

"Make yourself at home," Kusack said sourly. He wanted the monotony of his paperwork, not chitchat with Prince Charming. "Underpaid public servants are always at your disposal."

"It won't take long. I have new evidence that I believe weighs in Ms. Powell's favor. Are you interested, Kusack, or shall I wait until you finish your dinner?"

246

Kusack ran his tongue around his teeth and eyed the second half of his meatball sub. "Information is always welcome, Mr. De Witt, and I'm here to serve." At least until the bridge club clears out. "What is it you think you have?"

"I obtained copies of the documents in question."

"Did you?" Kusack's bland eyes narrowed. "Did you really? And how did you do that?"

"Without breaking any laws, detective. Once the copies were in my possession, I did what it seems to me, in my muddled civilian capacity, should have been done at the outset. I sent them to a handwriting expert."

Leaning back, Kusack picked up what remained of his dinner, used his free hand to motion Byron to continue.

"I just received my expert's report, via phone. I had him fax it to me." Byron took the sheet out of his inside pocket, unfolded it, and laid it on Kusack's desk.

"Fitzgerald," Kusack said with his mouth full. "Good man. Considered tops in his field."

So Josh had said, Byron thought. "He's been used for over a decade by both prosecutors and defense attorneys."

"Mostly for the defense—rich defense," said Kusack. He caught the whiff of Templeton influence. "Costs a goddamn fortune."

And has a very full schedule, Byron thought. Hence the delay in the report. "Whatever his fee, detective, his reputation is unimpeachable. If you care to read his report, you'll see—"

"Don't have to. I know what it says." It was small of him, Kusack supposed, but it gave him a little lift to tweak a man who didn't appear to have an ounce of extra fat on his body and who could wear a monkey suit and not look like a fool.

Byron folded his hands. Patience was, and always had been, his best weapon. "Then you've been in contact with Mr. Fitzgerald on this matter."

"Nope." Kusack dug out a napkin, wiped his mouth. "Got our own handwriting analysts. Got their final take in a couple weeks ago." Politely, he stifled a belch. "The signatures on the altered forms are an exact match. Too exact," he added before Byron could snarl. "Nobody writes their name the exact and precise same way every time. All the doctored forms have the same precise signature, stroke for stroke, loop for loop. Copies. Likely tracings of Ms. Powell's signature on the one 1040."

"If you know that, why are you sitting here? This is hell for her."

"Yeah, I figured that. Trouble is I gotta cross all my t's, dot all my i's. That's the way things work around here. We've got a few lines of inquiry going here."

"That may be, detective, but Ms. Powell has a right to know the status of your investigation."

"As it happens, Mr. De Witt, I'm finishing up my report on the progress of this investigation right now. I'll see Mr. Bittle first thing in the morning, and continue my investigation."

"You certainly don't believe Kate copied her own signature."

"You know, I believe she's smart enough to have done something just that clever." He balled up the napkin and two-pointed it into an overflowing wastebasket. "But . . . I don't think she's stupid enough or greedy enough to have risked her job and her freedom for a piddly seventy-five large." He rolled his shoulders, which had grown stiff after hours at his desk. "I don't believe she'd have risked it for any amount of money."

"Then you believe she's innocent."

"I know she's innocent." Kusack sighed a little and adjusted his girth. "Look, De Witt, I've been doing this job a long time. I know how to look into people's backgrounds, their habits, their weaknesses. My take is that Ms. Powell's weakness, if you want to call it that, was making a big splash at Bittle. Now why is she going to jeopardize something she wants that much for a little playing-around money? She doesn't gamble, she doesn't do drugs, doesn't sleep with the boss. If she needs flash, she's got the Templeton pool to play in. But she doesn't. She puts in sixty-hour weeks at Bittle and builds up her client list. That tells me she's hardworking and ambitious.''

"You might have indicated to her that you believed her.''

"It's not my job to soothe anxious souls. And I've got my reasons for keeping her on the hot seat. Hard evidence is what makes or breaks a case in the real world. And gathering hard evidence takes time. Now, I appreciate you coming by with this.'' He handed Byron the expert's report. "If it helps, you can tell Ms. Powell that the department has no plans to charge her with anything.''

"That's not enough,'' Byron said as he rose.

"It's a start. I've got seventy-five thousand to track down, Mr. De Witt. Then we'll finish it.''

It seemed he would have to be satisfied with that. Byron slipped the report back in his pocket, then eyed Kusack. "You never believed she was guilty.''

"I go into an investigation with an open mind. Maybe she did it, maybe she didn't. After I took her statement, I knew she didn't. It's the nose.''

Byron smiled curiously. "She didn't smell guilty?''

Laughing, Kusack stood, stretched. "There's that. You could say I've got a nose for guilt. I meant *her* nose.''

"I'm sorry.'' Byron shook his head. "You've lost me.''

"Anybody who dives headfirst into third and busts their nose to stretch a double has guts. And style. Somebody who wants to win that bad doesn't steal. Stealing's too easy, and this kind of stealing's too ordinary.''

"Sliding into third,'' Byron murmured, grinning foolishly. "So that's how she did it. I never asked her.'' Because Kusack was grinning back, Byron offered a hand. "Thanks for your time, detective.''

The crowd was thinning out by the time Byron arrived at Pretenses. Three hours late, he thought with a wince. The auction was obviously over, and only those lingering over their drinks or conversations were left. The fragrance of night jasmine blooming on the veranda mixed with the scents of perfume and wine.

249

He spotted Margo first, flirting with her husband. Even as he hurried toward her, he was scanning for Kate. "Margo, I'm sorry I'm so late."

"You should be." She touched pouty lips to his. "You completely missed the bidding. Now you'll have to come in next week and buy something very, very expensive."

"It's the least I can do. Still, you look successful."

When you bother to look at me, she thought, smothering a grin at the way he kept searching the room. "We raised just over fifteen thousand for Wednesday's Child. Nothing makes me happier than raising money to help handicapped children."

Josh wrapped his arms around her from the back, placed their joint hands protectively over her belly. It rippled under them, thrillingly. "She's trying not to look too gleeful over the number of requests to hold merchandise."

"It's a charity event," she said primly, then laughed. "And boy, are we going to clean up next week. In fact, Kate's in the office logging in all the holds."

"I'll go let her know I'm here. Actually, I—" He broke off, torn. Josh was her lawyer, after all. "No, I have to tell her first. Don't go anywhere."

He started across the room just as Kate swung through the office door. "There you are." She beamed at him. "I thought you must have gotten stuck in L.A. You didn't have to—" She stopped because he was staring at her as if he'd had a lobotomy on the trip home. "What is it?"

He managed to close his mouth, get his lungs working again. "Okay, who are you and what have you done with Katherine Powell?"

"Boy, a guy doesn't see you for a few hours, and—oh!" Her face lit up and she tried a sophisticated turn. "I forgot. Margo did it. What do you think?"

He turned first to Margo. "God bless you," he said fervently, then took Kate's hand. "What do I think? I think my heart stopped." He kissed her fingers, then, wanting more, her mouth.

"Wow." A little surprised by the dizzying depth of the kiss, she took a cautious step back. "Look what a little goop on the face and a push-up bra gets you."

His gaze shifted down. "Is that what's under there?"

"You're not going to believe what's under here."

"How long is it going to take for me to find out?"

Amused by his reaction, she toyed with his tie. "Well, big guy, if you play your cards right, we can—"

"Damn." He grabbed her hands. "It's amazing how a sexy woman can shut a man's mind down. I have news for you."

"Fine. If you'd rather discuss current events than my underwear."

"Don't distract me. I've just come from seeing Detective Kusack. It's why I'm so late."

"You went to see him?" The excited flush drained out of her cheeks. "He called you in? I'm sorry, Byron. There's no reason for you to be involved."

"No." He gave her a little shake. "Be quiet. I went to see him because I finally got the report I've been waiting for. I had the documents Marty Bittle gave me sent to a handwriting expert that Josh recommended."

"Handwriting expert? But you never told me. Josh never said anything."

Before her eyes could heat, he hurried on. "We wanted to wait until we had some results. And now we do. They were forgeries, Kate. Copies of your signature."

"Copies." Her hands began to tremble in his. "He can prove it?"

"He's one of the most respected people in his field in the country. But we didn't need him. Kusack had already verified the signatures. He knows they're forgeries. He doesn't consider you a suspect, Kate. Apparently he never really did."

"He believed me."

"He got his expert's report shortly before I got mine. He's going to take the information and his progress report to Bittle in the morning."

"I—can't take it in."

251

"That's all right." He pressed his lips to her brow. "Take your time."

"You believed me," she said shakily. "From the first day, on the cliffs. You didn't even know me, but you believed me."

"Yes, I did." He kissed her again and smiled. "It must be that nose."

"Whose nose?"

"I'll explain later. Come on, we have to fill Josh in."

"Okay. Byron—" She squeezed his arm. "You went to see Kusack before you came here. Was that what you'd call a white knight sort of thing?"

Sounds like a trick question, he thought. "It could be construed in that manner."

"I thought so. Listen, I wouldn't want you to make it a habit, but thanks." Grateful and touched, she pressed her lips to his. "Thank you very much."

"You're welcome." Because he didn't want her eyes swimming, but laughing, he traced a fingertip over her beautifully bared shoulder. "Does that mean I get to see your underwear?"

Chapter Sixteen

Kate had a long-standing concept of what Sunday mornings were for. They were for sleep. Throughout college she had used them for extra study time, or to finish up papers and projects. But once she entered the real world, she designated that time for indulgence.

Byron had a different agenda.

"You've got to resist both ways," he told her. "Mentally isolate the muscle you're working on. Right here." He pressed his fingers to her triceps as she lifted and lowered the five-pound weight, over her head, behind her back. "Don't flop your arm," he ordered. "You're pulling it up and pushing it down through mud."

"Mud. Right." She tried to envision a pool of thick, oozing mud instead of a nice soft bed with cool sheets. "And why am I doing this?"

"Because it's good for you."

"Good for me," she muttered, and watched herself in the mirror. She had thought she would feel ridiculous in the little sports bra and snug bike pants. But it wasn't really so bad. Besides, she got to look at him, too. A well-built man in a tank top and sweat shorts wasn't hard on the eyes at all.

"Now stretch. Don't forget the stretch. Go to the set of concentration curls. Remember?"

"Yeah, yeah, yeah."

She sat on the bench, frowned at the weight she lifted and lowered and tried to imagine her biceps growing. Good-bye, one-hundred-and-two-pound weakling, she thought. Hello, buff.

"And when we're finished here, you're going to make French toast, right?"

"That was the deal."

"I've got me a personal trainer and a chef." She flashed him a smile. "Pretty cool."

"You're a lucky woman, Katherine. Other arm now. Concentrate."

He moved her through flys and dead lifts, hammer lifts and extensions. Though he'd completed his Sunday routine before hauling her out of bed, they'd both worked up a nice sweat by the time he proclaimed her finished.

"So, I'm going to be buff, huh?"

He grinned, rubbing her shoulders, massaging his way down her arms. "Sure you are, kid. We'll put you in one of those little bikinis, oil you up, and shoot you into competition."

"In your dreams."

"Not my dreams," he said sincerely. "Believe me. I've discovered this latent desire for skinny women. In fact, it's starting to stir right now."

"Is that so?" She didn't object when his hands moved around her back and down to cup her bottom.

"I'm afraid it is. Hmm." His fingers roamed, clutched. "This reminds me. Tomorrow we work on the lower body."

"I hate those squats."

"That's because you don't have my vantage point." His gaze shifted to the mirror behind her, and he watched his hands take possession, watched her move against him, saw her

254

shiver when he lowered his mouth to that wonderful curve of neck and shoulder.

It was almost ridiculous the way he wanted her, the way the need would rise up time after time, again and again. Like breathing, he thought, nibbling his way up to her ear. Like life.

"I think we should finish off your morning routine with a little aerobics."

She managed a sound between a groan and a sigh. "Not the NordicTrack, Byron. I'm begging you."

"I had something else in mind." His busy mouth skimmed over her cheek. "I think you'll like it."

"Oh." She got the idea when his hand moved up to palm her breast. "You did say that for overall training aerobics is essential."

"Just put yourself in my hands."

"I was hoping you'd say that."

She gave so easily, he thought. So eagerly. The way her mouth moved on his, the mating of tongues, the press of bodies. All of his old fantasies about the woman of his dreams had faded and shifted and reemerged as her. Only her.

An image of her flickered into his mind. The way she'd looked the night before in that slim, shoulder-baring dress. All that smooth skin, those surprising curves. That wide, wet mouth.

And beneath the dress had been a wanton fantasy of black lace. The sight of her had been staggering, and so unexpected, so impractical for his practical Kate. It was a side of her he had loved exploring. Knowing she had been exploring it as well had been brutally erotic.

She was just as appealing to him now, in damp workout gear that he could hastily peel off.

Both of them were naked to the waist when they tumbled to the mat.

She laughed, rolling with him as they tugged at those last barriers. It was wonderful, wasn't it, to feel so . . . unbound. So completely liberated. She'd stopped questioning how it was he knew just where, just how to touch her. As if he'd always known. And his body was so strong, so hard. It was like making love with a dream. Rolling on top of him, she poured the sheer joy of it into a kiss.

Yes, touch me, she thought. And taste. Here. And here. Let me. Again. Always again, she thought as her heart pounded and her blood swam. Over and over, moment to moment, he could fill her with so many clashing sensations. The wave of heat, the chill of anticipation, a shiver of greed, the warmth of giving.

She wanted to hold him forever, to steep herself in him. Lose herself. And so she took him inside here, trembling to a gasp at that bright instant of joining. She arched back, savoring, tormenting herself with the power, groaning at the texture of his hands that slicked up her to torture her aching breasts.

She held them there, her tensed fingers gripping as she began to move.

It staggered him, the look of her. The dark cap of hair framed her glowing face. Breath heaved and hitched through her parted lips. That long swan's neck was bowed back, the doe's eyes closed. Sunlight poured in over her, so bright, so full, they might have been outdoors in some verdant meadow. He could see her there, a hot-blooded Titania, lusty and sleek.

He wanted her to feed herself, feed herself to satiation. But she increased her rhythm, driving him with her. Her moans and cries swarmed into his blood until they were thrust for desperate thrust.

He exploded beneath her, into her. With one long, glorying sigh, she slid down and crushed her mouth to his.

She sang in the shower. This was unusual even when she was alone. Kate was well aware that she did not have a voice like a bell. As they lathered and soaped he joined in for a miserably off-key, if heartfelt, version of "Proud Mary."

"Ike and Tina had nothing on us," she decided as she toweled her hair.

"Not a thing. Except maybe talent." Byron wrapped a

256

towel around his hips, rubbed his face, and prepared to shave. "You're the first woman I've showered with who sings as badly as I do."

She straightened, watched him lather up. "Oh, really? Just how many women might that be?"

"The mind boggles." He grinned at her, enjoying the laser gleam in her eyes. "And a true gentleman never keeps score."

She watched him swipe the razor through lather, leaving a smooth, clean path. It occurred to her she'd never actually watched a man shave before. Unless she included Josh, and a brother didn't count. But she refused to be distracted by the interesting male ritual. Instead she smiled sweetly and looked over his shoulder into the foggy mirror.

"Why don't you let me do that for you, darling?"

He lifted an eyebrow. "Do I look stupid enough to put a sharp instrument in your hands?" He rinsed the blade. "I don't think so."

"Coward."

"You betcha."

She snorted, nipped his shoulder with her teeth, then headed toward the bedroom to dress.

"Kate." He waited until she'd turned, aimed that smug look in his direction. "There's only one woman now." He watched her quick, almost shy smile spread before she slipped out the door.

Thoughtfully, Byron stroked off lather and stubble. The room was full of mist and heat, and their mixed scents. She'd hung her towel neatly and efficiently to dry. The little jar she used to moisturize her face sat on the counter. She'd forgotten to use it. She hadn't forgotten to put her workout clothes in the hamper or to replace the cap on the toothpaste. No, she would never overlook any practical detail.

It was the extras she forgot, particularly when they applied to herself. She wouldn't let herself browse through a shop, dreaming, and buy something foolish for herself. She wouldn't forget to turn off the lights or to give a faucet an extra twist to prevent a drip.

Her bills would always be paid on time, but stopping to eat lunch would slip her mind when it was crowded with other details.

She didn't have a clue that she needed him. Byron smiled as he lowered his head to rinse off the excess lather. Nor did she know what he'd just discovered. He no longer thought he might be falling in love with her. He knew that she, with all her contrasts and complexities, her strengths and weaknesses, was the only woman he would ever love.

He dried his face, slapped on aftershave, and decided this might be the perfect time to tell her. He stepped into the bedroom. She was standing beside the bed in black leggings and an old Yankees sweatshirt.

"See this?" she demanded, shaking a mangled rawhide bone at him.

"Yes, I do."

"It was in my shoe. How my shoe escaped the same treatment, I'm not sure." She tossed the bone to Byron, then scooped her hands through her hair to check for dryness. "It was Nip, that I am sure of. Tuck has much better manners. Last week it was that fish head he found on the beach. He has to be disciplined, Byron. He's very unruly."

"Now, Kate, is that any way to talk about our child?"

She sighed, put her hands on her hips, and waited.

"I'll talk to him. But I'm sure if you considered the psychology of it, you'd agree that he puts things in your shoe as a token of his great affection."

"And that includes the time he peed in it."

"Well, I'm sure that was just a mistake." He rubbed a hand over his mouth, too wise to let the grin show. "And it was outside. You took them off to walk on the beach, and . . . you're not buying it."

"I don't think you'd find it so amusing if he was using your shoes for his depository." As if on cue, there came the sound of frantic barking, of growing canine bodies thudding. "I'll deal with them," Kate stated. "You're too soft."

"Yeah, and who bought them collars with their names on them?" he muttered.

"What?"

"Nothing." Retreating, Byron opened his drawer for underwear. "I'll be down in a minute."

"To make French toast," she reminded him and rushed down to quiet the dogs. "Okay, guys, kill the racket. Keep it up and there's not going to be any walk on the beach. And nobody's going to play sock with either of you."

They rushed up and bumped against her, two alarmingly growing masses of fur and feet. Even as she started to ruffle them, they raced toward the front door and set up a fresh din.

"You know you go out the back way," she began, then the idiotic door chimes sounded. It seemed Byron had decided they were whimsical and had kept them. "Oh." Ridiculously pleased, she beamed at the dogs. "Pretty cool, guys. You were sounding the alarm. Listen, if it's anybody selling anything I want you to do this. Look, look—bare your teeth."

She demonstrated, but they only thumped each other with their wagging tails and offered canine grins.

"We'll work on it," she decided and opened the door.

Her bright mood plummeted. "Mr. Bittle." Automatically she grabbed collars to prevent the dogs from leaping joyfully on the new humans. "Detective."

"I'm sorry to disturb you on Sunday, Kate." Bittle eyed the dogs warily. "Detective Kusack indicated that he intended to speak with you today, and I asked to come along."

"Your lawyer said I would find you here," Kusack put in. "You're free to call him, of course, if you want him here."

"I thought—I was told I was no longer a suspect."

"I'm here to apologize." Bittle kept his solemn eyes on hers. "May we come in?"

"Yes, of course. Nip, Tuck, no jumping."

"Nice dogs." Kusack held out a beefy hand, and it was duly sniffed and licked. "Got me an old Heinz 57 hound. She's getting up in years now."

"Please, sit down. I'll just put them out." That task gave

259

her time to compose herself. When the dogs were racing maniacally over the yard, she turned back. "Would you like some coffee?"

"There's no need for you to trouble," Bittle began, but Kusack leaned back in the ancient recliner and said, "If you're making it anyway."

"I'll make it," Byron volunteered as he came down the stairs.

"Oh, Byron." Relief rippled through her. "You know Detective Kusack."

"Detective."

"Mr. De Witt."

"And this is Lawrence Bittle."

"Of Bittle and Associates," Byron said coolly. "How do you do?"

"I'll say I've done better." Bittle accepted the formal handshake. "Tommy's mentioned you. We had an early round of golf this morning."

"I'll put the coffee on." He sent a look to Kusack that said as clearly as words that anything of import would wait until he came back.

"Nice place here," Kusack said casually. Kate stood where she was, twisting her fingers together.

"It's coming along. Byron takes his time. He just settled on it a couple of months ago. He's, ah, having some things sent out from Atlanta. That's where he's from. Atlanta." Stop babbling, Kate, she ordered herself. Couldn't. "And he's looking for things out here. Furniture and things."

"Hell of a spot." Kusack settled into the recliner, thinking it was a chair that knew how to welcome a man. "House just down the road has a putting green right on the front lawn." He shook his head. "Guy can walk right out his front door and sink a few. Used to drive the kids down here. They got a kick out of the seals."

"Yes, they're wonderful." Gnawing her lip, she glanced toward the kitchen. "Sometimes you can hear them barking. Detective Kusack, are you here to question me?"

"I've got some questions." He sniffed the air. "Nothing like the smell of coffee brewing, is there? Even the poison down at the station house smells like heaven before you taste it. Why don't you sit down, Ms. Powell? I'll tell you again you can lawyer yourself up, but you're not going to need Mr. Templeton for what we have to talk about."

"All right." But she'd reserve judgment on calling Josh. She was not going to be lulled by small talk and paternal smiles. "What do you want?"

"Mr. De Witt showed you the report from his handwriting expert?"

"Yes. Last night." She sat on the arm of the couch. It was the best she could do. "It said the signatures were copies. Someone duplicated my signature on the altered forms. Used my signature, my clients, my reputation." She rose again when Byron came in with a tray. "I'm sorry," she said quickly. "For the trouble, here."

"Don't be ridiculous." He slid easily into the well-mannered host. "How do you take your coffee, Mr. Bittle?"

"Just cream, thank you."

"Detective."

"The way it comes out of the pot." He sampled the brew Byron offered him. "Now we're talking coffee. I was about to go over the progress of the investigation with Ms. Powell. I'm explaining that our conclusions jibe with those of your independent expert. At this point, indications are that she was set up to take the heat if the discrepancies were discovered. We're looking into other areas."

"You mean other people," Kate said, struggling not to clatter her cup in her saucer.

"I'm saying my investigation is moving along. I'd like to ask you if you have any idea who would focus on you as a scapegoat. There are a lot of accounts in the firm. Only those under your hand were touched."

"If someone did this to damage me, I don't have a clue."

"Maybe you were just convenient. The charges against your father made you prime, maybe gave someone an idea."

"No one knew. I only found out myself shortly before the suspension."

"Interesting. And how did you find out?"

Absently, she rubbed a finger over her temple as she explained.

"You have words with anybody? A tiff? A personality clash, maybe?"

"I didn't have a fight with anyone. Not everyone at the firm is a close friend and confidant, but we work well together."

"No grudge matches, petty grievances?"

"Nothing out of the ordinary." She set her coffee aside, nearly untasted. "Nancy in Billing and I squared off over a misplaced invoice during the April crunch. Tempers are high then. I think I snapped at Bill Feinstein for taking half my computer paper instead of going into stock himself." She smiled a little. "He stuck three cases of it in my office to get back at me for that. Ms. Newman doesn't like me, but she doesn't like anyone but Mr. Bittle Senior."

Bittle stared into his coffee. "Ms. Newman is efficient and a bit territorial." He winced as Kusack busily made notes. "She's worked for me for twenty years."

"I didn't mean she would do something like this." Horrified, Kate sprang up. "I didn't mean that at all! I wouldn't accuse anyone. You might as well say Amanda Devin did it. She guards her lone female partner status like a hawk watching for vultures. Or—or Mike Lloyd in the mail room because he can't afford to go to college full time. Or Stu Cominsky because I wouldn't go out with him. Roger Thornhill because I did."

"Lloyd and Cominsky and Thornhill," Kusack muttered as he wrote, and Kate stopped her pacing.

"You write whatever you want to write in that little book of yours, but I'm not going to go around casting blame." She lifted her chin, set it. "I know how it feels."

"Ms. Powell." Watching her, Kusack tapped his stubby pencil against his knee. "This is a police investigation. You're involved. Every member of your former firm is going to be considered. It's a long process. With your cooperation it can be shortened.''

"I don't know anything," she said stubbornly. "I don't know anyone who needed money that badly, or who would choose to implicate me in a crime. I do know I've already paid all I intend to pay for something I didn't do. If you want to ruin someone else's life, detective, you'll have to do it without me."

"I appreciate your position, Ms. Powell. You're insulted, and I can't blame you. You do your job, do what's expected of you, and go the extra mile. You see what you've been aiming for swing just into reach, then you get kicked in the teeth.''

"That's a nice and very accurate summary. If I knew who did the kicking, I'd be the first to tell you. But I'm not going to put someone whose only crime was to irritate me into the position I've been in.''

"Think about it," he suggested. "You've got a good brain. Once you set your mind to figuring it out, I have a hunch you'll come up with something."

The detective rose, and Bittle followed his lead saying, "Before we go, Kate, I'd like another moment of your time. In private, if there's no objection."

"All right. I—" She glanced at Byron.

"Perhaps you'd like to see the view, detective." Byron gestured, then led the way to the deck doors. "Did I hear you say you had a dog?"

"Old Sadie. Ugly as homemade sin, but sweet as they come." His voice faded away as Byron closed the doors.

"An apology isn't enough," Bittle began without preamble. "Is far from enough."

"I'm trying to be fair and understand the position you were in, Mr. Bittle. It's difficult. You watched me grow up. You know my family. You should have known me."

"You're quite right." He looked very old. Very old and very tired. "I've damaged my friendship with your uncle, a friendship that is very important to me."

"Uncle Tommy doesn't hold grudges."

"No, but I hurt one of his children, and that isn't easy for either of us to forget. I can tell you, for what it's worth, that none of us initially believed you would do anything criminal. We needed an explanation, and your reaction to the questions was, well, damning. Understandable now, under the circumstances, but then . . ."

"You didn't know about my father then, did you?"

"No. We learned about it later. There was a copy of a newspaper article in your office."

"Oh." As simple as that, she thought, and as stupid. She must have missed one when she'd stuffed them into her briefcase. "I see. That made it all look worse."

"It clouded the issue. I should tell you that when Detective Kusack contacted me, I was immensely relieved, and not terribly surprised. I could never reconcile the woman I knew with one who would cheat."

"But you reconciled it enough to suspend me," she said, and heard the brittleness of her own voice.

"Yes. However much I regretted it, and however much I regret it now, I had no choice. I have called each of the partners and relayed this new information. We're meeting in an hour to discuss it. And to discuss the fact that we have an embezzler in our employ."

He paused a moment, gathering his thoughts. "You're very young. It would be difficult for you to understand the dreams of a lifetime, and the way they change. At my age, you have to be very careful, very selective about dreams. You begin to become aware that each one may be your last. The firm has been mine for most of my life. I've nurtured it, sweated over it, brought my children into it." He smiled a little. "An accounting firm doesn't seem like something anyone would dream over."

"I understand." She wanted to touch his arm, but couldn't.

"I thought you might. Its reputation is my reputation. Having it damaged in this way makes me realize how fragile even such a prosaic dream can be."

She couldn't help but bend. "It's a good firm, Mr. Bittle. You made something solid there. The people who work for you work for you because you treat them well, because you make them part of the whole. That isn't really prosaic."

"I'd like you to consider coming back. I realize that you may feel uncomfortable doing so until after this matter is fully resolved. However, Bittle and Associates would be very fortunate to have you back on board. As a full partner."

When she didn't speak, he took a step toward her. "Kate, I don't know whether this will make matters worse or better between us, but I want you to know that this offer had already been discussed and voted on prior to this . . . this nightmare. You were unanimously approved."

She had to ease herself back down on the arm of the chair. "You were going to make me a partner."

"Marty nominated you. I hope you're aware that you always had his complete trust and support. Amanda seconded your nomination. Ah, I believe that was why she was so harsh when she believed you had taken the money from escrow. You'd earned the offer, Kate. I hope, once you've had time to think it over, you'll accept it."

It was difficult to deal with despair and elation at once. Not long before she would have leapt at such an offer, seized it, hugged it to her. She opened her mouth, certain that acceptance would pop out.

"I do need some time." She heard her own words with a kind of vague surprise. "I have to think it through."

"Of course you do. Please, before you consider going elsewhere, give us a chance to negotiate."

"Yes, I will." She held out a hand, just as Byron and the detective returned. "Thank you for coming to see me."

She was still dazed when she led Bittle and Detective Kusak out, said her good-byes. In silence she walked back into the house with Byron, stood staring at nothing.

"Well?" he prompted.

"He offered me a partnership." She said each word slowly, unsure whether she was savoring them or weighing them.

"Not just to make up for all this. They'd already voted on it before everything got screwed up. He's willing to negotiate my terms."

Byron angled his head. "Why aren't you smiling?"

"Huh?" She blinked, stared at him, then burst into laughter. "A partnership!" She threw her arms around his neck and let him swing her. "Byron, I can't tell you what this means to me. I'm too dazzled to tell myself. It's like—it's like being cut from the minors, then being signed to bat cleanup for the Yankees."

"The Braves," he corrected, home team loyal to the last. "Congratulations. I think we should have mimosas with that French toast."

"Let's." She kissed him hard. "And go light on the OJ."

"A dollop for color," he assured her, as they walked into the kitchen arm in arm. He released her to get champagne out of the refrigerator. "Well, aren't you going to pick up the phone?"

She opened the glass-fronted cabinet that held his wine glasses. "The phone?"

"To call your family?"

"Uh-uh. This is too big for the phone. As soon as we eat—" she grinned foolishly at the pop of the cork— "I'm going to Templeton House. This requires the personal touch. It's the perfect way to send Aunt Susie and Uncle Tommy back to France." The minute he'd finished pouring she lifted her glass. "Here's to the IRS."

He hissed through his teeth. "Do we have to?"

"Okay, what the hell. Here's to me." She drank, twirled once, then drank again. "You'll come with me, won't you? We'll get Mrs. Williamson to make one of her incredible dinners. We'll take the dogs, too. We can— What are you looking at?"

"You. I like seeing you happy."

"Get that French toast going and you'll see me ecstatic. I'm starving."

"Give the master room, please." He took out eggs and milk.

"Why don't we swing by your apartment and pick up a few more of your things? We can extend our celebration by having you stay another night."

"Okay." She was too high to think of objecting, though it broke her unspoken rule of staying more than two nights running. "I'll get it," she said when the phone rang. "You keep cooking. And use lots of cinnamon. Hello? Laura, hi. I was just thinking about you." Grinning, she swung over to nip at Byron's ear as he whisked. "We were going to come over later and invite ourselves to dinner. I have some news that I— What?"

She fell into silence and the hand she'd lifted to mess with Byron's hair dropped back to her side. "When? At the—yes. Oh, God. Oh, God. Okay, we'll be right there. We're on our way. It's Margo," she said, fumbling to disconnect the portable phone. "Josh took her to the hospital."

"The baby?"

"I don't know. I just don't know. It's too early for the baby. She had pain, and some bleeding. Oh, God, Byron."

"Come on." He clasped the hand that reached for his. "Let's go."

Chapter Seventeen

She was grateful that it was Byron behind the wheel. No matter how she ordered herself to be calm, she knew her hands would have trembled. Flashes of Margo ran through her head.

There were images of them as children, sitting on the cliffs, tossing flowers out to the sea and Seraphina. Margo parading around the bedroom in her first bra, smug and curvy while Kate and Laura looked on in flat-chested envy. Margo curling Kate's hair for the junior prom, then slipping a condom into Kate's bag—just in case.

Margo on her first visit home after running off to Hollywood to become a star. So polished and beautiful. Margo in Paris after she'd nagged Kate to come over and see the world as it was meant to be.

Margo at Templeton House—always back to Templeton House.

In despair after her world had crumbled, in fury when one of her friends was hurt. The determination and glassy bravado as she'd fought to rebuild her life.

As a bride walking down the aisle to Josh, so outrageously lovely in miles of white satin and French lace. Weeping as she rushed into the shop to announce she didn't have the flu but was pregnant. Weeping again when she felt the baby quicken. And cooing over the tiny clothes her mother was already sewing. Showing off her bulging belly, beaming when it rippled with a kick.

Margo, always so passionate, so impulsive, and so thrilled with the idea of having a baby.

The baby. Kate squeezed her eyes tight. Oh, God, the baby.

"She doesn't want to know if it's a girl or a boy," Kate murmured. "She said they want to be surprised. They have names picked out. Suzanna if it's a girl, for Aunt Susie and Annie, and John Thomas if it's a boy, for Margo's father and Uncle Tommy. Oh, Byron, what if—"

"Don't think about 'what ifs.' Just hold on." He took his hand off the gearshift long enough to squeeze hers.

"I'm trying." Just as she tried to block the shudder when he pulled into the parking lot in front of the tall white building. "Let's hurry."

She was quaking when they reached the door. Byron pulled her back, studied her face. "I can go and find out what's going on. You don't have to go in."

"Yes, I do. I can handle it."

"I know you can." He linked his fingers with hers.

Margo was in the maternity wing. As she hurried down the corridor, Kate blocked out the sounds and smells of hospital. At least this wing had familiar and good memories. Laura's babies. The rush and thrill of being a part of those births soothed away the worst edge of panic, urged Kate to remember what it was like to watch life fight its way into existence.

And to tell herself that this place was one of birth, not death.

The first face she saw was Laura's.

"I've been watching for you." Laura wrapped her arms around Kate in relief. "Everybody's here, in the waiting room. Josh is with Margo."

"What's going on? Is she all right? The baby?"

"Everything's all right as far as we know." Laura led her toward the waiting area and struggled to maintain the pretense of calm. "Apparently she went into premature labor, and she was hemorrhaging."

"Oh, my God."

"They've stopped the bleeding. They've stopped it." Laura took a slow breath to steady herself, but her eyes mirrored her inner fears. "Annie was just in to see her. She says Margo's holding her own. They're trying to stabilize her, stop the labor."

"It's too early, isn't it? She's only in her seventh month." Kate stepped into the waiting area, saw worried faces, and ruthlessly smothered her own fears. "Annie." Kate caught both the woman's hands in hers. "She'll be all right. You know how strong and stubborn she is."

"She looked so small in the bed in there." Ann's voice broke. "Like a little girl. She's too pale. They should do something for her. She's too pale."

"Annie, we need coffee." Susan slid an arm around her shoulders. "Why don't you help me get some?" After stroking a hand down Kate's arm, she led Annie away.

"Susie will take care of her," Thomas murmured. He often thought there was too little for a man to do at such a time, and too much for him to imagine. "Now sit down, Katie girl. You're too pale yourself."

"I want to see her." The walls were closing in already, thick with the scent of fear that meant hospital to her. "Uncle Tommy, you'll make them let me see her."

"Of course I will." He kissed her cheek, then shook his head at his daughter. "No, you stay here. I'll check on the girls while I'm at it. Though you should know they'll be fine down in day care."

"They're worried. Ali especially. She adores Margo."

"I'll tend to them. I'm leaving all my women in your hands, Byron."

"I'll take care of them. Sit down," he murmured and nudged both of them to a couch. "I'll help your mother and

Ann with the coffee." He saw their hands link before he turned away.

"Can you tell me what happened?" Kate asked.

"Josh called from his car phone. He didn't want to take time to call an ambulance. He was trying to sound calm, but I could tell he was panicked. He said she'd been feeling tired and a little achy after last night. When they got up this morning, she wasn't feeling well, complained of back pain."

"She's been working too hard. All that prep for the auction. We should have postponed it this year." I should have pulled more weight, Kate thought.

"Everything was fine at her last checkup," Laura put in, rubbing her brow. "But you may be right. She said she was going to take a shower, then she started shouting for him. She was bleeding and having contractions. By the time we got here, they'd admitted her. I haven't seen her yet."

"They'll let us see her."

"Damn right they will." Laura took the coffee Byron offered, remembering to thank him.

"The waiting's hell." He sat beside Kate. "It always is. My sister Meg had a bad time with her first. Thirty-hour labor, which translates to the rest of your life when you're pacing."

Just talk, he ordered himself. Just talk and give them something else to focus on. "Abigail was a hefty nine pounds, and Meg swore she'd never have another. Went on to have two more."

"It was so easy for me," Laura murmured. "Nine hours for Ali, only five for Kayla. They just sort of slid out."

"Selective memory," Kate corrected. "I distinctly remember you breaking all the bones in my hand while we were in the birthing room. That was Ali. And with Kayla, you—"

She sprang to her feet when a nurse stopped in the doorway. She stepped over the coffee table, prepped for battle. "We want to see Margo Templeton. Now."

"So I've been informed," the nurse said dryly. "Mrs. Templeton would like to see you. You'll have to keep it short. This way, please."

She led the way down a wide corridor. Kate blocked out the hospital sound of crepe-soled shoes slapping on linoleum. There were so many doors, she thought. White doors, all closed. So many people inside them. Beds with curtains around them. Machines beeped and hissed inside. Tubes and needles. Doctors with sad, tired eyes who came to tell you your parents had died, gone away. Left you alone.

"Kate." Laura soothed the hand that gripped hers.

"I'm okay." She ordered herself to stay in the now and relaxed her grip. "Don't worry."

The nurse opened the door, and there was the room. It was designed to be comforting, cheerful. A room to welcome new life. A rocking chair, warm ivory walls with dark trim, thriving plants and the quiet strains of a Chopin sonata were all pieces of the serene whole.

But the machine was there, beeping, and the rolling stool that doctors used, and the bed with its guarded sides and stiff white sheets.

Margo lay in it, glassily pale, her glorious hair pulled back. A few loose tendrils curled damply around her face. The bag hanging from the IV stand beside the bed dripped clear liquid down a tube and into her. She had one hand pressed protectively to her belly, the other in Josh's.

"There you are." Margo's lips curved as she gave her husband's hand a reassuring squeeze. "Take a break, Josh. Go ahead." She rubbed their joined hands over her cheek. "This is girl talk."

He hesitated, obviously torn between doing what she wanted and being more than a step away from her. "I'll be right outside." He lowered his head to kiss her, and his hand brushed over the bulge of her belly. "Don't forget your breathing."

"I've been breathing for years. I've almost got it down pat now. Go on out and pace like an expectant father."

"We'll make her behave," Laura assured him. She sat on the edge of the bed and patted his thigh.

"I'll be right outside," he repeated, and waited until he was in the hall to rub unsteady hands over his face.

"He's scared," Margo murmured. "You hardly ever see Josh scared. But it's going to be all right."

"Of course it is," Laura agreed and glanced at the fetal monitor that beeped away the baby's heartbeats.

"No, I mean it. I'm not messing this up. My timing's off, that's all." She looked at Kate. "I guess this is the first time in my life I've been early for anything."

"Oh, I don't know." Striving for the same light tone, Kate eased down on the side of the bed opposite from Laura. "You developed early."

Margo snorted. "True. Oh, here comes one," she said in a shaky voice and began to breathe slowly through the contraction. Instinctively Kate took her hand and breathed through it with her.

"They're very mild," Margo managed. "There's something in there that's supposed to be slowing them down." She flicked a glance toward the IV. "They'd hoped to stop them altogether, but it looks like the kid wants out. Seven weeks too early. Oh, God." She squeezed her eyes shut. Fear circled back no matter how hard she focused on willing it away. "I should have taken more naps. I should have stayed off my feet more. I—"

"Stop that," Kate snapped. "This is no time to feel sorry for yourself."

"Actually, labor's the perfect time for self-pity." Remembering her own, Laura stroked Margo's belly to bring comfort. "But not for blame. You've taken good care of yourself and the baby."

"Milked it for all it was worth." Kate arched a brow. "How many times did I have to run up and down the stairs at the shop because you were pregnant and I wasn't?" She wanted to weep, promised herself a nice long crying jag later. "And those cravings in the afternoons so I had to go over to Fisherman's Wharf and get you frozen strawberry yogurt with chocolate sauce? Do you think I bought that?"

"You bought the yogurt," Margo pointed out. "Actually, I wouldn't mind having some now."

"Forget it. You can chew your chipped ice."

"I'm going to do this right." Margo took a deep breath. "I know the doctor's worried. Josh is worried. And Mum. But I'm going to do this right. You know I can."

"Of course you can," Laura murmured. "This hospital has one of the best birthing wings in the country. They take marvelous care of preemies. I was on the committee that helped raise funds for new equipment, remember?"

"Who can remember all the committees you were on?" Kate commented. "You'll do fine, Margo. Nobody focuses on what they want and how to get it better than you."

"I want this baby. I thought I could will the labor away, but well, apparently the kid takes after me already. It's going to be today." Her lips trembled again. "It's so small."

"And tough," Kate added.

"Yeah." Margo managed a genuine smile. "Tough. The doctor's still hoping they can stop the labor, but it's not going to happen. I know it's today. You understand?" she asked Laura.

"Absolutely."

"And he's being snotty about delivery. Just Josh. I wanted you to be there. Both of you. I just had this image of a big, noisy, bawdy event."

"We'll have one after." Kate leaned down to kiss her cheek. "That's a promise."

"Okay. Okay." Margo closed her eyes and dealt with the next contraction.

"She's strong," Laura said to Kate as they walked back down the corridor.

"I know. But I don't like to see her scared."

"If the drip doesn't stop labor, she'll be too busy to be scared much longer. All we can do is wait."

Wait they did, as one hour passed into two. Restless, Kate paced the room, walked out to badger the nurses, drank too much coffee.

"Eat," Byron ordered and handed her a sandwich.

"What is it?"

"Any time a sandwich comes out of a vending machine, you don't ask what it is, you just eat it."

"Okay." She took a bite, thought it might have something to do with chicken salad. "It's taking so long."

"Barely three hours," he corrected. "Miracles take time."

"I guess." Considering it necessary fuel, she took another bite of the sandwich. "We should be in there with her. It would be better if we were with her."

"It's hard to wait. Harder for some." He combed his fingers through her hair. "We could take a walk outside, get you out of here for a while."

"No, I'm okay." She damn well would be. "It's easier concentrating on Margo than thinking about where I am. Phobias are so . . ."

"Human?"

"Dumb," she decided. "It was a horrible night in my life. The worst I'll ever have to go through, I imagine. But it was twenty years ago." It was yesterday if she let her mind drift. "Anyway, I handled the hospital both times Laura had kids. Maybe that was easier because I was in on it, and labor really keeps you busy. But this is the same thing. I want to be here."

Linking his fingers with hers, he tugged her into the moment. "You pulling for a boy or a girl?"

"I hadn't thought of it. How—how big does a baby have to be to have a good shot?"

"It'll be beautiful," he said, sliding over her question. "Think of the gene pool it's coming from. A lot of times you think a baby could get lucky and get the best features of his parents. You know, his mother's eyes, his father's chin. Whatever. This one strikes gold anywhere he turns. Going to end up being spoiled rotten."

"Are you kidding? You should see the nursery Margo and Josh put together. I'd like to live there." She laughed and barely noticed he'd handed her tea rather than coffee. "They bought this incredible antique cradle, and this old-fashioned

276

English pram they found in Bath. We were going to have the baby shower next week at Templeton House. All that loot . . .'' She trailed off.

''You'll have to make it an after-the-birth shower. What did you get?''

''It's silly.'' She turned the cup around and around in her hands, trying not to cry or scream or simply bolt up and break into the birthing room. ''Margo's got this thing for Italian designers. Especially Armani. They have this junior line. It's ridiculous.''

''You bought the baby an Armani?'' He burst out laughing, roaring all the harder when she flushed.

''It's a joke,'' she insisted. ''Just a joke.'' But she found herself smiling. ''I guess the first time the kid spits up on it, the joke's on me.''

''You're incredibly sweet.'' He cupped her face in his hands and kissed her. ''Incredibly.''

''It's only money.''

Comforted, she leaned her head against his shoulder and watched her family. Laura had come back from checking on the girls and was sitting with Ann. Her aunt and uncle were standing at the window. Uncle Tommy's arm was around her aunt's shoulders. There was a television bolted to the wall. The Sunday news on CNN rolled by, reporting on a world that had nothing to do with the room where people waited.

Others came and went, bringing with them frissons of worry, anticipation, excitement. She heard the hollow echoes of the PA system, the brisk, efficient footsteps of nurses, and occasional laughter.

She saw a young man leading his enormously pregnant wife down the hall, rubbing her back with intense concentration as she took slow, measured steps.

''Laura always liked to walk during labor,'' Kate murmured.

''Hmm?''

''Margo and I would take turns walking with her, rubbing her back, breathing with her.''

''What about her husband?''

277

"Right." Kate made a derisive sound, eyed Laura to make certain she was out of earshot. "He didn't have time for the Lamaze route. Didn't consider it necessary. I was her coach for both girls, with Margo pinch-hitting."

"I thought Margo was living in Europe during those years."

"Yeah, but she came back for the births. Kayla was a few days early, and Margo was on assignment. The plan had been for her to spend the last week with Laura at Templeton House, but when she called from the plane, Laura had just gone into labor. Margo ended up coming to the hospital straight from the airport. We were with her," she said fiercely. "Right there with her."

"And Ridgeway?"

"Breezed in after everyone was all cleaned up and tidy. Made what I'm sure he considered a manful attempt to conceal his disappointment that the babies didn't have penises, then gave Laura some elaborate gift and left. Creep."

"I've never met him," Byron mused. "I can't say I'd formed a favorable opinion of him from reports. Normally I prefer to form my own opinion on a firsthand basis." He was silent for a moment. "But I think I can make an exception in this case and just despise him."

"Good call. She's well rid of him. As soon as she stops feeling guilty for being glad she's rid of him, she'll be fine. Oh, God, why is it taking so long? I can't stand it." She sprang to her feet. "They've got to tell us something. We can't just sit here."

A nurse in green scrubs stepped into the doorway. "Then perhaps you'd all like to take a little walk."

"Margo," Ann choked out as she got to her feet.

"Mrs. Templeton is doing just fine. And Mr. Templeton is floating somewhere in the vicinity of Cloud Nine. As for Baby Templeton, I think you'd like to see for yourselves. Come with me, please."

"The baby." Ann reached out, found Susan's hand. "She's had the baby. Do you think it's all right? Do you think it's healthy?"

278

"Let's go see. Come on, Grandma," Susan murmured as she walked Ann out.

"I'm scared." Trembling as she followed, Kate gripped Byron's hand. "The nurse was smiling, wasn't she? She wouldn't have been smiling if something was really wrong. You can tell by their eyes. You can tell if you look in their eyes. She said Margo was fine. Didn't she say Margo was fine?"

"That's exactly what she said. They'll let you see for yourself soon. And look at this."

They approached a glass door. Behind it, Josh stood, the grin on his face breaking records. In his arms was a small bundle with a golden sprinkle of hair topped with a bright blue bow.

"It's a boy." Thomas's voice broke as he pressed a hand to the glass. "Look at our grandson, Susie."

"Five pounds," Josh mouthed, gingerly tilting his son for his family to view. "Five full pounds. Ten fingers. Ten toes. Five full pounds." He lowered his head to touch his lips to the baby's cheek.

"He's so tiny." With her eyes swimming, Kate wrapped her arms around Laura. "He's so beautiful."

"John Thomas Templeton." Laura let her own tears fall. "Welcome home."

They cooed at him, objecting noisily when a nurse came to take him away. When Josh came through the door they fell on him as villagers might fall on a conquering hero.

"Five pounds," he said again, burrowing his face in his mother's hair. "Did you hear that? He's five pounds even. They said that was really good. He has all the right working parts. They're going to check him out some more because he didn't cook enough, but—"

"He looked done to me," Byron put in. "Have a cigar, Daddy."

"Jesus." Josh stared at the cigar Byron handed him. "Daddy. Oh. I'm supposed to be passing out the cigars."

"Handling details is part of my job description. Grandma."

Byron handed one to Ann, who delighted everyone by popping it into her mouth.

"Margo, Josh." Laura took his hand. "How is she?"

"Amazing. She's the most amazing woman. He came out wailing. Did I tell you?" Laughing, he lifted Laura off her feet, kissed her. He couldn't seem to get the words out fast enough. "Just howling. And the minute he did, Margo started to laugh. She was exhausted, and we were both scared bloodless. Then he just slid out."

Baffled, he clasped his hands together and stared at them. "It's the most incredible thing. You can't imagine. Well, you can, but you had to be there. He's crying and Margo's laughing, and the doctors says, 'Well, it looks like there's nothing wrong with his pipes.' Nothing wrong with his pipes," Josh repeated, his voice hitching. "Nothing wrong with him."

"Of course not." Thomas closed Josh in a bear hug. "He's a Templeton."

"Not that we're not glad to see you." Kate brushed the hair back from Josh's face. "But when are they going to let us in to see Margo?"

"I don't know. In a minute, I guess. She had the nurse get her purse." His grin broke out fresh. "She wanted to fix her makeup."

"Typical." Kate turned and threw her arms around Byron. "That's just typical."

Chapter Eighteen

The week following the appearance of J. T. Templeton was hectic and complicated. Laura's schedule didn't allow for more than a few hours at the shop. With Margo involved with her new son, Kate was left to deal with the results of a successful reception. Early delivery had thrown their vague plans for interviewing and hiring a part-time clerk out the window.

Kate was on her own.

She opened the shop every day, learned to control her impulses to hurry browsers along. Though she would never understand the appeal of dawdling in a store, she told herself to appreciate that others enjoyed it.

She studied the inventory lists and tried to recognize the more esoteric items in Pretenses' stock. But why anyone would feel the need to own a designer pillbox with pearl inlay remained beyond her.

Simple honesty was sometimes taken for a credit, sometimes an insult. For every woman who appreciated being told an outfit didn't suit her, there were two who bristled at the information.

She persevered by remembering that for at least one hour every day she could close herself in the back office and be alone, blissfully alone, with her ledgers.

They didn't talk back.

"The customer is always right," Kate muttered to herself. "The customer is always right—even when the customer is an asshole." She marched out of the wardrobe room where one particular customer had just informed her that the Donna Karan was mislabeled. It couldn't possibly be a size ten, as it was too snug at the hips.

"Too snug at the hips, my butt. The old bat couldn't get one thigh in a size ten if she greased it with motor oil."

"Miss, oh, miss." Another customer snapped her fingers, like a diner signaling a particularly slow waitress to bring more wine. Kate gritted her teeth into a smile.

"Yes, ma'am. Can I help you?"

"I want to see this bracelet. The Victorian slide. No, no. I said the Victorian slide, not the gold cuff."

"Sorry." Kate tried again, following the direction of the woman's pointing finger. "It's charming, isn't it?" Fussy and foolish. "Would you like to try it on?"

"How much is it?"

There's a tag right on it, isn't there? Still smiling, Kate turned the tag around, read off the price.

"And what are those stones?"

Oh, shit. She'd studied, hadn't she? "I believe there's garnet and . . . carnelian and . . ." What was that yellow one? Topaz? Amber? Citrine? "Citrine," she hazarded, because it sounded more Victorian to her.

As the customer studied the bracelet, Kate scanned the shop. Just her luck, she thought. It was packed, and Laura was gone for the day. She had three hours to go, and in three hours she judged that what was left of her mind would resemble a mass of cold rice.

The sound of the door jangling made her want to whimper.

When she saw who breezed in she wanted to scream.

Candy Litchfield. Her long-standing enemy. Candy Litchfield, whose bouncy stride and perky looks, tumbling red hair and perfect nose hid the heart of a spider.

And she'd brought pals, Kate noted as her heart sank. Perfectly groomed, canny-eyed society matrons in Italian shoes.

"I never find anything I like in here," Candy announced in her bright and far-reaching voice. "But Millicent told me she'd noticed a perfume atomizer that might fit in with my collection. Of course, they overprice everything."

She strolled through, envy packed solidly in ill will.

"Can I show you something else?" Kate said to the customer, who was now studying Candy as carefully as the bracelet.

"No." She hesitated, but avarice won over and she took out her credit card. "Would you gift wrap it, please? It's for my daughter's birthday."

"Of course."

She boxed and wrapped, rang up and bagged, all the while keeping a weather eye on Candy's progress. Two customers left without a purchase, but Kate refused to give Candy's viciously criticizing tongue credit for it.

Feeling like Gary Cooper at the end of *High Noon*, she stepped out from behind the counter to face them alone. "What do you want, Candy?"

"I'm browsing in a public retail facility." She smiled thinly, and exuded a not-so-subtle whiff of Opium. "I believe you're supposed to offer me a glass of rather inferior champagne. Isn't that store policy?"

"Help yourself."

"I was told by a friend there was a perfume bottle that I might like to have." Candy cast an eye over the displays. Her gaze latched on to a gorgeous design in the shape of a woman's body, beautifully fashioned in frosted rose glass.

She would have revealed her own age before she would have shown a flicker of interest.

"I can't imagine what she was thinking of," she drawled.

"She probably mistook your taste." Kate smiled. "That is, she mistook you for having any. How's the pool boy these days?"

Candy, who had a reputation for enjoying very young men in between husbands, bristled. "How does it feel to be a shop clerk? I heard you were fired. Stealing clients' funds, Kate. How . . . ordinary."

"Someone must have pruned your grapevine prematurely, Candy Cane. You're way behind."

"Am I?" She filled a glass to the rim with champagne. "Am I really? Everyone knows that with the Templeton influence behind you, all your petty crimes will be brushed aside. Like your father's were." Her smile sharpened when she saw that shaft strike home. "But then, only fools would have you handling their accounts now." She sipped delicately. "Where there's smoke, after all. You're so lucky to have rich friends who'll throw you crumbs. But then, you always were."

"Always wanted to be a Templeton, didn't you?" Kate said sweetly. "But Josh never looked twice in your direction. We used to laugh about it. Margo and Laura and I. Why don't you finish your champagne and go diddle your pool boy, Candy? You're really wasting your time here."

Candy's skin darkened, but she kept her voice even. Her approach had been to divide and conquer. She'd never been able to score any real points when Kate had Margo or Laura around. But alone . . . And this time she had more ammunition.

"I've heard you're seeing quite a bit of Byron De Witt. And that he's seeing quite a bit of you."

"I'm so flattered you've taken an interest in my sex life, Candy. I'll let you know when we release the video."

"A smart, ambitious man like Byron would be very aware of the advantages of developing a relationship with the Templeton ward. Imagine how high up he can climb using you as a springboard."

Kate's face went blank, pleasing Candy enormously. Candy sipped more wine, her eyes alive with malice as she studied

Kate over the rim. The malice blurred into shock as Kate threw back her head and laughed.

"God, you really are an idiot." Weak with laughter, Kate took a few steps to the side so she could support herself against the counter. "To think we just thought you were a mean little snake. All this time you've just been stupid. Do you actually believe a man like Byron needs to use anybody?" Because her ribs were beginning to ache, she took several deep breaths. Something in Candy's eyes tipped her off. "Oh, I get it. I get it. He didn't look twice at you either, did he?"

"You bitch," Candy hissed. She slammed down her glass before stalking over to Kate. "You couldn't get a man on your own if you danced naked in front of a Marine band. Everyone knows why he's sleeping with you."

"Everyone can think what they want. I'll just enjoy it."

"Peter says he's an ambitious corporate shill."

Now Kate's interest peaked. "Peter does, does he?"

"The Templetons booted Peter out because Laura whined about the divorce. They were so concerned with protecting their darling daughter they ignored the fact that Peter is an excellent hotelier. All the years he worked for them, helped build the Templeton chain into what it is today."

"Oh, please. Peter never built anything but his own ego."

"He'll use his talents to open his own hotel soon."

"With Templeton money," Kate commented, thinking about Laura and the girls. "How . . . ironic."

"Laura wanted the divorce. Peter was entitled to financial compensation."

"You'd know all about making a profit out of marriage terminations." Kate decided Candy's visit wasn't such a pain in the butt after all—not when it brought along such interesting news. "Going to use some of your alimony to invest in Ridgeway's hotel?"

"My accountant, who isn't a thief, considers it a smart investment." Her lips curved again. "I believe I'll enjoy being in the hotel business."

"Well, you've spent a lot of time in them, on the hourly plan."

"How droll you are. Hold on to that sense of humor, Kate. You'll need it." Candy's smile was still there, but her teeth were set. "Byron De Witt will make use of you until he achieves the position he wants. Then he won't need you anymore."

"Then I guess I'd better enjoy the ride." She angled her head. "So you've set your sights on Peter Ridgeway. That's just fascinating."

"We've run into each other in Palm Springs a number of times and have discovered many mutual interests." She smoothed her hair. "Be sure to tell Laura he's looking extremely well. Extremely."

"I'll do that," Kate said as Candy headed for the door. "And I'll give Byron your best. No, on second thought, I'll give him mine."

She snickered, turning when the customer nearest the counter cleared her throat. The woman's eyes darted from the door to Kate, bright and wary as a bird's. "Ah, show me these evening bags. If you don't mind?"

"Sure." Kate beamed at her. For some reason Candy's visit had brightened her mood. "I'd love to. Have you shopped with us before?"

"Yes, actually, I have."

Kate took three ridiculously fussy jeweled bags from the shelf. "We value your business. Aren't these just fabulous?"

"And then she said how lucky I was to have rich friends throwing me crumbs." Kate stuffed a home-baked chocolate chip cookie into her mouth. "So thanks, since I suppose you're one of my rich friends."

"What an ass." From her position on the patio chaise Margo stretched up her arms.

"She hit me with the business about my father."

Margo lowered her arms again, slowly. "I'm sorry. Damn it, Kate."

"I knew I'd get smacked with it sooner or later. I just hate that it was her, of all people. I hate more that she could see she'd jabbed me. I wish it didn't matter, Margo."

"Everything about the people we love matters. I'm sorry I wasn't there." Her eyes narrowed in thought. "I'm really overdue for a manicure. I think Candy's day for the salon is Wednesday. Won't it be fun to bump into her?"

Well able to picture the event, and the outcome, Kate chuckled. "Give yourself a couple weeks to get back in shape, champ, then you can take her on. I knew I'd feel better if I came here to wallow."

"Remember that the next time you've got something eating away at your insides."

"Never going to let me forget that, are you?" Kate muttered. "I said I was wrong not to tell you and Laura. I was stupid."

"After you've said it at regular intervals for the next year or two, we'll forget all about it."

"I have such understanding friends. Christ, these are criminal," Kate mumbled through another cookie. "It must be great having Annie here baking and fussing."

"It really is. I never would have believed we could live under the same roof again, even for the short term. It was awfully sweet of Laura to insist that Mum stay here for a couple of weeks."

"Speaking of Laura." Kate had made a point of dropping by Margo's after work, knowing that Laura would be too busy for an early-evening visit. "Candy mentioned Peter."

"So?"

"It was the way she mentioned him. First she was on me and Byron."

"Excuse me." Margo indulged in a cookie herself. "In what way?"

"Well, she said how he's a corporate shill, and he's using me to earn points with the Templetons. You know, like he brings me to orgasm, and they give him another promotion."

"That's pathetic." She narrowed her eyes at Kate's face. "You didn't buy that?"

"No." She shook her head quickly. "No. I might have if it had been anyone other than Byron. It was a pretty clever chain to pull. But he's just not made that way. I laughed at her."

"Good for you. What does that have to do with Peter?"

"Apparently that's where she got the idea. At least partially. It sounds to me as if they've gotten . . . close."

"Jesus. What a frightening thought." She shuddered dramatically. "Two creeps in a pod."

"She wanted to make sure I mentioned it to Laura. I don't know if I should."

"Let it alone," Margo said immediately. "Laura doesn't need that. If she hears it, she hears it. Besides, with Candy's track record, it's probably already fizzled."

"I was leaning that way." Kate toyed with the rest of her cappuccino, studied the view. "It's so beautiful here. I never really told you what a terrific job you've done putting the place together. Making it like home."

"It is home. It was, straight off." Margo smiled. "I owe that to you. You're the one who told me about the place."

"It seemed right for you—you and Josh. Do you think you can tell sometimes if a place is where you want to be?"

"I know it. It was Templeton House for me. I was too young to remember anything before we came there, but it was home, always. My flat in Milan."

When Margo broke off, Kate shifted uncomfortably. "I'm sorry. Didn't mean to stir up old memories."

"It's all right. I loved that flat. Everything about it. I was home there, too. It was right for me at the time." She shrugged her shoulders. "If things had stayed as they were, it would be right for me still. But they didn't. I didn't. Then there was the shop." She smiled and sat up straighter. "Remember how I was so dazzled by that big, empty building while you and Laura rolled your eyes and wondered if you should cart me off?"

288

"It smelled of stale marijuana and spiderwebs."

"And I loved it. I knew I could make something there. And I did." Her eyes glowed as she looked out to the cliffs. "Maybe childbirth has made me philosophical, but it's not hard for me to say I needed to make something there. And I wouldn't have without you and Laura. Let me be sappy for a minute," she ordered when Kate grimaced. "I'm entitled. I've started to think that things move in a circle, if you let them. We're together on this, through varying circumstances. But we're together. We always have been. It matters."

"Yes. It matters." Kate rose, wandered to the edge of the patio where the ground spread green and bloomed with colorful blossoms. The autumn sky was still brilliantly blue, ranging out to the rocking sea and beyond.

This was a home, she thought. Not hers, though she felt at home here as she did at Templeton House. It worried her that she'd fallen in love with the bent cyprus, the blooming vines and wood and glass of a house on Seventeen Mile that wasn't her own.

"It was always Templeton House for me," she said, putting an image of the towers and stone over the image of multilevel decks and wide windows. "The view from my bedroom, the way it smelled after the floors were polished. I never felt that way about my apartment in town. It was just a convenient place to stay."

"Are you going to keep it?"

Puzzled, Kate turned back. "Of course. Why wouldn't I?"

"I thought since you were staying at Byron's—"

"I'm not staying there," Kate said quickly. "Not living there. I just . . . sleep over sometimes. That's entirely different."

"If you want it to be." Margo tilted her head. "What worries you about him, Kate?"

"Nothing. Exactly." Blowing out a breath, she came back and sat. "I was going to ask you—figuring you'd be the expert on such matters."

Margo waited, tapped her fingers on the arms of the chaise. "Well?"

"Okay, I'm working up to it." She braced, looked Margo dead in the eye so that she could detect any flicker. "Can you become addicted to sex?"

"Damn straight you can," Margo said without a single flicker. "If you do it right." The corners of her lips turned up. "I'd bet Byron does it very right."

"Rake in your winnings," Kate said dryly.

"And you're complaining."

"No, not complaining. I'm asking. I've just never . . . Look, it's not like I haven't had sex before. I just never had such an appetite for it as I seem to now. With him." She rolled her own eyes, chuckled at herself. "Christ, Margo, five minutes with him and I want to bite him."

"And since the taste suits you, what's the problem?"

"Because I wondered if you could get too dependent on certain aspects."

"On great sex?"

"Yeah, all right. On really great sex. Then people change, and move on."

"Sometimes they do." She thought of herself, and of Josh. Smiled. "Sometimes they don't."

"Sometimes they do," Kate repeated. "Candy got me thinking—"

"Oh, please. Damn it, Kate, you said you didn't buy that shit she was spewing."

"About him using me? Absolutely not. It just made me think about our relationship. If it is a relationship. We don't have anything in common really but, well, sex."

With a long sigh, Margo leaned back, helped herself to another cookie. "What do you do when you're not busy pounding each other into puddles of passion?"

"Very funny. We do stuff."

"Such as?"

"I don't know. Listen to music."

"You like the same music?"

"Sure. Who doesn't like rock and roll? Sometimes we watch movies. He's got this incredible collection of old black and whites."

"Oh, you mean the old movies you like."

"Hmm." She shrugged. "We walk on the beach, or he whips me through a workout. He's tough about that." More than pleased, she flexed her biceps. "I've got definition."

"Hmm. I guess you never talk, though."

"Sure, we talk. About work, family, food. He's got this thing about nutrition."

"Always serious, huh?"

"No, I mean we have a good time. We laugh a lot. And we play with the dogs, or he works on one of his cars and I watch. You know—stuff."

"Let me see if I have this straight. You like the same music, the same kind of movies, which translates into being entertained together. You enjoy walking on the beach, pumping iron, share an affection for a pair of mongrel dogs." Margo shook her head. "I can see the problem. Other than sex, you might as well be a couple of strangers. Dump him now, Kate, before it gets ugly."

"I should have known you'd make a joke out of it."

"You're the joke. Listen to yourself. You've got a terrific man, a wonderful, satisfying relationship that includes great sex and mutual interests, and you're sitting there looking for hitches."

"Well, if you find them before they happen, you can work around them."

"It isn't an audit, Kate, it's a love affair. Relax and enjoy it."

"I am. Mostly. Nearly." She shrugged again. "I've just got a lot on my mind." And, she thought, it might be time to bring up the fact that she'd been offered a partnership at Bittle. "There's some, ah, adjustments coming up," she began, but was interrupted as Ann came out, carrying the baby.

"The little man woke up hungry. I've changed him," Ann said, cooing as she carried him toward Margo's open arms. "Yes, I did. Changed him and put on one of his fancy suits. There's a lad. There's a darling."

"Oh, isn't he gorgeous?" Margo cuddled him, and smelling mother, J. T. sent up a call for dinner. "He's more beautiful every time I look at him. Just like a man, can't wait for a woman to open her blouse. There you are, sweetie."

He settled happily at her breast, his small fists kneading, his newborn blue eyes intent on hers.

"He's gained four ounces," she told Kate.

"At the rate he's going, he'll be ready for heavyweight status in another week." Charmed, Kate shifted to the edge of the chaise to stroke his downy head. "He has your eyes and Josh's ears. God, he smells so good." She drew in the powdery, milky scent of baby and decided to talk business another time. "I get to hold him when you're done."

"You'll stay for dinner, Miss Kate." Ann put her hands behind her back to end her struggle not to adjust the way Margo was holding the precious boy. "Mr. Josh has a late meeting at the hotel, and you'll keep us company. Then you can hold our baby as long as you want."

"Well . . ." Kate traced a fingertip over the curve of J. T.'s cheek. "Since you've twisted my arm."

The Bay Suite of Templeton Monterey was elegantly appointed. Black-lacquered tables held huge porcelain urns filled with exotic blooms. A curved settee in icy blue brocade was sprinkled with pillows that picked up the tones of a floor-spanning Oriental rug. The drapes on both sets of wide glass doors were open to invite in the glorious bleeding colors as the sun slowly sank into the sea.

The table in the dining area was conference size, graced with high-backed, ornately carved chairs with tapestried seats. Dinner was served on bone-white china, accented with a Fumé Blanc from the Templeton vineyards.

The meeting might have been held at Templeton House, but both Thomas and Susan considered that to be Laura's home. This, as pleasant as it was, was business.

292

"If there's a weakness in the Beverly Hills location, it's in room service." Byron glanced at the notes beside his plate. "The complaints run to the usual—the amount of time for delivery, mix-up in orders. The kitchen runs well as a whole. Your chef there is . . ."

"Temperamental," Susan suggested with a smile.

"Actually I was going to say frightening. I know he scared me. Maybe it was being ordered out by a very large man with a thick Brooklyn accent and a cleaver, but there was a moment."

"Did you leave?" Thomas wanted to know.

"I reasoned with him. From a safe distance. And told him, quite sincerely, that he made the best coquilles St. Jacques it had ever been my privilege to taste."

"That goes a long way with Max," Josh commented. "As I recall, the line chefs there work like machines."

"They appear to. They're terrified of him." Grinning, Byron sampled his tarragon chicken. "The problem doesn't seem to be in the preparation, but in the servers. Naturally there are certain hours when both the kitchen and the servers are backed up, but the room service staff has become undeniably lax."

"Suggestions?"

"I'd recommend transferring Helen Pringle to the Beverly Hills location, if she's agreeable, in a managerial position. She's experienced and efficient. We'd miss her here, of course, but I believe she would eliminate the problem in L.A. And she'd certainly be my first choice for a promotion."

"Josh?" Thomas turned to his son for verification.

"Agreed. She has an excellent record as an assistant manager."

"Make her the offer." Susan picked up her wine. "With the appropriate increase in salary and benefits."

"Fine. I think that closes Beverly Hills." Byron skimmed down his notes. San Francisco had been dealt with and tabled. San Diego required a personal spot check but posed no immediate need for discussion. "Ah, there is a little matter here at the flagship." Byron scratched his cheek. "Maintenance would like new vending machines."

Thomas raised a brow as he finished off his salmon. "Maintenance came to you about vending machines?"

"There was a problem with the plumbing on the sixth floor. Sabotage by a toddler who decided to drown his Power Rangers in the toilet. Hell of a mess. I went down to soothe the parents."

And ended up sending them down to the pool while he helped the mechanic stem the flood. But that was beside the point.

"I supervised the disgorging, so to speak, and the matter of vending machines came up. They want their junk food back. It seems candy bars and chips were ditched a couple of years ago and replaced with apples and fat-free cookies. Believe me, I got an earful about corporate interference in personal choice."

"That would be Ridgeway," Josh decided.

Susan made a dismissive sound, but held a napkin to her lips to disguise her grin. She had an image of Byron, elegant in a suit and polished shoes, wading through water and listening to a mechanic's gripes about snacks. "Recommendation?"

"Keep them happy." Byron shrugged. "Let them eat Milky Ways."

"Agreed," Thomas said. "And is that the biggest staff problem here at Templeton Monterey?"

"Just the usual hitches, nothing that isn't typical day-to-day. There was the dead woman in 803."

Josh grimaced. "I hate when that happens."

"Heart attack, died in her sleep. She was eighty-five, led a full life. Gave the maid a hell of a start."

"How long did it take you to calm her down?" Susan asked.

"After we caught her? She went screaming down the hall. About an hour."

Thomas topped off the wine, lifted his glass. "It's a relief for Susie and me to know that California is in good hands.

Some people believe that running a hotel means sitting up in the fancy office and pushing paper—and people—around.''

"Now, Tommy." Susan patted his arm. "Peter's no longer our problem. We can hate him for strictly personal reasons now." She beamed at Byron. "But I agree. We'll go back to France at the end of the week knowing things here are well looked after." She tilted her head. "Professionally, and personally.''

"I appreciate that.''

"Our Kate's looking very happy," Thomas began. "Very healthy and fit. Are you making plans?''

"Uh-oh, here it comes." With a grin, Josh leaned back, shook his head. "Sorry, By, I'm just going to sit here and watch you twist in the wind.''

"It's a reasonable question," Thomas insisted. "I know what the man's prospects are, obviously. I want to know what his intentions are.''

"Tommy," Susan said patiently, "Kate's a grown woman.''

"She's my girl." His face clouded as he pushed his plate aside. "I let Laura rush off her own way and look what that got her.''

"I'm not going to hurt her," Byron said. He wasn't as offended as some might have expected by the probing. After all, he'd been raised in the old school, where family interest and interference went hand in hand. "She's very important to me.''

"Important?" Thomas tossed back. "A good night's sleep is important.''

Susan sighed. "Eat your dessert, Thomas, You know how you love tiramisu. Working for Templeton doesn't require you to answer personal questions, Byron. Just ignore him.''

"I'm not asking as his employer. I'm asking as Kate's father.''

"Then I'll answer you in that spirit," Byron agreed. "She's become a major part of my life, and my intentions are to marry her." Since he hadn't fully understood that himself until this moment, Byron fell silent and frowned into his glass.

"Well, then." Pleased, Thomas slapped his palm on the table.

"It'll be news to her," Byron muttered, then let out a breath. "I'd appreciate it if you'd let me deal with your Kate in my own way. I haven't quite worked it out."

"I'll have him out of your way in a few days," Susan assured Byron. "Six thousand miles."

Thomas forked up creamy cake. "But I'll be back," he warned and shot Byron a wide grin.

He was a detail man, after all, Byron reminded himself when he let himself into his house. He knew how to handle sensitive problems. Surely he could handle something as basic as a proposal of marriage to the woman he loved.

She wouldn't want anything flowery, he decided. Kate wouldn't go for the down-on-one-knee routine. Thank God. She'd prefer the direct, the simple. It was all in the approach, he concluded and tugged off his tie.

He wouldn't put it as a question. Phrasing something as "will you" opened up too much leeway for the answer to be no. Better to make it a statement, being certain to keep it short of a demand. Because it was Kate, after all. And it would be wise, because it was Kate, to have at the ready a list of rational reasons why it would be sensible.

He only wished he could think of a single one.

He'd pulled off his shoes before he realized something was wrong. It took him another minute to pinpoint it. It was the quiet. The dogs always set up a greeting din when he pulled into the drive. But there was no barking. When he raced to the deck door, wrenched it open in panic, he saw that there were no dogs.

He called, whistled, hurried down the steps to check the fence that kept them safely in the backyard. His frantic mind whirled with the possibility of dognappers, newspaper articles about stolen pets sold for experiments.

The first happy bark weakened his knees. They'd gotten

through the safety gate, he thought as he strode toward the beach steps. That was all. Somehow they'd gotten through and gone for a run on their own. He'd have to give them a good talking-to.

They topped the stairs at a run, tails waving flags of devoted joy. They leapt on him, licking and wriggling with the trembling delight they displayed whether he'd been gone for hours or had simply run to the store for milk.

"You're grounded," he informed them. "Both of you. Haven't I told you to stay in the yard? Well, you can just forget gnawing on those ham bones I got from the hotel kitchen. No, don't try to make up," he said, laughing when they held up paws for shaking. "You guys are in the doghouse—for real."

"Well, that'll teach them." Kate climbed the last step and stood smiling at him in the moonlight. "But I have to take the heat on this one. I asked them to escort me down to the beach, and being well-bred gentlemen, they could hardly refuse."

"I was worried about them," he managed. He couldn't seem to stop staring at her. She was standing there, windblown, slightly breathless from the climb. Just there, as if he'd wished it.

"I'm sorry. We should have left you a note."

"I didn't expect to see you tonight."

"I know." Feeling awkward now, as she always did after following an impulse, she tucked her hands in her pockets. "I went by Margo's after I closed the shop, had dinner and played with the baby. He's gained four ounces."

"I know. Josh told me. He has pictures. About six dozen."

"I got to see videos. I loved it. Anyway, I started to head back to my apartment." Her apartment, she thought. Dull, empty, meaningless. "And I ended up here instead. I hope you don't mind."

"Do I mind?"

He wrapped his arms around her, slowly. Drew her close against him, gradually. For three humming heartbeats his eyes

297

stayed on hers. His mouth brushed hers, retreated. Brushed again, shifted angles. Then his lips covered hers, heated hers, parted hers. Soft and deep and welcoming, the kiss shimmered through her. Her hands stayed in her pockets, too limp to move. The muscles in her thighs went lax, her knees weak. When he drew away she could have sworn she saw stars dazzling her own eyes.

"Well," she began, but he was kissing her again, in that same drugging, devastating, delicious way. It was as if they had forever to simply be there, caught in soft sea breezes and quiet passion.

She gulped in air when his mouth lifted. His eyes were so close, so clear, she could see herself trapped in them. It jolted her back a step, made her fumble for a casual smile.

"I'd have to say, at a guess, you don't mind."

"I want you here." He took her hands, brought her palms, one at a time to his lips. And watched her. "I want you."

He could see that she was struggling to recover, to plant her feet back on the ground. He didn't intend to let her. "Come inside," he murmured, drawing her with him. "I'll show you."

Chapter Nineteen

Days later, she was still there.

Byron's idea of a break from weight training was a three-mile jog on the beach. It was difficult for a woman whose idea of a morning start had always been two very hot, very strong cups of coffee to adjust to the concept of running at dawn.

Kate told herself it was the experience that mattered. And, more important, the waffles he'd promised her if she stuck it out.

"So you, like," she puffed, huffed, and tried to concentrate on her pace, "really enjoy this."

"It's addictive," Byron assured her. He was going at a snail's pace to bring her along gradually, and admiring the way her legs looked in baggy shorts. "You'll see."

"No way. Only sinful stuff is addictive. Coffee, cigarettes, chocolate. Sex. Good stuff never becomes addictive."

"Sex is good stuff."

"It's good but sinful—sinful in a good way." She watched

the dogs race into the surf and shake themselves so that little bullets of water flew and sparkled in the strengthening sun.

She supposed there was something to be said for dawn, after all. The light was achingly beautiful, and the smells so fresh, so renewed, they seemed unreal. The air was just cool enough to be bracing.

She had to admit her muscles felt loose. Oiled, in a way, as if her body was becoming a well-tuned machine. It made her feel foolish to realize she'd accepted feeling unwell for so long simply because she'd found it too much trouble to change.

"Where did you run in Atlanta? No beaches there."

"We've got parks. Indoor tracks when the weather's bad."

"Do you miss it?"

"Bits and pieces. Magnolia trees. The sound of slow voices. My family."

"I've never lived anywhere but here. Never wanted to. I liked going to school back east. Seeing snow, frost on the windows. The way the leaves look in New England in October. But I always wanted to be here."

She saw the beach steps in the distance. Her aching calves all but applauded. "Margo's lived lots of places, and Laura's done much more traveling than I have."

"Someplace you'd like to see?"

"No, not really. Well . . . Bora Bora."

"Bora Bora?"

"I did this report on it in high school. You know, a geography report. It seemed so cool. One of those places I told myself I'd go when I took a real vacation. Just a hang-out-and-do-nothing vacation. Oh, thank goodness," she breathed and sank to the sand in front of the beach steps. "I made it."

"And you're going to cramp up if you don't keep moving." Unsympathetically, he hauled her to her feet. "Just walk. You've got to cool down. Why haven't you gone to Bora Bora?"

She walked, for three paces, then bent over at the waist and breathed. "Come on, Byron, real people don't just go to Bora

Bora. It's one of those daydreams. Do you think jogging can dislocate internal organs?''

"No."

"I was pretty sure I could hear my ovaries rattling."

He paled a bit. "Please." He handed her the bottle of water he'd screwed into the sand at the base of the stairs. He whistled for the dogs before starting up the steps with her.

"Normally, I'd just be getting up now, stumbling into the kitchen, where my timed coffee machine would be finishing up its last few drips. Leave the house at eight twenty-five, hit the office at eight forty-five. Have the coffee machine there brewing away and be at my desk with the first cup by eight fifty-five.''

"Eat the first roll of antacids by nine fifty-five."

"It wasn't quite that bad." She fell silent as they crossed from steps to lawn toward the house. The dogs winged through the gate, streaking toward their bowls in anticipation of breakfast. "I haven't had a chance to tell Margo and Laura about going back to Bittle.''

Byron hefted the twenty-five-pound bag of dog food out of the pantry. "Haven't had a chance?''

"All right—haven't found the right way." She shifted as the nuggets clattered into plastic. "I feel like I'm letting them down. I know that's not right. I know they won't feel that way. They'd understand this is right for me.''

Byron replaced the bag, signaling the dogs to chow down. "Is it?''

"Of course it is." She brushed back her hair. "What a thing to say. It's what I studied for, worked for. It's what I've always wanted.''

"All right, then." He gave her a friendly pat on the rump and headed in.

"What do you mean by that? 'All right, then'?" She rushed in behind him, scowling. "It's a partnership, with all the bells and whistles. I've earned it.''

"Absolutely." As a matter of habit, he started upstairs toward the shower. Kate followed at his heels.

"Well, I have. That whole business about the altered documents is just about cleared up. In any case, I'm clear. The rest is Detective Kusack's problem. And the firm's problem. I'll have more control over what's done after I'm a partner."

"Are you worried about it?"

"About what?"

He tugged off his short-sleeved sweatshirt, flung it toward the hamper. "About clearing up the escrow discrepancies."

"Of course I am."

"Why haven't you pursued it?"

"Well, I—" She broke off as he flicked on the shower and stepped inside. "I've been busy. There's not a hell of a lot I could do, in any case, and with Margo being pregnant, and the auction, and Laura tossing me all these details about this holiday fashion show she wants, I haven't had time."

"Okay," he said agreeably.

"That doesn't mean it doesn't matter." Disgusted, she stripped and joined him under the spray. "It just means I've had other priorities. It all came to a head a couple of weeks ago. The forgeries, the offer, the baby. It didn't seem fair to tell Margo and Laura I'd have to cut back at the shop just when Margo had to cut back herself. And until I do, and I'm back at Bittle, I don't see what I can do about finding out who tried to screw me and the firm. But once I'm there, you can bet your ass I'm going to find out who set me up."

"That makes sense."

"Of course it makes sense." Irritated for no reason she could name, she stuck her head under the spray. "Just like it makes sense for me to accept the offer. It's the most practical course."

"You're right. It's definitely the most practical. Pretenses is an investment. Bittle is your career."

"That's right." Instead of being soothed by his agreement, she bristled. "So what are we arguing about?"

"I don't have a clue." He gave her an absent kiss on the

302

shoulder and stepped out to dry off. "I'll get breakfast going," he announced, and chuckled his way down the stairs.

She was, he thought, as easy to see through as a chain-link fence.

Kate worked with Laura shoulder to shoulder throughout the morning. She told herself the minute they had a real break in traffic, she would sit Laura down and explain about her plans. She would, of course, continue to take care of the books. A few evenings a week, the occasional Sunday—that would be enough for her to run Pretenses' finances. Naturally, she would be very busy as a partner at Bittle, but she would also be in a position to delegate a great deal of the grunt work that she had been accustomed to handling herself.

She would have more leeway, more freedom. And, of course, more clout. Her schedule would be crammed, but she was used to that. Working at the shop had certainly kept her busy, but it had also given her large chunks of free time that weren't necessary.

She told herself she would be glad to have her hours prioritized again. That was her way.

And she would be thrilled not to have to chitchat with strangers. Not to be asked to give fashion opinions or have a say in gift-giving decisions. What a relief it would be to settle back at her computer and not have to speak to a soul for hours on end.

"My sister's going to be thrilled with that," a customer said, as Kate carefully removed the tag from a coral cashmere tunic.

"I hope she is."

"Oh, she will be. This is her favorite shop. And mine, too." The woman beamed at the varied selections she'd placed on the counter. "I don't know how I managed before you opened up. Look at the wonderful dent I've made in my Christmas shopping."

"Getting an early start," Kate commented and blinked herself back into focus. "I'd say everyone's going to be happy."

"My mother would never buy herself something as frivolous as this." The woman trailed a finger over the delicate lines of a crystal Pegasus. "That's what gifts are for. And where else but here could I find an antique pocket watch for my father, cashmere for my sister, sapphire studs for my daughter, a crystal flying horse for my mother, and a pair of navy suede Ferragamo pumps for me?"

"Only at Pretenses," Kate said, her own spirits lifted by the woman's exuberant good nature.

The customer laughed and stepped back. "You have the most wonderful place here. If you could gift-box everything but the shoes? I think I'll take one more turn around in case I missed something I have to have."

"Take your time." Smiling to herself, Kate began to box the selections. She caught herself humming as she settled the pocket watch in a bed of cotton. Well, what was wrong with humming? There was nothing wrong with enjoying your work, even though it wasn't your chosen field. Being temporary, it was like playing at a job.

She glanced up as Laura came down the winding stairs from the second floor, chatting with a customer. "I know Margo picked this up on a buying trip to London last year, Mrs. Quint."

"Oh, call me Patsy, please. I shop here so often I feel like we're old friends. And this is just what I was looking for." She gloated over the cherry slant-top writing box Laura set on the counter. "But then, I always find what I'm looking for here. That's why I'm here so often." She laughed at herself, then caught sight of the crystal horse. "Oh, how wonderful! How charming. Someone beat me to it."

"I did." The first customer straightened from her survey of jeweled compacts and smiled. "He's beautiful, isn't he?"

"Gorgeous. Tell me you have something else like him," she begged Laura.

"I think we have a winged dragon—Baccarat, that we haven't shelved yet. Kate?"

"In inventory, priced but not tagged. In the storeroom. I'll find it as soon as I'm done here."

"No, I'll find it. I hope. If you don't mind waiting a minute."

"Not at all. You know, even my husband likes to shop here," Patsy confided to Kate when Laura slipped into the back. "No small accomplishment that, since getting him to stop for a can of peas is a major feat. Of course, I think he likes to come in and look at the pretty girls."

"We're here to serve." Kate affixed a gold seal to the tissue she'd wrapped over the cashmere.

"This compact here." The first customer tapped on the glass. "The heart-shaped one. I think my sister-in-law would love it."

"Just let me get it out for you."

While the two customers chatted about the compact, Kate boxed the horse. A fresh discussion broke out when Laura brought out the dragon. When the door opened, everyone sighed.

"Oh, what a gorgeous baby!" Patsy pressed her hands together under her chin. "Why, he's an absolute angel."

"He is, isn't he?" Margo shifted the baby carrier to show off her son. "He's seventeen days old."

Business ground to a halt, as it was necessary to admire his fingers, his nose, to comment on how bright and alert his eyes were. By the time Kate brought the cradle out of the back room and John Thomas was settled in it, the women had bonded over the baby.

"You should have called me if you wanted to get out for a little while," Laura scolded. "I'd have picked you up."

"Mum dropped me off. She had some marketing she wanted to do. I think her plan is to stock my kitchen so that if we're locked in for a year, we'll have provisions." Margo settled in a chair with the cradle at her side. "God, I've missed this place. So, how's business?"

"The pair who just left?" Kate began, pouring tea.

305

"On their way to lunch, yes."

"They became fast friends about fifteen minutes ago over mythical glass animals. It was kind of fun to watch."

"This is the first time the shop's been empty since we opened this morning," Laura added. "We're getting a lot of those people who always have their holiday shopping done by Thanksgiving."

"And to think how I used to hate them," Margo sighed. "I checked with my doctor. He says if I keep it to mostly sitting behind the counter, I can start coming in a few hours a day starting next week."

"There's no need to rush," Kate objected. "We're handling it."

"I don't like you handling it without me. I can bring J. T. with me. Babies mist shoppers' brains."

"I thought you were going to interview nannies."

"We are." Pouting a little, Margo bent over her son, adjusted his blanket. "Soon."

"She doesn't want to share," Laura murmured. "I know how it feels. When Ali was born, I—" She broke off as a trio of fresh customers came in.

"I'll take them," Kate volunteered. "You two indulge yourself in mommy talk."

For the next twenty minutes, she showed one customer every diamond earring in stock while the second poked through the bric-a-brac and the third cooed over a napping J. T.

She helped serve tea, saved a frantic husband with a last-minute anniversary gift, and rehung the castoffs left in the wardrobe room.

Shaking her head at the way some people treated silk, she stepped out again. New customers were browsing amid a hum of female voices. Someone had switched on an Art Deco lamp to test the effect, and smooth golden light shimmered in the corner. Margo was laughing with a customer, Laura was stretching on her toes to reach a box for a purchase. And the baby slept.

It was a wonderful place, she thought suddenly. It was a magical little treasure chest filled with the sublime and the foolish. Crafted, she realized, by the three of them. From desperation, from practicality, and most of all from friendship.

How odd that she had ever considered it a business to be measured in profit and loss, overhead and expenditure. And odder still that she hadn't realized until this moment how happy she was to be a part of something so risky, so ridiculous, so entertaining.

She walked to Laura. "I have an appointment I'd forgotten about," she said quickly. "Can you handle things here until I get back? It should only take an hour or so."

"Sure. But—"

"I won't be long." She grabbed her purse from behind the counter before Laura could ask any questions. "See you later," she called out, and bolted.

"Where's she going?" Margo demanded.

"I don't know. Just out for a little while." Concerned, Laura stared through the glass after Kate. "I hope she's all right."

She wasn't sure that she was. It was a test, Kate told herself. Going back to Bittle, gauging her feelings. Her reaction would be a test.

The lobby was familiar, even comforting, with its quiet colors and no-nonsense furniture. Chrome and leather, efficient and easily cleaned, made up the small sitting area where stacks of *Money, Time,* and *Newsweek* were handy for the clients' perusal.

The main receptionist offered Kate a quick and slightly embarrassed smile. She took the steps, as was her habit and passed through the first floor. No nonsense here either, she mused. Clerks and computer operators went about their business, busy as bees and just as focused on the task at hand. One of the mailroom clerks pushed his cart along, passing out the afternoon deliveries. Someone's fax was clicking.

On the second floor, the hum of business continued. Account executives plowed through the daily routine in their own offices. The phones were active, reminding her that it was, after all, the middle of the last quarter of the year. Clients were beginning to call for advice on how to squeeze in more deductions, how to defer income until the next tax year, how much they might need to contribute to their Keoghs or IRAs.

Of course, she thought, twice as many would wait until the last week of December and call in a panic. It kept accounting interesting.

She stopped at her old office. No one had claimed it, she mused. Her computer and phone sat on the desk, but otherwise it was bare. The fax machine was silent, but she could remember the way it had beeped and clicked along.

The blinds were closed on the window behind the desk. She'd often left them that way herself, she realized. Working in artificial light, never taking notice of the view.

The shelf was a handy stretch away from the desk and would have held her research books, tax manuals, supplies. No tchotchkes, she thought. No distractions. And, she decided with an inner sigh, no style. Just another bee in the hive.

Good God, she was boring.

"Kate."

She turned, shaking off the moment of self-pity. "Hello, Roger."

"What are you doing?"

"Taking a good look in the mirror." She gestured toward her empty office. "No one's using it."

"No." His smile was a little weak as he glanced in. "There's talk about hiring a new associate. There's a lot of talk," he added, looking back at her face.

"Is there," she said coolly. "And?"

"I'm just surprised to see you here. That cop's been around a lot."

"That doesn't worry me, Roger. I didn't do anything to be worried about."

"No, of course you didn't. I never believed it. I know you too well." He glanced over his shoulder, the movement jerky and ripe with nerves. "Bittle Senior called a full staff meeting last week, made the announcement that you'd been cleared of any implication. Now everybody's looking at everybody else. Wondering."

"That's not surprising, is it?" Curious, she studied his face. "Still, only one person should be worrying as well as wondering. Don't you think, Roger?"

"The finger pointed at you," he said. "Who knows who it might point to next?"

"I think Detective Kusack knows how to do his job. Then there's the FBI."

"What do you mean, the FBI?"

"Tampering with tax forms is a federal offense."

"Nobody tampered with the forms filed with the IRS. Nobody fucked with the government."

"Just with me, and a few clients. You bastard."

His head snapped back as if she'd slapped him. "What the hell are you talking about?"

"You're sweating. You know, I don't believe I've ever seen you sweat before. Not in bed. Not when you told me one of my top accounts was transferring to you. But you're sweating now."

When she started to pass him, he grabbed her arm. "Don't be ridiculous. Are you actually accusing me of doctoring files?"

"You son of a bitch. You knew where I kept all my records. You knew just how to pull it off and point the finger at me. You found out about my father, too, didn't you?" Fury was pouring through her hot blood. "And you had the nerve to come on to me again after what you'd done. I couldn't figure out why you were suddenly interested in me again. Just another way to cover your ass."

309

"You don't know what you're talking about."

Yeah, he was sweating, she noted. Scared. Scared as a fucking rabbit caught in oncoming headlights. She hoped to God he suffered. "Take your hand off me, Roger. And do it now."

He only tightened his grip, leaned closer. "No way you can prove any of this. If you try to put this off on me, you're going to look like a fool. I dumped you. I got that account because I'm better, I'm more innovative. I work harder."

"You got that account because you slept with a lonely, vulnerable woman."

"Like you never slept with a client," he said in a furious undertone.

"No, I never did. And you took the money because you were greedy, because it was easy, and you'd found a way to set me up."

"I'm warning you, Kate, if you go to Bittle and try to put me on the hot seat, I'll—"

"What?" she tossed back, her eyes alight with eager challenge. "Exactly what?"

"Is there a problem here?" Newman glided down the hall in her eerily silent way. Her mouth was pursed, as usual, in disapproval.

Kate sent her a feral smile. "I don't believe there is." She jerked her arm out of his loosened grip. "Is there, Roger? I believe Mr. Bittle's expecting me, Ms. Newman. I called in on the car phone."

"He'll see you now. Your phone's ringing, Mr. Thornhill. If you'll come with me, Ms. Powell." Newman glanced over her shoulder once, measuring Roger as he stood grim-faced in the hall, then looked down when Kate rubbed her aching arm. "Are you all right?"

"I'm fine." She drew in a breath as Newman opened the door to Bittle's office. "Thank you."

"Kate." Bittle rose from behind his desk, held out a hand in welcome. "I'm very glad you called." He closed both hands around hers. "Very glad."

"Thank you for seeing me."

"Please, sit. What can we get you?"

"Nothing. I'm fine."

"Ms. Newman, inform the partners that Kate is here."

"No, please, that's not necessary. I'd like to speak just with you."

"As you wish. That'll be all, Ms. Newman." He took the chair beside Kate rather than the one behind his desk. "I wish I could tell you about the progress on the investigation. But Detective Kusack asks more questions than he answers."

"I'm not here about that." She thought of Roger. No, she wouldn't point the finger, not yet. She would let him stew, and sweat, and she would find a way to prove what he'd done. Then she'd watch him fry. "I came about your offer."

"Good." Pleased, he sat back, folded his hands. "We're very anxious to have you back. We're all agreed that the partners could use some fresh young blood. It's too easy for a firm such as this to become stodgy."

"It isn't stodgy, Mr. Bittle. This is a good firm. I've just started to realize how much I benefited from my years here."

Without any idea of what she was going to say, she, too, folded her hands in her lap. "First, I want to say that I've thought about what happened a great deal and come to the conclusion that under the circumstances you did what you had to do. What I would have done in your position."

"I appreciate that, Kate, very much appreciate it."

"My mistake was in not facing it, and maybe I'm starting to give myself a break about that, too. I can't always handle things by myself. I don't always have all the answers." She let out a little breath. That was a tough one to admit.

"Mr. Bittle, I had one goal when I got my M.B.A. That was to work my way up in this firm to a partnership. Working for you was one of the best experiences of my life. I knew that if I made it here, if I met your standards and became a partner, it meant I was the best. It was very important to me to be the best."

"This firm has never had an associate with a finer work ethic. While I realize the timing of our offer might worry you, I'll assure you again that our regret for your involvement in this police matter has nothing whatever to do with the terms of partnership."

"I know that. It means a great deal to me to know that." She opened her mouth, acceptance hovering on her tongue. Then shook her head. "I'm sorry, Mr. Bittle, I can't come back here."

"Kate." He reached out to take her hand again. "Believe me when I say I understand your discomfort. I expect that you'd be reluctant to accept until this matter is completely cleared up. We're certainly willing to give you time."

"It's not a matter of time. Or maybe it is. I've had time to readjust, reevaluate. For the past few months I've deviated from the path I set for myself when I was still in high school. I like it, Mr. Bittle. No one's more surprised than I am that I'm happy running a secondhand shop on Cannery Row. But I am, and I'm not willing to give it up."

He sat back, tapping his fingertips together as he did when he faced a knotty problem. "Let me talk to you a moment as an old friend, someone who's known you most of your life."

"Of course."

"You're goal-oriented, Kate. You've put all your time and effort into achieving success in your chosen field. A field, I might add, that you're eminently suited for. Now perhaps you've needed a break. We all do from time to time." He spread his fingers, tapped them together again. "But to lose sight of that goal, to settle in a position you're not only over-qualified for, but unsuited for, is a waste of time and talent. Any adequate bookkeeper could handle the daily finances of a shop, and a high-school girl can ring up sales."

"You're right." Delighted to hear it all put into logical, unemotional terms, she smiled at him. "You're completely right, Mr. Bittle."

"Well, then, Kate, if you'd like a few more days to sort out your thoughts—"

"No, I've got them sorted. I've told myself basically the same thing you've just said to me. What I'm doing makes absolutely no sense. It's illogical, irrational and emotional. It's probably a mistake, too, but I have to make it. You see, it's our shop. Margo's and Laura's and mine. It's our dream."

Chapter Twenty

She copped a bottle of champagne from the shop, then decided to go one better and attempt to cook a meal. She had a tacit agreement with Byron that he would cook and she would wash up, as he was light-years ahead of her in culinary skills. But since this was to be a celebration of a new stage of her life, she wanted to give it a shot.

She'd always considered cooking a kind of mathematical skill. She could handle the formulas, like calculus, calculate the answer, but she didn't particularly enjoy the process.

Wrapped in a bib apron, her sleeves rolled up past the elbows, she lined up her ingredients like elements in a physics lab.

First the antipasto, she decided, and warily eyed the mushrooms she'd washed. It couldn't be easy to stuff them with cheese, but the recipe claimed it could be done. She removed the stems and chopped them fine, as directed. Following the steps she cooked them with the green onions and garlic and found herself smiling at the scent.

By the time she'd finished with the bread crumbs and cheese and spices, she was enthralled with herself.

It wasn't long before she was happily smearing the stuffing mixture into the caps, then popping them into the oven.

There were cucumbers to marinate, peppers to slice, tomatoes to deal with. Oh, right—and the olives. She fought with the lid on a jar of plump black olives, cursing it as the oven timer beeped. Out came the mushrooms.

She was in control, she told herself as she sucked on the thumb she'd brushed against the hot baking dish. It was just a matter of efficiency. What the hell came next?

She sliced cheese, struggled over the perfect consistency for the basil and olive oil she wanted for the bread she intended to serve.

An emergency call to Mrs. Williamson, the cook at Templeton House, calmed her down enough that she could arrange the antipasto meticulously on a platter.

Where the hell was Byron? she wondered and nibbled her nails over the recipe for pasta con pesto. "Coarsely chopped basil leaves," she read. What the devil did "coarsely chopped" mean, exactly? And why the hell did you have to grate Parmesan when anybody with half a brain could buy a nice can of it in the market? And where was she going to find pine nuts?

She found them in a labeled canister in his cupboard. She should have known he would have them. The man had everything that had to do with eating, preparing to eat, and serving eats. The carefully measured ingredients went into the blender. Deciding that a little prayer couldn't hurt, she closed one eye, sent it up, and hit the switch.

Everything whirled satisfactorily.

Smug now, Kate put water on to boil for the pasta and set the table.

"Excuse me," Byron said from the kitchen doorway. "I seem to have walked into the wrong house."

"Very funny."

The dogs, who had been keeping her company, and keeping

an eye out for scraps, dashed to greet him. Since he'd followed his nose and his curiosity straight into the kitchen, he still had his briefcase with him. He set it aside now to pet the dogs and grin foolishly at Kate.

"You don't cook."

" 'Don't' doesn't mean 'can't.' " Anxious for feedback, she took a mushroom off the platter and popped it into his mouth. "Well?"

"It's good."

"Good?" She arched a brow. "Just good?"

"Surprisingly good?" he ventured. "You're wearing an apron."

"Of course I'm wearing an apron. I'm not getting splatters all over me."

"You look so . . . domestic." He slid his hands over her shoulders, kissed her hello. "I like it."

"Don't get used to it. This is pretty much a one-shot deal." She went to the refrigerator to take out the champagne. "I remember when Josh went through this phase and wanted to marry Donna Reed."

"Donna Reed." After opening the door to let the dogs streak out, Byron settled on a stool. "Well, she did look pretty hot in those aprons, now that I think about it."

"He got over it and decided he'd rather go for Miss February." With a quick, efficient twist, she popped the cork. "Of course, he always wanted Margo anyway. Donna and Miss 42-D Cup were just distractions."

She took flutes out of the cabinet and turned back with a wicked grin. "Now, if I have the line right, I say, 'And how was your day, dear?' "

"It was good. This is better." He took the glass she'd filled for him, toasted her. "What's the occasion?"

"I'm glad you realize there has to be one for me to go through this mess." She blew out a breath as she looked around the kitchen. No matter that she'd tried to be careful, there was a hell of a cleanup in store. "Why do you do it? You know, cook."

317

"I enjoy it."

"You're a sick man, Byron."

"Your water's boiling, Donna."

"Oh, right." She picked up the clear canister of pasta, frowned at it. "You take this stuff out of the box and put it in here. Okay for aesthetics, I guess, but how am I supposed to know how much is ten ounces?"

"Estimate. I know that goes against the grain for you, but we all have to live dangerously now and again."

He watched her worry over it, started to tell her she was putting in too much, then shrugged. It was her dinner, after all. In any case, he found himself easily distracted by the way the neat bow of the apron strings accented her tidy little butt.

Just how would it look if she was naked under that sturdy white apron?

At his laugh, she glanced around. "What?"

"Nothing." He drank more wine. "Just an unexpected and slightly embarrassing fantasy. It passed. Mostly. Why don't you tell me what happened to set you off on this domestic campaign?"

"I'll tell you. I was—Shit, I forgot the bread." Her brow furrowed as she slid the pan into the oven, adjusted the heat and timer. "There's no way you can hold a conversation and deal with all the details of a meal in progress. Why don't you put on some music, light the candles. Do that kind of stuff while I finish this."

"All right." He rose, started out, turned back. "Katherine, about that little fantasy . . ." Amused at himself, he shook his head. "Maybe we'll try it later."

Too preoccupied to pay attention, she waved him away and got back to business.

She thought she'd managed very well when they were settled at the table, scents wafting, candles flickering, and Otis Redding crooning on the stereo. "I could handle doing this," she decided after she'd sampled and approved the pasta. "About once a year."

"It's fabulous, really. And very much appreciated. It's quite a feeling coming home to a pretty woman and a home-cooked meal.''

"I had some excess energy.'' She broke bread, offered him half. "I thought about just dragging you up to the bedroom when you walked in, then I figured that could wait until after dinner. Anyway, I was hungry. My appetite's definitely improved in the last few months.''

"So has your stress level,'' he commented. "You've stopped popping aspirin and antacids like candy.''

It was true, she admitted. She had. And she certainly felt better than she remembered feeling in years. "Well, I've done something today that is going to either keep me on that same route or send me back to the pharmacy.'' She took a hard look at the bubbles in her wine, swallowed some. "I turned down the partnership.''

"Did you?'' He laid a hand over hers, toyed with her fingers. "Are you okay with that?''

"I think so.'' Out of curiosity she said, "You don't sound very surprised. I didn't know I was going to turn it down until I was sitting in Mr. Bittle's office.''

"Maybe your head didn't know it, but your gut did. Or your heart. You've wrapped yourself up in Pretenses, Kate. It's yours. Why would you give it up to be a part of something someone else had built?''

"Because it's what I've always wanted, always aimed for.'' A bit unsure of him, she shrugged her shoulders. "It turned out it was enough just to know I was good enough. It's a little scary, changing directions this way.''

"It's not that radical a change,'' he corrected. "You're partners in a business, in charge of accounts.''

"My degree, all that education—''

"You don't really believe that's wasted, do you? It's part of who you are, Kate. You're just using it in a different way.''

"I just couldn't go back to that office, to that—life,'' she decided. "It all seemed so rigid. Margo was in the shop today with the baby. People were fussing over him, and Margo was sitting there with the cradle beside her, and Laura had to look for this winged dragon, and I boxed a pocket watch and put away shoes . . ." Embarrassed, she trailed off. "I'm babbling. I never babble."

"It's all right. I get the drift. You're having fun working there, being part of it. You're enjoying the surprises of something you helped create."

"I never liked surprises. I always wanted to know the when, where, and how, so I could be prepared. You make mistakes if you aren't prepared, and I hate making mistakes."

"Are you doing something that feels right to you?"

"It looks that way."

"Well, then." He lifted his glass, touched it to hers. "Go for it."

"Wait until I tell Margo and Laura." The idea of it made her laugh. "Margo was gone when I got back, and Laura had to run pick up the girls, so I didn't have the chance. Of course, we're going to have to make some changes. It's ridiculous not to have a regular posted schedule of our work hours. And the pricing system needs to be completely overhauled. The new software I've just installed will completely streamline our—" She caught herself and found him grinning at her. "You can't change overnight."

"You shouldn't change at all. That's the kind of thing they need you for. Play to your strengths, kid. Which apparently include Italian cooking. This pesto is terrific."

"Really?" She sampled more herself. "It is kind of good. Well, maybe I could throw something together. On special occasions."

"You won't get an argument from me." Thoughtfully, he twirled pasta on his fork. "Speaking of special occasions, now that you're going to continue to be self-employed, you should be able to flex your schedule a bit. For a variety of reasons, I'm not going to be able to get back to Atlanta for Christmas, so I'm making plans to take a few days for the trip over Thanksgiving."

"That's nice." She refused to acknowledge the thud of disappointment. "I'm sure your family will be happy to have you, even for a few days."

"I'd like you to come with me."

"What?" Her fork paused halfway to her mouth.

"I'd like you to come to Atlanta with me for Thanksgiving and meet my family."

"I—I can't. I can't just fly across the country like that. There's not enough time to—"

"You have the best part of a month to arrange your schedule. Atlanta's not Bora Bora, Kate. It's Georgia."

"I know where Atlanta is," she said testily. "Look, besides the time factor, Thanksgiving's a family holiday. You don't just bring someone and dump them on your family on Thanksgiving."

"You're not someone," he said quietly. Oh, it was panic in her eyes, all right. He could read it perfectly. Though it irritated him, he determined to follow through. "It's traditional where I come from to invite the woman who's important to you to meet your family, to have them meet her. Particularly if it's the woman you're in love with and want to marry."

She jerked back as if scalded, nearly knocking over the chair as she sprang to her feet. "Wait a minute. Hold it. Whoa. Where did that come from? I cook one stupid meal and you get delusions of grandeur."

"I love you, Kate. I want to marry you. It would mean a great deal to me if you'd spend a few days with my family. I'm sure Margo and Laura would be willing to adjust the work schedule to accommodate a short trip over the holiday."

It took several tries before the sounds coming out of her mouth could be fashioned into words. "How can you sit there like that and calmly talk about scheduling in the same breath as marriage? Have you gone insane?"

"I thought you'd appreciate the practicality." Not sure who was irritating him more, himself or Kate, he topped off his wine.

"Well, I don't. So just stop it. I don't know where you got this brainstorm about marriage, but—"

"I wouldn't call it a brainstorm," he said, contemplating his glass. "I've given it quite a bit of thought."

"Oh, have you? Have you really?" Temper began to bubble beneath panic. Preferring it, Kate let it spew. "That's how you work, isn't it? That's how Byron De Witt works, in his quiet, thoughtful, *patient* way. I see it all now," she fumed, storming around the center island. "I can't believe I didn't see it all along. How clever you are, Byron. How canny. How fucking devious. You've just been reeling me in, haven't you? Taking over, step by little step."

"You're going to need to explain that for me. What have I taken over exactly?"

"Me! And don't think I can't see it all perfectly now. First it was sex. It's hard to think rationally when you're nothing more than one big throbbing gland."

He might have laughed, but instead carefully chose an olive. "As I recall, the sex was as much your idea as mine. More, actually, in the beginning."

"Don't try to confuse the issue," she spat out, slamming her hands on the counter.

"Far be it from me to confuse the issue with facts. Keep going."

"Then it was the let's-get-Kate-healthy campaign. Hospitals, damn doctors, medicine."

"I suppose it would be confusing the issue again to point out that you had an ulcer."

"I was handling it. I could have gotten myself to the doctor just fine on my own. Then you're cooking and feeding me all this healthy stuff. 'You've got to have a decent breakfast, Kate. You really should cut back on the coffee a little.' And before I know it I'm eating regular meals and exercising."

Byron ran his tongue around his teeth, stared down at his plate. "I'm so ashamed. Setting this diabolical trap for you. It's unforgivable."

"Don't you get glib with me, buster. You bought puppies. You tuned up my car."

He rubbed his hands over his face before he rose. "Now I

322

got the dogs and fixed your car in order to blind you to my evil plot. Kate, you're making a fool of yourself.''

"I am not. I know perfectly well when I'm making a fool of myself, and I'm not. You set everything up in clever little stages until I'm practically living here.''

"Honey," he said with a mix of affection and exasperation, "you *are* living here.''

"See?" She threw up her hands. "I'm living with you, without even realizing it. I'm cooking meals, for God's sake. I've never cooked for a man in my entire life.''

"Haven't you?" Touched, he moved forward, reached for her.

"Don't you do that." Still blazing, she retreated behind the island. "You've got a hell of a nerve confusing things like this. I told you you weren't my type, that it wasn't going to work.''

His patience straining, he rocked back on his heels. "The hell with types. It has been working, and you're perfectly aware of just how well it works with us. I love you, and if you weren't so damn pigheaded you'd admit that you love me.''

"Don't you assume my feelings, De Witt.''

"Fine. Then I'm in love with you. Deal with it.''

"I don't have to deal with it. *You* have to deal with it. And as far as your half-assed proposal of marriage—''

"I didn't propose marriage," he said coolly. "I told you I want you to marry me. I didn't ask you. Just what are you afraid of, Kate? That I'm a replay of that jerk Thornhill who used you until something more appetizing came along?''

She went cold. "Just how do you know about Roger? You've been poking around in my business, haven't you? And why am I not surprised?''

It was no use biting his tongue now. Better, he thought, to play it out. "When someone is as important to me as you are, her business is important to me. Her welfare is important to me. So I made it my business to find out. You mentioned his name to Kusack, I've kept in touch with Kusack.''

"You've kept in touch with Kusack," she repeated. "You know it was Roger who set me up."

He nodded. "And apparently so do you."

"I just figured it out this afternoon. But at a guess I'd say you've known a bit longer and didn't find it necessary to mention it to me."

"The trail led back to him. A personal clash between the two of you, access to your office. He made phone calls to New Hampshire around the time you were told about your father."

"How do you know about the phone calls?"

"Josh's investigator accessed the information."

"Josh's investigator," she repeated. "So Josh knows, too. But still no one thought it necessary to pass any of this handy information along to me."

"It wasn't passed to you because you'd have stormed right up into Thornhill's face and blasted him." The way, Byron admitted, he'd wanted to take Thornhill's face apart with his fists. "We didn't want him tipped off before the investigation is complete."

"You didn't want," she shot back. "Too bad, because I've already blasted him and ruined your neat plans. You had no right to work around me, to take over my life."

"I have every right to do whatever I can to protect you, and to help you. And that's what I've done. That's what I'm going to continue to do."

"Whether I like it or not."

"Essentially. I'm not Roger Thornhill. I'm not, and I've never used you for anything."

"No, you're not a user, Byron. Do you know what you are? You're a handler. That's what you do, you handle people. It's what makes you so good at your job—that patience, that charm, that skill at easing people onto your side of an issue without them ever really seeing they've been maneuvered. Well, here's a flash for you. I will not be handled. I sure as hell won't be maneuvered into marriage."

"Just a damn minute."

He shifted to block her path before she could storm out

324

When he closed his fingers around her arm, she yelped. Afraid that he'd misjudged his strength in temper, he jerked back holding her arm much more gently. But the bruises he saw on her arm were already formed. The haze that smothered his brain was dark and ugly.

"What the hell is this?" he demanded.

Her heart thudded hard into her throat as his eyes snapped to hers. "Let go of me."

"Who put these marks on you?"

Her chin angled in defense. The fury hardening his eyes was as lethal as the slice of a well-honed sword. "I've seen your white knight routine already, Byron. I'm not interested in a reprise."

"Who touched you?" he said, spacing each word carefully.

"Someone else who couldn't take no for an answer," she snapped. She regretted the words, bitterly, before they were fully formed. But it was too late. His eyes went carefully blank. Smoothly, he stepped out of her path.

"You're mistaken." His voice was cool and calm and deliberate. "I can take no for an answer. And since that seems to be the case, we don't seem to have anything left to discuss."

"I'll apologize for that." She felt the heat of shame burning her cheeks. "It was uncalled for. But I don't appreciate your interference in my business, or your assumption that I'd just fall into your plans."

"Understood." Hurt was a rusty ball of heat in his gut. "As I said, that seems to end it. It's clear you were right from the beginning. We want different things, and this isn't going to work." He walked over to the table, more to distance himself from her than because he wanted the wine he picked up and drank. "You can get your things now or at your convenience."

"I—" She stared at him, stunned that he could close the door between them so neatly. "I don't—I can't—I'm going," she managed and fled.

He listened for the slam of the door, then sat, as carefully as an old man. He put his head back, closed his eyes. It was

325

a wonder, he thought, that she could assume he was such a brilliant strategist when a blind man on a galloping horse could see just how badly he'd bungled it.

She went home, of course. Where else did you go when you were wounded? The scene she burst in on in the parlor was so cheerful, so familial, so much what she had just been offered and refused, that she wanted to scream.

Josh sat in the wing chair near the fire, the pretty lights from the flickering flames playing over him and his sleeping son. Laura, her younger daughter at her feet, poured coffee into pretty china cups. Margo snuggled on the end of the couch with Ali so they could pore over a fashion magazine together.

"Kate." Laura glanced up with a welcoming smile. "You're just in time for coffee. I bribed Josh to bring the baby over with one of Mrs. Williamson's honey-glazed hams."

"He might have left a few scraps," Margo added. "If you're hungry."

"I only had seconds."

"You had seconds twice, Uncle Josh," Kayla pointed out, and got up, as she had every few minutes, to peek at the baby.

"Stool pigeon." He tweaked her nose.

"Aunt Kate's mad." Ali straightened up on the couch in anticipation. "You're mad at somebody, aren't you, Aunt Kate? Your face is red."

"So it is," Margo drawled when she took a closer look. "And I think I hear her teeth grinding."

"Out." Kate pointed a finger at Josh. "You and I, we're going to go round later, but right now, go away and take your testosterone with you."

"I never go anywhere without it," he said easily. "And I'm comfortable right here."

"I don't want to see a man. If I do see a man in the next sixty seconds, I'll have to kill him with my bare hands."

He sniffed, feigning insult. But he rose. "I'm taking J. T.

326

into the library for port and cigars. We're going to talk about sports and power tools.''

"Can I come, Uncle Josh?"

"Of course." He gave Kayla his free hand. "I'm no sexist."

"Bedtime in thirty minutes, Kayla," Laura called out. "Ali, why don't you go keep Uncle Josh company until bedtime?"

"I want to stay here." She poked out her bottom lip and folded her arms over her chest. "I don't have to leave just because Aunt Kate's going to shout and swear. I'm not a baby."

"Let her stay." Kate made a grand, sweeping gesture with her arms. "She can't learn too early what men are really like."

"Yes, she can," Laura corrected. "Allison, go into the library with your uncle or go upstairs and have your bath."

"I always have to do what you say. I hate it." Ali stormed out, stomping up the stairs to sulk alone.

"Well, that was pleasant," Laura murmured, and wondered yet again what had happened to her sweet, compliant Ali. "What cheerful note would you like to add to that, Kate?"

"Men are pigs." She grabbed a cup of coffee and downed it like whiskey.

Chapter Twenty-one

"And your point is?" Margo said after a long moment.

"What do we need them for, anyway? What possible purpose do they have other than procreation, and with advances in technology we'll be taking care of that in a lab soon."

"Very pleasant," Laura decided and poured another cup. "Perhaps we don't need them for sex, but I still depend on them for large-insect disposal."

"Speak for yourself," Margo put it. "I'd rather kill spiders than give up sex. What crime did Byron commit, Kate, or do we get to guess?"

"The sneak, the conniving son of a bitch. I can't believe I was idiot enough to fall into a relationship with a man like that. You never really know a person, do you, never really know what's behind their beady little eyes?"

"Kate, what did he do? Whatever it is, I'm sure it's not as bad as you think." As Kate tore off her coat, Laura's gaze settled on the bruises. She was on her feet in a blink. "Dear God, Kate, did he hit you?"

"What? Oh." She dismissed the bruises with a wave of the hand. "No, of course he didn't hit me. I got this bumping into something warped at Bittle. Byron wouldn't hit a woman. It's too direct an approach for someone like him."

"Well, what for Christ's sake did he do?" Margo demanded.

"I'll tell you what he did. I'll tell you what he did," she repeated as she stormed around the room. "He asked me to marry him." When this was met with silence, she whirled. "Did you hear what I said? He asked me to marry him."

Laura considered. "And he has, what, a closet full of the heads of his former wives?"

"You are not listening to me. You are not getting it." Struggling for calm, Kate breathed deep, pushed at her hair. "Okay, he cooks, pushes vitamins on me, gets me working out. He gets my juices all stirred up so I'm ready to fall onto any handy surface and have incredible sex. He goes to see Kusack, he's been working with Josh behind my back, tries to get all the worry out of my life. He sees to it that I have a closet so that I can just start leaving my clothes over there. Of course, he's bought that house," she continued, pacing. "And those damn dogs that anyone with half a heart would fall for. My car hasn't run better since the day I drove it off the lot. And regularly, so you hardly notice, he brings flowers home."

"Not flowers." Margo pressed a hand to her breast. "Good God, the man is a fiend. He must be stopped."

"Just shut up, Margo. I know you're not on my side. You're never on my side." Certain of Laura's loyalty, Kate dropped down on her knees in front of her, clutched her hands. "He asked me to go with him to Atlanta over Thanksgiving and meet his parents. He says he loves me and wants me to marry him."

"Darling." All sympathy, Laura pressed Kate's hands. "I can see that you've been through an ordeal tonight. Obviously the man is deranged. I'm sure Josh can arrange to have him committed."

Stunned, Kate yanked her hands away. "You have to be on my side," she insisted.

"You want me to feel sorry for you?" The flash of anger in Laura's eyes had Kate blinking.

"No—yes. I—no. I just want you to understand."

"I'll tell you what I understand. You have a man who loves you. A good, considerate, thoughtful man who's willing to share the burdens of living as well as the pleasures with you. Who wants you, who cares enough to make an effort to make you happy, to make your life run a little more smoothly. One who wants you in bed and out. One who cares enough to want you to meet his family because he loves them and wants to show you off to them. And that's not good enough for you?"

"No, I didn't say that. It's just . . ." She got to her feet, staggered by the heat. "I didn't plan—"

"That's your problem." Laura—small, delicate-boned, and furious—rose as well. "It has to be in tidy order in Kate's plan. Well, life's messy."

"I know. I meant—"

Riding on a fury and frustration she herself hadn't guessed at, Laura barreled over Kate's protest. "And if you don't think yours is adequate, try mine. Try having nothing." And her voice was bitter. "An empty marriage, a man who wanted your name more than you and didn't even pretend otherwise after he had you. Try coming home every night knowing there's not going to be anyone there to hold you, that all the problems that need fixing come to you, that you have no one to lean on. And having your daughter blame you for not being good enough to keep her father under the same roof."

She stalked over to stare at the crackling flames of the fire while her friends watched in silence. "Try feeling unloved, unwanted, and crawling into bed every night wondering how you're going to make it work, how you can possibly make it right again, then come crying to me."

"I'm sorry," Kate murmured. "Laura, I'm so sorry."

"No." Exhausted and ashamed, Laura moved away from Kate's comforting hand and sat again. "No, I'm sorry. I don't know where that came from." She leaned her head back against the cushion a moment, her eyes shut as the last of the temper drained away. "Yes, I do. Maybe I'm jealous." She opened her eyes again and managed a smile. "Or maybe I just think you're stupid."

"I should have moved back in here after Peter left," Kate began. "I should have realized how much you were dealing with alone."

"Oh, stop. It's not about me. I'm just a little raw." Laura rubbed her aching temples. "That wasn't the first go-round Ali and I had today. It makes me edgy."

"I can move in now." Kate sat down beside Laura.

"Not that you're not welcome," Laura told her, "but you're not moving in."

"Blocked that escape route," Margo murmured.

"I'm not looking for escape." Kate struggled to get a grip on her tumbling emotions. "I could help with the girls, share the expenses."

"No. This is my life." Laura grimaced. "Such as it is. You have your own. If you don't love Byron, that's one thing. You can't tailor your feelings to suit him."

"Are you kidding?" Margo reached for the coffeepot. "She's been cross-eyed over him for months."

"So what? Emotions aren't any guarantee when it comes to something as big as marriage. They weren't enough for Laura." Kate sighed, shrugged. "I'm sorry, but they weren't."

"No, they weren't. If you want guarantees, send in your warranty card when you buy a toaster."

"Okay, you're right, but that's not the whole point. Can't you see he was playing me? He's been handling me all through this relationship."

Margo made a low feline sound. "Being handled by a strong, gorgeous man. Poor you."

"You know very well what I mean. You'd never let Josh push all the buttons, make all the moves. I'm telling you that Byron has a way of undermining things so that I'm sliding along in the direction he's chosen before I realize it."

"So change directions if you don't like the destination," Margo suggested.

"He called me a detour once." Remembering, Kate scowled. "He said he liked taking long, interesting detours. I actually thought it was sort of charming."

"Why don't you go back and talk this out with him instead of arguing?" Laura tilted her head, well able to imagine the scene that had taken place in Byron's kitchen. "He's probably feeling just as unhappy and frustrated as you are."

"I can't." Kate shook her head. "He told me to pick up my things at my convenience."

"Ouch." Margo looked at Kate with genuine sympathy now. "In that polite, mannerly tone of his?"

"Exactly. It's the worst. Besides, I don't know what I'd say to him. I don't know what I want." At a loss, she buried her face in her hands. "I keep thinking I know what I want, then it shifts on me. I'm tired. It's too hard to think rationally when I'm tired."

"Then talk to him tomorrow. You'll stay here tonight." Laura rose. "I have to put the girls to bed."

"She's made me so ashamed," Kate murmured when she was alone with Margo.

"I know." Margo slid closer. "At least all she made me feel was like killing Peter Ridgeway if he ever shows his sorry face around here."

"I didn't realize she was still so hurt, so unhappy."

"She'll be all right." Margo patted Kate's knee. "We'll see to it."

"I'm, ah, not going to go into another accounting firm."

"Of course you're not."

"Everybody seems to know what I'm going to do before I do" Kate griped. "Bittle offered me a partnership."

"Congratulations."

"I turned him down this afternoon."

"My, my." Margo's million-dollar smile flashed. "Haven't we had a busy day!"

"And Roger Thornhill is the embezzler."

"What?" Margo's cup clinked into its saucer. "That slimy weasel who two-timed you with your own client?"

"The very same." It pleased Kate to see that she could say something that got a rise out of Margo. "It was the way he acted when I ran into him at Bittle today. He's smart enough to have figured out how to siphon funds, and I was his main competition for the partner slot. He gets a little playing money and screws me at the same time."

"You've been to Kusack with this?"

"No, apparently Byron, the cop, and your husband, whom I will deal with shortly, already knew."

"And left you in the dark." Understanding perfectly, Margo pulled Kate to her feet. "Occasionally men have to be reminded that they are no longer hunting out of caves, fighting dragons, or blazing trails west while we huddle around the fire. I'll help you remind Josh."

At nine forty-five the next morning, Kate opened the till at Pretenses. She would run the shop alone that morning. She took some pride in her competence. Laura was at her office at the hotel, and Margo remained on maternity leave. She decided to relish these last few minutes before she unlocked the door, turned the sign to Open.

She'd brought her own CD's. Margo preferred classical. Kate preferred the classics. The Beatles, the Stones, Cream. After putting the music on, she went into the powder room, filled the copper watering can. She was going to enjoy the pleasant little duties of nurturing an elegant business, she told herself.

She was not going to think about Byron De Witt.

He was in the penthouse suite by now. Probably in some meeting or on a conference call. He might be glancing over an itinerary for a trip to San Francisco. Didn't he say he had to fly up?

Didn't matter, she reminded herself, and stepped out on the veranda to water the tubs of pansies and impatiens. He could fly anywhere he wanted—to the moon, for that matter. Her interest in his affairs was over. Finished. A closed book.

She had her life to worry about, didn't she? After all, she was beginning a whole new phase. A new career with a new goal to aim for. She had dozens of ideas to improve and expand the shop floating around in her head. Once Margo was back in gear, they would have a meeting. An efficiency meeting. Then there was the fashion show right around the corner. The advertising had to be placed. They needed to discuss other promotions for the holidays.

What they needed was a regular weekly brainstorming and progress meeting. She would set it up, fix it into the schedule. You couldn't run a successful business without regular structured meetings. You couldn't run a life without structure, without specific plans and goals.

Why the hell couldn't he see that she had specific plans and goals? How could he have thrown marriage at her, knocking down all of her carefully placed pins?

You didn't marry someone you'd known barely a full year. There were stages to a relationship, careful, cautious, and sensible stages. Maybe, just maybe, after two years, after you'd worked out the kinks in the relationship, after you fully understood each other's faults and foibles and had learned to accept them or compromise on them, you began to *discuss* the possibility of marriage.

You had to outline what you wanted out of marriage, assign roles and duties. Who handled the marketing, who paid the bills, who took out the trash, for God's sake. Marriage was a business, a partnership, a full-scale commitment. Sensible people didn't just jump into it without first fine-tuning the details.

And what about children? It was obvious who had the children—if there were going to be children—but what about assignment of responsibilities? Diapers and laundry, feedings and doctors' appointments. If you didn't nail down the details of responsibilities, you had nothing but chaos—and a baby needing to be taken care of by a responsible adult.

A baby. Oh, God, what would it be like to have a baby? She didn't know anything about having a baby. Think of all the books she would have to read, all the mistakes she was bound to make. There were so many . . . things you had to have for a baby. Strollers and car seats and cribs.

And all those adorable little clothes, she thought dreamily.

"You're drowning those pansies, Ms. Powell."

She jerked back, slopping water on her shoes. She stared blankly at Kusack while her mind whirled. She had just all but named a baby she hadn't conceived with a man she didn't intend to conceive it with.

"Daydreaming?" His lips curved in that now familiar paternal fashion.

"No, I—" She wasn't a daydreamer. She was a thinker. A doer. "I've got a lot on my mind."

"Bet you do. Thought I'd catch you before you opened up. Do you mind if we go inside?"

"No, of course not." Still fumbling, she set the watering can down and opened the door. "It's just me today. My partners are—aren't here."

"I wanted to talk to you alone. I didn't mean to spook you, Ms. Powell."

"No, that's all right." Her speeding heart seemed to have settled back to a reasonable rate. "What can I do for you, detective?"

"Actually, I just came by to catch you up on the progress of the investigation. I figured after the trouble you went through, you deserve to know how it panned out."

"Well, that makes one of you," she murmured.

"Your boyfriend nudged me toward Roger Thornhill."

"He's not my boyfriend," Kate said quickly, then set her teeth. "If you're referring to Mr. De Witt."

"I am." He smiled a bit sheepishly and tugged on his ear. "I never know how to refer to these kinds of things. Anyway, Mr. De Witt nudged me toward Thornhill. Fact is, I was already looking in that direction. You don't look shocked speechless by the news," he commented.

"I figured it out yesterday." She shrugged her shoulders, discovering it simply didn't matter any longer.

"Thought you would. Thornhill's got a little gambling problem. Gambling's one of the best reasons to need quick money."

"Roger gambles?" That did shock her. "You mean he bets on horse races, that sort of thing?"

"He bets on Wall Street, Ms. Powell. And he's been losing steady for the past couple of years. Overplayed his hand, so to speak, and lost his ante. Then there was his personal relationship with you. Then add in the information about your father and the fact that he was the one who found the newspaper article in your office and passed it to Bittle."

"Really." She nodded. "I didn't know that."

"A little too pat, to my way of thinking. Connections usually aren't coincidences in my line of work. You had a little run-in with him yesterday at Bittle."

"And how do you know about that?"

"Ms. Newman. She's got good eyes and ears, and a sharp nose." He grinned. "I asked her to report any unusual incident, officewise. She's another who didn't like the way Thornhill smelled, so to speak. And she stood by you from the start."

"Excuse me?" Kate tapped her ear as though her hearing had gone suddenly off. "Newman stood by me?"

"First interview I had with her on this business, she said if I was looking in your direction I was looking in the wrong one. She said Katherine Powell wouldn't steal so much as a paper clip."

"I see. I always thought she disliked me."

"I don't know whether she likes you or not, but she respects you."

"Are you going to bring Roger in for questioning, then?"

"Already have. I had to move a little quicker after I learned you'd had a face-off with him. So I paid him a little visit last night. He was already packed and on his way to the airport."

"You're kidding."

"No, ma'am. Had reservations for a flight to Rio. He's been living on the edge since you were cleared. Whatever you said to him at the office yesterday broke his nerve. He lawyered himself pretty quick, but we figure to cut a deal by the end of the day. They call this sort of thing a victimless crime. I guess that's a misnomer this time around.''

"I don't feel like a victim," Kate murmured. "I don't know what I feel."

"Well, I'd feel right pissed—if you'll pardon my French. But . . ." He shrugged his shoulders. "His career's in the toilet, and he's going to be paying off fines and his lawyer for a long time to come. And the federal government is going to have him as their guest for a while."

"He'll go to prison." As her father would have gone to prison, she thought. For a mistake, an error in judgment. A moment of greed.

"Like I said, we're cutting a deal, but I don't see him walking away without doing some time. You know, the way things work today, you could sue him yourself. Defamation of character, emotional pain and suffering, all that. Your lawyer would tell you."

"I'm not interested in suing Roger. I'm interested in turning the page."

"I figured that." He smiled at her again. "You're a nice woman, Ms. Powell. It's been a pleasure meeting you, even under the circumstances."

She thought about it. "I suppose I have to say the same, Detective Kusack. Even under the circumstances."

He stepped toward the door, stopped. "It's about opening time, isn't it?"

She glanced at her watch. "Just about."

"I wonder . . ." He tugged on his ear again. "My wife's got this birthday coming up. Tomorrow, actually."

"Detective Kusack," she beamed at him, "you've come to the right place."

Kate told herself she felt wonderful, revived. All of her troubles were behind her. She was starting the next phase of her life.

There was no reason to be nervous about going to Byron's. It was the middle of the day—lunchtime. He wouldn't be home. She would simply pick up her things, as he'd requested, and thereby close that chapter cleanly.

She would not regret. It was fun while it lasted, nothing lasted forever, all good things came to an end.

And if another cliché popped into her mind, she would scream.

She pulled into his driveway. The key she had meticulously removed from her own ring was in her pocket. But when she reached in to pull it out, she found herself holding Seraphina's coin. Baffled, she stared at it. She would have sworn she'd put that in the top drawer of her jewelry box.

She turned it in her hand. The sun caught the edge and shot out dazzling light. That was why her eyes watered, she told herself. It was the reflection off the gold, and she'd taken off her sunglasses. It wasn't because she felt a sudden, wrenching connection to that young girl, standing on the cliff, ready to throw her life away.

Kate Powell was not throwing her life away, she told herself firmly. She was facing it. Only the weak tossed away hope. She had years of happiness left in her life. Years. And she was not going to stand here and cry over some old coin and a misty legend.

This was reality. She blinked back tears. Her reality, and she knew exactly what she was doing.

She found the key, replaced the coin in her pocket. But it was harder than she'd imagined to use the key, knowing it would be the last time.

It was just a house, she thought. There was no reason for her to love it, no reason to feel this aching sense of welcome when she opened the door. There was no reason at all for her to walk to the glass doors and want to weep because the pups were napping in the sunshine.

And geraniums were blooming in gray stone pots. Wind chimes of copper and brass sang in the breeze from the sea. Shells that she had gathered with Byron from the beach were arranged in a wide-mouthed glass bowl on the redwood table.

It was so perfect, she realized, so simply perfect. That was why she wanted to weep.

When the dogs' heads popped up in unison, and they scrambled up to bark and race, she realized she hadn't heard the car. But they had. They reacted just that way whenever they recognized the sound of Byron's return home.

Jolted with panic, she turned around and faced the door as he came in.

"I'm sorry," she said immediately. "I didn't realize you'd be home early."

"I don't suppose you did." But he'd known, thanks to Laura's call, that she would be there.

"I came to get my things. I . . . I thought it best to come by when you were at work. So it would be less awkward."

"It's awkward now." He stepped toward her, eyes narrowed. "You've been crying."

"No, not really. It was . . ." Her fingers slid into her pocket, touched the coin. "It was something else entirely. And then I guess it was the dogs. They looked so sweet sleeping in the yard." They were at the door now, tails waving furiously. "I'll miss them."

"Sit down."

"No, I really can't. I want to get back to the shop, and . . . and I do want to apologize, Byron, for shouting at you the way I did. I really am sorry for that, and I'd hate to think we couldn't at least be civil." She closed her eyes on her own absurdity. "This is very awkward."

He wanted to touch her, badly wanted to touch her. But he knew his own limitations. If he so much as brushed his hand over that short cap of hair, he would want to touch more, have to touch more until he was holding her against him and begging.

"Then let's try being civil. If you won't sit, we'll stand. There are a few things I'd like to say." He watched her open her eyes, saw the wariness in them. What the hell did she see when she looked at him? he wondered. Why couldn't he tell?

"I'm going to apologize as well. I handled things badly last night. And at the risk of getting kicked in the teeth again, I admit that you weren't that far off the mark in some of your, let's call them . . . observations about my character."

He walked to the doors, jingling the change in his pocket. The dogs, still hopeful, sat sentry on the other side of the glass. "I do plan things out. We have that in common. I admit I eased you into living here. It seemed to me that it would help both of us get used to it. Because I wanted you here."

When he turned back to her, she struggled for a reply, but found none.

"I wanted to take care of you. You see vulnerability as a weakness. I see it as a soft, appealing side of a strong, intelligent, and resilient woman. It's in my nature to protect, to fix—or at least try to fix—what's wrong. I can't change that for you."

"I don't want you to change, Byron. But I can't change either. I'm always going to resist being guided along, however well intentioned it might be."

"And when I see someone I love stressed out to the point of illness, taken advantage of, hurt, I'm going to do whatever it takes to turn it around. And when I want something, when I know it's right, I'm going to work toward making it happen. I love you, Kate."

Her heart swam into her eyes, filled them. "I don't know how to handle this. I don't know what to do. I can't figure it out."

"I've figured it out. You know, every once in a while it doesn't hurt to let someone else figure it out."

"Maybe. I don't know. But there were points in all of this I had to come to myself. I didn't even realize some of them. They've arrested Roger."

"I know."

"Of course you do." She tried to laugh, then turned away. "When Kusack came by and told me, I wasn't sure how I felt at first. Relieved, vindicated—but there was more. I thought of my father. He'd have gone to jail, just as Roger will go.

It's the same crime, the same punishment. They're both thieves."

"Kate—"

"No, let me finish. It's taken me so long to get here. My father made a mistake, a criminal mistake. As much as it hurts me to know that, I also know that he never tried to shift the blame, implicate anyone else. He wasn't like Roger. He would have faced what he'd done, and he would have paid for it. I realized today that that made all the difference. I can live with that, and forgive, and remember what he was to me for the first eight years of my life. He was my father, and he loved me."

"You're a beautiful woman, Katherine."

She shook her head, brushed away tears. "I had to get that out. It seems I can always pull out what's inside me and hand it to you. It worries me how easy it is to do that."

"You worry too much. Let's see if I can help there. We'll try a simple logic test. I'm thirty-five years old. I've never been married, never been engaged, never formally lived with a woman before. Why?"

"I don't know." She dragged her hands through her hair, fighting to use intellect over emotion as she turned back to him. "There could be a dozen reasons. You resisted commitment, you were too busy sampling southern delights, you were too focused on your career."

"It could have been any of those," he agreed. "But I'll tell you what it comes down to. I don't like to make mistakes any more than you do. I'm sure there are other women I could be happy with, build a decent life with. But that isn't enough. I waited, because I had this image, this dream about the woman I'd share my life with."

"You're not going to tell me I was that image because I know very well I wasn't." She stared blankly at the handkerchief he offered. "What?"

"You're crying again." When she snatched it away and mopped at her face, he continued. "Some of us are more flexible in our dreams and can even enjoy when they take a dif-

342

ferent shape. Look at me, Kate,'' he said gently and drew her gaze to his. ''I've been waiting for you.''

''That's not fair.'' She pressed crossed hands to her swelling heart as she backed away. ''It's not fair to say things like that to me.''

''We said civil. We didn't say anything about fair.''

''I don't want to feel this way. I don't want to hurt this way. Why won't you just let me think?''

''Think about this.'' He did touch her now, drawing her in until their faces were close. ''I love you.'' And kissed her. ''I want to spend my life with you. I want to take care of you and be taken care of.''

''I'm not the kind of woman people say those things to.'' She thumped her hand on his chest. ''Why can't you see that?''

He'd have to make sure she got used to hearing those things, coming from him. His lips curved as he ran his hands up her back.

''No. I see it.'' She jerked back out of reach. ''I can actually see that look come into your eyes. Kate needs to be soothed and stroked and eased into it. Well, it's not going to work. It's just not going to work. I've just got things sorted out,'' she fumed, stalking around the room. ''I've got the shop. Isn't it enough of a shock to deal with that I love being there? How am I supposed to suddenly adjust to all of this? There aren't any rules to being in love. Oh, I figured that out all right, tossing and turning all night because you'd told me to pick up my things at my convenience.'' She spun back and seared him with a look. ''Oh, that was low.''

''Yes, it was.'' He grinned at her now, delighted with the image of her spending as miserable a night as he had. ''I'm pleased to see it hit the mark. You hurt me last night.''

''See? That's just what happens when you get tangled up in love. You hurt each other. I didn't ask to be in love with you, did I? I didn't plan it. And now I can't bear the idea of being without you, of not sitting at the table in the morning watching you cook breakfast, or listening to you tell me to concentrate when you've got me lifting those damn weights. Walking on the beach with you and those mangy dogs. And I want a baby.''

Stunned, he waited a beat. ''Now?''

''You see? You see what you've done?'' She sank onto the couch and buried her face in her hands. ''Listen to what I'm saying. I'm a mess. I'm insane. I'm in love with you.''

''I know all that, Kate.'' He sat beside her, pulled her into his lap. ''It suits me just fine.''

''What if it doesn't suit me? I could really screw this up.''

''That's okay.'' He kissed her cheek, nuzzled her head on his shoulder. ''I'm good at fixing things. Why don't we look at the big picture and work on the details as we go along?''

She sighed, closed her eyes, and felt blissfully at home. ''Maybe you'll be the one to screw it up.''

''Then you'll be there to put everything back in place. I depend on you.''

''You—'' Those words, the look in his eyes that showed he meant them, were more powerful to her than any declaration of love. ''I want you to. I need to know you do, and will. But marriage—''

''Is a practical, logical step,'' he finished and made her smile.

''It is not. And besides, you never asked me.''

''I know.'' He smiled back at her. ''If I asked you, there's a possibility you would say no. I'm not going to let you say no.''

''You're just going to ease me into it until it's a done deal.''

''That's the idea.''

''It's pretty smart,'' she murmured, feeling the beat of his heart under her palm. Fast and not quite steady, she realized. Maybe he was just as nervous as she was. ''I guess since most of my stuff's here already anyway, and I love you so much and I've gotten used to your cooking, it isn't such a bad idea. Being married, I mean. To you. So, it looks like your idea worked.''

344

"Thank God." He pressed her hand to his lips. "I have been waiting for you, Kate, all my life."

"I know. I've been waiting right back."

He tilted her head back and smiled into her eyes. "Welcome home."

Turn the page for a sneak preview of
Nora Roberts' final novel in the Dream *trilogy*

Finding the Dream

Available now from Piatkus

California, 1888

It was a long way for a man to travel. Not only the miles from San Diego to the cliffs outside of Monterey, Felipe thought, but the years. So many years.

Once he had been young enough to walk confidently along the rocks, to climb, even to race. He had defied the fates, celebrated the rush of wind, the crash of waves, the dizzying heights. The rocks had bloomed for him in spring once. There had been flowers to pick for Seraphina then, and he could remember, with the clear vision of age to youth, how she had laughed and clutched the tough little wildflowers to her breasts as if they were precious roses plucked from a well-tended bush.

His eyes were weak now, and his limbs were frail. But not his memory. A strong, vital memory in an old body was his penance. Whatever joy he had found in his life had been tainted, always, with the sound of Seraphina's laughter, with

349

the trust in her dark eyes. With her young, uncompromising love.

In the more than forty years since he had lost her—and the part of himself that was innocence—he had learned to accept his own failings. He had been a coward, running from battle rather than face the horrors of war, hiding among the dead rather than lifting a sword.

But he had been young, and such things had to be forgiven of the young.

He had allowed his friends and family to believe him dead, slain like a warrior—even a hero. That had been shame, and pride. Small things, pride and shame. Life was made up of so many small blocks. But he could never forget that it had been that shame and pride that had cost Seraphina her life.

Weary, he sat on a rock to listen. To listen to the roar of water battling rock far below, to listen to the piercing cries of gulls, the rush of wind through winter grass. And the air was chill as he closed his eyes and opened his heart.

To listen for Seraphina.

She would always be young, a lovely dark-eyed girl who had never taken the chance to grow old, as he was old now. She hadn't waited, but in despair and grief had thrown herself into the sea. For love of him, he thought now. For reckless youth she hadn't lived long enough to know that nothing lasts forever.

Believing him dead, she had died, hurling herself and her future onto the rocks.

He had mourned her. God knew he had mourned her. But he hadn't been able to follow her into the sea. Instead, he had traveled south, and had given up his name and his home. He had made new ones.

He had found love again. Not the sweet, first blush of love that he had with Seraphina. But something solid and strong built on those small blocks of trust and understanding and needs both quiet and violent.

And he had done his best.

He had children and grandchildren. He had a life with all

350

the joys and sorrows that make a man. He had survived to love a woman, to raise a family, to plant gardens. He had been content with what had grown from him.

But he had never forgotten the girl he had loved—and had killed. He had never forgotten their dream of a future, or the sweet, innocent way she had given herself to him. When they had loved in secret, both of them so young, so fresh, they had dreamed of the life they would have together, the home they would build with her dowry, the children they would make.

But war had come, and he had left her to prove himself a man. Instead, he had proven himself a coward. She had hidden her bride gift, that symbol of hope a young girl treasures, to keep it out of American hands.

Felipe had no doubt where she had hidden it. He had understood his Seraphina, her logic, her sentiment, her strengths and weaknesses. Though it had meant leaving Monterey penniless, he had not taken the gold and jewels Seraphina had secreted.

Now with the dreams of age which had turned his hair to silver and had dimmed his eyes and lived in his aching bones, he prayed that it would be found one day by lovers. Or dreamers. If God was just, he would allow Seraphina to choose. In spite of whatever the Church preached, Felipe refused to believe God would condemn a grieving child for the sin of suicide.

No, she would be as he had left her, more than forty years ago on these very cliffs. Forever young and beautiful and full of hope.

He knew he would not come here again. His time of penance was almost at an end. He hoped when he saw his Seraphina again, she would smile at him and forgive a young man's foolish pride.

He rose, bending in the wind, leaning on his cane to keep his feet under him, and left the cliffs to Seraphina.

There was a storm brewing, marching across the sea. A summer storm, full of power and light and wild wind. In that eerily luminescent light, Laura Templeton sat contentedly on the rock. Summer storms were the best.

They would have to go in soon, back to Templeton House, but for now, she and her two closest friends would wait and watch. She was sixteen, a delicately built girl with quiet gray eyes and bright bronze hair. And as full of energy as any storm.

"I wish we could get in the car and drive right into it," Margo Sullivan said and then laughed. The wind was fitful, and growing stronger. "Right into it."

"Not with you behind the wheel," Kate Powell sneered. "You've had your license a whole week and already have a rep as a lunatic."

"You're just jealous because it'll be months before you can drive."

Because it was true, Kate shrugged. Her short black hair fluttered. She took a deep gulp of air, loving the way it thickened and churned. "At least I'm saving up for a car, instead of cutting out pictures of Ferraris and Jaguars."

"If you're going to dream," Margo said, frowning at a minute chip in the coral polish on her nails, "dream big. I'll have a Ferrari one day, or a Porshe, or whatever I want." Her summer-blue eyes narrowed with determination. "I won't settle for some secondhand junker like you."

Laura let them argue. She could have diffused the sniping, but understood it was simply part of the friendship. And she didn't care about cars. Not that she didn't enjoy the spiffy little convertible her parents had given her for her sixteenth birthday. But one car was the same as another to her.

She realized it was easier, in her position. She was the daughter of Thomas and Susan Templeton, of the Templeton hotel empire. Her home loomed on the hill behind her, stunning under the churning gray sky. It was more than the stone and wood and glass that made it. More than the turrets and balconies and lush gardens. More than the fleet of servants who kept it shining.

It was home.

But she had been raised to understand the responsibilities of privilege. Inside her was a great love of beauty, of symmetry, and a kindness. Aligned with it was a need to live up to the Templeton standards, to deserve all she'd been given by birthright. Not only the wealth, which even at sixteen she understood. But the love of her family, her friends.

She knew Margo fretted at her own limitations. Though they had grown up together at Templeton House, as close as sisters, Margo's mother was the housekeeper.

When Kate's parents had been killed, she had come to Templeton House. An eight-year-old orphan. She was cherished, absorbed into the family, as much a part of Templeton as Laura and her older brother Josh.

Laura and Margo and Kate were as close as sisters who shared blood—perhaps closer. But Laura never forgot that the responsibility of Templeton was hers.

And one day, she thought, she would fall in love, marry and have children. She would carry on the Templeton traditions. The man who came for her, who swept her up in his arms, who made her belong to him would be everything she'd ever wanted. Together they would build a life, create a home, carve out a future as polished and perfect as Templeton House.

As she pictured it, dreams budded in her heart. Delicate color bloomed on her cheeks while the wind tossed her blond curls around them.

"Laura's dreaming again," Margo commented. Her grin flashed, turning her striking face to stunning.

"Got Seraphina on the brain again?" Kate asked.

"Hmm?" No, she hadn't been thinking of Seraphina, but she did now. "I wonder how often she came here, dreaming of the life she wanted with Felipe."

"She died in a storm like the one that's coming. I know she did." Margo lifted her face to the sky. "With lightning flashing, the wind howling."

"Suicide's drama enough by itself." Kate plucked a wildflower, twirled the stubby stem in her fingers. "If it had been

353

a perfect day with blue skies and sunshine, the results would have been the same.''

''I wonder what it is to feel that lost,'' Laura murmured. ''If we ever find her dowry, we should build a shrine of something to remember her by.''

''I'm spending my share on clothes, jewelry and travel.'' Margo stretched up her arms, then tucked them behind her head.

''And it'll be gone in a year. Less,'' Kate predicted. ''I'm going to invest mine in blue chips.''

''Boring, predictable Kate.'' Margo turned her head, smiled at Laura. ''What about you? What will you do when we find it? And we *will* find it one day.''

''I don't know.'' What would her mother do? she wondered. Her father? ''I don't know,'' she repeated. ''I'll have to wait and see.'' She looked back toward the sea where the curtain of rain was inching closer. ''That's what Seraphina didn't do. She didn't wait and see.''

And the rising wind sounded like a woman weeping.

Lightning jagged, a flashing pitchfork of brilliant white through the heavy sky. The blasting boom of answering thunder shook the air. Laura threw back her head and smiled. Here it came, she thought. The power, the danger, the glory.

She wanted it. Deep inside her most secret heart, she wanted it all.

Then there was the squeal of brakes, the angry pulse of gritty rock and roll. And an impatient shout.

''Jesus Christ, are you all nuts?'' Joshua Templeton leaned out of his car window, scowling at the trio. ''Get the hell in the car.''

''It's not raining yet.'' Laura stood. She eyed Josh first. He was her senior by four years, and at the moment looked so much like their father at his crankiest she wanted to laugh. But she'd seen who was in the car with him.

She wasn't certain how she knew that Michael Fury was as dangerous as any summer storm, but she was sure of it. It was more than Ann Sullivan's mutters about hoods and troublemakers. Though Margo's mother had definite opinions on this particular friend of Josh's.

Maybe it was because his dark hair was just a little too long and too wild, or the little white scar just above his left eyebrow Josh said Michael had gotten in a fight. Maybe it was his looks, for they were dark and dangerous, and just a little mean. Like a greedy angel's, she thought as her heart fluttered uncomfortably. Grinning all the way to hell.

But she thought it was his eyes. They were so startlingly blue in that face. So intense and direct and intrusive when he looked at her.

No, she did not like the way he looked at her.

"Get in the damn car." Impatience shimmered around Josh in waves. "Mom had a fit when she realized you were out here. One of you gets hit by lightning, it'll be my ass."

"And it's such a cute one," Margo added, always ready to flirt. Hoping to make Josh jealous, she opened the door on Michael's side. "It'll be a tight fit. Mind if I sit on your lap, Michael?"

His gaze shifted from Laura. He grinned at Margo, a quick flash of teeth in a tanned, hollow-cheeked face. "Make yourself at home, sugar." His voice was deep, a little rough, and he accepted the weight of a willing female with practiced ease.

"I didn't know you were back, Michael." Kate slipped into the backseat, where, she thought sourly, there was plenty of room for three.

"On leave." He flicked a glance at her, then looked back at Laura who still hesitated at the car door. "I ship out again in a couple days."

"The merchant marines." Margo toyed with his hair. "It sounds so . . . dangerous. And exciting. Do you have a woman in every port?"

"I'm working on it." As the first fat drops of rain splatted the windshield, he cocked a brow at Laura. "Want to sit on my lap, too, sugar?"

Dignity was something else she'd learned at an early age. Not sparing him a reply, Laura got into the backseat with Kate.

The minute the door closed, Josh sent the car streaking across the road and up the hill toward home. When her eyes met Michael's in the rearview mirror, Laura deliberately looked away, then back. Back toward the cliffs, and her place of comfortable dreams.